RELUCTANT BETRAYALS

RELUCTANT

BETRAYALS

A NOVEL BY

CLAUDE RENAUD

HUNTER

PUBLISHER: Hunter Publications

EMAIL: huntpubs1@gmail.com

First published as an eBook in August 2019
First published in Print in April 2020

NATIONAL LIBRARY OF AUSTRALIA
CATALOGUING-IN-PUBLICATION DATA

AUTHOR	Renaud Claude
TITLE	Reluctant Betrayals
ISBN	978-0-6487808-0-9
SUBJECTS	Novel
DEWEY NO	A823

To K.

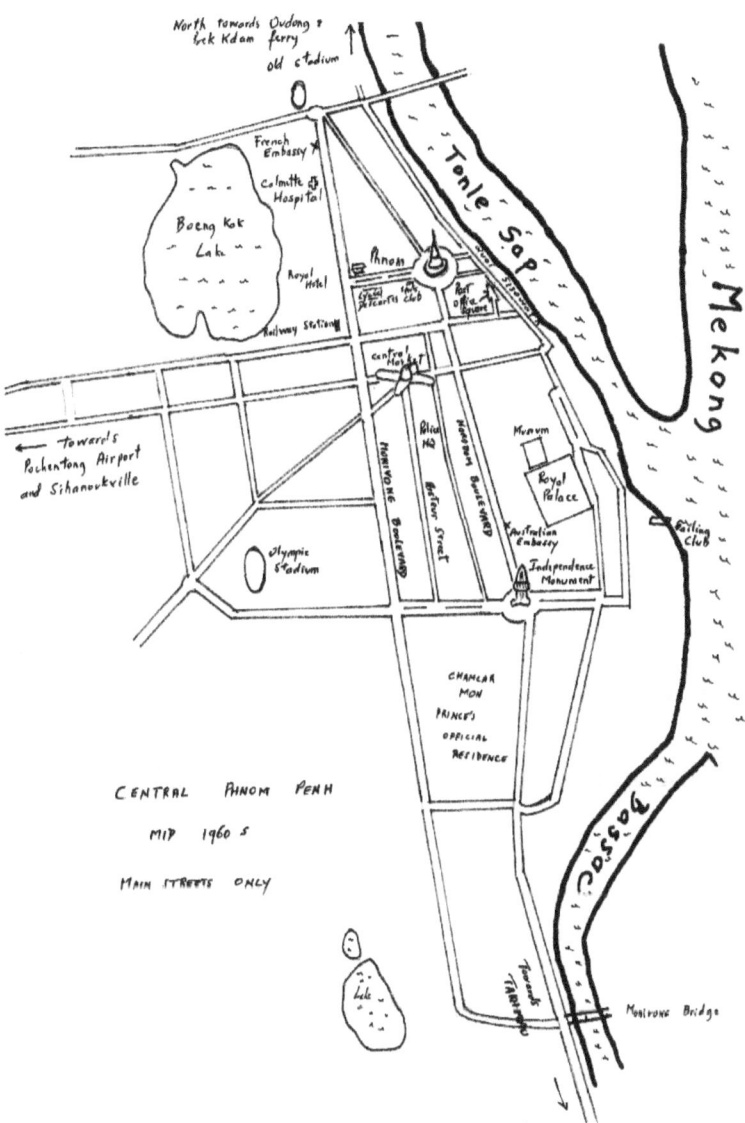

North towards Oudong &
Kek Kdam ferry
Old Stadium

French Embassy
Calmitte
Hospital

Boeng Kok
Lak

Phnom
Royal Hotel
Sporting Club
Railway Station

Tonle Sap

Post
Office Square

Central Hospital

← Towards
Pochentong Airport
and Sihanoukville

Bleu HQ
Norodom Boulevard
Horivong Boulevard
Balfour Street

Mekong

Museum

Royal
Palace

Australian
Embassy
Independence
Monument

Sailing
Club

Olympic
Stadium

CHAMCAR
MON
PRINCE'S
OFFICIAL
RESIDENCE

CENTRAL   PHNOM   PENH

MID   1960 s

MAIN STREETS   ONLY

Bassac

Lake

Towards TAKEO

Monivong Bridge

CONTENTS

Prologue

Sometimes it's easier to start at the end: in a village in Normandy, in north-western France, on the southern edge of that region where it merges into the *Pays de Loire*: a quiet, unassuming place with a pretty little chateau in need of upkeep, a robust country church pleasing in its simplicity, and not much else to tempt the passing tourist in search of local colour. Its name, *Champfleur*, sits well with its peaceful setting of ploughed fields and lush meadows which must be full of flowers in spring. A good place to end your days, especially if that's where you were born.

It wasn't always so peaceful. One afternoon in August 1944, two months after the Normandy landings, it was the scene of a fierce engagement as forward elements of General Leclerc's Free French 2nd Armoured Division, fighting as part of Patton's Third Army, pushed through some stubborn *Panzer* resistance on their way to Alençon, a few kilometres to the north – the first town in France to be liberated by Free French troops, and coincidentally Leclerc's birthplace. Soon afterwards Leclerc went on to liberate Paris itself, a much bigger prize, with the support of the 4th US Infantry Division, after an equally fierce clash between General de Gaulle, leader of the Free French, and US General Eisenhower, commander in chief of allied forces in Europe, who wanted to bypass Paris altogether. De Gaulle had his way, as he tended to do, after threatening to withdraw his forces from American command – which was lucky for the Parisians, as they had jumped the gun and started their own uprising, which would otherwise have been bloodily crushed.

But that is another story. Now, seventy years later, all that remains of those dramatic events is a few bullet scars and the fading memories of its oldest inhabitants. As I walk along the gravel paths of the little village cemetery, Lise, my guide, by my side, I think back to a different past altogether. Lise is a sturdy countrywoman in her fifties, with an open countenance and intelligent eyes which remind me of her mother. We talk quietly, as we walk past the serried tombs.

'You still speak excellent French, Philippe,' Lise remarks. 'You have no trace of an accent.'

'Thank you,' I say. 'I can thank my parents for that. They made sure I grew up bilingual.' Thinking, that's almost word for word the first conversation I had with Nicole, all those years ago. 'I am after all a son of the soil. I was born not far from here.'

'*C'est ici*,' says Lise, and we stop at a tomb, set back a little from the path: a plain headstone, free of wrought iron curlicues or plastic flowers in stone vases, with simple lettering:

Nicole Monique le Gallois, 1930-2015

épouse de Henri Robert Marchand, 1921-1967

'*Maman* always liked simplicity,' remarks Lise, as if to apologise for the lack of ornamentation, of gilt lettering.

'That's pretty well how I remember her.'

Lise kneels before the tomb, not in pious recollection but to remove a few weeds from the patch of gravel in front of it, and places a bunch of fresh flowers to replace the faded bunch she laid there last week.

'I usually come once a week,' Lise says, matter-of-fact. 'I tell myself I'll do this for a year.'

I stand silent, watching her, thinking of the woman I knew long ago in a faraway place, and of the mouldering bones beneath the ground, which must be all that's left of her now. It took months for her letter to reach me.

'How well did you know my mother, Philippe?' Lise asks as she stands up again, as if she could read my mind.

I nod, to show that I consider the question legitimate. But I choose my words carefully.

'It's probably fair to say that for a time I was closer to her and your father than just about anyone else in my life.'

She gives me a sidelong glance, and I know that's not the answer she wanted. But it's all she's going to get. Because there's no way I can tell her the truth. Nicole and Henri both made sure of that, all those years ago.

This is the tale of a young man, told by an old one.

11

PART I

My name is Philippe Roche – or Philip, depending on whether you're talking to me in French or in English. I'm Australian, but I was born in France, of French and English parents. And in 1966 at the age of 23 I went to Cambodia to work on a small magazine there, called *La Revue du Cambodge*.

Cambodia in those days wasn't widely known to the outside world, though that was to change dramatically a few years later. It's that small country in south-east Asia, next to Vietnam on the Gulf of Thailand, where the Khmer Rouge in the nineteen seventies managed to kill off nearly two million of their fellow Khmers before they were driven out by the Vietnamese in January 1979. *Khmer* is another word for 'Cambodian', usually reserved for the race and the culture rather than the nationality, and *rouge* of course is French for 'red', the colour of blood and communism (Cambodia being a former French colony, like Vietnam and Laos to the north); and the Khmer Rouge were a particularly bloodthirsty form of communism, who had seized power in April 1975, as a sort of by-product of the Vietnam War, after years of waging a vicious civil war of their own. When they left there was more civil war still, which only ended in 1991 with a shaky United Nations peace agreement and the return to Phnom Penh of the former Head of State, Prince Norodom Sihanouk (later restored to the throne). Since then the country has slowly returned to normal and foreign tourists can once again visit the ancient temples of Angkor in safety, in the north-west. But it remains backward and impoverished, beset by corruption and bad governance, a shadow of its former self. It will be another generation at least before the scars of that dreadful period are finally healed.

Then, however, things were very different. For one thing, it was at peace. The Vietnam War next door was fast hotting up – the first US combat troops had landed a year earlier and already numbered over two hundred thousand, with more to follow – and occasionally it spilt over the border in the shape of an armed incursion or other incident, but so far Cambodia had avoided being drawn directly into the conflict. The capital Phnom Penh was an attractive, cheerful city of six hundred thousand, mostly Khmer of course but with large Chinese and Vietnamese minorities and a diplomatic community which was the source of much social activity. Developed mostly by the French in the late nineteenth century, on the banks of the Mekong where it joins its tributary the Tonle Sap (and immediately splits up again into the lower Mekong and the Bassac, twin rivers which then make their way through southern Vietnam to the sea), it still retained a strong French influence and felt at times more like some sunny *préfecture* in the south of France than the capital of a modern Asian nation.

Cambodia was a kingdom, and the Head of State, Prince Sihanouk, had formerly been king, having been raised to the throne by the French in 1941 at the age of nineteen. But he had stepped down soon after independence in the mid-fifties, in order so he said to become a modern democratic leader. In practice that made little difference. Only one political party was allowed, his own (apart from a minuscule communist party, ancestor to the later Khmer Rouge, which kept a very low profile), and the press was similarly controlled: there were a handful of Khmer-language dailies, a few Chinese and Vietnamese papers for those communities, and half a dozen French or English publications, all supposedly independent but closely watched by the government, and in some cases dependent on it for financial support. It was one of these which had hired me.

2

Two days after my arrival I went to a party. It was a large, noisy gathering in the flat of one of the Australian embassy girls, near the city centre, of a kind I soon got to know among the English-speaking community: fifty or sixty people packed in a room meant for half that number, with the air-conditioners at full blast and music blaring out from a record player. Vietnamese servants in white carrying trays of drink somehow circulated through the throng without spilling any. I'd been told casual but I didn't want to take any chances – an embassy party sounded very imposing – and I'd come in a suit, despite the heat. I quickly got rid of the coat but that wasn't enough and soon I was sweating heavily. After an hour of shouting to make myself heard I developed a headache as well, and fled to the balcony outside in search of some peace, pursued by Herb Alpert and his Tijuana Brass. I wondered how the neighbours put up with the din.

I'd been there a few minutes, slowly recovering my wits, when a woman came out, a European, presumably for the same reason. For a moment we didn't speak, enjoying the relative calm in silence. Then I pulled out my crumpled pack of cigarettes and offered her one. In those days almost everybody smoked and this was an accepted way to strike up a conversation with a pretty woman on a balcony. By the light of the match I saw a curl of blond hair, a smooth, finely drawn cheek, and frank blue eyes fixed briefly on me before the light went out.

At first I thought she was Australian or English, like most of the guests. But as soon as she spoke I knew that she was French, and I switched to that language.

'You're French too.' She sounded faintly surprised.

'That's right. In part anyway.'

'Ah. And which part's that?'

'Well, my father's French, and I was born in France, but my mother's English and I've been brought up in Australia. My family migrated there when I was very young. I'm really more Australian than anything else.'

'But you've certainly kept up your French. You have no accent.'

'Thank you. My parents made sure we didn't forget it. And I've just spent a few months in France.'

'Whereabouts in France?'

'In Tours, where I was born. I still have relatives there.'

'I love the Touraine. It's a lovely part of France. And people say that's where the purest French is spoken.'

'That must be it then. It's rubbed off on me.'

As we talked I took a closer look at her. She was older than I'd first thought, in her early thirties perhaps, with that indefinable look which somehow told me she was married. She had wavy fair hair swept back from a sharp, intelligent face, a humorous mouth, she wore a green sleeveless dress which set off a firm shapely figure, and she looked altogether rather stylish. She also looked

16

very cool, despite the heat. I was conscious of my own crumpled and dishevelled appearance.

'Is it always as hot as this in Phnom Penh?' I asked.

'No, thank God. This is the worst, just before the end of the dry season. It gets cooler later on, when the rains start in earnest. And towards the end of the year it becomes quite pleasant. When did you arrive?'

'On Thursday. From Paris.'

'On a visit?'

'No, I've come here to work. I'm a journalist. At least,' I went on, anxious to avoid false pretences, 'I'm trying to become one. Do you know Monsieur Marcellin?'

'Yes.'

'I've just started working for him, as assistant editor on his magazine. I'm on a two-year contract with the Ministry of Information.'

'That must be interesting.'

I laughed.

'It's not as grand as it sounds. The magazine's very small, and it only comes out twice a month. I expect I'll mostly be doing translations for the English edition. But I'm surprised you don't already know that. Phnom Penh's such a small town, everyone seems to know what everyone else is doing.'

'It's still nice to meet someone new. And I'm sure you'll be very good at it. How did you get the job?'

'Sheer luck I think. I happened to see the ad when they advertised it in one of the French papers, and I applied.'

She seemed interested, and I explained. It was a relief to hear oneself talk, after the racket inside. I told her how I'd always wanted to be a journalist, and after university in Melbourne I had worked for a year as a cadet reporter on a suburban newspaper. But I was impatient to see the world, and at the end of that year I'd gone to France to try my luck there. I had an uncle in Tours, himself a journalist with one of the local papers. Thanks to him I'd been able to place a few articles, mostly pieces about Australia, and get some translation work. But apart from that I'd found it tough going. Part of the reason was that I was travelling on my Australian passport, which made it difficult to get employment.

(Had I been there on my French passport, to which I was entitled, I would have been liable for military service, which I had no intention of doing. I didn't tell her that.)

Then, providentially, that ad had appeared. It had been put there by the Cambodian embassy in Paris, and it was for a junior position in Phnom Penh. I didn't know much about Cambodia, and I didn't think I had much chance of getting it, but my uncle urged me to apply, and it turned out I was just what they wanted: young, yet with some experience, bilingual in French and English – the ad specified fluency in both languages – and, though I didn't realise its importance until later, a French-born Australian. Prince Sihanouk was strongly opposed to the war in Vietnam and pursued a neutralist policy, which put him at odds with the west – the Americans had closed their embassy the year before, after a series of violent anti-US demonstrations – but he had maintained close relations with two western countries, and these happened to be France and Australia. To the embassy officials who interviewed me I must have seemed the ideal candidate.

She listened patiently to all this, and in return I learnt a few facts about her, though she was more reserved at a first meeting. She was a Norman, from somewhere near Alençon, she had two children, and she had been living in Cambodia for nearly three years now. Her husband, also French, was an adviser to the Cambodian Ministry of Finance, on loan from the French government. They had previously served in Africa.

'You must have seen him in there – there he is, talking to that Indian woman.' She pointed him out through the balcony doors, a tall greying man who looked much older than her. I barely had time to register the fact when another shape appeared at the balcony door, a shorter, spare young man with gingery hair plastered over a domed skull, who came out towards us. This was Rick McPherson, who had brought me to the party. His face glistened with sweat and he looked as bedraggled as I felt, but his eyes lit up when he saw us.

'What a terrible crush in there!' he exclaimed. 'They shouldn't allow it in this heat. Have you two met? Good. I meant to introduce you.'

'Perhaps you should,' she said. 'We've talked a lot, but we still don't know each other's name.'

'Don't you? How typically French. Nicole, Philippe – sorry, I should say *Madame Marchand, Monsieur Roche.* I keep forgetting how formal you are in French.'

I smiled. Rick spoke French with a strong Australian accent – and I hardly knew him as yet – but already he'd struck me as a man who didn't forget much about anything.

What he was, however, was clearly a good friend of Nicole's. They called each other *tu* and chatted with easy familiarity about various events and people in Phnom Penh, while I stood to one side, wondering if I should leave them to it. But then she looked at her watch and said she had to leave.

'We still have a dinner to go to. But we're giving a dinner ourselves soon. In two weeks. Can you come Rick? I'll send you a card.'

'Thank you. I'd love to.'

She hesitated, then turned to me. 'Perhaps you'd like to come too, Monsieur Roche. It must be lonely, staying in a hotel when you don't know many people. Can I get in touch with you through the magazine?'

'Certainly. Thank you very much, *Madame.*'

She smiled, held out her hand, and went back inside towards her husband. Rick gave me an amused glance.

'You've made a conquest. Nicole doesn't issue invitations lightly.'

I didn't believe him, though it was nice to hear, and as I headed back into the fray I thought she was easily the most attractive woman I had met that evening. But that was just a passing thought, for the heat was getting to me and I longed for nothing more exciting than a shower and my bachelor bed. I resisted McPherson's own invitation to go and sample the bars, and went quietly back to my hotel instead. There'd be time for that later, I thought, when I had more money and the address of a good tailor.

The Marchands lived in a leafy, exclusive part of town reserved for diplomats and wealthy Cambodians, just north of the small hill which gives Phnom Penh its name (*phnom* means 'hill' in Khmer, and there is a shrine on it, a bell-shaped stupa which houses the remains of a lady hermit who once lived there, called Penh – the Lady Penh.) Strangely enough I have much vaguer memories of the dinner I attended there two weeks later – mainly I think because it's too overlaid with later memories. There was a large house, a solid rambling two-storied villa set in a big garden, with lofty rooms linked by tall archways and ventilated by ceiling fans with the wingspan of an eagle. I had already discovered that expatriates lived rather better in Phnom Penh than back home, but I was still impressed by the size and style of the establishment, the number of servants, the self-assurance of the guests, most of whom that evening were French, from the local business community. I was glad I'd had time to buy a new light-weight suit, which I inaugurated that evening. No one could have survived long in that climate, socially or physically, in the thick and battered clothes I had inherited from my student days.

But it takes more than clothes to shine in society, and although I did my best to fit in I felt gauche and out of place and stayed mostly in the background. In fact the only person I spoke with for any length of time was Henri Marchand, Nicole's husband. This was my first meeting with him but Rick had told me that Henri, born and largely bred in Indochina, was something of an authority on the region, and taking that as my cue I managed to ask him a few reasonably intelligent questions, my mind still full of the books I'd read in France before coming out. He answered them with interest, even with pleasure, but also a kind of mild diffidence, as if he wanted to apologise for an undeserved reputation. Yet he clearly knew what he was talking about. I guessed he was a shy man at heart. Certainly his reserve contrasted with his wife's polished and rather brittle social manner.

One thing which struck me was that he was very tired. He looked indeed much older than his wife at close range – I thought he must be in his fifties, though in fact he was only forty-seven – with the lined face of a man who spends too much time at his desk. He also had the disconcerting habit at times of breaking off in the middle of a conversation, as if withdrawing into a private reverie for a moment. It happened once or twice while we were talking, and I saw his wife glance at him with a mixture of concern and irritation, quickly controlled, and make some remark which brought him back to earth. Towards the end of the evening he became downright taciturn, and I sensed hidden relief when the guests stood up. But he accompanied us all to the door and was alert enough to remember me when I said goodbye.

'We have a houseboat of sorts on the river,' he said, 'and we often go there on Sundays when it's fine, for a picnic and some water-skiing. Why don't you join us this Sunday? Rick knows where it is, he can bring you.'

I accepted gratefully, though it all seemed rather grand, and I wondered how I would fit in with the Marchands' circle of friends. The evening had been a little starchy for my taste.

I needn't have worried. Sundays on the river, it turned out, involved a very different crowd from the formal dinners which the Marchands gave from time to time, and I had no difficulty getting accepted into their entourage – or should I say Nicole's, to be more accurate? Most of them were closer to Rick's age and mine, and some of them at least were more attracted to Nicole than to Henri, whom they regarded with tolerant amusement, as a sort of avuncular presence who had to be humoured at times, when he became a little moody and preoccupied. One or two of them in fact were quite possessive about her and looked me over with distrust before they made room for me.

I didn't like them all, even as I learnt to mimic them on occasion. But Henri didn't seem to mind them. And as I came to know the Marchands better I saw that he even encouraged his wife to cultivate them, as if he feared that his company alone might pall on her, that she needed more colour and excitement than he could give her. I felt a little uneasy when that thought first occurred to me. I wasn't a prude but my parents had led very conventional lives and there was no clue there, or among the few married couples I'd known, as to how one should behave in that situation.

21

But Henri showed no sign of resenting them. And if I wondered sometimes about his relationship with his wife, I could put it down to the difference in age and temperament. Nicole was still young (though older than I'd first thought: all of thirty-six) and liked attention, and Henri preferred to be left alone, and to get on with his work. Sometimes it embarrassed me when she flirted with me, but that was due to my inexperience. Nicole flirted with at least four other young men, including Rick, without any suggestion that it went any further – whatever the gossips might say.

It wasn't perhaps the way I would want my own marriage to be, but each to his ways – and besides, it wasn't any of my business.

4

In any case the Marchands only took up a small part of my life, in those early days. As a young and reasonably presentable bachelor, and one of the few foreign journalists then allowed in the country, I was soon much in demand, and led a busy social life. Phnom Penh might be small but it was very welcoming. Hostesses invited me to their dinners (who cared if it was to make up for a last-minute defection), the young asked me to their parties, even diplomats sought me out at embassy receptions as a useful contact. There was much there to tempt and flatter a young man, and for weeks on end I rarely spent an evening at home.

Much of that I owed to Rick McPherson. He was himself a young diplomat, Second Secretary in the Australian embassy, and I had met him the morning of the party, when I had gone to the embassy to register and called on him as part of a round of diplomatic calls which Marcellin, the editor of the magazine, had asked me to make. He wanted me to take over that side of the work. Rick's curiosity was piqued when I told him I had French as well as Australian nationality.

'An Aussie Frog,' he said. 'Don't you feel conflicted about it? A clash of cultures?'

'Not really, no. It's not as if the two countries were at war. Except on the rugby field sometimes. Then I usually end up supporting the losing side.'

He laughed at that.

'And just to complicate things I have British nationality too, through my mother.'

'Ah. A Bloody Pom as well! I wouldn't boast too much about that around here if I were you.'

'Why not?'

'Well, the Prince seems to like us, for whatever reason. Mainly I think because we've always been nice to him. And he loves France of course, de Gaulle's his poster boy. But he doesn't like the Brits very much. He thinks they're too close to the Americans. Which is rather odd, considering we're the ones with troops in Vietnam, and we're representing American interests here as well since they left.'

He gave me a shrewd look.

'I'm not being too frank, am I? You're not the kind that betrays a confidence?'

'I should hope not!'

'Good. I think you'll do. Just bear in mind that we're here to help, if you get into trouble. Feel like going out tonight? One of our girls is giving a party. Where are you staying?'

'Hotel Monorom.'

'I'll pick you up. It's just down the road.'

Personal chemistry works in mysterious ways. McPherson was a clever man with an acerbic sense of humour and little tolerance for fools, but somehow he took to me from that first occasion, and we quickly became friends. He was only a few years older than me but I looked on him as a man of sense and experience, and he slipped easily into the role of older brother, full of good advice, ready to guide me in the right direction.

It was McPherson who led me to the bars.

5

There wasn't much of a night-life in Phnom Penh at that time. The departure of the Americans the year before, following the sack of their embassy, and Sihanouk's version of a state-controlled economy, had seen to that. There was a government-owned establishment out near the airport at Pochentong, the *Dancing d'Etat*, where for a stiff fee you could spend an hour or two practising the *paso doble* or the rumba with some bored and supercilious hostess, and a few restaurants of course, but apart from that all the town had to offer by way of legalised debauchery was a small cluster of bars near the Central Market – most of them rather seedy but one or two with a better reputation.

The first one we tried was *Chez Martin*, on the waterfront. Martin was a stumpy little *Auvergnat* who had lived in Indochina most of his adult life, since jumping ship in Saigon at the age of sixteen, several decades earlier. He was a shrewd, tough, sentimental man with a fund of reminiscences and I was immediately fascinated. In better times he had owned five establishments at the one time, in Saigon. That was before he came to Phnom Penh, in the days of the first Indochina war, against the Vietminh. He told colourful stories of Foreign Legionnaires breaking up his bars, of grenades and *plastique* explosions, and of rough rides through the outer suburbs, when he drove his staff home in the early hours and they ran the gauntlet between Vietminh infiltrators and French patrols. Once, he said – he swore – he found bullet holes in his car when he got home.

You never knew how much to believe Martin, but that didn't matter to me. He took such pleasure in the past, and the people he'd known, back in the days of the *Corps Expéditionnaire*.

'All of them, I tell you, I knew them all. Most of them are dead now of course. But they all came to see me, at the end of their leave, before they went back on operations, and we'd shake hands and they'd sign my book and I'd shout a last round, and a week or a month later a friend would drop in and say so and so's copped it. All their signatures, their units, their addresses in France...' His voice would drop to a dramatic whisper, in which regret and child-like pride still mingled, all these years later.

'That book...I've still got it, in France. *C'est un document historique, une vraie pièce de musée...*'

But when I knew Martin, times were lean. Customers no longer stood three deep at the bar. That was partly his fault. He was a man of principles, and there were no girls in his bar.

Madeleine, manager of the *Cochon d'Or*, near the market, had no such inhibitions. I hesitated, the first time Rick took me there.

My imagination ran to seedy dives full of pimps and hard-faced whores, and I wasn't sure what I'd find. I was soon reassured. Certainly it was safer to stay away from the whisky, and some of the girls, even under the subdued lighting, had seen better days. But provided you stuck to beer the place was harmless enough. Most of the girls were still very young, learners at the trade, and they had charming names: Kantha, Jacqueline, Hoa, Thérèse, Marie-Chantal. They dressed neatly in their best clothes, they said thank you when you bought them an orange drink, and they didn't talk too much. Madeleine watched them closely to make sure they behaved properly, and ran her establishment with a firm velvet paw. She was very pleased when Rick introduced me. She knew most of the European bachelors of Phnom Penh and many of the married men as well by their first names, and she quickly accepted me into her circle, giving me motherly advice and letting me run my bar bill from one month to the next if need be. She greatly facilitated my role when, still unsure of myself, I hesitated to do what was expected of me.

'Of course you can take Hoa home afterwards. Just ask her. She's a nice girl, very affectionate, and intelligent. She won't cause you any trouble.'

I couldn't have made a better choice. There's a song by that French *chansonnier* of the sixties, Georges Brassens, which always reminds me of Hoa:

'*Qu'elle soit pucelle, qu'elle soit putain,*
Mon Dieu qu'elle était belle,
La première fille qu'on a pris dans ses bras...'[1]

Brassens was right. Who cared if she was closer to whore than to virgin? Hoa wasn't my first girl, but close enough to it, and she taught me the highways and the byways of her body as if it was for her too a revelation. We had no illusions, and it didn't last long. Soon there were others. But I've forgotten most of them, and I remember her.

---

[1] Whether whore or virgin
How beautiful she was
The first girl I held in my arms

It was in the Cochon d'Or too that I first met Mick Forbes, otherwise known as Shagger. It was an appropriate setting. Forbes was another Australian, a tall, broad-shouldered man who worked as a technician on one of Cambodia's many aid projects, and he had earned his evocative nickname according to Rick early in his posting by bedding as many of Phnom Penh's female population as he could manage and still get up in the mornings. Added to his drinking it was a heroic endeavour, which aroused much admiration among his friends, but which in that trying climate was beginning to leave its mark. I'm sure it's no coincidence that, if you look up the word *priapic* in the Shorter Oxford, you learn that in ancient times a statue or image of the god Priapus was 'often placed in gardens to protect them from depredators, or as a scarecrow'. For there was always something a little disreputable about Forbes – with his baggy, sweat-stained trousers, his rumpled shirt, and that weather-beaten face of his in the mornings, when he turned up late for work, breathing whisky fumes and literally cross-eyed with exhaustion, which made his success among women somewhat implausible. But women don't fall for tailor's dummies, and Forbes had other qualities besides energy. If he was often crude and unmannerly, he was also a warm-hearted, quixotic man who hated cant and hypocrisy, defended his friends behind their back, and always sided with the underdog. Generous to a fault, he would have given his shirt to the first beggar he saw in the street. I once saw him slip five hundred *riels* to a bar-girl with tooth-ache, out of simple humanity; and more than once I had to restrain him when, incensed by some careless remark about one of his many girl-friends, he wanted to push someone's face in and teach him a few manners.

Unfortunately, even in that Asian context, where girls were cheap (that sort of girl anyway) and you could go a long way on ten dollars, this combination of generosity and sexual prowess had proved too much for his salary, and he was in debt all over town. He'd even borrowed from me, before the month was out, despite Rick's warning and my own slender resources. But it was a measure of the man that you could never resist him, and none of us really minded. Besides, he only borrowed from those who could afford it. And when you considered the number of girlfriends and *cyclo*-drivers that he supported at any one time, you felt he was doing more, on his own modest scale, to raise the standard of living than half a dozen aid projects.

Forbes' role was never more than marginal in my life, and I only mention him out of nostalgia. But he did me a good turn, in those days of my innocence, when I was too embarrassed to ask Rick. He sent me to Fouchet.

7

Fouchet is another of those colourful, faintly disquieting figures which loom, larger than life, in my memory. In his case it's no exaggeration, for he was a huge bear of a man, with a completely bald head and the hairiest forearms I had ever seen. He had a long, fleshy, sceptical nose which quivered as he talked, and his little eyes, screwed up behind rimless glasses, held an expression of mistrust which at first I found rather sinister.

Fouchet was a doctor, a former surgeon-major with the *Corps Expéditionnaire*. He ran a clinic near the Central Market and was I knew a close friend of the Marchands, where I had first met him. But it wasn't until two or three weeks later that I got to know him more personally. I had been worried about my health, and following the advice of the knowledgeable Forbes I called on him one morning on my way to work. I had no appointment and I was a little embarrassed when he made me come in ahead of his other patients, who were all Cambodian. But no one protested, and I gathered this was common practice. In his consulting room I diffidently explained my symptoms, keeping a nervous eye on the nurse. I half-expected a lecture, but he wasted no time in moralising. Brushing my explanations aside he told me to drop my trousers, gave me a quick examination, then shrugged, laughed, and clapped me on the shoulder.

'Nonsense, my boy! You're suffering from nothing worse than the pricks of a puritanical conscience. Who was it, a bar-girl?'

'Yes,' I said, blushing, and greatly relieved.

'You were lucky then. Next time take a few precautions. You're too young to go catching their diseases.'

He glared at me for a moment, then suddenly his manner changed and he became kind and affable.

'We've already met, haven't we. You're that young Australian Frenchman who's just arrived – a journalist or something.'

'That's right. I work for the *Revue du Cambodge*, under Monsieur Marcellin.'

'Ha! That old goat!' he exclaimed. 'I bet it wasn't him who sent you.'

I laughed, and explained about Forbes. Fouchet evidently knew him well, professionally as well as personally, for he launched at once into a long monologue about Forbes' exploits, with scant regard I thought for discretion. Soon we were deep in discussion, his waiting room forgotten. Fouchet loved nothing better than an argument, about anything – sex, religion, politics especially, always taking opposite ends of the discussion and ready to switch sides if you threatened to agree with him. It turned out that he was a good friend of Rick's as well, and on the strength of that acquaintance, before I'd left him that morning he'd invited me to dinner.

It was easy to make friends with Fouchet.

8

I found it harder to like Marcellin, though he too was an unusual man and in retrospect perhaps the most fascinating of them all. Like Fouchet and Henri Marchand an old Indochina hand, there was in addition an element of mystery about his background which gave rise to some colourful rumours.

Marcellin was already in his fifties when I met him, a bachelor, and he had lived in Cambodia for many years. Like Martin he had come over from South Vietnam soon after independence in the mid-fifties, in the early days of Ngo Dinh Diem's regime there, apparently in a hurry. For reasons I never fully understood it seemed he had fallen foul of Diem and his American backers and he had left Saigon only a jump ahead of Diem's police, to be treated with great suspicion at first by the Cambodians – it was said they even put him in gaol for a time. How much truth there was in all that I never found out, but it would help to explain his strong anti-Americanism, which he rarely wasted an opportunity to put into print.

There were other, darker stories about him. According to these he had been a collaborator in France during the war – some even said a *sous-préfet* in the Vichy administration – and he had come to Indochina in the first place by a circuitous route and using a false name. Others claimed he was an agent of the French and their man in the palace. And to top it all there was a widespread belief that he was a rampant homosexual, at a time when homosexuality was still not quite respectable, even in a former French colony. Of course these stories could easily be true, separately or together, but again I have no evidence for any of them, apart from the fact that he never made a pass at me. Admittedly his appearance counted against him, for he had the rotund body, the squeaky voice and the white flabby hands of a court eunuch, a role which in another era he might well have filled.

Whatever the truth about his origins, Marcellin was a professional journalist, and a good one. He had himself founded the magazine where I worked, the *Revue* for short, which he edited with some help from the government, and over the years he had become a kind of *doyen* of the small band of French expatriates who then made up almost all of the foreign press community.

More important, he had earned the trust of Prince Sihanouk, who often used him and his paper as an unofficial mouthpiece. This gave him a privileged position, and he was one of the best-informed men in Cambodia, much courted by foreign diplomats, who knew that the government subsidised him and believed that he could in turn influence Sihanouk and put in a good word for them. They were wasting their time. Sihanouk and Marcellin were both too clever for that. But years of serving the Prince had left their mark and developed in him some less attractive qualities: a sense of self-importance, a taste for intrigue and calculation, a tendency to pomposity and a cold-blooded mistrust of everyone around him, only rarely redeemed by an occasional flash of warmth or whimsicality.

Perhaps I'm being unfair to the man. It would have been difficult for anyone living for years under the shadow of a latter-day Renaissance prince (however gifted) not to become a little warped in the process; and there's no doubt that Marcellin had plenty of talent for the job – how else could he have survived – including a genuine love of his craft and a knowledge of Cambodia and the Khmers which many scholars might have envied.

Marcellin behaved on the whole correctly towards me, and I learnt a lot from him. We had no choice of course, but to work closely together, for the staff was small – he had himself requested an assistant. My one complaint was that he remained cold and distant and wouldn't hand enough of the really interesting work to me. I was kept down to routine chores and trivial articles and spent much of my time as I'd told Nicole translating from French to English and vice-versa: for the magazine came out in two editions, week about (though never quite identical – that helped to boost our sales a little). After a few weeks I felt I had learnt enough about the job to be entrusted with more interesting work from time to time. But this was slow in coming, and he gave no sign that he regarded me as more than an apprentice, a sort of odd-jobs man who still had to pass some undefined test before I could be fully trusted. It was a little frustrating, after coming all that way.

Sometimes on free evenings he would unbend a little and we would go out together for a few drinks and dinner, at the *Venise* or the *Café de Paris*, often ending up *chez* Martin. He was a solid drinker when he got going and I earned many a hangover trying to keep up with him. On the whole I enjoyed these occasions, for he then became more talkative and almost friendly. But try as I might I never got him to talk about himself. And his sense of discretion remained as firm after six or eight whiskies as during office hours. No doubt that explained why the Prince trusted him. To the best of my knowledge these minor escapades were his only weakness.

9

Rick had warned me that Marcellin didn't like 'Anglo-Saxons' (as Sihanouk used to call the British, Canadians, Australians, or indeed anyone else who might be suspected of supporting US interests in their absence), and that he might well disapprove of our friendship, if he chose to read anything into it. And so I wasn't surprised one day when Marcellin turned to me and said, in his usual mildly caustic manner:

'I hope you're being careful with your diplomatic friends, and not heading into trouble.'

'What do you mean?' I asked, looking innocent.

'I mean the kind that a young man could easily get into, if he weren't on his guard. You seem to be in great demand, always going out to dinners and receptions, and I certainly don't want to stop you. You're young, full of energy, by all means enjoy life.' His hand sketched a small gesture of deprecation. 'But beware! These people may seem very friendly, but they're professionals first and last, and it may not be your fascinating personality which attracts them so much as your job and your position, whether you can hold your drink – and even,' he paused, 'whether you can be bought.'

'Bought?' I echoed. 'Whatever for? I haven't got anything to sell, apart from the drafts of next week's translations.'

He smiled thinly.

'I know that. But they don't.'

My first reaction was to shrug it off as an attack on Rick's character and the fact that I preferred his company out of office hours to that of many others in Phnom Penh, diplomat or plain civilian. Rick had never asked me an improper question, and if he wanted to drop a bag of gold into my hand he was very slow about it. But there was no point in trying to explain this to Marcellin. And I reflected instead that perhaps he meant his warning in a more general sense. If so he was being very alarmist. Who could possibly be interested in the indiscretions in or out of drink of a very junior journalist? The French? They had other fish to fry, especially if he was working for them. The Chinese? The Russians? I knew a number of communist diplomats, like Rassimov of the Soviet Embassy, a smooth multilingual man who was to be seen at all the embassy receptions. But these people looked too sober for that sort of nonsense, and although some of them might have welcomed a secret or two, there was bigger game for them to concentrate on. Marcellin, I decided, was either letting his imagination run away with him or having a dig at me, perhaps to keep me in my place. I shrugged again, and forgot about it.

But Marcellin was no fool, as I discovered soon after; though the approach, if it was one, came in such a roundabout way that at first I barely noticed it; and it wasn't the sleek and clever Rassimov who made it, but one of his colleagues, a tall bony man who looked much too old for his lowly position of Third Secretary (Press). His name was Kalyakin and he spoke a horrible brand of French.

I had been to dinner at Kalyakin's house, with others, and later the two of us had gone to the bars. Kalyakin insisted on buying most of the drinks, and towards one or two in the morning he gripped my arm in the intimate manner he sometimes affected, when he wanted to be especially friendly.

'*Mon cher Philippe*,' he said – we were on first name terms by then – 'I wonder if you could do me a small favour.'

'By all means,' I said unsuspectingly.

'It's very simple. As you know I'm in the press section, and one of my responsibilities is to place articles about the Soviet Union. But as you also know, anything which comes out with an embassy by-line invariably gets thrown into the wastepaper basket. People think it's propaganda and they don't even bother to read it.'

I nodded sympathetically, being guilty of that myself often enough.

'Now what I'd like to do,' he went on, giving me a laborious death's head grin, 'with your help if you agree, would be to publish an article or two about my country in your magazine from time to time. Once a month or so, for example. No propaganda, nothing like that, just general information, on our history, our economy...'

'But you don't need my help for that,' I said. 'Surely if you approach the editors of a few papers yourself, one of them's bound to publish it.'

'My dear friend, you're being very polite. You can see that I speak French badly, and write it even worse. It needs to be written by a native speaker, and a professional journalist, before any editor's going to look at it, not by an embassy official.'

I hesitated.

'Of course,' he pressed on, 'we'd supply you with all the material you need, statistics, photos...we've got a good research library. And my dear fellow, we certainly wouldn't expect you to do this for nothing. You'd obviously have to be remunerated. Say two or three thousand *riels* an article, depending on the length and the time you put into it?'

'Oh, it's not that,' I cried. At that time the Cambodian *riel* stood at seventy to the US dollar on the black market. 'I mean that's obviously a reasonable offer. But I don't see how I could. I only write what I'm told to write about. I can't just put in an article and say, print that.'

'Oh, but I'm sure, if you had a good article to put forward, Monsieur Marcellin would look at it seriously. Only the other day he was saying that it's hard to get good copy. Who knows? You couldn't lose by trying, anyway.'

I was getting embarrassed by Kalyakin's insistence, though the financial aspect was tempting enough. I hedged, and finally put him off by saying I'd think about it. And the next time I saw Rick I asked for his advice.

'What do you think, Rick? Do you think they're serious about it or just trying to see if I'm susceptible to money?'

'I don't know,' he said cautiously. 'Do you need the money?'

'I'm not flat broke, if that's what you mean, though it would certainly help. Shagger's just touched me for another thousand *riels*.' I shook my head. 'I don't really intend to accept. I just wonder what I should do next.'

'Why don't you talk it over with Marcellin? See what he says. If he agrees, there's no reason why you can't accept.'

Marcellin's comment was sharp and to the point.

'No. If we publish one country's stuff, we'll have all the others clamouring at our door. In any case I intend to run a series of special country supplements soon, getting all the embassies to submit material for it. If he's interested he'll get his chance then.'

He asked for details, and his mouth pursed when I mentioned money.

'Have you told anyone else about this?'

'No,' I lied.

'Good. It's best to keep this sort of thing to ourselves. But let me know if they persist, and I'll have a word with them myself.'

Did I detect a hint of the conventional, the rehearsed, about Kalyakin's disappointment when I gave him my 'considered response'? At any rate he didn't insist. And when, breaking professional discretion for the second time, I mentioned it again to Rick, he commented that they'd probably only tried it as a matter of routine, just in case, and to test my reaction.

'Just as well you did refuse, you know. I've heard of cases which started like that. Get someone working for them, very innocently at first, occasionally slipping them a bit of money, against a signed receipt of course, for the embassy accounts. Then, when they'd gathered enough of these, they started applying pressure. Receipts can be interpreted in different ways, if they fall into the wrong hands.'

'You should have told me!' I said, rather shaken. 'What if I'd accepted?'

He smiled.

'Maybe I wanted to test your reactions too.'

10

That episode, I must confess, didn't worry me much at the time. It was no doubt intoxicating to be a target for Soviet espionage, and with greater experience I might have read more serious warnings into it. But I was too busy, too excited with my new life to look on it as more than an amusing, vaguely tantalising incident.

I had been in Phnom Penh almost three months, and it had been one of the happiest times in my life. It had all gone very fast, and yet I felt I'd achieved many things. I had a job I liked, and which promised great things if I didn't make too many mistakes along the way. I lived in a happy, colourful, exotic land where none of the inhibitions of mid-sixties Australia, and few of the social restrictions of Europe, seemed to apply. My salary, though small, was enough for my needs. I'd started learning Khmer, though that was hardly necessary, as nearly everyone I met spoke fluent

French. I was young, I was liked, I had many friends. I had my own flat, a maid, I could even entertain at home, modestly. After Melbourne, the disappointments of Tours, it was as if I'd come into my own. I was independent.

The Ministry had even given me a car by now – I owed that too to Marcellin – an old, rattling Soviet-aid *Moskva* which groaned and belched clouds of smoke but proved surprisingly reliable and gave me freedom to go where I liked, at a time when Cambodia knew neither curfews nor army road-blocks. My father had given me a Leica as a going-away present and I loved nothing better than taking photos. On fine afternoons I roamed along the flat delta roads, thin levees above the flooded paddy fields which stretched away into the distance, repetitive and yet never dull, like Cambodian music, infinitely varied by the tall sugar-palm trees with their small top-knot of spiky leaves – nearer the coast, dishevelled coconut trees. Bullock carts on country roads, the shaft, curiously inlaid with tin and copper, curving high above the heads of the oxen. Sunsets in the water, streaked with the curving rice. Returning to Phnom Penh in the evening, to the warm nights, friendly as an animal's fur, conniving gently at the innocent sins of youth, was like coming home. I felt I could easily spend the rest of my life there, and caught myself dreaming of it, becoming part of the scenery like Fouchet or Martin, and never wanting to leave.

Of course it couldn't have happened. It was just a day-dream. In time I would have got tired of the monotony and the languid, easy-going life, and started to long for something harder, more exacting. Already sometimes I could feel stirring inside me a vague, barely conscious anticipation of something else, something more than the pleasurable existence I had so easily grown into. In the midst of my happiness I caught glimpses of myself as others might see me, a harmless and shallow young man in the first flush of hedonism, uncertain of myself, unused to people, self-centred and without real responsibilities. But these were only passing moods, hints of later dissatisfaction perhaps, not enough yet to do more than ruffle my sense of well-being and self-satisfaction. Above all I was still an innocent.

PART II

Chapter One

1

I began to lose my innocence, very quietly, one morning when I met Nicole Marchand near the post office. By chance, that was also the day the articles began.

It was a Friday, in late July, soon after my twenty-fourth birthday. I had been to the printer's for the magazine, the old *Imprimerie Royale* on the Quai Sisowath, and on the way back to the office I decided to stop for a drink at a small restaurant in the post office square, called *La Taverne*. I parked in the shade, around the corner, and took a table on the terrace, facing the square. I ordered a Radeberger beer. When it came I drank half of it in one gulp, then sat back in my chair, took off my sunglasses and began to enjoy the morning.

It was a splendid morning, despite the heat: one of those clear, blue and gold mornings such as you often got in Phnom Penh, by some paradox, in the heart of the wet season. The restaurant was an old-fashioned place which dated back to colonial times but it had a pleasant, homely atmosphere and at that time of day it was very quiet. The Cambodian waiters with nothing else to do moved slowly among the tables, setting for lunch, or simply stood in the wings staring at one another, their faces dark and impassive against the white of their mess jackets. Deeper inside the restaurant the woman at the *caisse*, an attractive *métisse*, sat slumped at the counter with her head in her arms, chatting quietly with the Chinese headwaiter. Overhead large ceiling fans slowly stirred the air.

Outside the scene was equally peaceful. The terrace was sheltered from the heat by a large awning and a row of huge pot plants, forming a kind of hedge, but there were gaps between the plants and I had a good view over the square: the old post office opposite, another memorial to the past, grey and peeling in the sun, further up the dun-coloured police station with its flag hanging limp over the doorway. There was little traffic: a few cars parked in front of the post office steps, and people coming in and out with their mail, at a slow, leisurely pace, as if reluctant to

38

disturb the morning with unnecessary bustle. There were moments of such calm that I could hear the click of scissors from the barber's shop three doors down. From time to time a ferry hooted on the river, a hundred metres away and out of sight.

I finished my drink and I was about to leave when I glanced once more across the square and saw Nicole. She had just come out of the post office, a neat trim figure in a blue shirt and a white skirt which gleamed in the sun, looking at that distance no more than eighteen. She paused in the doorway to adjust her sunglasses, then walked briskly down the steps and started across the square towards me. Involuntarily I smiled. I waited until she came closer. Then when she was about to pass by on the other side of the hedge I stood up, poked my head out and called out to her.

'Nicole!'

She saw me then, stopped, and came towards the hedge.

'Philippe!' she cried. 'You startled me. What are you doing here?'

'Having a rest. Come and join me. I'm about to order some coffee.'

'Oh I can't – I'm in such a hurry –'

'Just a quick one. I have to go myself in a minute.'

She hesitated, looking at her watch. 'Alright then, just a quick one,' and found an opening between two plants while I pulled up another chair. Instinctively I glanced at her knees as she sat down. She had good legs, smooth and well-shaped and brown from much water-skiing. Nicole caught the direction of my glance and gave me a mischievous smile. Like most Frenchwomen she was proud of her legs and not afraid of showing them.

A waiter came up and I ordered two *cafés-filtres*. He moved off silently on his rubber soles, leaving my glass and empty bottle on the table. Nicole nodded at them and gave me another smile, more rueful this time.

'You're starting early today,' she chided gently.

'Carrying on from last night, rather. I didn't get to bed until three.'

'Again? You'll wear yourself out if you keep going like this. What were you doing this time? Or shouldn't I ask?'

'Oh, it was all very proper, I assure you. I was out with Marcellin.'

She laughed. 'I didn't know you two were such friends. What were you doing out with him?'

'Just drinking. I work for him, remember. Besides, he's not such a bad sort, when he gets out of the office. But he will insist on staying up late, and drinking more than he should. I practically had to put him to bed in the end.'

'Is that safe with him?'

I laughed. 'Come on Nicole. You know me better than that. Anyway, enough of me. What about you? Any news of the children?'

'Yes. I had a letter yesterday from my mother. I've just sent them a parcel. They'd forgotten some of their toys.'

'How are they? Enjoying their holidays?'

The Marchands' two children had been sent off a month earlier, to start their summer holidays in France until their parents could join them. I had memories of two well-scrubbed boys, one eight and fair like his mother, the other four, dark and silent like his father.

'They're fine,' she said. 'But she complains that they're getting more spoilt each year.'

'She doesn't have a horde of servants to look after them.'

'That's it of course.'

The waiter returned with the coffee, two gleaming cylinders balanced precariously on their cups, and while we waited for it to percolate I studied Nicole's face. Not for the first time I considered that she wasn't really pretty: the cheekbones were too sharp, the mouth too strong, the nose a shade too pronounced. But it was a frank, intelligent face, and the more I saw of it the more I liked it. I noted with sudden sympathy the tiny wrinkles, an air of strain. With her sunglasses off she looked nearer her age.

She looked up suddenly and I felt myself blushing.

'You must be looking forward to that holiday too,' I said quickly. 'When are you going?'

'I don't know – we haven't decided yet.' She looked thoughtful. 'In fact we may not be going at all, this year.'

'Why not? I thought it was all arranged.'

'No. Henri wants to wait until the visit's over before we take a holiday. And by then it'll be too late.'

'Which visit's that? You mean de Gaulle's? He's not due for months yet.' There'd been much talk lately of a state visit by the French president, but so far no firm date had been announced.

'They've changed the dates again. He's coming in September now, Henri says.'

'I didn't know that.'

She frowned. 'You'd better keep that to yourself. Henri said it wasn't official yet.'

'Of course. In any case we'll soon hear about it at work. But what a pity for you. You were so looking forward to it. Why don't you go by yourself? You could easily spend a month there and be back for the visit.'

'I suppose so. But it's Henri who needs the holidays, more than I do. It wouldn't be fair to leave him alone with all this work. Maybe we'll go off to Japan instead when it's over.'

She spoke calmly enough, as if it had all been thought through already, but there was something in her manner – something more than disappointment, a shade of resentment perhaps – which made me wonder if she was entirely sincere. Henri Marchand I knew had a lot of work. Although technically he was only an adviser to the Minister of Finance, in practice he took a direct hand in much of the Ministry's work and carried a lot of responsibility – among other things he made sure that people like me were paid regularly. Clearly he couldn't drop everything at this stage, with a state visit pending, reports to be written, and no doubt detailed requests for economic aid to be submitted in advance. But I couldn't help thinking – not for the first time – that there must be something else, something a little off key about the Marchand marriage, which gave Nicole that weary, almost gaunt look at times. She too had her worries. Henri wasn't in very good health, he spent far too much time at his desk. Was this the whole reason? I had known them less than three months – first as social protégé, now as a friend – but I had seen enough of him in some of his moods, when he shut himself up with his books for hours on end, and I couldn't help wondering if he wasn't overdoing his work a little. Sometimes it looked as if he was neglecting her.

But of course I said nothing of that to her. Instead we finished our coffee, and she looked at her watch.

'Now I really must go. I have to see my dressmaker at eleven.' She stood up as I paid the bill. 'Are you going to the party tonight?'

'Of course. I wouldn't miss that.' Some French teachers had organised a party for that evening, which promised to be exciting. Almost everyone I knew was going.

As we walked out I looked around for her car, couldn't see it.

'Where's your car?' I asked.

'It's being repaired. Henri borrowed it last night and he broke one of the shock absorbers. That's why I have to hurry, I came by *cyclo.*'

'Let me drive you then – or better still, why don't you take mine?' She made to protest but I insisted. 'Really, I don't need it this morning. There's hardly anything to do at the office today.'

'You're sure?'

'Yes. I'll come round and pick it up this afternoon. But you should tell Henri to leave your car alone. He's got his own.'

'I know, but he likes to use mine from time to time, he says it makes him feel young. You'd better come to lunch then.'

'You're sure? I don't want to be a nuisance.'

'Don't be silly. About one? Henri should be home by then.'

I stood watching as she drove out of the square with a roar and a jerk of unfamiliar gears. Then I turned back towards the restaurant and a cluster of strange vehicles under a nearby tree. These were the *cyclos*, short for *cyclo-pousse*, the local equivalent of taxis: ungainly three-wheeled machines like the back end of a bicycle grafted on to a wheel-chair, with the driver perched high over the rear wheel and the passenger seated between the two front wheels, to act as human shock absorber in case of an accident. The drivers had drawn the canvas hoods up and sat there dozing and resting from the heat. They were dressed in rags and looked exhausted but they were fit and strong with muscles like rope. I tapped one of them gently on the shoulder. He sprang up to make room for me on the tired cushions, pushed his machine forward for momentum, then jumped into the saddle and we floated silently down the square, while I signalled the way with my hands.

The cyclo dropped me off twenty minutes later and more than a kilometre away, in a short side street between the Rue Pasteur and the Boulevard Norodom. I paid the driver thirty *riels* in ragged notes, which must have been twice the normal fare to judge by his grin and the way he took his cap off to me. Then I walked up to an old, narrow, two-storeyed villa with a wooden placard over the doorway which said:

> *La Revue du Cambodge*
> *Direction*
> *Editeur-en-chef : Jean Marcellin*

This was where I worked. Not much of an office perhaps for one of the country's leading publications. The building itself wasn't unpleasant, but it was very run down: the plaster, once a pale ochre, was now that dirty grey-brown which the French call *caca d'oie* or goose-shit and had flaked off altogether in places to reveal the brickwork beneath, the shutters hadn't been painted for years and the picturesque roof, I had soon discovered, leaked like a tea-strainer. For the magazine wasn't rich. For all its influence it only had a small distribution, five or six thousand copies, mostly to government departments and the various embassies, and it wouldn't have survived without its regular government subsidy. It couldn't afford the luxury of a face-lift.

Inside the effect was even more Dickensian. The ground floor consisted of one large room, dusty and shadowy, with pillars running down its length and a creaky staircase disappearing up the wall on the right. No carpets of course, and by way of furniture two plain desks, two chairs, and a battered switchboard which was the cause of many complaints. Its occupants, on this and every other morning, were an elderly Cambodian man, our *planton* or runner, who slept with his head in his arms and didn't stir as I came in; and at the other desk near the switchboard a young Cambodian woman who sat cleaning a typewriter. She wore a pink frilled blouse, faintly luminescent in the filtered light, and a long black skirt reaching down to her ankles, the traditional *sampot*. This was Mademoiselle Sovannareth, much more alert, who would have been quite pretty save for the cast in her left eye. She looked at me reproachfully with the other.

'Monsieur Roche!' she cried. 'Where have you been?'

'At the printer's, Mademoiselle. Why?'

'Monsieur Pherson's been trying to ring you all morning. He rang again just now before you came in.'

'Monsieur Pherson?' I echoed. Mademoiselle Sovannareth, like most Cambodians, never managed to cope with Rick's surname. They kept dropping the *Mac*, as if it was a nickname perhaps, or some strange form of address. 'What did he want?'

'He didn't say. But he asked if you could ring him back.'

'Right. I'll do that in a minute. Is the boss in?'

'Yes, but I'd be careful with him. He's not in a very good mood.'

She smiled, lowering her voice in a conspiratorial whisper, and I thought of making some clever comment about his night-life, to hide a small flutter of alarm, but wisely refrained. Instead I pointed to a white flower which she wore in her hair, tied by a thread.

'That's a pretty flower,' I said. 'What is it, jasmine?'

'I don't know the name in French. It's called *champa* in Khmer.'

'It's beautiful. It really suits you.' She giggled a little, the way Cambodian girls do when you pay them a clumsy compliment. 'Would you like it? Here.' She reached up to untie it, heavy breasts lifting under her blouse, and I took it from her and put it behind my left ear, hoping the gesture didn't carry too much symbolism. I liked Mademoiselle Sovannareth, gentle, helpful, and so poorly served by nature, and it would have been unkind to let her read anything in my occasional compliments. As I walked up the stairs I wondered how much it would cost to have her eye operated on.

As Marcellin's chief assistant I had an office to myself, on the first floor next to his. It was only a cubby-hole, scarcely better furnished than the reception downstairs, but it was the first office I'd ever had, and I still after three months walked into it with an enjoyable feeling of ownership.

I picked up the phone, and after the customary wait got my connection. Rick McPherson's voice came down the wire faint and tinny as if calling from another country.

'Philip?' he asked in English. 'I was hoping you'd ring. I've been trying to reach you. Have you got a moment this morning?'

'Yes, in a while. I've just got back to the office. What's the problem?'

'No problem,' he went on more calmly. 'But the other day your boss mentioned something about a special supplement, and said I should talk to you about it.'

'Right. But there's no rush. I don't know if he explained, but we're doing all the embassies in turn, and your turn isn't due for another month.'

'I know, but I thought I might as well start on it while I've got time. You're not coming over this way by any chance? I'm waiting for a couple of calls and I can't leave my office right now.'

I sighed. 'Alright. Twenty minutes?'

'Fine. See you then.'

I hung up and tidied my desk, a little puzzled by Rick's insistence. The special supplement was Marcellin's latest project: he'd decided to run a series of feature articles over the next few months on each of the countries represented in Phnom Penh – in each case at the cost of the embassy concerned. It was little more than a gimmick, which wasn't expected to boost our sales very much, but it would bring in some extra revenue and, as he said, add variety to a publication which tended to concentrate too much on Cambodian affairs. It was my job to contact the embassies and collect their material. It was the East German supplement which I'd taken to the printer's that morning – a stilted, unconvincing piece about a People's Paradise and the warm and friendly relations it enjoyed with the peace-loving Khmers and their enlightened ruler. I didn't expect Rick to get very excited about it, but perhaps he too had got caught up in the spirit of the thing. I walked across the room and knocked on Marcellin's door.

'*Entrez!*'

The voice had a curt ring to it and I went in cautiously. During office hours, and indeed at all times except for our occasional

45

evenings out, Marcellin had a dry, pedantic manner which discouraged familiarity and I treated him with respect at the best of times – let alone when he had a hangover. I found him sitting unhappily at his desk under his autographed portrait of Prince Sihanouk, with the window shutters closed against the light and his own large, normally pink baby's head abnormally pale in the shadows, turning painfully towards me.

'What is it?' he asked.

'I've just come back from the printer's,' I said for the third time in ten minutes. 'The proofs should be ready first thing in the morning.'

He grunted and rubbed the back of his neck.

'You'll have to go alone,' he said. 'The Head of State is giving a press conference in the morning, at eight, and I'll have to attend of course.'

'Anything important?' I asked, stifling a pang of envy. Sihanouk's press conferences, though not as rare as some foreign diplomats might wish (for he often used them to announce some dramatic turn in foreign policy) were major events in Phnom Penh, attended only by the select group of senior journalists who could be relied on to interpret his thoughts to the outside world. I kept hoping that Marcellin, as leader of that group, would take me along, but so far he had shown no desire to do so, and I waited in vain this time too for an invitation. Instead he gave me a dyspeptic stare and I remembered the flower behind my ear. I took it off and held it in my hand, feeling foolish.

'My dear Philippe,' he said testily, 'the Head of State doesn't call a press conference unless he has something important to say. I suppose he'll make some announcement about de Gaulle's visit, but apart from that I don't know any more than you. One thing for sure, we'll both have a lot of work tomorrow.'

'Do you think I should put off my visit to Battambang, then?' I asked. As a rare treat Marcellin was sending me to do a report on the northwest provinces, near the Thai border, and I was looking forward to it.

'We'll see. With luck we may get everything finished in one day.'

46

He looked down at his desk and I hesitated, standing on one foot in the doorway.

'Then I'll be off, if you don't mind. McPherson wants to see me about his supplement.'

'A bit early for that, isn't it?'

'Well, he seems keen to get on to it, so I might as well get it out of the way,' I said casually, instinctively protecting Rick. 'The Indians are handing in their material next and I've got the Japanese lined up the week after, and there may not be much time after that if he's got to send away for his stuff.'

'I suppose so,' he said, losing interest. 'Off you go then. In any case I think we can close up early today.'

He nodded and gave me a rare smile of friendly approval and I left, careful not to slam the door. Outside I reflected that I had never heard him refer to Sihanouk by name: it was always the Head of State, or *Monseigneur*, as the French called him, translating from the Khmer *Samdech*: My Lord. Maybe he considered it undignified to do otherwise. He was a very formal man.

Then I shrugged. It was too fine a day to worry about such matters. I put the flower in my pocket and went out to see Rick.

3

The cyclo was still waiting for me outside but I waved him away and started to walk. Rick's office was only a short distance away, on the Boulevard Norodom, Phnom Penh's premier avenue, named after the Prince's great-grandfather, King Norodom the first. The embassy was housed in a two-storeyed villa which had been extended at the back, next to the British embassy. A year earlier – long before my arrival – Cambodian police had stood protectively outside as a howling mob of demonstrators attacked the British embassy, which was then the target of Sihanouk's displeasure, helpfully directing the rioters next door. Since then the British had repaired the damage and repainted the building, which now looked in fact much grander than our own. Five hundred metres down the road the Independence Monument stood gleaming in the sun like a large pink asparagus.

In the lobby Mara, the Cambodian receptionist, rang up to announce me. She knew me well from previous visits, and unlike Mademoiselle Sovannareth she was careful to pronounce Rick's name correctly. She was a pretty, cheerfully pregnant woman who according to Rick was forever adding to Cambodia's population.

'He'll be down in a minute.'

I sat down and thumbed through the latest Australian magazines. A moment later the swing door behind Mara opened out and I looked up, expecting Rick. But it was the First Secretary, Chris Norton, escorting a visitor to the front door, and I recognised Rassimov from the Soviet embassy. I would have preferred not to meet him there but his practised eye caught sight of me and he paused on the way to shake my hand, greeting me with a show of cordiality which seemed a little excessive. There was a cold quality to his eyes which didn't go with his smile and made you think of steel-rimmed glasses, even though he didn't wear any. At that moment Rick appeared. Rassimov gave us both a little bow and went out, still smiling.

'Sorry,' Rick said as he led me through the security barrier and up to his first floor office. 'I wouldn't have kept you waiting if I'd known he was in the building. But I had to see the Ambassador for a minute.'

'Don't you have a warning system, when they're around?' I asked.

'We're supposed to mention it, but people keep forgetting,' he said, taking my question more seriously than I meant. 'Not that it matters much I guess. He probably thinks you're already working for us. Just out of curiosity, have they come back at you, since that business with Kalyakin?'

'Not that I could notice. Maybe they decided I'm not worth the trouble. I still think you were reading too much into it.'

'Possibly. The trouble is, you never know with them until too late.'

Rick's office was not much bigger than mine, but much better furnished, with Scandinavian teak furniture and a colourful rug on the tiled floor. An air conditioner in the wall clattered and wheezed like an asthmatic but managed to keep the temperature below blood heat.

Rick motioned me to a chair, sat down facing me, and offered me a cigarette from an embossed silver box. He grimaced when I took out my own crumpled Gauloises instead. 'Still smoking that French shit, are you?' he enquired amiably, but he took one too, and soon we were wreathed in layers of blue smoke. I waited for him to start.

'I'm afraid,' he began, looking serious once more, 'that I've got you here under false pretences.'

'I wondered why you were in such a hurry. What's up?'

'Nothing much, probably. I just didn't want to say too much on the phone.'

He turned round, picked a magazine off his desk and handed it to me.

'Do you know this?'

'I've seen it before.' It was a monthly magazine of Time or Newsweek format, published in Hong Kong and entitled '*East of Suez*'. This issue had a full-face portrait of Prince Sihanouk on the cover. The Prince could be a handsome man but this photo, taken it seemed in the middle of a heated speech, made him look almost demented. 'Not this issue though. We don't get it at work. What does it say about him?'

'See for yourself.' He opened the magazine at a page marked with a red Action sticker and passed it back to me. I read the banner headline:

'*Is the Cambodian tightrope too tight?* From our special correspondent in Phnom Penh.'

'I didn't know they had one here,' I said.

'One what?'

'Special correspondent.'

'Neither did I, until I saw that. But read it first.'

As everyone knows, the article began, *who has taken the trouble to visit the country lately – not an easy task for a foreign journalist these days – Cambodia is that little kingdom by the sea, half-way between Saigon and Bangkok on the map but a lot closer to Peking on the political line-up, where everything has been for the best since American aid was so dramatically rejected three years ago and economic policies took a sharp turn left on the road to socialism. We all remember the headlines which greeted this great event. The new nationalisation measures, we were told, would end once and for all the abusive practices of unbridled capitalism and put the country on a new footing. Corruption, the scourge of so many developing nations, would become a thing of the past. And with external trade, internal distribution, the rice harvest, and such diverse industries as glass manufacture and dance halls coming under direct state control, productivity would increase by leaps and bounds, prices would drop, and the whole country in short would enter an era of prosperity unequalled since the golden age of Angkor.*

Alas, even at the time, among the fanfares and the speeches, it sounded a shade too familiar, too much like the pipe-dreams of other fellow-travellers the world over; and while we would not accuse Samdech Norodom Sihanouk of lack of imagination, recent developments have shown once again that there's quite a gap between the promise and the performance, and that his version of a socialist utopia, when you look at it more closely, falls rather short of expectations...

I looked up curiously. 'Where did you get this?' I asked.

'In Hong Kong. A friend sent it over.'

'In the mail?'

He hesitated fractionally. 'In the bag,' he said.

'I was going to say, they would have had a fit at the Post Office.'

It was common knowledge in Phnom Penh that all mail in and out of the country was subject to censorship – except for diplomatic bags of course. The censors weren't always very efficient, but they would hardly have let something like that get through. One of their jobs was precisely to stop subversive publications from entering the country. And the article, whatever its merits, was decidedly unfriendly. Running into a three-column analysis of the Cambodian economy with a wealth of details which – assuming they were accurate – suggested the author had access to inside information, it accused the government not only of inexperience and lack of foresight, but also of ineptitude, nepotism, graft and corruption of every kind, and indeed of such callous disregard for the people's welfare that it looked as if the country must be about to erupt in bloody revolution. Not content to expose the failure of Sihanouk's policies, the author went on with equal relish to lay into his private life as well, including the multitude of in-laws and relatives who profited from his protection to run with impunity the most scandalous of rackets, from gambling dens and smuggling to prostitution. Even the Queen Mother got a mention. No, whatever the censors thought about it – even if they secretly agreed with it – they weren't about to let this through to the local newsagents. I shook my head in rueful admiration.

'Whoever wrote this certainly put some steam into it. Who was it, do you know?'

'Why, I thought you might tell me,' Rick said, fixing me with a sharp eye. 'It wasn't you by any chance, was it?'

'Me?' I cried. 'You're not serious! I work *for* the Cambodians, not against them! What on earth gave you that idea?'

'Well, you never know. You wouldn't be the first person to do some free-lancing on the side. I believe they pay rather well.'

'Now look here!' I said indignantly. 'What do you take me for! Just because I let the Russians proposition me doesn't mean –'

'I know. I know.' He held up a placatory hand. 'Take it easy. I was only pulling your leg.'

'Were you? You sounded bloody serious to me. Believe me, I think there's probably a lot of truth in that article, but I like this place, and my job here, and the last thing I'd do is go and write something like that about it. Besides, it's not my style.'

'I'm glad to hear it.' His smile faded. 'But seriously though. Someone did write it, and I'd very much like to know who.'

'Someone in Hong-Kong, I expect. You don't want to be taken in by that bit about 'our local correspondent'. It's quite a common trick, faking a dateline.'

'That's what I thought too at first. But take another look. Look at all these figures, and these details.' He pointed to several passages, which had been sidelined in red. 'And here, all those names of public officials. I checked, they're all correct. Some of them only got their jobs a month ago. Does that look as if it was written by a sub-editor in Hong Kong? That takes real local knowledge, believe me. I couldn't have done it, and I've been here a year.'

I re-read the article, noting the initials scribbled on the red Action sticker.

'What does your ambassador think?' I asked. 'Has he read it?'

Again Rick hesitated, then he nodded. 'Yes. He agrees with me, he thinks it's a local job. But that's just between us.'

'Of course,' I said. 'But what if it's a plant? You know, deliberately put in, by the Americans, say. I mean, they could easily do this, couldn't they? And they might like to give Sihanouk a black eye, after some of the things he's been saying about them lately.'

He shook his head. 'Maybe, but I don't think so. It's over a year since they left, so they'd have their own problems getting all the information. Besides, it doesn't fit the current mood. If anything they've been trying hard not to antagonise the Prince lately. I don't see what they could gain by it.'

I nodded, thinking that Rick probably knew more than he was letting on. Following their departure the Americans had asked Australia to represent them in Cambodia, and no doubt they relied on Rick and his colleagues to keep them informed as well about what was going on inside the country: in which case Rick was hardly likely to make a fuss about the article if he thought they were behind it. On the contrary, he'd want to play it down.

'What I'm saying,' he went on, 'is that it could only have been written by someone with recent and first-hand knowledge of this country.'

'And there hasn't been a visiting journalist in this place for...I don't know. Three months at least. The Prince won't let them in.'

'Exactly. So who does that leave?'

'What, me, or one of my colleagues? But that's preposterous.'

'Is it? I don't mean you of course. But what about the others?'

'Surely not. There's only about seven or eight foreign journalists in the country. And apart from Wilberforce who's a communist and hardly likely to criticise Sihanouk for going left, all the others are on contract to the government, like me. You don't see Marcellin writing this, do you? Or Brunner or Chalandon?' I said, naming a couple of others. 'They're much too well entrenched and afraid of losing their jobs. It must be a Cambodian.'

'A Cambodian would never write like that about the royal family, whatever else he might think. Besides, they're even more frightened of stepping out of line.'

We looked at each other for a moment.

'Well then, who?' I asked. 'Unless you think the Russians did it.'

'Exactly. Now do you see why I asked you to come over this morning?'

'Well, not really. I mean I'm glad you've shown it to me. But apart from what I've just said I don't see how I can help.'

He sighed.

'Let me put it this way. What do you think Monseigneur's going to say tomorrow morning when he finds this on his breakfast table?'

'The Prince? What makes you think he's going to read it? For one thing it's in English.'

'Which he reads as easily as French. And don't forget that press-cutting service of his. Twice a day he gets a bundle of press clippings as thick as your wrist from all over the world, in French, English, German, Chinese, Russian, and for all I know Hindustani as well. Everything that's written about Cambodia. And he reads them, what's more, in translation if need be. If he spent half as much time attending to the economy as he does worrying about what people are saying about him articles like this would never get written. Oh he'll read this one alright, if he hasn't already. You can bet your balls on that. And now you see what's going to happen, don't you. Because we both know our Prince. He's not stupid, and he doesn't take kindly to criticism either – to put it mildly. If you think this is a nasty piece of work, you can guess how he's going to react. And he'll very quickly come to the same conclusion as us. It's an inside job. And then he's going to turn round to someone on his staff and say, find out who wrote that. I want his guts. And then there'll be a nice little witch-hunt behind the scenes. And that's where you come in. Because one of the first people they'll be looking at is you.'

'Me?'

'Of course. As you say, we've eliminated just about everybody else.'

'But I didn't write it, I tell you!'

'So what? They don't know that. Look at all the evidence against you. You're bilingual –'

'That's why they hired me in the first place!'

'And you've only just arrived, whereas the others have all been here for years. And as you say, they're all much too worried about their future to take a risk like this.' He paused, as if to let his words sink in, while I stared at him. 'Oh, I'm not saying they'll look only at you, or try to pin it on you regardless. Sihanouk will take this much too seriously to want an innocent hanged for it. He'll want the real culprit. But they may well be taking a close look at you over the next few weeks, and you'd better be ready for it.'

'In case I get a funny feeling I'm being watched?' I laughed, shaken in spite of myself. 'Thanks, Rick. I'm sure you're right, but they're welcome to search my desk. They won't find anything incriminating.'

'Of course,' he went on more mildly, 'I may be wrong. Sihanouk's not infallible, and there's always a chance he won't get to hear about it.'

I thought of my brief conversation with Marcellin.

'No, I think you're probably right. I've just remembered. He's giving a press conference in the morning.'

'I didn't know that.'

'Marcellin told me just before I came here. Keep that to yourself. He mightn't approve if he knew I'd told you.'

'I'll have to tell my ambassador. He'll want to listen to it.'

Sihanouk's press conferences were usually broadcast live on Radio Phnom Penh.

'Okay, but make sure nobody knows I told you.'

'Of course. And you'd better keep quiet about our little chat too. Or we'll be accused of collusion, on top of everything else.'

Briefly I thought of telling him about the changed dates for de Gaulle's visit. As our friendship had deepened over the weeks I'd got into the habit of sharing useful information like that with him, and I had no scruples about passing on bits of office gossip if I thought it could help him. To that extent perhaps Marcellin was right in viewing our friendship with suspicion – I didn't tell

Rassimov and his colleagues any more than I had to. But I drew the line when it came to Nicole. I had after all promised her my discretion.

'And now,' Rick was saying, 'we'd better talk about this supplement of yours. Marcellin said something about a fee.'

'That's right. Standard advertising rates. Four thousand riels a page.'

'What? That's extortion! Are you telling me *we* have to pay *you* to provide you with material?'

'In advance too if you don't mind. Don't blame me! It's Marcellin's idea. He feels we're not earning our keep. Of course the others have all agreed.'

'That, you bastard, is known as blackmail!'

4

I'd already dismissed the article from my mind when I got home. It was well after twelve and I was bathed in sweat, for the lunch-hour crowd had taken all the cyclos, and although the sky had clouded over during the past hour there was no breeze and the heat was even more oppressive. I asked Chi Hai, my Vietnamese maid, to make some coffee while I changed. She was just preparing lunch and she clattered the saucepans noisily in the kitchen to show her displeasure. But the coffee came and I drank it on the balcony, looking at the sky with apprehension. It was now a menacing sea-grey colour, and the rain might start before I reached the Marchands' house, on the other side of town, where my umbrella had preceded me on the back seat of my car. I decided to risk it.

The rain caught me with three hundred metres to go. The streets were deserted, everyone had gone to ground. A few large drops splattered and steamed on the pavement, there was a lull during which I could smell the coming rain, and then the heavens burst. I started to run, but within seconds I was soaked to the skin. I swore angrily. Why were there no taxis in this bloody city? I thought of turning back, but I'd gone too far for that. And then, amused at myself, I decided to enjoy it. At least I was cool now, which was a relief. I threw my arms open and raised my face to the sky, eyes clenched against the pelting rain. The water streamed from my hair and down my throat, stuck my shirt in cold sheets against my ribs and turned my trousers into a shapeless mass. My shoes sent up little plumes of spray and I waded through the deepest puddles.

Nicole, true French mother, let out a cry of dismay when she saw me and scolded me like one of her children.

'Why didn't you wait for the rain to stop? Now I feel so guilty about taking your car.'

'It doesn't matter,' I laughed, shaking myself like a dog on her veranda. 'I haven't walked in the rain like that for years. May I take my shoes off, before I make a mess?'

'Of course! Come upstairs and dry out, before you catch a chill. I'll get you some of Henri's clothes.'

I followed her inside, skirting the carpets and the furniture, leaving a trail of wet footprints on the tiled floor.

'Where's Henri?' I asked.

'He should be home soon. He's probably been held up at the garage.'

At the top of the stairs she turned and set off down a corridor as if my life depended on getting to a towel in time. As I hurried to keep up with her my bare feet slipped on the tiles and I lost my balance. I waved my arms around uselessly, my feet shot out from under me, the next moment I was skating out of control along the corridor, vainly clutching at the walls, until I fetched up with a thud against a doorway. Nicole turned at my cry to find me all of a heap on the floor, clutching my right leg.

'Are you alright?' she exclaimed.

'I'm sorry,' I gasped, as she bent over me. The pain made me dizzy, and for a moment I thought I would throw up. 'It's alright,' I said at last. 'I should have been more careful.' But my leg felt on fire, and when I stood up Nicole had to hold me. She helped me to a chair, where I sat down regardless of the cushions.

'You're very pale,' she said. 'You haven't broken anything, have you? There's blood on your trousers.'

I rolled up my trouser leg and examined the damage. The pain was beginning to ease but a large purple bruise was forming halfway up the shin, and blood trickled from a cut in the centre. I took out my sodden handkerchief to stop the flow.

'That looks nasty,' she said.

'It's only a cut,' I said, inwardly agreeing with her. 'But you may find a piece of your wall missing. Can I use your bathroom to wash off the gore?'

'Of course. I'll get some water boiling. You can take your wet clothes off in there, there's a towel behind the door.'

She hurried out while I hobbled to the bathroom. I locked the door, turned on the shower and stepped under it fully clothed. I'd stripped off to my underpants and I was washing the wound when she knocked on the door.

'Wait a minute,' I called.

'Hurry, this water's scalding.'

I turned the water off, slipped a towel around my waist and opened the door a fraction. But she disregarded my outstretched hand and came in, holding a kettle. She went to a medicine cupboard on the wall, took out a small bowl and a bottle of disinfectant, and poured water into the bowl.

'I can do all this,' I protested.

'Just sit down,' she said firmly. 'This won't take a minute, and you'll only make a mess if I let you. I took a first aid course once.'

'It's not that bad you know.'

'Don't argue. Sit down and hold out your leg.'

Taken aback by her efficient hectoring I took the nearest seat I could find, which was the toilet seat, and without further ado she knelt on the floor and started to wash the wound. She worked quickly, deftly dipping bits of cotton wool into the steaming bowl without scalding her fingers, then gently rubbing the blood away from the centre of the cut, just like the manuals say. It reminded me of scenes from my childhood, when my mother washed the dirt out of my scraped knees after a fall. But I was no longer a whimpering child, and Nicole, with her fair hair a few inches below my eyes and her soft hands and the scent of her perfume still perceptible against the smell of disinfectant, was not my mother. I felt idiotic sitting there like a Roman emperor with Nicole like a slave at my feet, and a little embarrassed too, but it was by no means unpleasant, and I was fast acquiring a taste for the feel of her hands and her equivocal presence in the overheated bathroom. Outside the rain beat steadily on the roof, cutting us off from the world. I was almost sorry when after a final twitch of my leg she stopped and said:

'There, it's clean now. Did it hurt much?'

'Yes, but I won't admit it. And you're a splendid nurse.'

She smiled at me, her face flushed from the steam. A few strands of hair had stuck across her forehead, and glancing involuntarily down the line of her neck I saw, where a button of her blouse had come undone, the swell of a breast, an edge of white cotton. Suddenly I felt warmer than the temperature justified. I held my breath when she put her hand on my shoulder to stand up, and concentrated on the water trickling between my toes. She went to the cupboard and brought out a roll of bandages and a tube of disinfectant.

'Get your dress alright this morning?' I asked.

'Yes, they made a good job of it for once.'

There was a sound from downstairs, a door closing, a man's deep voice.

'That's Henri,' she said, a little breathless. 'You can do the rest yourself, can't you? I'll put some clothes on the bed for you.'

She went out before I could say anything.

I dressed quickly in the bedroom. I felt like an intruder now, stepping with faint distaste into the alien crutch of Henri's trousers (they were too long and I had to roll the legs up). But I couldn't resist taking a look around the room, as if it might contain some answers to the questions which again came to mind – but there were none, or I couldn't find them. The double bed with its neat blue bedspread, the framed photos of the Marchand children on the bedside table gave nothing away. I surveyed the heap of sodden clothes on the bathroom floor, decided to take them downstairs and carefully cleaned up all trace of my passage before leaving.

They seemed to be having an argument as I came down. I could hear Nicole's voice, sharp and disappointed, from the little sitting room to the left of the stairs. 'Why couldn't you?' she was saying. 'Just for once! Instead of telling me at the last minute.' Henri's indistinct reply, and Nicole again. 'I know it's not your fault, but it's always the same, isn't it! Why couldn't you say for once that you couldn't do it? He's got no business making you do his work for him, and you've got other things to do, like looking after your family for a change. Really, Henri!' They stopped as I reached the foot of the stairs, and then Nicole came out, her face set and angry.

'I'll take those!' she said curtly, seizing the clothes from my hands. She went into the kitchen, where I soon heard her snapping at the cook.

Henri was standing at a sideboard pouring himself a drink when I walked in: a tall, spare man with greying hair and the beginning of a stoop, staring introspectively at the bottle in his hands. His face was lined and there were shadows under his eyes and he looked for a moment sad and disturbed and rather lonely. He recovered when he saw me, putting his hand out with a smile and a touch of relief in his voice.

'You've been breaking up the house, Nicole tells me,' he said. I started to explain but he cut me off. 'Don't be silly. Nicole told me about the car. I'm the one who should be apologising. How's the leg, not too painful?'

'Not too bad. It's only a bruise.'

'Here, I've poured you a cognac. You look as if you need it.' I took the glass and swallowed a gulp. It burnt my throat and made me blink a little, but I soon felt its warmth spreading. I took a chair and he sat down near me and stretched out his long legs. When he stopped smiling his face settled into deep folds and his eyes took on a brooding expression, as if he had forgotten my presence. I was sufficiently used to his ways not to be surprised, but it was a little awkward and I searched for something to say, rejecting the various platitudes that came to mind. Henri also had a way of looking at you, when you made some witless remark, which made you wish you hadn't.

'I hear de Gaulle's visit is being put forward,' I ventured at last.

Henri stared at me and for a moment I thought he hadn't heard. But then he nodded.

'That's right. But it's not official yet. He may be here before mid-September.'

'That's pretty soon.'

'Yes. It doesn't leave much time.' He relapsed into silence. Trying to have a conversation with him, when he wasn't in the mood, was like using a Cambodian telephone: you kept getting switched on and off inexplicably. He sipped his drink moodily, still staring into space, while I began to wish I'd picked another day to come for my car. Then he got up to add some whisky to his glass and pour me another drink. He nodded at my leg.

'Nothing like anaesthetic. Feeling better now?'

'Much better, thanks. Don't worry about it. It won't stop me from having fun tonight.'

'Tonight? You're going to that party, are you?'

'Of course. Isn't everyone?'

'Taking anyone in particular?' he asked again, ignoring my question. I smiled. Phnom Penh parties weren't the sort to which you 'took' anyone, unless you were married or had a steady girl-friend from whom you couldn't bear to be separated for an evening. People just went, in groups or singly or in couples, and often came out again in a different combination. But Henri wasn't interested in our social habits. After a further silence he turned to me.

'Could you do me a favour? Take Nicole there for me?'

'Nicole? Aren't you going there yourself?'

'I can't. I've got to go back to the office this evening. There's a paper I have to finish for the Minister first thing in the morning. I meant to get it done earlier but I've had nothing but interruptions the last couple of days.' He shrugged, then smiled, a rueful boyish grimace which made him appear briefly years younger.

'To tell you the truth I'd forgotten about that party until Nicole mentioned it just now. But don't tell her that.'

So that was the altercation I'd heard. No wonder Nicole was upset.

'Could you do that for me?' he insisted, almost pleading. 'If it's not imposing too much –'

'Of course,' I said quickly. 'If Nicole doesn't mind. But it's a pity you can't come. It should be quite a party.'

'Oh, you know,' he said with a deprecating gesture, 'I don't really enjoy all those noisy parties very much anyway. I'm getting too old for them. But Nicole's been looking forward to it, and I'm sure she'd enjoy it more if you were there as an escort.' He smiled benignly. 'Tell you what, the easiest would be if she picks you up this evening. It'll save you using your leg. That's if I can borrow your car in exchange until tomorrow. The Fiat's still at the garage. I'll drive you back after lunch, how's that?' he added, as if tossing in a final compensation. I almost laughed. For a man of his intelligence he was transparent as a child in his eagerness to get out of a difficult situation.

'Fine,' I said. 'I'd be happy to. If Nicole's happy with it.' I was by no means sure of that. Nicole came back then and stared at us ominously.

'What were you saying about me?'

'We were talking about the party, my sweet,' Henri said blandly. 'Philippe's kindly agreed to accompany you in my place. But he's afraid you'd mind.'

'What nonsense is this!' she retorted. 'Philippe's got much better things to do. I'm sure you dragooned him into it.' She glared at each of us, while Henri took on a look of surprised innocence. I stepped rashly into the breach.

'Not at all,' I said. 'I'd be delighted. If that's OK with you.'

'So I should hope!' She was still staring at Henri, who pretended not to notice. Then she gave a light, barely perceptible shrug. She turned to me, and I thought for a moment she would give me the edge of her tongue too. But she nodded.

'Thank you Philippe. I accept. And now let's eat, before it gets cold.' She led the way decisively into the dining room.

I tried to take a nap that afternoon, but sleep wouldn't come at first. Too much coffee at lunch, and my leg ached. I lay naked under the sheet in my darkened bedroom, listening to the rain pelting down on the balcony outside, while the ceiling fan above my feet wobbled and swayed as if possessed of a life of its own. The first few days I'd been afraid it might come loose and cut me to pieces as I slept, but so far it had held firm and I was now used to it. Instead I thought about the morning, letting images form in my mind, following the rhythm of the blades. Marcellin, Rick, the article, my forthcoming trip to Battambang. If de Gaulle's visit was being put forward, a busy month lay ahead for us all. Should I really take Rick's warning seriously, expect the worst, an inquiry, pointing to me as a likely suspect?

More pleasant images, of Nicole Marchand. Nicole at parties, in her bikini on Sunday afternoons at the houseboat on the river. Nicole at La Taverne that morning, and then her disturbing physical nearness in the bathroom before lunch. Had she thought of it that way too? Unlikely. Twelve weeks earlier she was a total stranger, two months ago I still called her formally by her surname, *Madame Marchand*, we'd only recently started using the familiar *tu* – and tonight I was standing in for her husband. Funny. A little embarrassing perhaps, but a definite, almost tangible excitement. Which was stupid, I told myself. Better look on it as what it was, a social duty, a service rendered. Nicole had nothing of the wayward wife. It was true that she fed gossip from time to time, surrounded by her little court of admirers, but where was the harm in that? If she liked to flirt on occasion it was no more than a sign of youth, a social game, at worst a mild escape from a too-serious Henri. Phnom Penh was the kind of town where you could never avoid gossip, no matter how virtuous you were. For that matter, what did people say about me behind my back? Playing the bars too frequently of late?

One thing they couldn't do, the gossips, was link my name with Nicole. I had always stayed well within the bounds of friendship. Lack of opportunity perhaps, and a crippling ineptitude at flirting. Ill at ease with the vocabulary of *galanterie*, I was especially afraid of making a fool of myself. Nothing worse than a clumsy unwanted advance. And – let's be fair – scruples too, towards Henri.

But really, the man was asking for trouble, if he couldn't look after his wife better. What if one day she got caught at her own game? There's no such thing as a totally harmless friendship between a man and a woman. I didn't know it then, but I was beginning to suspect it.

Chapter Two

I didn't much enjoy the party that night. Apart from that it was a great success. Pelletier, himself one of Nicole's admirers, shared a house with several cronies near the centre of town and together they entertained on a lavish scale. By the time we arrived there were over a hundred guests in the large garden, with more inside the house, and the street was lined with cars for two blocks in either direction. There was even a policeman at the gate to control traffic. A live band played on a terrace, a dozen Vietnamese servants navigated with trays among the crowd, and in a corner of the garden, over a large pit of coals, two whole sheep sizzled on the spit. The noise was terrific. Luckily the rain had stopped.

Inside the gate our host swept down upon us. He was a large young man with a hearty manner and a bushy black beard like some nineteenth century criminal, a mass poisoner perhaps. He led us at once to a nearby table where a servant poured glasses from a huge bowl of punch.

'Compulsory initiation!' he cried. 'You're not allowed in until you've sampled this!'

Nicole spluttered over her glass. 'What did you put in?' she asked. 'Saltpetre?'

'Aphrodisiac of course!' he roared. 'Don't rush, there's lots more inside.' He laughed and clapped me on the back. 'Where's your husband?' he asked Nicole. 'I thought you were going to bring him.'

'He couldn't make it,' she explained, and conveyed Henri's regrets. 'What a pity,' said Pelletier, his own regret equally conventional. He shot me a quick bright glance. 'Well, tonight I'm exercising *droit de maître* over every pretty woman who comes without her husband. *Tu permets*, Philippe?' He seized her hand and led her off towards the dance floor, leaving me to hold her handbag. She wore her new dress, pale gold and very low-cut, causing heads to turn in her wake. She looked set to enjoy the evening, Henri or no.

I wasn't. I had finally managed to sleep during the afternoon, to wake up bad-tempered and dyspeptic at seven when Chi Hai thundered on the bedroom door. Now my mouth was dry, my head unclear, and I felt anything but sociable. I looked sourly after Nicole as she followed Pelletier (throwing me a look of mock-despair over her shoulder) and thought this was hardly an auspicious start. Stiff competition could be expected for her company as the evening wore on. I looked dubiously at the punch, decided to stick to safer spirits, and wandered off in search of a whisky, until I came upon Rick in the crowd. He was talking to a Cambodian girl, a pretty dark-skinned girl who looked vaguely familiar. She wore a sampot of dark blue silk embroidered with gold thread, and the design reminded me of bees. I didn't catch her name at first but I was sure I'd seen her before.

'I live three doors from your house,' she explained with a shy smile. 'I've often seen you in the street. But I was wearing my ordinary clothes then, and you wouldn't recognise me.' She spoke excellent French, with just a trace of the throaty Cambodian accent.

'Surya's just finished first year Arts,' Rick said. 'She very nearly topped her year too.'

'I had some help with my English,' she said, with a sidelong glance at him. She gave a little laugh, and soon after left us to join a group of other Cambodian girls nearby.

'What an attractive girl,' I said. 'I didn't know you were a teacher in your spare time.'

'Just occasionally. I know her father, he's in the Ministry of Agriculture. Nice chap, trained in France, one of the old school. I must introduce you some time.' He spoke casually, but sounded a shade self-conscious. He changed the subject.

'Had any more thoughts about the article?'

'Only one, for what it's worth. Do you remember a couple of journalists who came through here about two months ago? A man and a woman, I think he was Swedish and she was French. I don't remember what paper they worked for but I'm pretty sure they were based in Hong Kong.'

'I don't think I met them,' Rick said. 'It must have been while I was on a bag run to Bangkok. Why, do you think they had something to do with it?'

'I don't know. The trouble is I hardly remember anything about them. I know they came into the office and talked with Marcellin, but they met lots of people. I didn't pay much attention to them. But I can ask around.'

'Be careful. Better not draw attention to yourself. By the way, I found out about the press conference. It's going to be broadcast live over the radio. So that'll give us something to listen to in the morning.'

'Maybe he won't talk about that,' I said, and now I told him about de Gaulle's visit. Then we came upon Nicole, momentarily alone. She looked pleased to see us, but Rick quickly led her off to dance and once more I was left standing. I emptied my glass and found another, then searched for someone to talk to. I saw Surya with her friends and started towards her, then stopped. I couldn't work up much enthusiasm for polite conversation, even with such a pretty girl. I looked for another drink.

Three whiskies later, I felt even more depressed. I'd only managed to have one dance with Nicole before others came to claim her, and the alcohol, instead of kicking the fire of competition into me, only made me dull and surly. There was a brief flurry of excitement when Shagger Forbes drunkenly attempted a Filipino pole dance, and had to be carried from the floor with a cracked ankle. Then tedium and dissatisfaction returned. I went into the house. Upstairs, looking for a toilet, I heard music and laughter behind a closed door and went in. I found a group of people, young men and women, all European, sitting about in semi-darkness on the floor, listening to jazz from a record player. It was a reflective, intricate sort of jazz, which suited my mood, and I sat down in a corner next to a French girl I knew.

'Hello Suzanne,' I said. The girl looked at me hazily. She was a nurse from the Calmette Hospital, a lively, buxom lass with a low-cut blouse and the kind of uplift bra which pushed her breasts together like an offering of tropical fruit – mangoes perhaps. In other circumstances it would have been tempting to reach down and take one. But even that failed to cheer me up.

'Well, if it's not our Philippe,' she said at last, with exaggerated merriment. She gave me a sly look. 'You look lonely. What's wrong? Has Nicole deserted you? Here, have one of these, *mon chou*, and tell me about it.' She held a cigarette box up to me and I took one absently, thinking about what she'd just said. Had people noticed something? Or was she just being catty, and by chance hitting the mark? Suzanne was a friend of Nicole's, which wouldn't stop her from making any kind of snide remark if she thought it was funny.

Then I looked more closely at the cigarette. It was handmade, and it didn't take a genius to know it wasn't tobacco. Now I understood the odd atmosphere in the room: the faces which seemed to slip a little, the hoots of laughter for no apparent reason. I looked into the box. There were at least a hundred.

'Make all these yourself?' I asked.

'Yes. Took me all afternoon,' she said proudly. 'Come on. Let yourself go. You look as if you could do with one.'

'Some other time.' I sighed, and put the cigarette back. 'It wouldn't work tonight. I've had too much to drink.'

'Don't be a spoilsport.'

I shook my head. I'd only smoked marijuana once before, at a similar party a few weeks earlier, and I hadn't enjoyed it. People say it gives you a lift, makes you happy and relaxed, but in my case it had had the opposite effect: instead of the euphoria I expected all sorts of secret anxieties had come welling up as if from some deep and murky spring in my mind, to such an unpleasant extent that I'd gone and locked myself in my car, where a friend found me at three in the morning, gibbering incoherently and unable to drive. Maybe I'd had too much to drink, or I was simply not receptive – whatever the reason, I had no wish to repeat the experience. Suzanne made one last attempt to keep me next to her, while Forbes, sitting opposite with his foot stretched out dramatically on a cushion, gave me a cynical leer, but I resisted both and went out.

I found my toilet, and then wandered along the corridor until I came out on a small balcony, partly hidden by a tree from the lawn below. It was empty except for a cane chair and I sank gratefully into it, propping my leg Forbes-like on the railing. What was the matter with me tonight? I asked myself. Why couldn't I recapture the sunny mood of the morning? Was it just drink, or tiredness? Usually I could stand the pace much better. Was it *le Cafard*, one of those sudden and brutal fits of depression which sometimes fell on people, on Europeans anyway, in Phnom Penh? I'd been told about it, and I'd seen it happen to others. That insulated, inbred atmosphere got on your nerves after a while, caught you unawares when you were tired and made you suddenly detest everything around you – all those faces you met every day, that same frighteningly predictable company, evening after evening, week after week…but surely that only happened after prolonged exposure, like a tropical liver from years of cognac-sodas, it couldn't be happening to me, still fresh from a European spring, barely settled into the country. Only that morning I had told myself how much I liked the place, my life there, my work… Was it Nicole's pleasure with others' company, my own failure tonight to make on her the dashing impression I wanted to create, which had sent me running off like that, sulking like a child? With the thought that I might be jealous came a fierce desire to throw my cane chair down at the crowd below, as if somehow they were to blame.

But I'd noticed a change of rhythm, and I stood up to look over the balcony. The guests were no longer milling about on the lawn, but were preparing to eat, forming a queue, handing chairs around. Two servants lifted a sheep off its stand and carried it to a table where a third began to carve it up. I saw Rick walking towards Surya carrying two plates of food, and I looked for Nicole but couldn't find her. No doubt Pelletier or some other young man was now attending to her. I swore at myself, and at that moment heard her voice behind me, reproachful and relieved.

'So this is where you've been hiding! No wonder I couldn't find you. Are you alright? You look very pale.'

For a second I was on the verge of snapping at her. Then common sense returned.

'Yes. Yes I'm fine. Sorry. I think I drank a bit too much earlier on, and I came here to wear it off.'

She gave me a worried look.

'I'm okay. Really. Shall we go down? I think they're serving dinner.'

I levered myself up and followed her downstairs. But she insisted on making me sit down again while she went to get food.

When she came back with two plates and a bunch of cutlery she half scolded me, amused at herself.

"Here. Now eat this, before it gets cold. You hardly ate at lunch.'

We ate in silence for a while, sitting on patio steps, while people were spread around us on the lawn.

'Have you met Rick's new girlfriend?' I asked. 'Surya?'

'That pretty Cambodian girl? Yes. He introduced us. Though I'd met her before. Henri knows her father, we had dinner at their house once. But I didn't know there was any attachment with Rick, did you?'

'No, he's never mentioned her before. But there was an odd look about him tonight, don't you think?' I said, deliberately exaggerating. 'Very protective. It made me wonder.'

Nicole smiled.

'Do you think he's been storing her away, waiting for the right moment to bring her out?'

'Why not? He's quite capable of it. Though I'm surprised we haven't caught him at it. It's not the sort of thing you can keep quiet for long in Phnom Penh.'

'Oh, you'd be surprised what people get away with in this town, if they try,' she said drily.

'Really? Anyway, good luck to him. It's time he had a real girl-friend.'

I remembered once, soon after my arrival, Rick in a bar, flanked by two clinging hostesses. *That's the trouble with this life,* he'd said ruefully, *you work like a bastard all day and race all over town at night from one bloody reception to another, and when you feel like something more personal all you have time for is to grab for the nearest arse.* I'd thought then that he was trying to justify himself, for I was still disconcerted by the casual promiscuity which was such a natural part of life in Phnom Penh. But there had been a deeper sincerity in his words, and I guessed his life must be a lonely one at times.

'What about you?' she asked suddenly. 'Have you got someone tucked away somewhere, that you're not telling us about?'

'Not I,' I said gloomily.

'Why not?' she persisted. 'A young man like you, fresh to Asia, in search of local colour, I would have thought you'd be breaking your neck to get at girls like Surya.'

'Not necessarily,' I said, thinking of the Cochon d'Or, and the girls I knew there. A far cry from well-bred young ladies like Surya. And yet they'd served me well enough up to now.

'In any case they don't grow on trees, you know. That's one of the first things you learn here. How hard it is for a foreigner to meet one of these girls from a good family. I don't know how Rick did it, but it can't have been easy – what with parents and relatives behind every door, and prying neighbours. Not to mention the young lady's own maidenly modesty. Too many hurdles, before you can even find out if she's worth it. It's a wonder Cambodians manage to get married. I suppose it's easier if you know the customs.'

'A lot of these marriages are arranged by the families,' Nicole said. 'Using professional matchmakers if need be. But what about a European girl then? There's enough talent here, surely, among all those young teachers and nurses – or do you find us all too tame and colourless, in this exotic context?'

'Not at all,' I protested, thinking that it was typical of a woman to load the question like that, with the use of the word 'us'. And I wondered why she was so insistent. She'd never asked me so many personal questions before. It needed a careful answer. On the one hand there was Suzanne, bosomy, friendly, probably available if I went about it the right way, and yet who failed to excite me except in the most basic and fleeting manner. And on the other there was Nicole...

'I haven't yet found anyone who's available and who interests me enough,' I said lamely. Nicole laughed.

'What a cautious condemnation!' she said mockingly. 'But that doesn't leave you much, does it – bar girls, I suppose?'

'Well, what's wrong with that?' I said defensively. I had never made a secret of the fact that I went to the bars – I would have been an exception otherwise – though my occasional forays among the brothels to which Rick had also taken me had been conducted on more clandestine lines. But I had no wish to parade my list of easy conquests before Nicole. In her company they looked less enticing than at two in the morning in the cheap intimacy of the Cochon d'Or or wherever. And to be honest, how many of those girls would have come home with me afterwards, if they didn't have to earn a living?

'Come come,' she said gently, with unconscious cruelty. 'Don't be so modest. Ask any of those young men over there.' She gestured towards the groups which were reforming near the band. 'They'll tell you how many girls they've slept with, and probably add a few.'

'You forget,' I said, 'that I'm half English. It's considered vulgar to boast of one's virility. If you must know, I was pretty much virginal when I came here. I've had a sheltered upbringing. But I can assure you this is no longer the case.'

'I should hope not. A red-blooded young man like you.'

'Indeed.'

I thought of Hoa, the girl I'd known in the Cochon d'Or, and felt a stab of guilt. What would she say if she could see me now? That I was no different from other men? She and her kind didn't often get invited to parties like this, and if they were, they were expected to pay in kind for the privilege.

There was a silence. As if Nicole had sensed my mood, she gently seized my hand.

'Come and dance with me. And promise me you won't run away again.'

I no longer had any wish to.

After that the rest of the evening went by very quickly. I had two or three more dances with Nicole, which gave me the satisfaction of overtaking whatever rivals, real or imaginary, lurked about lusting for her. My own lust I kept under control largely because I felt more tenderness than anything else at that moment – and gratitude. I brushed my cheek against hers, surreptitiously buried my nose in her hair, and she didn't resist when I pressed her gently against me. The lights were low, and past a certain time every male partner was allowed a degree of licence, or else the gossips would have had a field day.

Then, soon after midnight, Nicole decided to call it a night. I would have liked to stay longer, but the party was beginning to degenerate as the pot smokers came out in the open, and Nicole had even less taste for marijuana than I did. Pelletier tried in vain to hold her back.

'I promised Henri I'd be home early,' she said tactfully as she pushed his hands away. 'Besides, Philippe's tired and I said I'd drop him home.' This wasn't quite true, but I didn't argue. I had no desire to stay without her.

Once in the car however she seemed in less of a hurry to go home.

'I'll just see if Henri's back yet,' she said as we drove off, and we made a detour past the Marchand house, which wasn't far. She slowed down past the gate. The downstairs lights were on but everything was in darkness upstairs and there was no sign of my car, unless Henri had parked it out of sight in the garage.

'Maybe he's already asleep,' I suggested. 'Do you want to go past his office, to see if he's still there?'

She hesitated. 'No,' she said, and drove on towards the Boulevard Monivong. But there, instead of turning left towards where I lived, she swung right towards the Calmette Hospital and drove slowly in a long loop which brought us up past the French embassy, across to the Tonle Sap river and the Japanese bridge, and then back down the Quai Sisowath towards the Chinese quarter.

'You don't mind?' she asked. 'Just for a breath of fresh air. Unless you'd rather I dropped you off at one of the bars.'

'You don't mean that, surely!'

She didn't answer, and we drove on in silence for a while, along deserted, ill-lit streets. Phnom Penh, so colourful in the morning, took on the look of a ghost town after midnight. The cinemas with their huge hand-painted posters were already closed, the central market was a gaunt and sprawling shell under the sodium lights. Even the Chinese quarter, always the last to shut down, was quiet now, its shop fronts grilled and shuttered. Only the bars showed any signs of life – Chez Martin on the Quai

Sisowath, where the doorman followed us with sleepy incurious eyes (to judge by the empty pavement Martin was having another lean night), closer to the market little islands of animation in narrow side-streets – a squadron of cyclos, a few bent strips of neon, purple, red, canary yellow. The Mocambo, the Green Jade, the Cochon d'Or, tiny places with their doors shut tight to keep the customers inside the fragile cocoon of conditioned air, ageing hit-tunes, the hip-and-thigh intimacy of clinging bar-girls. No doubt the Dancing d'Etat was still open out on the airport road, and *La Mère Chum* down past the Independence Monument, where for fifty riels you could lie on a mat in a dim cubicle and smoke a pipe of tourist-grade opium while one of the girls gave you a rough massage – for some reason they always had gritty hands. Down along the river too the little brothels would still be doing business, catering for late-comers who'd missed out elsewhere earlier in the evening, but the cyclo-girls who plied their trade near the railway station or in front of the Café de Paris had long ago found their client, been picked up by the police, or retired home in despair.

Then we were driving down Pasteur, across Samdech Pann where Rick lived, and then the smaller street where I had my flat, on the top floor of an old two-storeyed house with my Cambodian landlord downstairs. Nicole pulled up and I spoke the lines I'd been rehearsing for the past half hour.

'I'd ask you up for a drink, if I thought you'd accept.'

She didn't laugh, or refuse as I expected, though she may have smiled to herself in the darkness. She said nothing, seemed to consider the idea for a moment, then switched off the engine and followed me up to my flat, up the dark twisting staircase where I held her hand to keep her from stumbling and stopped myself just in time from putting my arms around her there and then. My heart was beating in my throat, I didn't trust myself to speak until we were inside under the safety of lights and I made my next speech, taking advantage of the fact that it was such a long way to go down again so soon.

'There's not much choice I'm afraid. Whisky or beer or plain cold water is all I have. Unless you'd like a lemonade.'

Nicole chose a whisky, and I went into the kitchen to get it. When I came back she was busy inspecting the living room and the few possessions it contained. She had been there before, once to lunch with Henri and Rick and a few friends, but then it had been daylight and I had dressed it up for the occasion. Now she saw it in its natural state: the cheap furniture, the tired settee, the rattan bookshelves with their heaps of periodicals, papers and a typewriter on a corner of the dining table which Chi Hai wasn't allowed to touch. Tourist posters and a piece of Cambodian silk hanging on the wall failed to hide the cracks and patches of damp. I wasn't very houseproud, and the room was nothing to be proud of – just the living quarters of a transient and not very affluent bachelor. But I liked it, it was a warm room, lived in, with its share of dreams and ambitions, and although Nicole instinctively patted cushions into shape and straightened the edge of the worn cotton mat with her foot, I guessed from her smile that she didn't find it unpleasant. Perhaps it was the contrast with the orderly interior of her home.

'Would you like a record?' I asked. 'Some Segovia?'

'If you like.'

I gave her her glass, added water, then we clinked glasses and smiled over the rims and I put on a record. *Fantasy for a Courtier*, by Rodrigo. No cheap seduction music for this occasion, something grand and stately which would lend dignity and a sense of purpose to any gaps in the conversation. She listened to a few bars, approved with a nod of the head, and nodded again towards the typewriter on the table.

'Do you like working at home?' she asked.

'Whenever I can. There are too many interruptions at the office. But that's not work,' I said hastily, when she glanced over a sheaf of papers. 'Just personal notes.'

'For when you write a book about us all one day?'

'Who knows?' I asked rhetorically. 'Actually it's more of a nervous tic, a hangover from my student days. I have a mania for collecting notes on odd events. Always of course with the thought that they'll come in handy later on, when I'm famous and publishers come begging for my memoirs.'

'Henri used to do that too,' she said.

'Used to?'

'Yes. He even started a book once. But he gave that up.'

74

'Why did he give up?'

'Why?' she stood still, reflecting. 'I'm not really sure, to tell you the truth. Lack of time, certainly. Lack of real interest perhaps…Henri has a tendency to give things up these days – although in other ways he can be quite stubborn.'

She spoke in a matter-of-fact tone, and kept her back turned to me while she studied the bookshelves, her head leaning alternately right and left as she read the spines: Hall's *History of South-East Asia*, Coedès, *Les Peuples de la Peninsule Indochinoise,* and another, *Recherches sur les Cambodgiens*, by Groslier. She took it out to look at the end papers, said: 'That's the *Conservateur d'Angkor*, isn't it – Henri knows him well. No, 1911. Must be his father.' She put it back and went on in the same dispassionate voice.

'And you, Philippe? Are you the kind of person who gives up?'

'It depends.' I turned the volume down. 'In Tours before I came here I was close to giving up and going back home. Until that ad turned up.'

'But you didn't, did you.'

'No. I'm not sure why. Obstinacy, perhaps, like Henri.' And sometimes I thought, obstinacy takes over where common-sense leaves off. Nicole laughed.

'Here's a book about Buddhism, written by a man called Christmas.' She glanced at another book. 'How do you spell Apollinaire?'

'I know. Two *l*'s. The bookbinder near the market lost one of them.' This, I thought, is where obstinacy verges on lunacy, becomes suicidal. The *Fantasy* reached a crescendo, rolled through my head amplified. I drew in my breath and in the silence that followed, before the soloist took up the theme again, I said distinctly, looking at her back:

'*Tes seins sont les seuls obus que j'aime.*'

'I beg your pardon?'

'*Your breasts are the only bombs I love.* He said that, not I. Apollinaire. While he was in hospital with his head wound, during the First World War. It's one of my favourite lines.'

She laughed a little, closed the book and put it back on the shelf.

'I was going to say, how would you know?'

'Right. I don't know. But I would very much like to.'

She turned and faced me. 'Why did you say that, Philippe?'

'Because it's true.'

'Is it? Why? Because you're a little in love with me, or think you are? Or do you just want to go to bed with me, like those other young men tonight, who made you feel jealous so that you ran away and hid on that balcony? Because that's what it was, wasn't it.'

'Yes, that's what it was.' I returned her stare. "I do want to go to bed with you, as you say. Though not perhaps as crudely as you seem to think. As for love...I'm not sure. I want to find out, Nicole.'

'Do you? If you're not sure...' She hesitated, bent her head to look away, while I kept my eyes fixed on her. 'I'm twelve years older than you.'

'I know. You're married to Henri and you have two children. I know that. I also know that you're not very happy.'

'And you want to take advantage of that?'

'Yes. I wouldn't have said all that otherwise.'

There was a pause then, a long silence, which no amount of music could bridge this time. We both stood still, facing each other across the room, with her eyes fixed on the knot in my tie and my mind racing with all sorts of questions which even now I couldn't answer. Why do you hesitate, Nicole? I wanted to ask. Do you dislike the way I've put my proposition? It had been put baldly, but she had never been afraid of words, or ideas, and she liked, if anything, my blunt talk. Was it because I hadn't put my arms around her and lied a little, exaggerated my feelings for her, wrapped them in sweet words which she could then pretend to believe? She herself more than liked me, I knew that now. She had perhaps been secretly hoping for that moment, at least she had done nothing to avoid it. Was it the thought of her age, or of Henri, that stopped her? But she knew that whatever she gave me she wouldn't be taking away from Henri, who had long ago withdrawn into himself those private antennae of intimacy between them. She could be Henri's wife, and my lover, at the same time. And you wanted to then, didn't you?

Why was it then that she didn't move forward, push her head into my shoulder, as she had, I know, dreamed of doing? She knew my body, she had studied it, she liked it. She was as drawn to it as I was to her, as curious to know how we would fit together. Why then did she leave me standing there, stock still with my hands by my side, while she picked up her handbag and held it indecisively in her hands until finally I looked away, turned away, picked up my glass and turned off the record?

There are moments for words and moments for action, and if I'd been older and more experienced there would have been less of the first and more of the second. I would have known what to do, even if, for other reasons, I might not have done it. But I was drunk, not with whisky only but with rhetoric, and I didn't want to seduce her in the ordinary way, by taking her in my arms as I should have on the stairs. I didn't know that you can love, and make love, without using words of love, and I didn't want to use those words because I didn't want to cheat, with my feelings or hers, and because it was a dramatic moment and I didn't want to spoil the drama of it.

Perhaps she sensed that, and perhaps she enjoyed the suspense too in her own way, because she made the best and only exit she could:

'I'm not sure Philippe. I'm not sure either.'

Then she left and went down the stairs, and I made no move to follow her.

Chapter Three

That week-end stands out in my mind, fifty years later, more for its mood of pervasive listlessness than any particular event – though it was also a very busy time. That was probably due more to exhaustion than anything else, but my first thought when I woke up the next morning was that I had committed a terrible blunder with my fumbled declaration to Nicole, and that feeling stayed with me like a pall of gloom for the next few days. Of course I had a hangover as well, and to make things worse I slept in that Saturday morning and missed the first half of the Prince's press conference on the radio: an unforgiveable lapse if Marcellin had found out. Luckily Henri had returned my car earlier, while I was still senseless. I barely had time to rush to the printer's and back (avoiding any detour via the Post Office square this time), and get a quick rundown on the Prince's comments from Mademoiselle Sovannareth before Marcellin returned from the palace, full of bustle and self-importance. I had a splitting headache by then and all I wanted to do was go and hide somewhere, but he paid no attention and started at once preparing his reports and editorials, with me to help him sort out his notes and tape recordings. We were at it all day.

Two things emerged from the Prince's speech that morning. First, as Rick had predicted, he had read the article. In fact he hardly spoke about anything else, for close on two hours. The Prince was not a man to mince words, and he used some alarming language to describe its authors. By the end of those two hours everyone in the country within range of a radio knew what to think of the despicable *plumitifs*, the hacks, saboteurs and dismal pen-pushers who dishonoured their profession by writing such offensive lies about a country which had done them no harm whatever.

Second, however, for all the strength of his feelings, he didn't so much as hint that they might have been helped by someone inside the country – even, if Rick was right, someone in his entourage. This calmed my nerves a little, until I remembered Rick's warning, and thought that the Prince might prefer to keep silent on that point until he had some evidence – which in turn could only mean that any witch-hunt would be conducted very quietly.

Then, towards the end of his broadcast, he made another announcement, which I'd forgotten about: he confirmed that de Gaulle's visit had been brought forward to the end of August.

Altogether there was enough work there to keep me from thinking too much about Nicole, until six o'clock that evening, when Marcellin put his notes away. Faced with the prospect of going home to my dreary thoughts – and having to decide whether to join the Marchands the next day on the river, where they were organising a picnic – I took the first escape route I could think of. Asking Marcellin if I could bring my trip north forward by a day, I caught that night's train to Battambang.

I spent three days in the north-west. I travelled to Pailin, Angkorborei, Sisophon, visited agricultural centres and rice mills, pagodas and ruby diggings, taking copious notes and photos for future articles. It was a straightforward assignment, and I would have enjoyed it thoroughly if my mind hadn't been so preoccupied with Nicole. I kept going over and over that evening, my behaviour at the party and in the flat, Nicole's words, even her gestures and tone of voice, as if somehow I could retroactively change what had happened. I tried to guess what she must be feeling now. Would she take me for a presumptuous fool, and drop me from her list of friends? Would she treat it simply as a moment of weakness, smile indulgently and never mention it again? I tried to find comfort in her parting words, but one way or another I knew our friendship had changed, and probably for the worse. To make matters worse my leg ached insistently, and I suffered the final indignity of an attack of dysentery which completely spoilt my trip to Pailin.

When I got back to Phnom Penh the first thing I did was call on Dr Fouchet at his clinic near the market, to see about my leg. He was busy when I arrived and his receptionist made me wait in a spare consulting room. I sat down and glanced through his magazines. In front of me the connecting door to the surgery was ajar and I could see, framed in the crack, part of Fouchet's back. He was coming to the end of a consultation and I heard his voice giving gruff, friendly advice in French: 'Organically there's nothing wrong with you,' he said, 'apart from low blood pressure. You're drinking too much of course, which doesn't help. But your main problem is that you're very tired. You're run down. You need a holiday, and soon, if you want to last much longer. *Sinon, d'ici un an ou deux...*' Fouchet closed the door and the rest was lost to me. But a moment later, when it reopened to admit his vast bulk, I caught a glimpse of his other patient. It was Henri Marchand.

Fouchet's favourite form of greeting was to crush his friends, male or female, to his chest as if he hadn't seen them for years. This he now did to me, laughing and rumpling my hair as if I was one of his nurses. Then he sat down to examine me. He pursed his lips when the bandage came off.

'That's nasty,' he said. 'When did you do this?'

"Last Friday. I couldn't come earlier.'

'You should have, you know. You could easily catch an infection.' He called a nurse to wash and dress my wound, talking fluent Khmer which I couldn't follow. I watched apprehensively as she prepared a needle.

'Antibiotics,' he said. 'You're lucky I don't fill you up with a few vitamin shots as well. You look as if you haven't slept for a week.'

'I've had a busy time,' I said, and told him about my trip north, while the nurse made me lie down on a couch and roll down my trousers for the injection. I bore it stoically, but when I stepped down my rump felt on fire.

'How much did she put in?' I complained. 'Now I've got two legs I can hardly walk on.'

'Think yourself lucky she didn't hit the sciatic nerve. I've seen that happen in my time.' He chuckled as if over some happy memory.

'What does that do?' I asked.

'It cripples you for life. And it really hurts.' Then, reassuringly: 'Don't worry. My nurses are well trained. They don't do that very often.'

After discussing my intestinal disorder and Fouchet had scribbled a prescription, I stayed to talk. Knowing he was a strong anti-Gaullist I took a minor revenge by mentioning the visit. The result was predictable.

'What a waste of time and money!' he cried out in disgust. 'Who wants to see him anyway? That great windbag! When I think of the taxes we pay –'

'Is it true what I hear,' I asked mischievously, 'that the Cambodians are drawing up a list of potential trouble-makers and they're going to send them off to the coast during the visit?'

'Ha!' Fouchet gave a snort. 'And you think I might be asked to join them? My dear fellow, you don't think I'm going to rush at the beast with a scalpel, do you? I know that's better than he deserves, but I'm not a homicidal maniac. Besides, I'd have to sterilize the instrument afterwards. But they'll have to wait a long time before I queue up to shake his hand!'

He scowled and looked ferocious, and I changed the subject, happy with my small victory.

'Anything new happen the last few days? I haven't seen a newspaper since Saturday.'

'Nothing. *Monseigneur* hasn't made any further announcements. There's some big operation going on in Vietnam, just over the border, but that's nothing new of course. They're always killing people over there.'

Fouchet yawned. He was normally just as outspoken in his anti-Americanism as he was against de Gaulle, and rarely missed an opportunity to lecture me on the evils of the American presence in Vietnam. But this time he wasn't interested. Instead, with the abrupt manner which sometimes frightened people before they got to know him, he barked at me.

'When are you coming to dinner? And don't say no this time. I'm sick of your excuses.'

'I can't help it if you always ask me at the last minute,' I said. 'At least give me two or three days' warning.'

'Next Saturday then. Bortsch and couscous.'

'With pleasure.'

'Good. It'll just be friends. The Marchands are coming, and that man McPherson.'

I nodded, feeling an inward surge of alarm and elation mixed together. I remembered the scene of a moment before and blurted out:

'How's Henri, by the way? Is he sick?'

'Henri?'

'Well, yes...I saw him in there when you came in. He hasn't been looking well lately.'

Fouchet shrugged, an ample movement of his shoulders beneath his white smock, and seemed for a moment to ignore the question – perhaps debating the propriety of discussing one man's illness with another, and a mutual friend at that. But the result, knowing him, was a foregone conclusion, and when he spoke it was with his usual frankness.

'Henri Marchand's one of those damn fools who don't follow their doctor's advice and take a rest while there's still time. No, he's not sick. He's just wearing himself out working too hard and trying to keep up with a wife who's too young for him. If he doesn't watch out very soon he's going to have a breakdown.' He rose, signifying that the conversation was over, and walked with me to the outer door. With his hairy arms folded massively across his chest he looked over the street for a moment, lost in gloomy speculation.

'Take my advice,' he said at last. 'Do like me. Don't get married. And take a rest, do you hear? Or you'll get old before your time too.' He grinned, crushed my hand in his paw, and shot back inside. 'And don't forget next Saturday,' he cried before closing the door.

On my way home I stopped at the office, and sat for a long while at my desk, fighting an urge to call Nicole. I didn't have any idea what to say to her, but that didn't stop the urge. Finally I gave in and rang her number.

'Hello.'

'Nicole? It's me. Philippe.'

'You!' she said emphatically, and stopped. I wondered what that meant. 'I wondered if you'd call. When did you get back?'

'Just now. Two hours ago. How are you?'

'Fine, thank you. Did you have a good trip? How's your leg?'

'Much better. I've just seen Fouchet about it. He talked about a dinner on Saturday night. He said you'd be there.'

'Yes.'

'Look, I'm sorry about Sunday. I wanted to come but –'

'I can't hear you. This line's all funny.'

'I said – I said I hope you weren't too tired on Saturday morning.'

'No. I wasn't too tired.'

There was another pause, while I hunted for something to say. She wasn't making it easy.

'Any chance of seeing you before Saturday?' I asked, trying to sound casual.

'I – let's wait until then, Philippe. I've got too many things on right now.'

'Okay. I understand.' I swallowed my disappointment.

I was about to say goodbye when she spoke again.

'Philippe? Are you still there?'

'Yes.'

'Philippe…thank you for Friday evening.'

Then she hung up. I stared at the phone, not sure whether to smile or throw the instrument at the wall.

That was on the Wednesday. On the Thursday, the radio announced that in the course of large-scale search-and-destroy operations in Loc Ninh and Tay Ninh provinces, just across the border in South Vietnam, *'Americano-Sud-Vietnamien'* aircraft had overflown the border and strafed a Cambodian village, destroying a number of huts and killing three villagers.

Chapter Four

'Cambodia: a haven of peace in a war-torn Asia', as Sihanouk was fond of proclaiming, in some of his more dramatic flights of oratory. Sadly, that description wasn't to apply much longer, but at the time it was accurate enough, allowing for some hyperbole. Next door, the war in Vietnam lurched from one crisis to another, like an incurably sick man with years of pain still ahead of him, while Laos to the north looked like a stick of celery, split down the middle by the thin front line of conflicting ideologies, communist *Pathet Lao* to the east, pro-American rightists to the west, and ineffectual neutralists in the middle. Even in Thailand trouble was beginning to stir in the outer provinces and Bangkok, so people said, was like an occupied city, a glorified field-brothel for American troops on R&R. Somehow, whatever his failings, Sihanouk had so far spared Cambodia any of that. There, when people shot or stabbed each other, they did it for passion, for love or greed or revenge, all sound, basic human motives – and not for politics.

But the war was never far away. The press wrote about it, the radio gave daily news of it, people talked about it all the time. Sometimes in the night, especially during the wet season when large areas of the countryside lay under water, windows rattled suddenly and you might even hear in the stillness the distant rumble of bombs from the south-east. The border was less than sixty miles away, and the sound of a B-52 raid carries a long way over water. And on the following Saturday I learnt at first hand what happens when you get too close to the firing line.

I was reading the latest news reports when Marcellin called me in. 'Got you camera? Good. Then get to the airport as fast as you can. The ICC's going out to look at the scene of that incident last Thursday, and the Ministry's asked if you can go. Brunner's sick, apparently. You'd better hurry, the plane leaves in half an hour.'

I wasted no time. The ICC was the International Control Commission, a tripartite body which had been set up at the end of the first Indochina war, against the French, to monitor the peace agreement, and Sihanouk, who was well aware of the threat that the present war in Vietnam posed to his country, called on it to investigate whenever there was a serious border incident. In half an hour I was at the airport, twenty minutes later I was on board a Royal Cambodian Air Force DC3, heading east. The plane was packed, for the Cambodians wanted to give maximum publicity to the incident; and apart from the three commissioners of the ICC, the Poles, the Indians and the Canadians, who never seemed to agree on anything, they had invited representatives from every diplomatic mission in Phnom Penh. There were North Koreans, Chinese, North Vietnamese, Indonesians, Filipinos; from the Soviet embassy both Kalyakin, shambling and badly dressed as usual, and Rassimov, smooth and blandly smiling; the French, British and Australian military attaches; Yugoslavs, Bulgars, and Germans East and West; and a host of others, including newsreel cameramen and army photographers, intelligence officers from the *Deuxième Bureau* of the Cambodian army, plus Wilberforce, the English left-wing journalist, Rick McPherson, and myself – all summoned at short notice and apart from the military, who always seem to have a uniform on hand, dressed in a variety of fashions from office suits with tie and matching handkerchief to shorts, sandals and Hawaiian shirts. No wonder the tourists waiting in the departure lobby stared at us as we boarded the plane.

It was my first air trip since arriving in Phnom Penh and I made the most of it, strap-hanging in the aisle and craning to get a look through the nearest port-hole. The view was spectacular. The Mekong had overflowed its banks and spread over the countryside in a vast sheet of water which stretched as far as one could see, unbroken except for the top of trees. Phnom Penh itself was dwarfed to village size by the flood, a small green island with thin straight lines radiating out like spokes, roads raised on their levees above the water line. It was at least twenty minutes before we saw land again, and then it looked at first more like a primeval swamp. I could see why in ancient times Cambodia was called the Water Kingdom. It would hardly have been surprising to see a giant reptile down there, staring up at us.

Further east towards Kompong Cham and Mimot the land gradually reasserted itself. At first it was only a canal, barely visible against the glinting surface, a string of barges between two pencil strokes; then the outline of paddy fields, houses on stilts, patches of dry ground covered with rough scrub. As the water receded, trees formed into clumps, the clumps merged into woodland and denser jungle, presently we were flying over a rolling carpet of vegetation so dense it looked from the air as if green foam had been sprayed over the ground. Here and there a square had been cut out of it, a village or a banana plantation inserted. As we lost height, the dark battalions of rubber trees came into view, a glimpse of ochre buildings, a small airstrip – Mimot plantation.

At Mimot we lunched. Hospitality for the Cambodians was an ancient tradition which you could never avoid. We ate curry in the district chief's headquarters, and drank pale beer in pint glasses with fist-sized lumps of ice floating in it, while a convoy of jeeps and army trucks waited outside. We still had a long way to go, and some grumbled at the delay, but it gave me a chance to catch up on some basic information, which Colonel Purdue from Rick's embassy obligingly supplied, as I still didn't know where we were going. A grizzled veteran in faded jungle greens, he made room among the glasses for his map-case and shook his head.

'To tell you the truth, I'm not sure myself. Map references are in short supply today. But as far as I can tell it's roughly here.'

His finger followed the blue line of the Mekong, hovered over the town of Kompong Cham and came to rest further down, on the Vietnamese border and next to a red china-graph cross.

'About here, I think.'

'What's that cross?' I asked.

'That's Anlong Tres. You should know all about that, your magazine mentions it often enough.'

I nodded. Anlong Tres had been the scene of a particularly bloody incident two years earlier, with ground incursions across the border, severe fighting and many casualties among the local population. It had been a major landmark in the decline in American-Cambodian relations, and the press, as Colonel Purdue had pointed out, still frequently referred to it.

'Any ground fighting this time?' I asked.

'No. But I don't know any more than what I heard on the radio.'

Rick was standing by, and I took him aside. 'Were they American or South Vietnamese planes?' I asked.

'Americans, I think,' he replied in a low voice.

'Doesn't look good, does it.'

'Couldn't have come at a worse time. It's over a year since there was anything so serious.'

He stopped, looking over my shoulder. I turned, to find Rassimov coming towards us, with a smirk on his face.

'Well, Monsieur Roche,' he said in his precise French. 'Enjoying our little excursion? Your first trip to these parts?'

'Yes,' I answered incautiously. 'I don't often get the chance to come out on assignments like this.'

'Quite,' he nodded. His eyes moved to Rick. 'In fact it would be perfect, don't you think, if a few villagers hadn't got themselves innocently killed to give us an excuse for coming. Perhaps we should send a letter of thanks to the American High Command in Saigon.' He spoke louder than necessary, and there was an unpleasant edge to his voice, but he didn't labour the point, and walked off, leaving us standing there searching for a reply. There was none of course, in a way, though Rick summed it up better when he said after a moment: 'That was too good to resist, wasn't it. Bastard. I don't suppose he gets opportunities like this very often.' Then he added, quietly as if to himself, 'That man bears watching though. He's even nastier than he looks.'

From Mimot we went by road, along *Route Nationale 13*. Before the war, before the first Indochina war especially, this road had been one of the major arteries of Indochina, linking Vientiane in Laos with Saigon, and it went through towns with exotic names: Thakhek, Savannakhet, Paksé in Laos, Stung Treng and Kratié further south. To the east, the provinces of Rattanakiri and Mondulkiri, rolling hills rising to the Annamitic Range and the Vietnamese border.

Below Kratié the road swung in a wide bulge which brought it close to the border, through the fertile *terre rouge* country of the rubber estates: Snuol, Mimot, Chup on the Mekong with 7 million trees. The big plantation trucks which carried the latex to the wharf at Kompong Cham had badly damaged the road, and in the back of the Landrover which I shared with half a dozen others we slid about and grappled with each other, trying to soften our landing after the worst potholes. Through gaps in the trees I caught glimpses of a hump on the horizon, a faint blue isosceles triangle, huge even in the distance: *Nui Ba Den*, which the Americans called Black Virgin Mountain, near Tay Ninh, just across the border. It was said to be a Viet Cong stronghold, and the current operation was aimed at clearing them out. In the fields as we passed black-clad peasants stared at us, expressionless. These were Khmers, like the soldier who rode with us and with whom I exchanged cigarettes, coughing over the harsh Cambodian tobacco. Brown men, not yellow, with strong faces and muscular bodies, but it was easy to imagine the smaller, more delicate-looking yet tougher Vietnamese in the jungle, only a few kilometres away, who tortured and assassinated government officials and lived daily under a rain of bombs; and the thousands of Vietnamese workers on this side of the border, the Tonkinese tappers on the plantations, who woke every night to the rumble of B-52 raids just across the border. These too were said to be Viet Cong sympathisers. They had stared unsmiling at us at the airfield and at Mimot plantation.

We still had a long way to go, and it was another two hours before we reached the scene of the incident itself. By this time any hope of getting back early to Phnom Penh had vanished. The roads had become steadily worse after leaving the highway, finally degenerating into a swampy track which proved almost too much even for our four-wheel-drive vehicles, slowing us down even further. As we neared the border too a certain uneasiness began to spread among the leaders. At one point the Indian Commissioner, who as Chairman of the ICC had overall control of the expedition, refused to go further without an armed escort. This took time to arrange – and in the event proved unwise – but he stood his ground, until an extra platoon of Cambodian infantry arrived and we set off again.

In due course we emerged from the forest and arrived at a hamlet. We were still some distance from our destination, but the track ended here and we stopped to talk to the inhabitants. One of them, who wore black pyjamas but had a soft city look about him, had his arm in a sling and a bandage around his neck, much stained with mercurochrome. He explained that he was a politician, a local candidate for the next elections, and that he had come that morning from Phnom Penh to distribute rice to the villagers, when he was caught up in another raid. Two helicopters this time. His wounds weren't serious – some shrapnel scratches at most – but this news caused consternation. The three ICC Commissioners retired for another debate, while Rick and I took a leak in the nearby undergrowth, unaware until too late of a peasant woman who stood staring at us. She nodded a civil greeting before she left.

At this point a new factor entered the situation: the appearance of a light aircraft to the south east, towards the border. At first it was just a small black cross flying in circles against the gathering clouds, but the circles widened and slowly brought it closer until it was directly overhead. Colonel Purdue, studying it through binoculars, declared that it was an L-19, an observation plane often used in Vietnam for target identification and fire control. Presently a second plane joined it, and people stopped talking to look up at them. Someone suggested that perhaps we shouldn't be standing out in the open. By then the two planes had stopped circling and were heading back towards the border, but this development had caused some alarm, and this time the Indian Commissioner's reluctance drew support. It was too risky to go on, several said. The military attaches stood firm, insisting we'd come too far to turn back. They argued that we could easily complete the inspection and be back with our vehicles within an hour, and that in any case our appearance was too civilian to be mistaken for a band of Viet Cong. This was true enough: white shirts still outnumbered khaki two to one, one of the North Koreans wore a floppy straw hat with a pink ribbon, and the Chinese press attaché had knotted a handkerchief over his scalp. We looked more like a party of picnickers. But still the Chairman hesitated, and we looked like getting nowhere, when one of the Cambodians stepped forward: a slender, elegant man in gum-boots and a pale grey safari suit, who cut through the discussion by striding resolutely down the path towards the border. This was the Province Chief, who had arrived to accompany us; and the rest of the group, shamed by his example, straggled off after him.

Half an hour later, sweaty, muddy, with trousers rolled up and shirt-tails flapping, we finally arrived. It was hardly a village: two rows of huts on stilts, a few banana and sugar-palm trees, beyond the huts some shallow fields, the stalk of young rice sticking up through the muddy water. 'Where's the border?' asked Rick, and a Cambodian pointed towards the tree-line, three hundred metres away. But someone else immediately pointed in the opposite direction. I looked around for signs of damage, but couldn't see any, though the huts were flimsy structures of bamboo and palm-leaf which looked as if they could hardly withstand a storm, let alone an air-raid. One disquieting detail: the village was deserted. Even the scrawny fowls, the dogs and the funny black piglets which you normally saw in the countryside had disappeared. There were no buffaloes in the fields, and the few tools and utensils left lying about indicated the inhabitants had fled rapidly.

No military operation is complete without a briefing. An army major provided it in the centre of the village, pointing out landmarks on a blackboard. In essence, he said, the first raid had been carried out by jets using incendiary and high explosive rockets. The major exhibited fragments of shell casing with English-language markings. Three people had been killed, he said, a pregnant woman who had not reached shelter fast enough, and two small children who drowned when their mother jumped with them into a water-filled trench and in her panic didn't realise that the water was above their heads. The major spoke flatly, unemotionally, as if describing a simple everyday occurrence, his guttural French adding unusual emphasis to his words. In answer to questions – most of them from the Communist representatives – the major said the village had never been used as a military base, either by the Viet Cong or the Cambodian army; that the villagers never traded across the border; that the trenches which we could see nearby had been dug by the villagers for their own protection; and that the attacks had been totally unprovoked. Rick asked if we could talk with some of the villagers, but the major explained that they had taken to the woods and couldn't be found. Wilberforce, Rassimov and their colleagues looked discreetly satisfied, the rest of us maintained serious, non-committal expressions. Cameras clicked, and we moved on.

For some reason the attacks had concentrated on the last ten huts of the village, separated from the rest by empty fields. And here at last we could observe the damage. All but two of the huts had been razed to the ground, and those that were still standing showed gaping holes and split timbers and looked about to collapse. The others were heaps of sodden ashes and charred wood. Here and there a stilt or a post stood at a crazy angle. Scraps of thatch littered the ground, mingled with baskets, broken pots and shredded leaves. On the ground were bits of jagged metal. I picked one up as a souvenir.

For some time I'd become aware of an unpleasant smell, as of dead rabbits, which became stronger as we moved through the village, and I imagined the worst: but it was no more than a dead buffalo lying in a field, bloated and spotted with flies. A dog was tugging at its entrails, and round about little sticks had been pushed into the ground, with bits of white cotton tied to them, presumably to mark other shell holes.

At first there were no other signs of death, and the major explained that the children's bodies had been taken away by their parents. But the dead woman's coffin had been left for us to inspect, and he led us to it next: a long, lumpy shape covered with a plastic rain sheet. The plastic sheet was a vivid pink, incongruous against the greyness of the scene. The major walked briskly up to the coffin and pulled off the rain sheet, and I saw that the lumps were branches heaped over the coffin, for incineration. Two soldiers lifted the branches off and people gathered round, preparing their cameras. One man fiddled with his light meter. I looked on for a moment, then turned away and walked back towards one of the huts that were still standing. There, under a thatched lean-to which had been left oddly intact, I found a tea-pot, with a cracked porcelain cup. There was still some tea in the pot and I poured some out and tasted it, then spat it out. I lit a cigarette instead.

Presently Rick joined me. He sat on the damp ground, and we smoked in silence for a minute or two. He looked pale.

'What do you think happened?' I asked uncertainly. He shrugged.

'Who knows? Perhaps there really were Viet Cong in the village, two days ago. Perhaps the villagers helped them. The Cambodians won't tell us, if they even know. Or perhaps the pilots made a mistake, shot at the wrong village. That happens too.'

'I've never seen a dead body.'

'I have, and I don't like it.'

I heard a sound and looked up. One of the spotter planes had returned, flying in slow circles as before, like a hawk gliding over a field. People stood about following it with their eyes, no longer alarmed by it.

'Look,' said Rick. He pointed to the south-east, where three small dots had appeared against a bank of cloud and were chasing their tails in circles, high up and very fast. They seemed to be a long way off, but their wide loops gradually brought them closer, until we could no longer hear the drone of the spotter against the roar of their engines. And now we could see more clearly their smooth, cigar-shaped bodies, sharpened at the front, with wings raked back, and what looked like rocket pods under their wings.

'Jets,' someone said unnecessarily. Colonel Purdue tried to follow them through his binoculars.

'F105's' he grunted. 'Thunderchiefs. That's odd. I didn't think they used them so far south. They're usually kept for missions over the north.'

'What do you think they're after?'

'Let's hope it's not us.'

'It can't be. Surely they can see we're harmless. Guerrillas don't sit around on the grass like this when enemy planes are around.'

'Maybe not. But I think we should head back for the trucks.'

'Too late for that.' The Canadian Commissioner raised his voice above the noise. 'Look!'

The spotter had stopped circling and was now on a straight course which brought him down diagonally across our front, heading for the trees. It jerked, a thin wispy trail appeared under its wings, followed almost at once by a burst of smoke from the tree line, two or three hundred metres away, and a sharp crack. The Canadian turned and waved his arms at us.

'Take cover!' he shouted. 'Everybody get down! They're coming in!'

We stood uncertainly for a few seconds, then everybody ran for shelter. Some dived under the hut, others headed for nearby shrubs or simply threw themselves on the ground. I was slow off the mark, and by the time I started to move every bit of shelter was already taken. I spotted a small trench a few feet away, leapt into it feet first as the first jet began to dive. My feet struck something soft, there was a muffled cry, and I sprawled on the ground, half in and half out. I tried to burrow deeper but whoever was in there wasn't about to make room for me. Somewhat aggrieved I crawled out again, found a slight ridge on the ground and lay face down in the mud and grass behind it.

The next few moments were nothing but chaos, sound and fury and the chattering of my teeth. There was a roar, which struck like a blow on the back of my head, a shock-wave of air, and a black arrow-head hurtling past overhead, very low, very fast. The roar increased until it sounded like a runaway train, the ground shook, then the thunder slowly receded. A brief lull as the arrow-head shot upwards and out of sight, and then the next one came in. After the third or fourth pass I began to hear a new sound, the crump of explosions and the crack of splintering timber from the tree line. I bit my lips and pressed my face against the mud.

It's sometimes a tiny detail which restores a sense of balance. When I opened my eyes again I saw, six or seven centimetres away, a blade of grass with a beetle clinging to it. Every time a plane dived the blade of grass trembled and the beetle tightened its grip. As I watched the beetle, so much like myself, my fear began to leave me, and I started to relax. Turning my head I saw where one of the Indians, a very young man in stovepipe trousers and a white shirt, was crouched under a bit of palm tree, his rear in the air like a Moslem at prayer.

'For Christ's sake put your coat on! Your shirt stands out like a fucking beacon!' I recognised the voice of Parodi, the French press attaché. 'Look at that fool over there!' he went on in disgust. 'Waiting to get a rocket up his arse. Hey you! Get down in the mud like everybody else! You're not a fucking neutral any more!'

93

We all laughed, except the Indian, who paid no attention. I saw nearby a heap of dried palm branches, with several bodies tightly packed underneath. One of them propped himself up on an elbow and I recognised the North Korean by his straw hat. Rick lay next to him, almost in his arms, and from another plumper shape rose the quavering tones of the Polish commissioner:

'What a stupid way to die this would be, lying in this shit with all my paperwork still unfinished at the office.'

'I don't even know if I'm in Vietnam or Cambodia,' Rick remarked. 'How will that look in my obituary?'

They are not shooting at us,' the North Korean said calmly, looking towards the trees. 'They are aiming at the smoke marker.'

'How very reassuring,' said the Pole, as another rocket exploded, much closer this time. We all ducked. Then suddenly the thunder stopped, the sky was empty. Bodies rose cautiously from under leaves and out of trenches. Someone handed cigarettes around, someone else made a joke, and I looked at my watch. It was four thirty and the whole episode had lasted less than ten minutes.

Chapter Five

'What I don't understand,' Rick said that night, 'what nobody could work out, is why the whole thing happened at all. It wasn't I suppose the fault of the jets. At that speed the pilots couldn't have seen much of what was happening on the ground. It was the spotter which guided them in. But why did he? Was there really something there, some concentration of Viet Cong among the trees? Even with all that racket you'd think we would have heard something! Of course we were all too busy getting away from the place to go and look. But even so, it seems unlikely. Did the spotter pilot take us for a bunch of VC then? God knows we didn't look like one. And we weren't trying to hide or anything, not until the shooting started. Besides, if they were shooting at us they made a poor job of it. The nearest rocket landed at least a hundred metres away.'

'You don't suppose,' said Henri Marchand, 'that it was done deliberately, do you? I mean a display of some sort –'

'To frighten us, you mean, and discourage us from going near sensitive areas like that in future?'

'Something like that.'

Rick shook his head.

'Too risky,' he said. 'Even if they could have known we were coming. Those rockets did land pretty close, even if they weren't meant for us. It wouldn't have taken much of an error to land one among us.'

'Can you imagine,' I added sarcastically, 'what an international incident that would have caused!'

Laughter all round.

'Mind you,' Henri added, 'the Cambodians mightn't have minded so much, to see someone else get killed for a change instead of their villagers.'

'Not to mention the publicity. But whatever the reason, if the aim of the exercise was to frighten us it certainly succeeded. I've never seen a sorrier bunch of diplomats, including me, when it was all over.'

It had indeed been a shaken group that returned to Phnom Penh that evening, by a circuitous route which made the trip out look more than ever like a picnic in comparison – a picnic suddenly interrupted by some natural disaster, an earthquake or a bolt of lightning. Faces were pale beneath the mud. Some found relief in hilarity – the crouching Indian, a man seen diving headlong into a puddle of water, made for repeated jokes – but most of us took refuge in silence and exhaustion. Only one man became mildly hysterical, and kept complaining in a shrill voice long after we'd left the scene. He was going to write to the American High Command, to the Pentagon, to the White House if need be, until we all received an apology and compensation, and he went on in this vein until we told him to shut up. We had enough cause for exasperation without him. As if the raid had been a signal for everything else to go wrong, the arrangements for our return quickly fell apart. It started to rain soon after we left the village, and we lost precious time when vehicles broke down in the mud. It was nearly dark when we got back to the airfield, to find that the plane had already left. After that, an interminable drive back to Phnom Penh, two hours to cross the Mekong by ferry at Kompong Cham in pitch darkness and under a pelting downpour, and then a stiff cold ride over the last hundred kilometres in a Chinese bus with the wind and the rain whistling through the slatted blinds. It was after ten by the time Rick and I had showered and changed and made our way to Fouchet's house. He thought we'd forgotten his invitation.

Now we were sitting on his veranda, after dinner, over coffee and liqueurs: Fouchet, the Marchands, three or four other guests. The Boisjolys, a French couple from Siemreap, in town for the week-end, Suzanne, the young nurse from the Calmette Hospital, still showing lots of cleavage but less provocative than at the party the week before. A picture of middle-class comfort and security, tropical version, with rattan chairs and unobtrusive servants. At first Rick and I hadn't wanted to make too much of our adventure, not from modesty so much as a kind of moral reluctance at exploiting the underlying grimness of it. But we couldn't very well keep quiet about it, the subject was too fascinating, and the others soon got most of it out of us. I let Rick do the talking, while I sat back and thought about the afternoon. He was a good story-teller, and managed with a mix of hyperbole and self-deprecation to make it seem both exciting and funny. For that's what it had been, really, an exercise in mock-heroics; and although I would have preferred not to talk about it I could see that he was right to talk about it in that way, to reduce what had been for a time a chaos of noise and sickening fear to the level of an anecdote, an amusing incident on a troublesome border. But my mind went back to the thunder and the fear, and the deserted village, the heap of ashes, the rotting buffalo and the woman in the coffin, also rotting, that I hadn't had the stomach, or the callousness, to look at. And I thought how naïve I had been about the war until then. I thought I knew all about it, I had read the clichés, seen the newsreels. But I really had no idea. I had never seen death before. Because that's what it came down to, in the end. Bodies in rice fields, children drowned in a water-filled trench, cameras clicking around a coffin. Putrid tea in an abandoned tea-pot, and the stinking sweat of fear. Rassimov had a point, and I felt ashamed of my earlier excitement.

Perhaps Rick felt this too, because he also fell silent, as the others ran out of questions. But the others, the men at least, were now launched on a track of their own. Fouchet had served as a young army surgeon, Monsieur de Boisjoly had also fought in Indochina, and as often happened with Frenchmen of their generation in Phnom Penh they were now talking of their war, the war against the Vietminh, and comparing it to the present one, the essentially foreign conflict which was being waged on their old stamping ground. Nostalgia and patriotic pride taking a hand, the Americans inevitably got little support – though, to give Fouchet his due, he loathed all war, regardless of who fought it or for what motives. He had seen too much of the damage it causes. But Monsieur de Boisjoly was made of sterner stuff, and his little moustache bristled with eloquence.

'When I think of the way we had to fight, with worn-out equipment and half the men the Americans have, and we held out for close on ten years! And,' he leaned forward, fixing us with a fierce stare, 'what's more we were spread over the whole of Indochina, Laos and Cambodia as well, and all of Vietnam from the north to the south. Whereas all the Americans have to do is control the south. And look at the mess they're making of that.'

'It's not quite the same sort of war,' Henri tried to say, but Monsieur de Boisjoly swept in again.

'Of course it's not!' he exclaimed triumphantly. 'That's just what I'm saying. Why, we only had a tenth of their equipment – what am I saying, a hundredth! None of these countless planes and helicopters, those Thunderchiefs and B-52s, we fought on foot. After the Korean War we were even outgunned! No, I repeat, ours was a real man's war!'

Une guerre d'homme! The phrase had an epic ring alright, like something from the Song of Roland. And maybe there was some truth to it. But it was lost on Fouchet, who gave a derisive snort. Earlier he had been the first to condemn the Americans for flying around in their supermachines calmly annihilating everything below. Now, with typical lack of scruple he reversed his position. 'Next you'll be telling me it was a more humane war! You forget we burnt villages too, and used napalm and torture with no greater moral hesitation. And in any case, what does it matter if people die of napalm or a bullet. The result seems much the same to me.'

'Not on the same scale –'

'Perhaps,' said Henri quietly, 'because we didn't have the means –'

'Means!' Monsieur de Boisjoly cried. 'Of course we didn't! That's just what I'm saying. If we'd had the Americans' means, we wouldn't have lost…'

And so it went. I looked at Nicole, who sat to one side, talking quietly with Madame de Boisjoly. We had hardly spoken since my arrival. She had listened with attention to our exploits, but now that the conversation had swung to this sort of debate she had lost interest and only pricked up her ears at the more dramatic outbursts. She had an air of minding her own counsel and I hesitated to approach her. Then Madame de Boisjoly stood up to go out of the room, Nicole looked at me, and I plucked up my courage and went to sit next to her. She got up too, and I thought she meant to avoid me. But she smiled. 'It's hot in here,' she said. 'Let's go out to the garden for a moment.'

I followed her, Rick glancing in our direction. We halted just beyond the edge of light, and sat on a little stone rampart which separated the lawn from the gravel driveway.

'You look exhausted,' she said. 'Was it really so frightening? Or would you rather not talk about it?'

'No, I don't mind. It wasn't so bad, after the initial fright, and anyway I think we deserved it in a way.'

'Why do you say that?'

'Oh, the way we carried on. We were like critics with free tickets to the theatre, who complain because the seats were too hard, or someone let off a bad smell in the audience. Because that's what we were, really, paid spectators, hired for the occasion, ready to go and watch the fun at someone else's expense. Looking at bodies, at burnt huts, taking photos...If one of us had been killed, it would have been the result of pilot error, or a blunder somewhere, not some sort of retribution for our political opinions, for taking a stand. We had no attitude. We were the safe men, the smooth people who come after disasters to spin words about them...which is why I suppose some of us behaved afterwards as if our dignity had somehow been violated.'

'But it was your job to go. You didn't have any choice.'

'I know that, and that goes for the others too. But there's still something unpleasant about it all. No one should have the right to go and look at war, as a way of spending the afternoon.' Again I remembered Rassimov's comments that morning. And yet to judge by his expression later on he'd been one of those who most resented the indignity inflicted on him.

'I went through something like that once,' Nicole said. 'When I was young, during the war.'

'Yes, you told me. When Leclerc came through your village and drove the Germans out. '

'No, this was different. It was earlier, before the Allies broke through. I was visiting a cousin, in another village. We were out in the fields, a group of us from the village, when some planes came and bombed the railway station. American planes. There was nothing there, no Germans or anything, just some old carriages in a railway siding. We were only about three hundred metres away. No one was hurt. But it was all pretty frightening.'

'What did you do?'

'Nothing. What could we do? Some of the younger children started to cry, but the older boys told them not to be scared, and they stopped. Then a woman living nearby called us over and we hid in her cellar until it was over.' She laughed briefly. 'There was a panic afterwards, one of the children had gone missing, people thought he must have been hit, and everyone went looking for him. Eventually they found him sitting happily in a burning railway carriage stuffing himself with sugar meant for the Germans.'

I laughed with her.

'At least he got something out of it. I don't think there were any winners today. But I shouldn't complain too much. I learnt one useful lesson.'

'What's that?'

'That I'm not necessarily a coward.'

'Why, did you think you were?'

'I wasn't sure. It's all very well imagining being brave watching war films, but I've never been in a war, I was too young during the war to remember it. I haven't even done any military service. I've always wondered how I'd behave under fire. It was pretty frightening at first, but I discovered I could stand it, and at least I didn't scream, or pee in my pants as someone did this afternoon. I suppose that's something to be thankful for.'

'I never thought you were a coward. Even if at times you have to force yourself a little.'

I smiled. 'I wasn't very brave tonight. I almost didn't come, you know. It was Rick who made me.'

'Have you told him –'

'Of course not! I know we're friends, but not that close. No, he just thought it would do me good, and it would be nicer to Aristide.' I paused, then said firmly: 'I'm not sorry about Friday night, Nicole, whatever you may think. I know I shouldn't have said those things I said. But I'm glad I did.'

Nicole was silent for a moment, letting that little piece of bravado hang in the air. Then she stood up, and pulled me up with her.

'I'm glad you did too.' She put her arm through mine and led me back inside. 'Now let's go back, before they start wondering what we're up to.'

Chapter Six

1

I didn't see much of Nicole over the next month, but that due more to circumstances than any desire to avoid each other. On the contrary, when we did meet we seemed to be drawn together and establish a mood of friendly complicity with very few words – as if that last exchange had taken us to a new level of comradeship, without yet leading any further. To me at least this was one of my happiest memories of that period, the private excitement of seeing Nicole, of my thoughts and feelings about her running like an invisible thread through the mounting tension which gripped Phnom Penh, in that month of August 1966, as it made ready for the French president's visit.

An odd change came over the city, as the state visit drew nearer. I was used to the sleepy pace of life, and I was amazed by it. Gangs of workers now roamed through the streets, sweeping, cleaning, clipping hedges and lopping branches, painting lamp-posts and street signs and traffic lanes along the roadways. Even the kerbs received a coating of whitewash – though that was soon washed away in the rain and had to be reapplied closer to the event. In the grey stillness of dawn fire-trucks clanked through the city, hosing down the dust. The street dogs all disappeared, and police in crisp new uniforms descended on householders whose front path wasn't swept clean by nine in the morning. Whole streets were tarred, where dusty lanes ran before, and building projects which had been paralysed by lack of funds suddenly shot up. In some districts the skyline changed daily.

After the cleaning came the decorating. Overnight, coupled flags of France and Cambodia appeared on all the lamp-posts, the next morning blossomed on every window sill. Huge portraits of the two heads of state oversaw the traffic at key intersections. The electricity network disappeared under bunting, and squads of workmen on precarious ladders struggled to erect large signs across the major avenues, each bearing a message of eternal friendship:

Le peuple Cambodgien souhaite la bienvenue à l'Eminent Visiteur

Le Cambodge salue le Grand Homme d'Etat des Temps Modernes

Vive le Président! Vive le Prince!

The Boulevard Norodom became a tunnel of colours, a carnival world.

The same single-minded concentration reigned at work, where everything that didn't relate to the visit was pushed aside. My days were now taken up with long fulsome articles about de Gaulle, with special supplements and colour plates in off-set printing, with programmes for the visit and proofs to the printer's, with corrections and re-corrections. The rest of the world, the war in Vietnam, even the border were relegated to the back pages. In my spare time, what little I had, I wrote pieces for my uncle's paper in Tours, which couldn't afford to send its own representative.

It was a heady atmosphere. At first amused and sceptical about these frenzied preparations, I was soon caught up in the mood. I watched in awe as the foreign press began to arrive – the great names of international journalism, who'd been given a special dispensation for the visit, and who seemed to me almost as prestigious as de Gaulle himself. Representatives of the major newspapers of the world, who covered wars, assassinations, the fall of dynasties, and made history by their presence. They sat near the pool at the Hotel Royal, drinking Chinese beer and swapping anecdotes, while the more anonymous technicians of publicity, the ones who held the microphones and the newsreel cameras and seemed to look at the world Cyclops-like through an invisible photoelectric cell in their forehead wandered, monstrously laden, among the few bewildered tourists who had managed to keep their rooms. The bars were doing a roaring trade. They hadn't seen anything like it since the Americans had left. I hovered on the sidelines and felt especially favoured when some of them, running out of ideas, came to me for comments:

'Tell me about the rice crop. How much of it gets to the Viet Cong?'

'Do you think de Gaulle will contact the North Vietnamese while he's here?'

'What's this rumour that the Khmer Serei rebels – how do you spell that again? – are going to attack Angkor Wat when de Gaulle goes there? I hear the army's sending two battalions of troops there. Is that true?'

If anything was needed to make the tension almost unbearable, it was this hint of possible danger. I hadn't seriously believed that the authorities would round up all the anti-Gaullists in town and pack them off to the coast, but they did exactly that – though I was glad that Fouchet was spared. And that was only part of the security precautions. Troops were not uncommon in Phnom Penh, but suddenly they were everywhere. Patrols in the streets, roadblocks where cars were searched, identity checks. Orders to households along the presidential routes to stay off their balconies and keep their shutters closed, while petrol stations were made to empty their tanks and fill them up again with water (petrol fumes on their own are easily ignited) so that long queues formed at the few outlets that still operated. And one evening at the Cochon d'Or I saw four strangers, large squat men with close-cropped hair who talked in monosyllables and drank even Madeleine's whisky without ill-effect. I asked a discreet question, was given a quiet answer: these were *les gorilles*, the president's bodyguards, come to look the place over in advance.

All this bustle and effervescence left me little time to think about Nicole. She herself had gone down to the coast for a few days, to get away from the atmosphere in Phnom Penh, and I was beginning to fret a little. It seemed to me sometimes that I was building a lot of daydreams on very little, that it wouldn't take much to upset the delicate balance of our friendship.

Then one morning I was called downstairs to meet a visitor – an elegant young German who asked, in tones that sang like the Lorelei, if I could discuss the political situation with him. He was pretty as a Dresden shepherd, and had I been made differently I would have been tempted to throw everything aside and go off with him into the morning. But I was very busy that day. At that moment the phone rang again, for the twentieth time in an hour. I hurriedly made an appointment to see him again later and as I rushed upstairs I caught a glimpse of the magazine under his arm. '*Was ist ein moderner Mann?*' it enquired appropriately.

'*Allo ! Roche à l'appareil !*' I barked into the phone.

It was Nicole, a merry, wistful Nicole, who had been back nearly a week and reproached me for not coming round to see her.

'Oh God, Nicole, this place is like a madhouse. I'll come round, I promise, as soon as I can. How are you? How's Henri?'

'I'm fine. As for Henri, he's like you, I hardly see him, he's up to all hours preparing for conferences and briefings. On top of which he's getting a cold. Are you going up to Angkor? Everyone says it's going to be grand.'

'I hope so. There's a special plane for the press and I'm trying to get on it. And you?'

'We may drive up. Perhaps I'll see you there? If you have time that is.'

'Don't be unkind, Nicole. If you knew how much I miss you.'

'I bet!' she said, and laughed gaily as she hung up.

2

I didn't go to the airport for the arrival. Instead I sat on my balcony, watching the presidential jet as it circled over the city, and thought enviously of Marcellin, the Marchands, even Rick, whose status entitled them to an invitation. Then I went down into the street. I had only gone a few yards when I heard my name and saw Rick's friend Surya standing at her front gate. I had to look twice to recognise her, in faded jeans and an old checked shirt hanging loose. She waved and smiled and asked where I was going.

'To the Boulevard Norodom, to see the Prince and the President come past. Want to come with me?'

'Oh, I can't go like this,' she exclaimed, looking down at her clothes, but I guessed she was more concerned about her reputation. Cambodian girls of good families didn't go walking in the streets with young foreign men – not if they wanted to avoid some unpleasant comments. But this was such a special occasion, surely the rules could relax for once.

'Come on,' I urged. 'People won't notice. They'll be too excited, and besides it'll soon be dark anyway. I'll wait for you to change if you like.'

She looked about to refuse, then changed her mind; and a few minutes later she was walking beside me towards the Boulevard, dressed more conventionally in *sampot* and blouse.

We were among the last to arrive. The crowd, as we turned the corner, was immense. It stretched ten deep along the footpath on both sides of the street as far as I could see, and was only prevented from spilling out on the roadway by two lines of troops which stood, facing outwards, a metre apart and arms at the port. There were regiments of school children in blue and white uniforms, each holding a stick with a small French or Cambodian flag, bands of musicians practising their scales, police at every intersection and roadblocks on every side street. We passed a group of young men carrying wicker shields and spears and drums and pipes of unusual design, and I thought at first that these were *Montagnard* tribesmen, come all the way from their distant hills to pay homage to the great white chief from across the sea. But Surya recognised them and said they were students from the Faculty of Fine Arts, *en costume folklorique*. They'd been practising for weeks.

Apart from the bands and occasional police whistles, the crowd was strangely silent. Only its feet could be heard, thousands of feet shuffling along like the sound of rain on gravel; and this quietness, the tense expectation in the fading daylight and the glare of the street lamps and the hundreds of coloured bulbs strung in zig-zags across the Boulevard, gave me an eerie feeling. If, as I surmised, this scene was repeated all the way from the airport to the Prince's residence at Chamcar Mon, where de Gaulle and his wife were staying, the city was cut in two as effectively as if a torrent in flood ran through it. Only a carrier pigeon could have got across.

We found an empty place along a fence and Surya climbed up on a post, gripping my shoulder for balance.

'I'm sorry I couldn't take you to our office,' I said. 'We would have had a better view from the balcony. But no one's allowed up there today.'

'This is fine. I can see all the way to the Phnom. Can you see?'

'On tip-toe I can.'

A whistle blew in the distance, a siren wailed. Heads turned, policemen ran across the road, the bands tensed and the

105

wickerwork warriors took up poses. But it was a false alarm, a solitary jeep racing down the Boulevard to check the route, and only some of the school children missed their cue and began to wave their flags prematurely. The crowd relaxed, there was scattered laughter, and a small child fell headlong off the kerb and retreated in confusion into the ranks.

'Standard procedure,' a Frenchman standing nearby said. 'They do that to relieve the tension when there's a long wait.'

'I hope they don't take too long,' Surya said. 'I'm getting cramps in my legs.' And she leaned more heavily on my shoulder. The Frenchman gave her an appreciative glance, and me a brief envious smile.

It happened very quickly, in the way of great moments, so that later I would have difficulty remembering all the detail. There was a hush, then a faint sound of surf, gradually swelling until we could hear the rumble of car engines and the mounting roar of the crowd, with sirens and police whistles bobbing up as it were in front of it. Orders shouted. The police and the soldiers stiffened, officers threw salutes, already the first cars were drawing abreast, while the blue and white children became a field of waving flags and the crowd broke into clapping. Police jeeps with whip-lash aerials, truckloads of troops sitting at attention, more jeeps skimming the edge of the kerb, here and there among the uniforms the squat civilian shape of a presidential bodyguard sitting sideways, eyes scanning the crowd and right hand near his open jacket. A flat-topped truck so packed with cameramen that it seemed they'd all fall off at the first pot-hole, zoom lenses bristling to the rear like cannon barrels. I couldn't have heard myself scream. An arrowhead of motorcycle police sweeping the street from gutter to gutter like the prow of an aircraft carrier, drowning even the clapping and the shouting in the thunder of their exhausts. The air was electric blue with fumes.

The great man came twenty metres back, standing upright in an open car, the Prince sitting beside him. A tall, gaunt figure towering above the crowd and the hedgerow of troops, a huge, lonely silhouette who at that moment truly seemed an embodiment of history. Stretched to the limit of my aching ankles I saw the pale uniform, striking for its absence of braid, the plain *képi* with its two stars, the craggy head, and the myopic eyes and endless nose which no cartoonist could exaggerate. Two hands raised and lowered in Olympian salute. Beside him the Prince was small and plump like a child – then it was hulking shoulders, a back hunched with age like an old wolf's. Paroxysms of applause. The crowd was unleashed. The bands played their lungs out, unheard. The warriors, as if released by springs, leapt and fell on each other in ritual battle, and tears sprang to my eyes as the vision swept past, heading towards the pink floodlit Independence Monument that stood like a beacon on the edge of the night, drawing in its wake the countless glossy limousines of the official party, all suddenly insignificant.

What an impressionable creature I am, I thought afterwards in more sober mood. But as I helped Surya down from her perch I could see that she was even more excited. Her eyes were shining, she gave my hand a quick tight grip of gratitude before she settled down to a more sedate walk beside me. We scarcely talked until we were back at her front gate.

'I suppose you can hardly wait to go to France now,' I said. 'Didn't you say you're planning to finish your studies in Paris?'

'Yes, but not until next year. My father thinks I'm still too young to go and live alone in France, with all those students. He's very old fashioned.'

'Don't you have any friends or relatives there, who can look after you?'

'I have an aunt in Bordeaux, but I want to go to Paris,' she said firmly.

'I agree, Paris is more exciting. What are you going to study there?'

'I'm not sure yet. I think I'd like to do political science.'

'And then?'

She laughed a little, embarrassed by my persistence. 'I don't know. I haven't thought that far ahead.'

'Maybe you'll come back and become a politician.'

'Certainly not! I only want to study it. Perhaps I'll become a teacher.'

Clearly she didn't want to think beyond Paris at that stage, and I didn't blame her. I remembered my own excitement when I had landed in France. I also remembered my later disappointments, and my joy when I had been accepted for the job in Phnom Penh. That was not so long ago. I had certainly had no cause to regret it, and I wished her similar luck with her dreams.

For a minute I even shared her longing to be away from Phnom Penh. If this had been Australia or France I could have asked her out to dinner, and afterwards we could have walked along the waterfront, mingled with the crowd and talked of ourselves. But that was a dream too because I knew she couldn't accept. Whatever she might want she knew she had gone as far as public morality allowed in that place, and although I was tempted to ask, common sense prevailed and I walked home alone.

3

The euphoria which swept through the country during the visit was still running strong two days later, for de Gaulle's last evening in Cambodia. The visit had been a total success. Sihanouk had been a splendid host, de Gaulle the perfect guest. It was true that he had caused quite a stir the day before, addressing a massed crowd at the National Stadium, by calling for the neutralisation of all of Indochina, and Phnom Penh was buzzing with rumours of some secret meeting with a North Vietnamese envoy, but these calculated moves were such a firm endorsement of the Prince's foreign policy that he would have been the last to object. On the contrary, Sihanouk had as much cause to be pleased with de Gaulle as the latter had to be gratified at his welcome. At that very moment, in fact, 320 kilometres to the north, final preparations were being made to round off the visit with a sound and light performance in the ancient temple of Angkor Wat, the likes of which no one had seen before or would see again for a very long time.

In the midst of all this pomp and magnificence however there were those, such as myself, who were beginning to wilt under the strain. In overall terms I had no cause for complaint, as I was also at Angkor, having managed to get a seat on the press plane that morning. But by the third day of the visit the foreign journalists, harassed by deadlines, hemmed in by protocol and security restrictions and always on the move, were a haggard, ill-tempered lot, and the experience of spending a day with them in the wake of the President had been a sobering one. Many of my youthful illusions had been crushed in the process. It was now seven o'clock in the evening and I was standing on the steps of the dining room at the hotel, the *Auberge des Temples* at Angkor, where we were all staying, having at last escaped from them, and all I wanted at that moment was a bout of strong solitary drinking. Then I saw Nicole in the courtyard below. She had just come in through the gate, apparently alone, and seemed to be searching for someone. My first instinct was to pretend I hadn't seen her. I needed more time before I felt ready to face her. But she had seen me, and waved, and I had no option then but to go down to her. She wore a shimmering dress of Thai silk and a cashmere shawl draped over her shoulders, though the evening was warm, and she looked chic and expensive and rather formidable. I spoke the first words which came into my head.

'You look ravishing! Don't tell me you drove all the way from Phnom Penh like that!'

"Of course not. We came up this afternoon and changed at the hotel. Henri managed to get a room for us both in town.'

'Is he here too?'

'He had to stay in town for some last minute meetings. He'll be here soon with one of the official cars.' In town meant Siemreap, four kilometres away, where the bulk of the official party was housed. 'I came ahead for some fresh air. I thought I might find you here.'

'That's kind,' I said, starting to feel better. 'Let's have a drink at the bar then, if you have time. I need some cheering up.'

'Why, have you had a hard day?'

'Well, it's been educational, if nothing else. Let me tell you about it.'

In retrospect the day had not been without its lighter moments. The journalists had spent much of the time when not bickering among themselves, quarrelling with any official who stood in their way, and a running battle had started from the moment we'd landed at the airport, lasting through the day. Altercations over luggage, which, they knew, was either lost or about to be; over the airport tax, which they refused to pay; over the allocation of rooms at the hotel, where a matronly lady journalist from a right-wing French daily found herself – one assumes in error – sharing a room with an East German communist cameraman (who reacted to the prospect rather more courteously than she did). And a host of other reasons, all equally vexatious. But this was nothing to the hullabaloo which followed when officialdom, taking a suitably impersonal revenge, placed us not at the head of the convoy, where we should have been to cover the President's movements, but sealed in a bus right at the other end. And there, despite our protests, we spent the rest of the day, fuming and pleading in vain with the driver to overtake the endless queue of cars ahead of us. He was clearly under orders to keep his place, and he knew no French anyway. At one moment there was a ray of hope when he lost his way in the maze of temple roads, was misdirected on purpose, took a short cut, and somewhat implausibly brought us to the next stop on the itinerary from the wrong direction and before the President had actually left it. With a cry of joy we all rushed out, cameras at the ready – only to be dislodged by the herd of security guards who sprang at us from the surrounding bushes. The French lady was pushed (perhaps by the East German, in the confusion) and sat down in the mud, several heavy men ran across my feet, we were shoved this way and that, and when the President at last emerged from the temple grounds there was such a flurry of bodyguards and officials about his person that all we saw was an umbrella (it was raining steadily, even the weather conspired against us), his grey head bending down to get into a car, and then the black limousine tearing away in a wail of sirens.

'You should have heard them howl!' I said with feeling, starting my second whisky. 'And again tonight at dinner, when someone announced that cameras won't be allowed in the temple for tonight's performance. By order of the Province Chief. I thought they'd tear the place down. They're still arguing about it inside. I ran out and missed out on dessert.'

Nicole laughed. 'Poor Philippe. No wonder you looked so fierce when I saw you on the steps. I was almost afraid to speak to you.'

'Really? I find that hard to believe. But I'm much better now, thanks to you and those two drinks. What about you? How was your day?'

'Not nearly so exciting. We left Phnom Penh at ten, had a quick lunch at Kompong Thom, and got here about two thirty. And Henri's been closeted with the President's aides ever since, just like yesterday. His cold's better though, which is a relief. I wandered around Siemreap this afternoon, bought a couple of nice sarongs to pass the time, and here I am.'

'You're going back tomorrow, are you?'

'Yes, we'll probably leave in mid-morning. Unless Henri goes back by air, with the official party. He says they'll probably have things to discuss right up to the last minute. In which case I'll have to drive back alone. A bit of a bore, but I've done it before. And you?'

'Oh, we'll all go back by plane tomorrow morning. If they let us into the airport after this morning's performance. I'm not looking forward to it.'

'Why don't you come back with us, then? Or with me, as the case may be? There's enough room in the car.'

'Thanks. I'd like to, but I can't.' I toyed briefly with the thought of accepting. 'I have to be back early at the office.'

'Go on!' she teased gently. 'Don't tell me you're indispensible. A few hours won't matter.'

'You tell that to Marcellin. He's the one who told me to get back early. I'd stay here all week otherwise. What's the time, by the way?'

'Seven thirty.'

'I'd better go. We're supposed to be there before eight, they won't let anyone in after de Gaulle arrives, and I need a shower first. There's Henri now, why don't we all meet again here afterwards? You don't have to rush back to town straight after the performance, do you?'

'No, that's a good idea.'

'Here in the bar then.' I waved to Henri and hurried off, much refreshed, to my long awaited shower.

111

The next two hours I spent on one of the hard wooden seats reserved for the press, on a grassy embankment in front of the temple of Angkor Wat, oblivious to all discomfort, the mosquitoes, my tiredness, even Nicole's presence a few rows away with Henri and the official party. As the narrator's voice sprang out on the still night air, the temple which that morning had been grey stones, dead stones glimpsed hurriedly through the bus window, blossomed forth before us like a tropical flower, petal by petal.

Abrupt silence, darkness. Then, from a gallery, pitch-black at first, rose the slow stanzas of an ancient prayer, like some Gregorian chant of the Buddhist world, intoned by a hundred monks, suddenly revealed the next moment in a bar of saffron light which glowed like a fresh ingot on the sea of night. A timeless moment, stretching infinitely before the last lament fell back softly into the darkness.

A change of focus. Next the central terrace became a stage, as dancers emerged from the stone pillars with slow, gliding steps – the Royal Ballet, dancing with bare feet on the smooth worn stones where seven hundred years before their ancestors had danced, praying to be transformed for an hour into Apsaras, the dancers of the gods whom mortals can only imitate, dancing to the shrill woodwind music that changed imperceptibly from the gentle sigh of the wind to the enervating whine of bees on a summer afternoon. Gilt and brocade and silk, crimson and gold and peacock blue and the glint and sparkle of rubies. For a moment the mind forgot the arc-lights and the microphones, the wires running under the parapets, and drifted back to that golden age of seven centuries earlier, the greatness of Angkor, before the Thai armies poured in from the west to burn and pillage and enslave, before the marauders came to dig and desecrate and scratch away the gold leaf and crack open the statues of Buddha and of earlier gods in their greed for treasure, before the jungle crept in to smother the sacked and ruined temples and the carved sandstone began to rot like a leper's skin under the monsoon rains and the beating sun and the corrosive droppings of a million bats. For an hour or two the old ghosts were reborn. As the mimes and players of a later age stepped forth in stately procession out of the night, it was the legends of the bas-reliefs that came to life, the cohorts of Khmer and Cham warriors marching along the walls of the galleries, the generals in their chariots and the caparisoned elephants, the Sacred Monkeys Hanuman and Sugriva, and the God-King Suryavarman himself, who had this temple built for his own apotheosis on the back of a myriad slaves, it was these who were reborn in the hollow boom of the conch-shells, in the jingle and creak of harness and the slow tread of the elephants.

The vision slowly faded, the temple slid back into the darkness to brood alone once more like a cold volcano. We walked back in silent procession along the causeway, the way lit fitfully by young boys with torches. Near the entrance and the upturned head of a sacred Naga, the seven-headed cobra whose stone body, long fallen into ruin, had once formed a balustrade to stop fools from tumbling into the moat on moonless nights such as this, I waited for a moment for the Marchands to emerge from the crowd. Then when I didn't see them I headed across the road towards the bright lights of the hotel and the twentieth century of the bar.

The place was packed, and it took me a while to find them. To judge by the number of faces I knew most of Phnom Penh's foreign community had come up for the occasion, although for many of them it would mean driving back that night. Struggling through the throng I came upon Rassimov, who stood to one side with a glass in his hand and a speculative look on his face. He nodded and smiled at me and I wanted to ask him what he thought of all this pre-revolutionary splendour. But we were pushed apart and I moved on, until I came upon them standing in a corner with Rick and the Boisjolys, the couple I had met at Fouchet's house. They squeezed up to make room for me.

'Aha!' Monsieur de Boisjoly exclaimed. ''Our young friend from the wars returning. What did you think of it? Wasn't it splendid?' He waved his free hand in a sweeping gesture, somewhat risky in that confined space. 'The Field of the Cloth of Gold! Francis the First greeting Henry the Eighth couldn't have done it better!'

Rick grinned. 'Yes,' he shouted back. 'But Francis the First was a spendthrift who nearly sent France broke. Who's paying for tonight's extravaganza, I wonder?'

Henri winced, as well he might. France, it was rumoured, had just signed a generous aid agreement with the Prince. How much of it had been used up in tonight's blaze of glory? But Rick was not in the mood for diplomatic tact. Contorting himself to catch a passing waiter he produced a whisky which he shoved into my hand.

'Drink up, my boy,' he cried. 'Who cares anyway? Drink and be merry, for tomorrow we sink into bankruptcy.' He lowered his voice. 'And just you wait and see what they write about this!' Over the rim of her glass Nicole gave me a wink, and I settled in for some serious drinking. There didn't seem much hope of seeing her alone again that night. Should I have accepted her offer of a lift, and risked Marcellin's displeasure, on the off-chance that Henri went back by air? I grinned and nodded and joined in the jokes, but inwardly I felt rather annoyed with myself.

Then, about midnight, the place began to clear. Rick was the first to go, pretexting tiredness and an early start in the morning, then the Boisjolys left ten minutes later. I saw them go with mixed feelings, for I knew my time was up. Soon there would be no one left to drink with apart from Rassimov. Henri looked at his watch, finished his drink, and helped Nicole on with her stole as he paid his bill. Then he signalled me to one side.

'I've got a problem,' he said, keeping his voice low. 'You don't feel like driving back to Phnom Penh tonight, by any chance?'

'Are you going back now? I thought you weren't leaving until tomorrow.'

'That's right, but I'm going back by air, with the official party. There's still some unfinished business to discuss and it's our last chance before they leave. But Nicole has to take the car back and she'd prefer to leave tonight, if she can find someone to go with her. Would that be imposing too much?'

I stared at him, then glanced over his shoulder at Nicole, who gave me an almost imperceptible nod. 'She'll need to change,' I said lamely, and Henri nodded. 'Of course. She can do that in the hotel. Is that alright?'

It looked as if they were only waiting for my agreement. Had they been arguing? There was a faint nervous flicker to Henri's left eyelid, and he looked even more tired than usual, but otherwise impenetrable. Poor bastard, I thought with sudden pity, you've had a worse week than any of us.

'Fine,' I said. 'No problem. When do you want to leave?'

'As soon as you're ready.'

'I'll go and get my bag then.'

'We'll wait in the car.'

5

It was warm in the car, safe as a cocoon. Nicole drove well. We sped past trees, silent fields, sleeping villages, took the little humped culverts like ski jumps. The ghosts of the past, of the Angkorian forest, fell away like distant voices shouting against the wind. Four hours ahead lay Phnom Penh, soft beds, known faces with known expressions, all the familiar routine, welcome and depressing after the excitement of the past weeks. We would arrive spent in the pre-cock crow stillness before the dawn.

'Cigarettes in the glove box, please.'

I lit hers before passing it over, musing on the inconsequential intimacy of the gesture. Watching her profile I thought of Surya, Surya's smile, shy, trusting and innocent. She would offer a warm, dry friendship. Why couldn't I find something like that, and be satisfied with it? Why must I complicate life, coveting my neighbour's wife?

'I suppose you haven't had much time to think about me over the past month,' she said suddenly.

'I've been so busy I've hardly had time to think about anything. But no, I haven't changed my mind, or turned my attention elsewhere. Why? Did you think I was so faithless?'

'The trouble with you, I never know where truth ends and flattery begins.'

Somewhere after Kompong Thom she slowed down and drove off the highway, along a narrow lane that ran into the fields

115

towards some distant hamlet. There was no moon, with the lights off it was dark and close like the inside of a hollow tree. Bullfrogs throbbed, resonant as drum skins. Fireflies winked in flight like monstrous solitary eyes. We sat in silence for a moment, listening to the engine ticking.

'You realise I'm not free, don't you, and that if you fall in love with me you risk getting hurt?'

'I know. But that applies to you too. I hope you see that.'

'Yes. But I can look after myself. It's you I'm worried about.'

'I'll take that risk. And I promise I won't interfere in your marriage.'

She turned to me.

'Promise me you won't do or say anything that might hurt Henri. I don't want him to know about this, ever.'

'I promise. I'll never do anything to hurt him. Or you.'

She kissed me. It was an oddly clumsy kiss at first, sweet but inexpert, as if she'd forgotten how, but we soon warmed to it. Whether by chance or design she had dressed for the trip in a light blouse and skirt. When I pulled her skirt up to start caressing her thighs she kissed me more fiercely. *Wait*, she said. The car had reclining seats and she let them down, then pulled me down with her. In our haste we hardly bothered to undress. She pulled off her knickers, loosened her blouse and bra while I struggled off with my pants. Her breasts fell into my hands like the forbidden fruit. *Tes seins sont les seuls obus que j'aime.* She gasped at first when I entered her and eased herself gently on me, but soon we were locked in a passionate embrace, clutching and lunging at each other like blind wrestlers in the dark and grunting with effort. When she came she collapsed on me with a shuddering groan. *Oh Philippe I wanted you so much.* My heart beat like a drum out of control and we were covered in sweat.

Afterwards we lay still for a long while, saying sweet things, beautiful things, and later we made love again, more gently this time, and in the early morning, as the sky took on the pastel tints of a pigeon's wing and our eyes smarted against the light, we drove slowly back to Phnom Penh.

PART III

Chapter One

1

Perhaps I shouldn't go into details of my relationship with Nicole over the next few weeks. After all, one love affair must be very like another, apart from circumstances of time and place there can't be much that hasn't been written on the subject. But there was more to this for me than a simple *aventure* with an older woman, and some of the circumstances at least merit a closer look. Phnom Penh wasn't just the sleepy tourist paradise of the travel brochures. It was a small, isolated, introverted community with many of the drawbacks of a French provincial town – the hidden tensions behind the social ritual, the gossip and petty jealousies – there were other dangers as well of which we weren't aware, and we wouldn't have lasted long if we hadn't, almost from the start, taken great care not to be found out, behaving at times more like spies or secret agents than lovers. Looking back on it now, what surprises me most is that we managed to get away with it as long as we did.

2

We met in my flat at first, in the afternoon. By the second time her influence was making itself felt, with a noticeable improvement in tidiness. But on her third visit we came close to discovery, when Rick unexpectedly dropped in. He wanted to discuss the article on Cambodia which, as he had predicted, had come out soon after de Gaulle's visit and attacked the Prince for his extravagance at a time when the country could ill afford it. At any other time I would have been fascinated. On this all I could think of was Nicole, hiding behind the door as in some bedroom farce: one sneeze and the game was up. I sighed with relief when Rick left half an hour later and it was safe for her to come out.

'Thank God you came by cyclo,' I said. 'He'd have spotted your car at once.'

'I can't come here again, Philippe. It's too risky.' She was even more shaken than I was.

'It's alright as long as we're careful,' I said. 'I'll make sure the bottom door's locked in future.'

'I don't mean only Rick. What if your maid starts to gossip?'

'She won't. She's very reliable, and she likes her job.'

'No doubt. But servants talk, you know. Especially if they know something funny's going on. You can't stop them.'

I tried to reassure her, but she was right, we couldn't go on meeting like that for long without being found out; and who wants to make love with one ear cocked for footsteps on the stairs? Lulled into a false sense of security by the happiness of spending two hours with her, I had forgotten what a dangerously small place Phnom Penh could be. But apart from the flat there weren't many alternatives. Hotels were out of the question – they were even more risky. Rent another flat, as a Cambodian friend had done to escape from his wife and arrange lunch-hour assignations with his secretaries? A Cambodian might get away with it, but I doubted if we could, and besides I couldn't afford it. That left the car; but we'd already done that, and it wasn't a real solution. Discomfort aside, there wasn't a country road within thirty kilometres where you didn't run the risk of interruption, or worse, from happy village youths. I wasn't going to subject Nicole to that.

Yet, half an hour later, we still hadn't found anything else.

'Damn it!' I burst out. 'It's stupid to be at the mercy of small things like that. And you must think I'm a pretty useless lover not to have thought of it earlier.'

'Don't be stupid. If you were the kind of womaniser who plans all these details in advance I wouldn't be here with you.' She sat cross-legged on the floor in my dressing gown, looking absurdly young, like a school-girl dressed for a part in a play. She looked at her watch.

'I'll have to go in a minute. Henri will be back soon.'

'I'll drive you home. Tell him you've been shopping. But first we've got to find a solution.'

'Of course there is a way,' she said. 'We could use the houseboat.'

'Your houseboat? On the river?'

'Yes.' She gave me a level look. 'I know it sounds grim, but can you think of anything else? It's about the only place where we can be sure of meeting without being seen, provided we go there at night.'

'Don't you have a watchman there?'

'No. Fouchet keeps his boat at the Club Nautique, during the week. It's just locked up.'

I knew the houseboat well, from the Sundays spent there on the river, picnicking and water-skiing with the Marchands and their friends. The *maison flottante*, as it was called, a large wooden structure floating on drums, with a bedroom and a store-room and a covered veranda. It was only used on week-ends, we would be safe there. But it was a long way from town, down along the Bassac river, past the Monivong bridge and a series of warehouses and timber yards with their rotten smell of soaking bamboo. We would only be able to go there after dark. It seemed a devious and complicated way of solving the problem.

'Please, Philippe,' she pleaded. 'I know what you're thinking. It's underhand, and complicated, and not the kind of place you'd imagine for an idyll. But there's no other way. I need you, Philippe. I don't want to have to give you up because we can't find a bed to sleep on!'

She frowned, looking for a moment almost close to tears – whether of frustration or something else I couldn't tell. *Need*, I thought. I hadn't heard her use that word before. I knelt down and put my arms around her.

'Here,' I said. 'Who's talking of giving anybody up? We'll go there, I promise, and it'll be just the thing. But so you know, let me tell you. I love making love to you. That's pretty obvious. But don't think that's the only reason – bed. There's a lot more besides.'

She leaned her head against my chest. 'I know' she said. 'I know.'

3

We went there three days later, in her little Fiat, while Henri was out at a men's dinner. She parked off the road, under an overhanging tree which should screen the car from passing headlights. Then, with the river only fifty metres away we took a narrow muddy path which led off at right angles, along the corrugated iron wall of some disused warehouse. On the right, a vegetable garden, with a few small huts beyond. A dog yapped hysterically at our passing and we trod warily in the dark, afraid to use the torch, but no one paid attention. At the edge of the bank we paused. The river level was high with recent rains but there was still a drop of two or three metres down a series of rough and slippery steps cut into the earth, and we half tumbled, half slid down the slope, pulling up just short of the water. The houseboat a few paces away was a looming hulk slightly darker than the sky, linked to the bank by a narrow plank which dipped under our weight. We stood on the ledge while I fumbled with the key like a clumsy burglar. I listened, but the dog had shut up and the bank behind us was deserted. All I heard was the soft slapping sound of water against the planks, the call of a night bird.

Then we were inside, and with no risk of being seen I switched on the torch: there was the small boat-harbour, empty now, where water glistened like black oil, beyond that wooden walls, a corridor, bedroom to the left, the upstream side, store room and toilet to the right, all opening on the veranda which ran the length of the structure, facing the river and protected from the rain when not in use by a heavy tarpaulin lashed to the railings.

In the store-room, crammed with cane furniture, the tables and chairs which came out on the veranda for picnics, I found a hurricane lamp and lit it. Its yellow light gave some warmth to the scene, but some of my earlier doubts returned. By night the bare walls looked shabbier, the smell of mud and mildewed timbers and cold motor-oil seemed stronger than on those cheerful Sunday afternoons, when people laughed and shouted and splashed about in the water outside. The bedroom was a tiny cubicle, most of it filled by a heavy wooden bed-frame big enough to accommodate a baby elephant, while the kapok mattress on it looked indeed as if it might at one time have been used by one. I stared at it for a while, then hung the lamp on a nail and opened a small shutter in the wall, to let in some fresh air. Fifty yards upstream I could just make out the heavy bulk of a rice barge, with the rickety superstructure aft where the barge keeper slept with his family. No danger from that quarter, and from the river no one would notice anything odd, even if they saw the glow of the lamp. Only fishermen used the river at night. But I remembered the tawdry little floating brothels further down the river, at Takhmau: they weren't very different, and I'd made love on beds like that before, except that I'd been half-drunk and no one there wore perfume as expensive as Nicole's.

I closed the shutter, on the night and on my thoughts. It was too late for misgivings. I turned to Nicole, who sat on the bed displaying her legs, and gave myself the uninhibited pleasure of looking at her. I could never tire of looking at her, dressed, undressed, or as now about to be. Suddenly the room was warm and friendly and conniving, and the blood began its familiar beat in my temples.

'There's a little of the wanton in me,' she said, laughing a little and tugging at her skirt, 'but I think there's something of the prude too.'

'That's one of the things I like about you.'

'What's that? The mixture?'

'Yes. The fact that you can be both at the same time. And the way the wanton has of coming out at the right moment.'

I turned the light down and sat down beside her.

'You'll see,' she whispered. 'It doesn't look much now, but it's ours, and we'll make it cheerful and friendly...we will be happy here.'

'Yes, we will.' She too needed reassuring. I wondered if she had done this before with someone else, a former lover. I pushed the thought aside. Unlikely, I told myself. But even if she had, it didn't matter. It was now which counted, the present and what we could make of the future.

4

Afterwards I dragged out two cane chairs and rolled up the canvas blind and we sat out on the veranda, in the dark, watching the glimmer of lights on the opposite bank. One of them moved slowly upstream and the flutter of a small engine reached across the water. The houseboat rocked minutely on small waves. It was very peaceful. With my earlier distaste for the place quite forgotten I could have stayed there all night, waiting for the dawn, if Nicole hadn't had to go home to Henri.

I thought of him now with discomfort. It was over three weeks since I had last seen him in Siemreap. Since then I had avoided going near the Marchands' house, had even avoided mentioning his name more than necessary. I don't want to exaggerate my moral sense about Henri, then or later. I didn't feel guilty towards him. After all, I told myself, I hadn't seduced Nicole all by myself, if I was now her lover he himself was no doubt partly responsible. But I liked Henri, he had been a friend, and if betrayal seemed an old-fashioned word for what I was doing to him, there was nevertheless too much deceit about it for my peace of mind. I wasn't looking forward to our next meeting and wondered how long I could keep putting it off.

Not very long, it seemed. Nicole, who must have guessed my thoughts, brought the subject up herself later that evening, as she drove me home.

'We're giving a dinner soon,' she said suddenly. 'Thursday of next week. Can you come?'

'Next week?' I echoed dimly.

'Yes. Henri's invited Marcellin and a few others, and he'd very much like you there too. He says you can help with the conversation.'

'That's kind of him. But I can't remember if I'm free. Can I let you know tomorrow?'

'If you like,' she said. 'But you should come, you know. Henri's been asking about you, he's wondering why you don't come round any more.'

I sighed. I knew very well that I had nothing else on that evening, and I didn't want to invent some transparent excuse.

'Aren't you afraid it may be a little embarrassing?' I asked.

'For you or for me?'

'For both of us I suppose.'

'Perhaps.' She shrugged lightly, staring ahead at the pools of darkness on the road, from which a cyclist could at any moment emerge, dressed in black. 'Look, I know how you feel, Philippe. But you'll have to surface sometime, you know. You can't solve a difficult situation by turning your back on it. If it's any consolation I'm not looking forward to it much either.'

I suppose that's what made up my mind: the thought that whatever my reluctance she had a much more difficult role to play, and I wasn't helping by hanging back.

'Alright,' I said. "I'll come.'

'Good,' she said briefly, as if that settled it. By then we'd reached my flat. She stopped the car and turned to me and I waited, expecting some further comment. Instead she changed the subject.

'You're not in any sort of trouble, are you Philippe?' she asked.

'Trouble? No, why?'

'Your work. The other day, when Rick came to the flat, I couldn't help overhearing...'

'Oh that!' I laughed. 'It's nothing. Some journalist in Hong Kong's got a bee in his bonnet about this place and keeps writing articles about it. It's nothing to do with us.'

'Are you sure? Rick sounded rather worried.'

'Of course I'm sure. Rick's a diplomat, and a very good one no doubt, but he does fuss over small things. There's nothing to worry about.'

'I suppose you're right,' she said doubtfully. 'I don't know much about your work...' She hesitated. 'Be careful, Philippe. Rick's been here longer than you, he knows this place...I'd hate to see you getting involved in anything.'

'Are you afraid something might happen to me?'

'Yes. I know it's silly, you know what you're doing, but I feel very vulnerable sometimes. I don't want to lose you.'

I put my arm around her and kissed her and a wave of tenderness washed over us, erasing the faint hostility of a moment earlier.

'I know,' I said. 'I feel like that too sometimes. But don't worry. I'm not going to do anything stupid. I don't want to lose you either.'

A moment later I stepped out of the car and stood on the pavement, watching its tail-lights disappear around the corner. I meant what I'd said, and right then, with the taste of her mouth on mine I felt much too strong to be vulnerable. But I looked over my shoulder as I walked to the front gate. The street was quite empty – there wasn't even a dog in sight.

Chapter Two

1

The Marchands' dinner went off much better than I feared. I went there expecting an ordeal, and discovered instead that I could play the dissembler as smoothly as if I'd had years of practice. Does that sound complacent? There was one awkward moment, right at the start, when Henri with unconscious irony thanked me for accompanying Nicole back from Siemreap, and reproached me for staying away so long. 'We've missed you,' he said. 'Have you been working very hard?' But my blush passed unnoticed, I managed not to fumble my lines, and after that took my cue from Nicole, who carried out her role as hostess with her customary poise. There was just a shade of affectionate irony in the smile she gave me from time to time, as if to say, you see how easy it can be, there was no need for all that hesitation. The thought crossed my mind that she was enjoying the situation more than she might admit. What woman could resist a glow of satisfaction at seeing her husband and her lover sitting together in such a friendly manner?

I wasn't so sure about Henri. He was affable enough, and did his best to look relaxed, but there was an air of tension about him, a hint of effort in the way he followed the conversation about the table, as if his mind had to be brought back reluctantly from some private and not very pleasant speculation. I thought he looked tired. But there was nothing in his manner to suggest what his thoughts might be, and if he had any suspicions about us he kept them well hidden. Maybe I was simply too tense myself, and inclined to over-react; but the wine was good, I drank enough to still my qualms, and turned my attention instead to Wilberforce, thereby providing the sole incident of the evening.

I had been a little surprised to find him there, as Nicole hadn't mentioned him, and I didn't think he and Henri had much in common. He was the left-wing English journalist who lived in Phnom Penh with the Prince's blessing, the only foreign journalist in fact who wasn't employed in some form or other by the Cambodian government. But politics aside, he and Henri shared a genuine interest in the region, and Wilberforce was too clever to push his views forward at such a gathering. At one point during dinner the conversation turned to the Vietnam War, and someone asked him how long it would be before the whole of Indochina became communist. I expected him to say it was just a matter of time, but he swerved away from that and played the neutralist card instead, thereby pleasing the French and supporting Sihanouk's dearest foreign policy. This was crafty of him, and good sales talk as well. There was no doubt from what Rick had told me that he was a communist sympathiser, if not an actual party member, and he didn't hide his admiration for the North Vietnamese. But he derived his market value as a free-lance writer from a careful façade of objectivity. He maintained at all times that the North Vietnamese were nationalists first and communists second, that they mistrusted the Chinese even more than they hated the Americans, and that it was most unjust to accuse them of violating Laotian borders or Cambodian territory to bring arms and men to the South. Ho Chi Minh was a gentleman above all. I remembered a photo of Uncle Ho which Wilberforce had shown me one day, one he had taken himself on one of his trips to Hanoi: a serene-faced contemplative wreathed in cigarette smoke, the halo of wispy white hair an outward sign of some inner holiness. It was an excellent photo, but I wondered how much it showed of the true nature of the man. It was hard to see in it the subtle revolutionary, the ruthless master-mind of the Vietminh – too much uncle. Just as it was hard to find in Wilberforce's own jolly red face the cunning propagandist that he undoubtedly was. Success had fattened him, mellowed the outline of his face, he lived these days in bourgeois affluence on the royalties from his books and his films. It was just possible at times to catch a glint of the eyes, a flash of his foxy teeth, and get the feeling that he could be pretty ruthless too. Or maybe it was just a trick of the light and he was doing a job like anybody else.

I didn't particularly like Wilberforce, but I had no intention of picking a quarrel with him when I found myself sitting next to him after dinner, as we regrouped in the sitting room for coffee and liqueurs. We began to talk about various novelists who had made a name for themselves out of Indochina, like Graham Greene and

Morris West, and the conversation was friendly enough up to that point, even if we didn't agree on every detail. But then I mentioned Lartéguy, author of *The Centurions*, who described graphically among other things the ordeal of French paratroopers in Vietminh prison camps (he was later accused of plagiarism). Wilberforce, who had been doing his own steady drinking over dinner until his face was now quite flushed, lost his natural caution and gave a derisive snort which rang through the room like a sneeze.

'Ha! That detestable man!' he said. 'Don't tell me people are still reading him. I thought they'd buried him long ago.'

'Oh come on, he's not so bad,' I said, secretly amused. 'You don't have to agree with everything he says.'

'Everything? I wouldn't agree with anything the man writes! He's nothing but a fraud.'

'I thought his early books at least were remarkably well documented.'

'Documented?' he repeated. 'I've never read anything more tendentious, more distorted and packed with half-truths in all my life. The man's a fascist.'

'I would have called him a romantic myself.'

'Most fascists are. That's why they lose in the end.'

These were strong words, and I'd got as much from him as I could hope. What I hadn't foreseen however with all that drink inside me was that I would get caught up in the game. I had always enjoyed Lartéguy's books, whatever their faults, to some extent my interest and indeed my presence in Indochina were due to them, and I felt I owed it to come to his defence. I made a rambling speech to the effect that while no one could deny that Lartéguy was a partisan observer, and that in some ways he could be accused of defending the indefensible, on purely literary grounds there was a lot to recommend him: he had style and vigour and the ability to explain complex situations and make whole battalions of characters come to life. In short he might be biased but he was a rattling good novelist. Wilberforce heard me out impatiently and then turned on me like an irate schoolmaster.

'What nonsense!' he said, and snorted again. 'You know, that's the trouble with you young fellows, you get taken in by all that superficial claptrap and facile exoticism and you just overlook everything else. It's very easy to write that sort of book, pick a subject like Dien Bien Phu and make it appear exciting, anyone can do it, providing you don't look too closely at the truth of it all. But the fact is that he sets himself up as a chronicler of real and major events, of things which have had immense historical significance, and conveniently distorts and drops three quarters of the truth out of them. He's nothing but a sensation seeker. It's all very well if that's what you're looking for and it's obviously earned him a lot of money, but only the very young can find any appeal in him. For somebody who wants to study this place seriously I would have expected you to show better judgement.'

'Hold on!' I cried. 'This is getting a bit rough.'

'Is it?' he shrugged. "I'm sorry if it hurts, but it happens to be true.'

'Maybe, but what about the others then? How about putting yourself on trial too? You're not entirely free of bias yourself you know – and you're hardly in a position to blame him for making money out of it.'

'And what's that supposed to mean?'

'Well, you're not doing so badly yourself, are you! I hear your latest series is selling very well in the US. Are you sure you're condemning him for the right reasons, and not simply because he's not on your side?'

That was not a well-advised remark, even if it was true. But his words had stung me and my blood was up. At that moment there was a lull in the conversation and several heads turned towards us. And then suddenly, stupidly, we both lost our temper.

'What do you know about sides?' he shouted, slamming his glass down. 'Young men who come out here in nice cushy jobs, think you know all the answers just because you've read a few books. Think I'm getting soft, do you? Making too much money? Let me tell you what I write about I've found out the hard way, tramping those paddy fields and mountains while the rest of you sat safely on your arse when you weren't still at school. I've seen men die because they took sides, so don't talk to me about sides, lad, you don't know what the word means.'

'Not as well as you, that's for sure!' I retorted. 'Those friends of yours out there, what were they doing, handing out flowers? If they got killed it's only because someone else got in first. You're no doubt a brave man, Mr Wilberforce, and you're entitled to your views, but don't pull your experience on me, because if that's what you call journalism I want none of it.' And to hell with you, I thought angrily, you and Rassimov, you make a good pair. We glared at each other, while around us the other guests looked on with varying expressions of interest. Then Nicole materialised at my elbow, with her best hostess manner. 'How are your drinks, would you care for another *citronnelle*?' she said smoothly. 'Philippe, why don't you come and sit over here, we've hardly talked all evening. Chi Ba?' She beckoned a maid over, someone made a remark about the heat which raised a laugh, and I let myself be led away, still belligerent but glad of the chance to escape.

'What are you trying to do?' she hissed. 'Start a brawl? You were meant to be helping tonight.'

'Oh, I don't know. I wasn't doing too badly, I thought. Anyway he was asking for it.'

'And you're asking for trouble, if you keep on drinking like that. You should see yourself.'

'No thanks, I'd much rather look at you. You're really very pretty when you're angry, has Henri ever told you that? Besides it was a bloody awful evening until I started that argument, you ought to be grateful to me. Oh hell!' I said, suddenly contrite. 'I'm really rather drunk, Nicole. I think I'd better go home before I do something really stupid.'

'No you don't. Drunk or not I need you here, so just sit still and behave yourself.' That was the nearest she came to admitting that she too had found the evening something of a strain. 'And if you've got any sense you'll go and make your peace with him before it's too late,' she added with great practicality. 'Otherwise you'll end up not speaking to each other, and you can't afford that in your job.'

She was right, and it sobered me to think of the consequences of making an enemy like Wilberforce, in Phnom Penh. I didn't much enjoy making my apologies, but he accepted them, though his manner thereafter remained cool towards me. Perhaps it served as a reminder that he didn't have a monopoly on truth. The two people who took it best were Henri, who said I had a great future on television, and, most surprisingly, Marcellin. I expected a lecture from him but all he said as we walked a few steps to my car afterwards was: 'You'll have to watch that tongue of yours. You're still a bit green to take on big game like that.' I think in fact he was hugely amused.

2

Memories of my brush with Wilberforce rankled for some time, and I was still smarting from it the next time I met Nicole on the houseboat. This time she was more tolerant.

'It was silly to provoke him like that,' she said, 'but I don't really blame you. Wilberforce is a crashing bore at times, I don't know which I like least, him or Marcellin. And you didn't do too badly. I don't suppose it was a very pleasant evening for you. But you had to come, you see that, don't you?'

'Of course,' I said, as much to please her as anything. It obviously meant a lot to her, and no doubt she was right. What puzzled me was that I couldn't make up my mind about that evening: whether to feel ashamed for the way I was deceiving Henri, or instead rather proud of the way I'd carried it off. Something kept telling me that I should be feeling at least some remorse, and that I was guilty of a serious moral breach for not having any. I wasn't helped by the fact that I didn't know how Nicole herself felt about it, deep down. There was too much I didn't understand. It was time to look for some answers.

'Are you sure he doesn't suspect us?' I asked.

'Henri? Quite sure. Why should he? We're being very careful.'

'I know, but Phnom Penh's such a small place, it wouldn't take much to tip him off...what would happen if he did find out, do you think?'

'He'd hate it, what do you think? Though it would depend on how he found out, to some extent. If he thought that I meant to leave him, or that I had stopped loving him, he would be very hurt. And he'd certainly resent it if there were any scandal, any public knowledge. Which is another reason why we have to be very careful, quite apart from the fact that I don't want him to find out anyway. But sometimes I think he mightn't mind terribly much. If he thought I knew what I was doing, and that I wasn't making a fool of myself.'

'He'd mind that more, would he?'

'Let's say he'd be…disappointed, as well as hurt.'

I considered this for a moment. Then: 'I don't follow. Look, I know it's none of my business, what's between you and Henri is yours, and I shouldn't pry into it. But seriously, what goes on between you two? When I see you together, some days you look the best of friends, the most compatible of couples. As if you were sharing a private joke against the world. And other times you sound like complete strangers. You've just said you love him –'

'Did I say that?'

'That's what it sounded like. Why, don't you?'

'Yes. Yes I do.'

'Then what are you doing here with me? Am I the private joke?'

'Of course not!' she cried. 'How can you say that?'

'Because I don't understand, that's why,' I said more gently. 'You don't love me –'

'Don't say that, Philippe. I like you very much.'

'But it's not the same thing, is it!'

She sighed. 'We've been over that before. I don't know. For that matter you don't know either.'

'I'm not – ' I began, and she completed the sentence for me. 'You're not being unfaithful to someone else, is that it?'

'I was going to say, I'm not sure any more. I mean – I think I am falling in love with you.'

'Philippe,' she said gently. 'I warned you.'

'I know, I know. You told me not to expect too much. Have you heard me complain? I said I'm falling in love with you, I didn't say I was unhappy about it. Anyway I can take care of myself. It's you we're talking about. You and Henri. I like Henri, you know. That's why I haven't particularly wanted to see him since we… since we became lovers. I won't say I lost my head that night. I knew perfectly well what I was doing. But then I

132

didn't think I was doing him any great harm.' I spoke in a rush, before she could interrupt. 'Whereas now...now I'm not so sure any more. There are all sorts of things still between you two,' I finished lamely. 'Things you didn't mention before.'

'Would it have made any difference if I had?' she said sharply. 'Be honest Philippe. It's a bit late for scruples now.'

'Don't be unkind!' I retorted, and we glared at each other. Then I shook my head. 'Sorry. You're right. I had no business speaking like that. It's just that...I'd feel easier in my mind if I didn't like both of you quite so much.'

She didn't answer straightaway. She took out a cigarette and lit it, and then walked to the edge of the veranda railing, where she stood in silence for long seconds, staring at the black river. Then she turned back to me.

'Would it help,' she said, 'if I told you Henri has a mistress?'

'What? Henri?'

'Yes.'

I was speechless with surprise. Henri, with a mistress! Of all people. I would have picked him last as a philanderer. And yet...a new doubt rose in my mind. 'Is that why you...'

'Why I took you as a lover?'

'Yes.'

'No! That's not the reason.'

'Then I still don't understand.'

'Now listen to me, Philippe,' she said firmly. 'I didn't say that to give you an excuse for my unfaithfulness. There's no excuse, and I'm not looking for one. I'm not here for revenge, I'm here because I want to be. Because part of me is in love with you too. Yes, I've admitted it! And I also like you very much, which is yet another thing. I've tried to be honest with you from the start. But there are some things I won't discuss with you. Maybe because I don't understand them fully myself. Henri's life with me...you're right, when you say we're very close friends. In many ways we are. In others we're worlds apart. There are aspects of him I don't understand, and probably never will. I know he's not happy, and I've tried to work out why, for years I've tried to understand what it was in me that failed to make him happy. I've tried to talk it over with him, I've even offered him a divorce if he wanted one –

133

though God knows I didn't – but he's never explained. He's always told me that he needs me, that he wants to keep on living with me, that the day I leave him will be the end of him. And I believe him.'

'You didn't discuss his mistress with him?'

'No. That was before. Much before…at least before I found out.'

'Do you know who she is?'

'Some local girl. No one you know. He meets her in town sometimes in the evening, instead of going to the office.'

'How do you know all that?'

'I followed him once. Look,' she went on quickly, before I could ask more questions, 'Don't try and understand it all. There's a lot about Henri that I don't understand too. Maybe you consider him weak, and strange, but you mustn't judge him. In some ways he's much better than we are. And he wasn't always like this. When we were first married, the early years…the thing is, Philippe, that I love him. I'm prepared to put up with him as he is, even if it isn't always easy. And he needs me too. That's what matters, between him and me, not the differences.'

'And me…?'

She put her arms around me, kissed me gently.

'You? You're the part of me that's young and irresponsible. You're what might have been. Can't you accept that, me, us, as we are?'

'Yes,' I said. 'Yes I will.'

3

Thinking about it afterwards, I wasn't fully convinced by Nicole's explanation of Henri, of her inner life with him. It had only been a glimpse, and it raised more questions than it answered. Henri, no longer the distrait, dreamy, rather grey husband too preoccupied with his work to care properly for his wife, but a stranger now, a man with a secret life, a man in pain. What pain though? If I could now understand better why Nicole had taken a lover, it was not at all clear to me why Henri had taken a mistress in the first place. Of course many men have mistresses, and Frenchmen, by reputation,

134

more than most. And these include intelligent and sensitive men, considerate husbands and good fathers, not simply the gross or the self-indulgent. But a man who took a mistress, I thought, must be moved by a lack in his life, a need to compensate elsewhere for some major deficiency at home. Men with fat and ugly wives, or dull wives, shrill wives, wives who demanded too much or were satisfied with too little. Any of a thousand reasons could drive a man to it. The trouble was that none of these descriptions applied to Nicole, who was lively, desirable, intelligent and devoted to Henri, and by his own admission loved and needed by him. It just didn't make sense that he should have turned away from her. Especially as he didn't give the impression of being driven by great hungers of the body. There must be something else, some other reason which Nicole didn't want to tell me. For I wasn't satisfied either by the sort of escape clause that she used to cut off further discussion, that there was much to Henri that she didn't understand. What! After ten years of marriage, between two people as intelligent as those two, that she should claim incomprehension, ignorance of the dark side of her husband? Surely by now they should be all but transparent to each other.

But when I tried later to get further revelations from her, she refused gently.

'There's nothing more to tell,' she insisted, smiling at my disbelief. 'And if there were I wouldn't tell you. It wouldn't be fair to him.'

Loyalty at least I could understand, and asked no more questions. Having given me the minimum explanation required in the circumstances – and only because I'd forced it from her – to lie back in the darkness now, after making love, and calmly discuss the secret life and hidden personality of Henri, would be disloyal to him in a way very different from unfaithfulness of the body or even of the heart – a breach of the most fundamental trust. By the same token I knew that Nicole would never be disloyal to me, now or later, by discussing my private failings with Henri – or with anyone else.

'It's partly that, yes,' she agreed. 'But more than that too. Here, it's only the two of us that count, you and I. When I come here, I leave everything else behind. It's like entering another life. I want to keep it that way. Does that sound very selfish?'

Yes, I thought, but no more than anything else – no more than I was. And her selfishness in its way required more moral courage than I could say for mine. What baffled me now was the way she seemed able to keep the two sides of her life separate. She was not frivolous, and she admitted to loving us both. How could you love two people at once? She laughed at my ignorance.

'I don't love you both in the same way. You're such different people, how could I have the same feelings for each of you? That wouldn't be disloyal, it would be downright impossible.'

'You make it sound very logical,' I grumbled. 'I'm sure there's a flaw somewhere.'

'It all comes from this terrible word 'love',' she said earnestly. We were lying on the big ugly bed, if not that night then another one, at that moment of physical satiety when the mind wanders most freely into abstract theories. '*L'amour*, what a useless word. At least in English you have the two, *love* and *like*, and even then you can't say what you mean. How can you summarise all the complexities of emotions, all the nuances of affection and attraction, of violence and gentleness, in one or two simple words?'

'Is that why you use them so rarely then? I must say it's much simpler to me. When I say I love you, it does seem to my primitive mind to express all the feelings I have at the moment. It all depends on the way you say it.'

'Now you sound like a Frenchman,' she said. 'A stage Frenchman.'

And also, I thought, I'm not divided between two people. I don't have to use the word in two directions at once. That was the problem, and no amount of semantics could cover it up.

4

But that I decided was a problem for a later time. We met to make love, not just to talk about it. We didn't meet just for sex of course. We met because we wanted to be together, because we felt so good together. If we'd had the time, if we'd been free to go about openly, we would have done many other things – gone for drives, for long walks, out to dinner, talked. As it was we talked almost non-stop, our meetings were a constant dialogue, we never ran out of things to say. But sex was very much at the core, and we went at it with great enthusiasm.

It was a joyous, exhilarating time, full of excitement and discoveries. Nicole had the advantage over me in age and maturity, but in matters of sex she wasn't much more experienced. She'd only had one lover before me, many years earlier, before her marriage: a young man, barely older than her, a fellow student. They hadn't lived together but they had been very close, had talked of marriage, before he was killed in a car accident. It had taken her a long time to get over his death. She still spoke of him with sadness.

'When Henri came along I didn't love him at first. I liked him, he was sweet, and kind and intelligent – unlike other men he wasn't forever trying to get me into bed. It wasn't until we were married that I really began to love him…Are you surprised, that I haven't had more lovers?'

'A little. But I'm glad.'

'What did you think, when we first began to know each other? Did you think I was having affairs? All those young men, circling round, you must have wondered. Did you wonder if I was sleeping with any of them?'

'I did a bit at first. Then I decided you probably weren't.'

'Why not?'

'Oh, I don't know. Maybe it was wishful thinking. I was starting to be very attracted to you. But I thought you had too much class, to be sleeping around. Too much…dignity, I think. Deep down you were too serious. I told myself it was probably just a game.'

'You were right. I've never wanted to sleep with any of them. I've only loved three men in my life, Philippe. Jean-Luc (that was the young man's name), Henri, and now you. I don't want to love anyone else.'

Perhaps the biggest discovery was the extent of my sexual ignorance. It would be hard for anyone growing up nowadays to imagine what it was like in the late fifties and early sixties in

Melbourne, capital of the state of Victoria in southern Australia. The western world's sexual revolution – at least the English-speaking world – was still just beginning, books like *Portnoy's Complaint* hadn't yet been written, and television shows like *Sex and the City* – never mind the *Naked News* – would have been unimaginable. But the dead hand of censorship in Melbourne was something else. Not only novels like *the Catcher in the Rye* and *Lady Chatterley's Lover*, but even the book of the famous trial in London in 1961, when Penguin Books were prosecuted for publishing it, were totally banned. As for Henry Miller or Jean Genet, they were considered the devil incarnate, by those who'd even heard of them.

Nicole laughed, when I tried to explain it to her.

'You really never had sex, before you came here? Didn't you have any girlfriends in Melbourne?'

'I did. I had one girlfriend especially, at university. We were pretty serious too. But we always stopped short of having sex. Full sex I mean. Just putting my hand up her skirt was pretty heavy. In the end she dumped me for one of my friends.'

'Maybe that's why,' she teased. 'But you've caught up since, haven't you. All those bar-girls. And now me.'

'Right.'

'Do I fuck as well as they do?'

'Come on, Nicole!'

I was mildly shocked when she said this. It sounds less crude in French – she used the word *baise,* which literally means to kiss, though it's more commonly used to mean having sex, even in polite society. The American *screw* might be a better translation.

'No, I want to know.'

'There's no comparison.'

And that was another revelation. I was used to the simplicities of sex with compliant bar-girls, with its own set of rules – which essentially meant being kind to them – but with Nicole I was in another dimension. Here no rules applied, other than the overarching principle that we would never want to harm each other. At first I was cautious, hesitant, afraid of appearing uncouth, to the extent even that she reproached me for being too gentle. 'I'm not a china doll you know. You don't have to treat me as if I'm going to break.' Nicole might have had a sheltered life but she was neither naïve nor ignorant, and she liked sex, as much as I did. When we met in public we were always on our guard, careful not to give by word or gesture a hint of our feelings. But once inside the safety of the houseboat we cast all restraint aside. We would pull our clothes off and go about half-naked, then make passionate love where the mood took us – on the bed, on a chair, standing up, even facing the river sometimes as she leaned forward on the darkened veranda with her hands on the railing and I took her from behind, her muted cries carried off on the breeze. Afterwards we would lie together for as long as we dared, caressing each other and talking quietly, until it was time to go.

'Do you think I'll be punished for this one day? For being so happy with you?'

'I don't see why you should,' I said. 'It's not as if we're harming anyone. As long as no one finds out.'

And what about Henri, I wanted to ask. In truth I didn't know the answer to that. All I wanted was for it to last, as long as possible, without worrying too much about the future.

We were lucky. Only once was there any hint of danger, when we stayed too long on the houseboat one evening and Henri returned home ahead of her, from his office – or his mistress. She pretended that she'd gone for a drive in the countryside, and he became upset when she said she'd gone as far as Oudong, thirty kilometres away. 'The roads aren't safe,' he said. 'What if you had an accident, or a breakdown? Promise me, when you get bored, that you won't go out of town like that. Please...go and see a friend, or invite someone over. I don't want to think of you wandering alone over the countryside.' I thought he was overdoing his concern for her safety – perhaps to cover his guilt for neglecting her. But we were more careful after that, and it seemed clear that neither Henri nor anyone else suspected anything.

Chapter Three

We couldn't meet very often, naturally. Nicole was a busy woman, she had her family, a household to run, like all diplomatic couples the Marchands led an active social life which took up much of their time, we were lucky if we met once a week. By and large I didn't mind that, though there were times when I felt a little despondent that I should be so dependent on her crowded timetable. But it kept the risks to a minimum, and let me get on with the rest of my life unhindered.

And so I remember that period not only for Nicole but for other things as well, and in particular for a lot of hard work. In Cambodia things never stood still for long, and September brought a renewal of political activity which kept all diplomats and journalists extremely busy, long after de Gaulle's visit had faded into the background.

It started with elections to the National Assembly, in mid-September. They're of little interest now, but at the time they seemed important enough. For the first time it looked as if Sihanouk's grip might begin to slip.

At first no one was very excited about them. Only the Prince's party was allowed to present candidates to the polls, apart from the communists, who kept out of sight. This wasn't as undemocratic as might appear, as almost everyone with political ambition belonged to the party anyway, and voters were still given a fairly wide choice. But whatever its composition the new Assembly wasn't expected to be more than a rubber stamp for the Prince.

But then something unexpected happened: whatever the population at large thought of the elections, the participants at least took them seriously. No sooner were the elections over than every unsuccessful candidate in the country began to challenge the result. For a time there were so many accusations of vote-rigging and tampering that it looked as if they might have to be annulled altogether. But that too that was part of the game. Commissions of enquiry were set up, the votes were recounted, the original results validated and the new Assembly moved into is seats.

Then came a second surprise.

The new Assembly's first task was to elect the new Prime Minister. The Prince was known to favour two candidates, amiable nonentities who could be relied upon to carry out his policies without asking questions, and once again the result seemed pre-ordained. But the Assembly contained a lot of new blood, eager to show its mettle, and this time it did succeed in surprising everyone by rejecting the Prince's nominees and electing instead a man of its own choice, General Lon Nol, a right-winger, and seen as a man of substance – at least in those days.[2] The Prince was not pleased, but he let it pass, and retired instead for a few days to the Calmette Hospital to follow a dietetic cure. He let it be known that he might follow this up with a trip to France and a private clinic on the Riviera, as he was in the habit of doing from time to time when he needed a break from the cares of office.

Next the new Prime Minister succeeded in getting his new cabinet, which consisted mainly of conservatives, approved by the Assembly, which included a number of vociferous left-wingers. The Prince was now less pleased. He disliked several of the new ministers, and he objected that the new cabinet, with its right-wing bias, went against his policy of balancing the forces of right and left. As his calorie intake at the Calmette Hospital had been reduced to 1000 a day, people began to predict an outburst. These dietetic cures were known to have a depressive effect on his temperament. But the Prince was never short of ideas, and he quickly adapted his tactics.

First, from his hospital bed he issued a statement disclaiming all responsibility for the new Assembly and the Lon Nol government.

Next, he instituted what he called 'Cambodia's first democratic experiment': gathering together several ministers from the

---

[22] He proved a dismal failure later on, after the coup d'état of 1970 in which he and Sihanouk's cousin Prince Sirik Matak overthrew Sihanouk, when he became president of the new Khmer Republic. Unlike Sirik Matak, a much abler man, who had the courage to stay and face the Khmer Rouge when they marched into Phnom Penh in 1975 – and paid for it with his life – Lon Nol fled to America to retire in comfort and obscurity.

previous government, passed over by Lon Nol and better known for their dislike of him than for their past achievements, he added a sprinkling of hard-line leftists, gave them the title of 'Counter-Government', and set them up in official opposition, with the unofficial but very clear task of harassing the new government until it fell.

The Prince was a careful man, who knew the dangers of reckless experimentation. To make sure this one didn't get out of hand he instructed the new shadow cabinet to 'act constructively' and to refrain from 'recalling the past': meaning that it should not rake up too much mud about the new ministers, because once it started to fly no one was sure of emerging unstained. In compensation he allowed it to use government facilities to print its own press releases, identical in format to the official daily bulletins from the Ministry of Information, so that for a while we had two press reports to read at the office every morning, each a mirror image of the other. Finally, to make sure he could dissolve it without difficulty once he no longer needed it, he called the Counter-Government 'extra-constitutional'. Then, having set everything in motion, the Prince went back to his diet of raw carrots, announced that his trip to France had been put off indefinitely, and sat back to watch the fun.

The result was not hard to foresee, though by then it was only late October, the end of the wet season, and it would take several more months for the battle to run its course. Lon Nol was no pushover, and his ministers formed a capable team. After widespread floods in September had threatened to ruin the rice crop he had earned a lot of support by bringing quick aid to the farmers. But the game was stacked against them. The Assembly by then had scented the wind, and saw no contradiction in bringing down the cabinet which it had elected a few weeks earlier. One by one his ministers fell around him. He fought a valiant rear-guard action, but an army on the retreat rarely wins; and when in March the following year he cracked his ankle in a car accident and was likely to be bed-ridden for weeks, he knew it was time to quit. No one thought the worse of him for it.

But that, in October, was to look forward to a time when I would have more troubling problems of my own. For the present I was too engrossed to worry much about the future. I watched and learned, fascinated by these antics, occasionally earning a grunt of approval from Marcellin, and scoffing at Rick when he showed me the articles which still kept appearing in the Hong Kong magazine, *East of Suez*, drawing predictable fulminations from the Prince. He was right to be concerned, for they were to have unfortunate consequences for me later on. But so far none of his predictions had come true. The enquiries, the threatened witch-hunt – if it had ever taken place – had passed me by, and in any case what did I have to worry about? Apart from Nicole my life was an open book, I had nothing to hide. I felt secure.

It was a hectic time, full of variety and colour, with occasional reminders of a grimmer reality. More border incidents: a peasant boy machine-gunned in a rice field, a row of coffins along a village track, with the stinking remains of women and children hit by mortar fire. I went along as a matter of course now, and my hands no longer shook when I took photos.

Buffoonery: two politicians, co-owners of a daily newspaper, took opposite sides in the political dispute and fought like fishwives for control of the paper. Their wives joined in, one of them slapped the other in public, and Phnom Penh talked of nothing else for a week.

Pageantry, never far from public life in Cambodia: the Water Festival, to mark the end of the wet season. Boat races on the river for three days, illuminated barges by night, religious ceremonies, fireworks and classical dances by the Royal Ballet. I went with Henri and Nicole, who looked dazzling in a white dress and made me feel very possessive. The funeral of a leading bonze, taken to his incineration on a huge catafalque of scarlet and gold, shaped like a stupa and mounted on a truck like a carnival float, with cohorts of shaven monks in attendance. The catafalque was so tall that wires had to be cut along the route to let it pass and we were without electricity for two days. In November Ganefo, the Games of the New Emerging Forces, long forgotten now, with teams from Communist China, North Korea and Burma. Marcellin promoted me sports writer.

Mid-December. Cooler nights, dustier days. Long files of ox-carts on the roads heading for Phnom Penh and the Mekong: for this was *prahoc* time, when the fishermen gathered along the banks to prepare their evil-smelling fish paste, basic ingredient of the Cambodian diet, and peasants came from as far as the coast to barter their produce for a year's supply.

The fields had dried out. Christmas was approaching, and after that, the rice harvest.

By then, things weren't going nearly so well for us.

Chapter Four

1

'Your reputation seems to be improving these days,' Nicole had said to me one evening. 'You don't go to the bars any more, you don't take girls home any more, it's been weeks since you had a night on the town. Rick was commenting on it the other day. He couldn't work out what's come over you.'

'Yes, he's made various remarks to me too.'

'Aren't you worried that people might wonder what lies behind this sudden change?'

'What if they do? Everyone's entitled to mend their ways, it's time they learnt I'm not just a fly-by-night,' I said. 'Not that it'll make much difference. They'll just think I've got a girl tucked away somewhere. But that's alright, as long as they don't get too close to the truth. Why? What's wrong?'

'Nothing – except that it makes me feel a bit guilty. I give you so little of my time, so little of myself – I mean it's not as if we were living together. You've got your own life to lead, your friends...what I'm trying to say is that I won't mind if you want to go out with other women from time to time.'

'Wouldn't you feel jealous if I brought home a girl from time to time?'

'Not if you don't tell me about it,' she said practically, and I laughed.

'I mean that,' she cried. 'It worries me sometimes, that you're letting your life revolve too much around me. I'm selfish enough as it is, I don't want you to feel that you're missing out on something because of me, because of some...exaggerated loyalty towards me.'

'Hey, what's brought this on? Can't you see that if I don't run around town any more, chasing girls and living it up, it's because I don't want to? I'm not jealous of Henri because he's taking up more of your life than I am, if that's worrying you. I'm simply not interested any more. If I went to a bar now I'd be bored stiff. I'd much rather be at home reading a book when I'm not with you. Seriously. And it's not loyalty that brings me here either. You should know that.' And taking her in my arms I set about giving her the best proof I knew, which not even the lumps on the big ugly bed could make any less convincing.

2

Then one day I had an accident.

I was driving home from work, about to turn into my driveway, when a young Chinese boy on a bicycle ran into the back of my car. Luckily he wasn't badly hurt – grazed hands and a bump on the knee, plus a twisted pedal on his bike. But by the time I'd helped him up and checked him over people had begun to gather, with that instinct for blood which can conjure a crowd out of an empty street in minutes in Asia, especially when a foreigner's involved. I stood uncertainly, wondering what to do next, when someone spoke up angrily in Khmer. I looked around, and saw a small nuggety Cambodian in the front row, who stared back at me truculently and repeated his comment. He spoke too fast for me with my basic knowledge of the language to follow him, but there was no mistaking his hostility. There was a murmur from the crowd, and although someone offered to interpret there was now so much noise that it was impossible to hear anything.

Over their heads I saw Chi Hai my maid near the front gate and waved her over. She too joined in the discussion, but she was of little help, her basic French being little better than my Cambodian.

'He says it was your fault,' she said, scrupulously translating. 'He says you must give the boy five hundred riels.' Her voice rose ominously.

'Five hundred riels? He's out of his mind!' That was nearly ten dollars, an exorbitant sum in those days by the standards of instant roadside compensation. 'Tell him I have no intention of paying.'

I turned to the man, forgetting he spoke no French. *'Vous êtes cinglé ma parole! Vous me prenez pour un millionaire?'*

That only made things worse. Everybody started to argue. Chi Hai threw her hands up in the air and began babbling away at the top of her voice in an incomprehensible mixture of French, Vietnamese and Khmer, more people were coming from every direction, and I began to fear for my safety.

I felt a touch on my arm. I turned round, ready to defend myself, and was startled to find Surya, Rick's friend, the Cambodian girl who lived three doors away.

'What's going on?' she asked. 'Are you in trouble?'

I explained, and concerned for her safety, tried to make her leave. She simply laughed.

'You'll be here all day at this rate. There's nothing Cambodians like better than an argument. Is this the man?'

And turning to him she launched into a spirited debate which soon reduced him to silence. I understood even less of what she said, but she evidently had a gift for street oratory as several times she had the crowd laughing with her. By the time she'd finished all sign of danger had disappeared. The angry man had slunk away, clearly defeated, people drifted away, soon there were only a few bystanders left, amiably discussing the incident. Reverting to her normal gentle manner she turned to me:

'It's alright now. But you'd better give the boy some money, for form's sake.'

I was only too happy. I shoved a fifty riel note into the boy's hand, helped him on his bicycle – someone had obligingly twisted the pedal back into shape – and sent him on his way, clearly relieved himself at the outcome.

'I don't know how to thank you,' I said. 'You were marvellous.'

I wanted to ask her inside, but she hesitated, and I understood why. She was dressed very casually, in an old sarong and a faded blouse which she would normally only wear at home, only the urgency of the situation could have caused her to come out like that. If she followed me inside people would jump to the worst conclusions.

'Why don't you come along in a while?' I suggested more wisely. 'Give me time to put the car away and tidy up. I mean it. I want to thank you properly.'

'Alright,' she smiled. 'Give me half an hour.'

Surya didn't believe in half measures. When she came forty-five minutes later she had changed into a formal *sampot* and blouse, she had brushed her hair up and put on some make-up, and she carried a small basket of fruit: *sapotilles*, grey-green and egg-shaped, and mangosteens the colour of old burgundy.

'I'm the one who should be offering gifts,' I said as I accepted hers. I smelt a faint but expensive scent. '*Fleurs des Cardamomes*?' I asked innocently, naming a well-known Cambodian perfume.

'*Marcel Rochas*,' she answered grandly. Then she giggled. 'I'm sorry I took so long, but my father had just come home – and I couldn't come dressed like one of my maids, could I?'

'Clearly not,' I said tactfully, though I preferred her as she had been earlier, less sophisticated, more natural. But she certainly hadn't wasted her time. 'Your father didn't mind that you came?'

'He doesn't know I'm here. He's rather old-fashioned, and I...well, I thought it was easier to say I was going to see my cousin. She lives not far away. I won't be able to stay long.'

Chi Hai had used my best jasmine tea, which I poured for her. Although she was shyer at first than she had been in public, before long we were chatting away merrily. I showed her my records – she had a good knowledge of western music – and she looked over my books. I wondered if she would pick up the spelling mistake in Apollinaire's name. She didn't, and picked instead Verlaine's *Fetes Galantes*, more appropriate no doubt to the occasion. A small warning flashed in my mind: displaying books of poetry might one day be my undoing.

I noticed her hands, which were long and slender. As she fiddled with a thin silver bracelet on her wrist her fingers arched backwards, supple as young rice in the wind.

'You look like those dancers from the Royal Ballet,' I said. 'You know, the way they bend their fingers back at all angles.'

'Like this you mean?' she asked, and pushed each finger back in turn until the tip touched her forearm. It seemed impossible to do this without tearing them out of their joints, but she showed no pain. She laughed and did the same with her thumb, then took off her sandals and repeated the whole performance with her toes.

'It's incredible,' I cried. 'Where did you learn to do that?'

'I took ballet lessons for a long time.'

'At the Royal Palace?'

'Yes, until I was fifteen.'

She stood up and struck a pose from one of the dances, standing on one bare foot with her left leg bent double behind her – she had smooth long calves the colour of dark honey – her arms held out at complicated angles, one stiff with elbow locked, palm upwards and fingers arched back and the other bent towards her, forefinger and thumb meeting at the tip, her back supple as bamboo. It had to take amazing muscular discipline – and the joints of a contortionist – but she held the pose for a long moment, then slowly revolved on the heel and ball of her right foot, with no sign of strain and hardly a muscle moving above the knee, until she had turned full circle.

'That's amazing,' I said. 'I've never seen anything more professional. Even the Royal Ballet couldn't do it better.' She grinned, and sat down again. 'Why did you stop studying?'

'My father made me.'

'Your father? Why?'

'Oh...' she laughed. 'Because...fifteen's rather a dangerous age for a ballerina.'

'Why's that?'

'Well, you see, the Palace is full of young princelings with nothing better to do than chase after the girls after practice...'

'And they started chasing you.'

'One of them did. And my father thought it safer to take me away. I didn't really mind. I didn't want to become a dancer. He only sent me there as part of my education.'

'Well, he obviously had your best interests at heart. But it does seem a pity. You looked so good.'

'Not really,' she said modestly. 'I was only an average pupil, you know. And besides it was very hard work. It takes years to become a good dancer. You have to start very young, before your bones harden. I didn't have enough endurance for it. All I ever danced was the monkey roles, with the funny masks.'

149

It was almost dark and nearly two hours later when Surya left, taking a handful of my books under her arm. I went downstairs with her but stayed out of sight inside the gate.

'I hope you'll come again,' I said.

'I'd like to…but my father may not give me permission.'

'Do I have such a bad reputation?'

'Of course not. But you know Asian fathers, they're very conservative.'

'What about your cousin? Can't you use her again?'

'He might check up…' She looked quickly up and down the street, then darted out the gate. 'I'll try though,' she whispered, and rushed away.

Chi Hai was clearing up the cups and saucers when I went back upstairs.

'Oh, Monsieur,' she cried, still shaken by the incident. 'I was so afraid. Cambodians are so wild, they get so excited. *Cambodgiens, moi très peur!* Better pay and finish quick.'

That Chi Hai should be afraid of anyone seemed most improbable. She was built like a Japanese Sumo wrestler, with huge fat arms and a back twice as broad as mine, enormous by any standards, let alone for a Vietnamese. But obviously this didn't reckon with her. Cambodians had fierce fiery eyes, and knitted their brows when angry and spoke threatening words in that guttural language of theirs, and she, after all, was nothing more than a frail Vietnamese woman, with all her ingrained fear of the alien, the darker-skinned.

'*Moi très peur Cambodgiens,*' she repeated, rolling her eyes in her fat moon face. '*Eux en colère très méchants!*' She wrung her hands together, each the size of a small ham.

'And what about Mademoiselle Surya? Are you afraid of her?'

'Oh no!' she replied. 'She's different. I like her.'

4

I didn't tell Nicole about the accident at the time, nor about Surya's second visit a few days later. There was no reason to keep them from her, but it was more than a week before I could see her, and she had more important news.

'We're off to Japan,' she announced, when next we met on the houseboat. 'I've finally talked him into it.'

'Congratulations. When are you going?'

'In ten days' time, as soon as we've got the visas and the tickets, and before he changes his mind again.'

'He'd better not. It'll be winter there soon, if you don't hurry up.'

Nicole had good reason to be pleased. She had been trying for weeks to persuade Henri to take some leave, before it became too cold there. His work-load had if anything increased since de Gaulle's visit, and he was reluctant to leave the country at such a fascinating time. But Nicole wasn't going to be put off a second time. 'No one's indispensible,' she said firmly. 'Not when it comes to choosing between your health and your job. Either we go away now, together, before it's too late, or you'll have a breakdown by the end of the year.' When Henri stalled she sulked, she nagged, she kept at him until it was easier to give in. Now they were taking three weeks off, going to Japan, Hong-Kong, the Philippines, leaving the children with friends. We talked of nothing else during our last hurried meetings on the houseboat.

It hurt me a little to see her go. I knew this was selfish of me. She too needed a break, her own happiness was involved. But her single-minded anticipation, her excitement, were such a clear reminder of the secondary role I played in her life that, for the first time, I found it insufficient.

'You'll miss me, won't you?' she asked. 'You won't fall for anyone else while I'm away?'

'What do you think?' Of course I'd miss her. Would she miss me though, away from the place? It was too late then to mention Surya. She might have misunderstood, read a warning where none was intended, and I didn't want to spoil our last evening together. In any case I had no intention of looking elsewhere for consolation during her absence. The fact that, by the time the Marchands returned, Surya had become a regular visitor, was little more than a coincidence.

5

Even coincidences sometimes need a helping hand. A few days after the accident I sent Chi Hai to return Surya's fruit basket, filled with hibiscus flowers this time and with a note to say that I looked forward to her next visit and another demonstration of classical Khmer dancing. There'd been no sign of her since her visit, and there was just a chance she was waiting for me to confirm my invitation before she came again. More probably, I thought, she would accept the gesture as a friendly compliment and leave it at that. Under the strict rules of Cambodian morality, unmarried girls of good family did not call unescorted on young foreign bachelors – not if they wanted to keep their reputation. I didn't expect to see her that same afternoon. She brought another basket of fruit and a young brother to keep her company, eight years old, who shook my hand formally and then disappeared into the kitchen with Chi Hai.

'Thank you for the flowers,' she said brightly in her best English. 'It was very kind of you.'

'Not at all. I couldn't send you back an empty basket.'

'I hope you don't mind my calling on you again so soon,' she went on, reverting to French. 'I saw your car in the drive-way. But I should have checked first, to see if it was convenient for you.'

'On the contrary, it's a pleasant surprise.' We sounded like something out of Jane Austen. 'I was wondering what to do with myself. How are you getting on with those books?'

'I haven't finished them yet,' she said apologetically. 'May I keep them a little longer? I've started *Brideshead Revisited* but it's rather hard and I keep stopping to look up words in the dictionary.'

'Bring it along next time. We can go over the difficult bits together. If that doesn't sound too much like homework.'

'Oh no, I'd like that – as long as it doesn't impose on you.'

'Of course not. It'll be a change from the translations I have to do at work.'

As Chi Hai laid out what remained of my tea, with a few rather mouldy biscuits on a plate, I talked to her about my work. We sat on my tired rattan couch, a careful arm's length between us. Some of the high excitement of her previous visit had gone, making way for a more cautious, formal mood. She was too reserved still to ask many personal questions but I could feel her observing me. I got up to put on a record.

'Did you get your father's permission to come here today?' I asked. 'Or are you still visiting your cousin?'

'He's gone out this afternoon. I didn't ask him.'

'Will he be angry if he finds out?'

'Oh, Sarin won't tell him.' Sarin was her younger brother. She blushed a little, a darker tan on the mat honey of her skin. 'Actually it's not him I'm worried about,' she went on. 'I'm sure he wouldn't mind really. It's my aunts, my mother's sisters. They're very old-fashioned and since my mother died they've decided to look after my education. They're always going at him about the way he lets me do what I want. They wouldn't approve at all.'

'Do they live with you?'

'No, fortunately. They're both married and they live on the other side of town. I couldn't bear to have them around all the time. It's bad enough having to listen to them when I go and see them. You should have heard them when they found out about Rick –' She caught herself, then gave me a sheepish smile. 'You know Rick, of course.'

'I met you at a party with him once, remember?'

'That funny evening at that French teacher's place, where everyone was smoking marijuana. You were dancing with Madame Marchand. Did you have some too?'

'No,' I said, and went on before she remembered too many details. 'Did you often go to see him at his place?'

'Rick? Only once or twice. But I went to a few parties with him and that's how they found out. You can't keep anything quiet in this town.'

'I know. There's always some well-intentioned friend to come along and tell your family. It's the same among the foreigners. Was it your aunts who told your father?'

153

'He knew already. He and Rick are good friends. But they went on about it so long that he gave in in the end, and told me I'd better wait until I get to Europe before I start going out with Europeans, because here it causes too many misunderstandings. He was very nice about it, really, not like them. All they can think of is the family's reputation, and getting me married off. They don't even want me to go to France, do you realise? And they tried to get my father to take me out of the Lycée Descartes, after my mother died, and put me in a Cambodian school so I wouldn't mix with all the young French boys! What do they think I am? Thank goodness he's not like them. He can't stand their shouting any more than I can. That's the trouble of course. He trusts me, but he wants to be left in peace.'

She stopped, caught my eye, and we smiled at each other in complicity. There was something very appealing about her, a spontaneous warmth, a faith in the future, which made me feel almost old by comparison. I remembered the way she had gone into battle for me.

'I'm sorry,' she said. "I shouldn't bore you with all these family matters. But you can see now why I have to be careful, and why I didn't want to tell my father.'

'Of course. I'm glad you told me. It makes me appreciate your visits even more. I only hope these problems don't stop you from coming again.'

'I'd like to. But I don't want to be a nuisance.'

'You won't be. I'm usually home by four, unless there's something special on at work, so you needn't worry about ringing me up first or anything. Just come over when you feel like it. *Ça me fera vraiment plaisir.*'

6

Surya took me at my word. She came often over the next few weeks: timidly at first, but with growing confidence as time went on until it became a habit for me to stand on my balcony, about four o'clock, two or three times a week, and watch as she came scurrying through the gate and up the side path, clutching some books or another basket of fruit. She rarely stayed long, an hour at most, and usually went on to her cousin afterwards. We read aloud to practise her English, listened to records, sometimes tried out a new dance step. But mostly we talked – of her plans, her ambitions, France, her studies. Some of her questions were very naive, and she said some funny things at times. Under the influence of one of her former teachers, an anglophobic Frenchman who for no clear reason taught English at the Lycée Descartes, she mispronounced words in the strangest manner, saying *angle* for *angel* for instance, and she firmly believed that all Anglo-Saxons were lechers – an impression which her short friendship with Rick, who was anything but, had somehow failed to dispel. *Non Angli sed angeli*, said I wittily.

She was better informed about the local scene. She had a wealth of gossip at her fingertips about various personalities, most of it scandalous but told with such innocent pleasure that no one could have accused her of being malicious: old Mr Prak Sokhun, a well-known official, had quarrelled with his son after discovering they both shared the favours of the same taxi-girl from the Dancing d'Etat. Mr Peng Seng Huot, Chinese millionaire, fat and nearly senile, had paid thirty thousand *riels* for his latest bride, a young Vietnamese girl of fifteen. 'Those dirty old men,' she remarked succinctly, 'that's the only way they spend their money, buying up virgins from poor families. Thank God my father's not poor. I'd rather die than marry a man like that.'

She was more reserved at first about the European community, but she had some revealing comments about them too, the Anglo-Saxons in particular coming in for criticism as a snobbish, closed circle to which few Asians were admitted. So-and-so was mean to his servants, such-and-such was often drunk at ten in the morning, Monsieur Untel and Mrs Whatsit were carrying on with total lack of discretion. I was glad to see that Surya liked the Marchands – Henri especially – and that Rick had a good reputation as a man who understood and liked Cambodians. For my part I was thankful that my own way of life had been quiet lately. If in earlier times she had seen me sometimes come home at night in female company, she was tactful enough not to mention it.

Altogether these sessions were an enjoyable way of passing the time, and it passed quickly. The Marchands had already been gone for two weeks, sending me a cheerful scribbled postcard from Manila, between the lines of which I could read almost anything except any urgent desire to return to Phnom Penh. How were they doing, I wondered. I often thought of Nicole, but sometimes I told myself I wasn't missing her as much as I should. What would she say if she knew how I spent my afternoons now? Would she feel betrayed, accuse of me of fickleness? She was the one who had urged me to find other friends and not rely on her too much; and there was nothing in my growing friendship with Surya to which she could object – no flirtation, no ambiguity. If, as sometimes happened during the golden afternoons, I felt a stir of interest as I caught a glimpse of her breasts down the front of her blouse, and wondered how she would react if I were to make a gentle pass at her, dismiss me as a typical *obsédé sexuel* or slide softly into my arms, this was no more than a young man's reflex, a passing thought to quicken the blood and then be pushed aside. Surya was a very attractive girl, but she was clearly virginal, and so was our friendship, and I wanted to keep them both that way.

I certainly didn't want anybody to get hurt over it – least of all Rick.

Chapter Five

1

I had been seeing less of Rick lately – not for personal reasons so much as political ones, of the kind which often affect private lives in countries like Cambodia. Since de Gaulle's visit, and in parallel with internal developments, Sihanouk had embarked on a new phase of foreign policy which made contact with western embassies delicate, even for a foreigner like me.

'*France acknowledges and respects Cambodia's independence, neutrality and territorial integrity within its present borders,*' de Gaulle had declared during his visit. This apparently innocuous statement had in fact acted like a time-bomb, by reviving Cambodia's interest in the sensitive border question.

More precisely, it had brought back to Sihanouk's mind his long-standing desire to obtain some formal guarantee of Cambodia's borders with Thailand and South Vietnam, parts of which the Vietnamese and the Thais refused to accept. This was a complex problem, the origins of which went back deep in Cambodia's history, but the short of it was that the Vietnamese laid claims to some off-shore islands and stretches of territory which in Cambodian eyes were strictly Cambodian; while the Thais could not forget that they had once controlled all of Cambodia's northwest, Sisophon, Battambang, even Angkor Wat itself, before France had seized it back for Cambodia early in the twentieth century, and they had not given up hope of one day regaining those territories. No one knew this better than Sihanouk, and he had been quick to seize the opportunity offered by de Gaulle's declaration: now he was asking all the other countries represented in Phnom Penh to issue a similar statement, in the hope that this would provide at least some safeguard against future take-over bids by his neighbours.

The communist countries, not on terms of close friendship with either the Thais or the South Vietnamese, complied readily enough. They had nothing to lose by such a declaration, which made them look good with the Prince, and they probably reasoned that the wording was too general to tie them down to any specific commitment. It also had the advantage of putting the onus on the western countries to follow their example, and prove that they too were Cambodia's friends. The trouble was, the west was in no hurry to do so.

By western countries here I mean mainly the Anglo-Saxons, which were on much closer terms with both Thailand and South Vietnam. To do them justice, they had other reasons as well for dragging their feet. It is true that they were conscious of their interests in those two countries, and reluctant to irritate them by appearing to take Cambodia's side in such a long-standing dispute. But there was also an underlying concern with facts and objectivity which didn't seem to bother the communist countries overmuch. In many areas the border was vague on the ground, there were conflicting maps; and whatever the Thais' attitude, the Vietnamese at least had a war on, and bigger worries than could be solved by debating a frontier alignment which the Viet Cong disregarded with impunity every day. To make grandiose statements before these questions were settled, they felt, simply because de Gaulle and the communists had done so – for reasons which had little to do with Cambodia's interests – would not only fail to solve the problem, but would debase the currency of international obligations.

Personally I thought this was splitting hairs too fine, and the Anglo-Saxons got themselves badly outflanked on the question. They should have treated it as a simple exercise in public relations. But that's neither here nor there. What mattered was that the Anglo-Saxon countries were taking a long time to make up their mind, and Sihanouk was getting impatient. Various alternative formulae were put up, which he rejected one after the other. Nothing would do but de Gaulle's own wording. Sihanouk was beginning to consider their attitude a betrayal of Cambodian friendship, and he started to apply pressure.

There were several ways of doing this, but I remember two in particular, for they affected us personally. There was the overt pressure, which involved an increasingly hostile press and radio campaign: as my job now included the drafting of political articles for Marcellin's signature, some of them of a decidedly anti-western nature (France excepted), this put me in a very uncomfortable position towards Rick. I found it difficult to adopt the right tone of shrill denunciation, and I've never liked polemics anyway. But when I took my scruples to Marcellin, all I got for my pains was a sermon.

'Your duty,' he reminded me, 'is to the Cambodians. They hired you, they're feeding you, and you're working for them. It may not be very pleasant to say hard things about your friends, but that's what you're paid for right now, and there's no getting away from it. It's all politics anyway, I'm sure they won't take it personally.'

Now I knew the meaning of the word 'mercenary'! But it could have been worse – at least I didn't have to sign the bloody things. And Marcellin, whatever his faults, had his own sense of loyalty too. He didn't tell the Cambodians about my attitude, as well he might have done. That would have meant a quick end to my contract.

The second form of pressure, even less attractive and scarcely more discreet, was to put a police watch on all the embassies. Diplomats were used to being watched in Phnom Penh, and even to provocation (like the man who kept appearing at the Australian embassy, saying: 'I want to work for the CIA'), but this time the Prince went further – though in the interest of fairness he didn't stop at the west. Plain-clothes police in black priest's hats, Hawaian shirts and sunglasses – clothes which in Phnom Penh were anything but plain – stood outside every embassy in town, questioning visitors and writing down number-plates, and there was even a cyclo-driver outside Rick's house at night, polishing his machine for hours on end and refusing all custom. It would have been laughable, if it hadn't also been a little sinister. What happened to people whose names went on record too often? The measure was aimed mostly at isolating western diplomats from the local population, and it wasn't supposed to affect other foreigners. I could come and go without having to fill in a form each time. But it was still a nuisance. I couldn't even have a drink at Rick's house without someone making a note of it. In the end Rick – who didn't seem to hold any grudge against me over my articles – decided that it might be safer to space out our contacts, and I stopped going to his house. Instead he sometimes came to my flat,

159

when he thought the coast was clear, and he didn't use the phone any more than he had to.

2

What happened next was thus predictable: when Rick, who knew nothing of Surya's visits, came unannounced to the flat one afternoon and found us in close tête-à-tête. Chi Hai, who should have been on hand to guard against that sort of surprise, had gone out. Surya was sitting close to me, her hand I think was on my arm, and to anyone not aware of the nature of our relationship it could be very misleading.

Rick was too self-controlled to show his feelings before Surya, and she in her innocence simply looked glad to see him. I was the one who felt most embarrassed. But he looked pale, and he didn't stay long, and when I followed him down to the gate he turned on me: 'Bastard!' he said succinctly, and walked off, leaving me feeling even more uncomfortable.

'How long is it since you last saw Rick?' I asked Surya when I went back upstairs. We were on very familiar terms now, calling each other *tu.* 'About two months...' She blushed a little, but went on. 'I told you, my aunts made a fuss –'

'Did you tell him about it?'

'Yes. He said he understood...You're worried about him, aren't you. Look, there's no reason. We were just friends, like you, and there wasn't anything between us...'

Wasn't there? I wondered. I too had assumed from what she'd said that it had been just a casual friendship, and no doubt from her point of view that's all it was. But Rick was not a demonstrative man, and perhaps Surya had penetrated his bachelor defences more deeply than she knew. To find us sitting like that, shoulder to shoulder, not prevented by my job or her family from seeing each other, must have struck him as a rather nasty trick, a sort of betrayal on my part. Perhaps I'm exaggerating his feelings – he didn't confide them to me. He simply stopped coming.

The difficulty was that there wasn't much I could say to him, apart from assuring him I had no design on Surya. He'd have to take my word for that, I couldn't go and back it up with proof that

160

I was involved elsewhere. And he probably wouldn't want to believe me. I brooded over it for some days, feeling sheepish, and then I went to see him. I found him dressed in shorts and an old floppy hat, crouching in a corner of his garden, a jungle of bamboo clumps and plants with large fleshy leaves like a painting by the *douanier* Rousseau – even his gardener had stopped coming, frightened by the secret policeman at the gate. He was transplanting frangipani shoots and he didn't look up as I walked up to him.

'I'm sorry, Rick,' I said, 'but I think you've misunderstood. There's nothing going on between Surya and me. She's just a friend, to coin a phrase, who comes in from time to time to listen to records and talk about France and get away from the atmosphere in her house. She's lonely and we spend an enjoyable hour or two like that every so often, and then she goes home. There's never been any suggestion of anything else, you know. I wasn't trying to cut you out. In fact I thought you weren't interested.'

Rick stood up. The filtered light threw green shadow over his face, and there was a smudge of earth on his forehead. He didn't smile at my outburst.

'And her?'

'Her?'

'Yes. Have you thought about the effect you may be having on her? How does she consider this...this relationship?'

'I don't know... the same as me, I expect. I mean we haven't discussed it, obviously. But I haven't done or said anything to make her think there was anything more to it.'

That wasn't quite true, and I suddenly knew it. What about the books of poetry I had lent her, the Brassens records we listened to together, the flowers I had sent her? What symbolism could a young Asian girl, impressionable and probably at the most romantic age, read into the offering of a hibiscus blossom? I tried not to show my doubts, but I was worried.

'I hope you're right,' he continued. 'I don't want to sound Victorian but Surya's a very fine person and I wouldn't like to see her get hurt, for whatever reason.' He rubbed his hands on his shorts, stuck his trowel in his hip pocket and said: 'Anyway, thanks for telling me.' Then he went back to his digging and I left him, scarcely more comfortable than when I'd arrived.

I was also rather worried. What if he was right? I had enough emotional problems of my own without adding to them. Nicole had just come back, and I was trying to work up the courage to tell her about Surya. But if he was right I didn't see what I could do about it. I couldn't discuss it with her, it would only embarrass her and might bring out into the open things which were better left unsaid. Either way, I thought, the safest thing was to keep quiet, and see what happened. With a bit of luck, Surya herself might give me a clue.

Which is what happened, though not quite as I expected. One afternoon she arrived laughing and out of breath from running up the steps.

'My father knows!' she declared.

'Knows?' I echoed.

'Yes! That I come to see you.'

'How did he find out? Did someone tell him?'

'I told him,' she said simply. 'Oh, I think he'd been suspecting for some time that I wasn't always going out to see my cousin. But yesterday he found one of your books, with your name inside the cover...and he asked me straight out, and I told him. I said I'd been coming here regularly to see you, alone, that you were nice and hadn't tried to seduce me, that you lent me books and records and never let me drink anything alcoholic, and that the only reason I hadn't told him earlier was that my aunts would get to know and start making a fuss the way they did over Rick.'

'I see.' I sat down weakly. 'And what did he say to that piece of youthful defiance?'

'He gave me a lecture. He told me about young European men, and the way they behave when they come to Asia, how they all want to have an affair with a local girl and how one has to be very careful with them because when they do have an Asian girl-friend they don't really want to marry her, and even if they do it rarely works out anyway...all things I knew before,' she added airily. 'And then you know? He really took my breath away. He said: be careful. Don't tell your aunts, and don't let the neighbours see you, or they'll talk. And don't...'

'Yes?'

'Don't fall in love with him, whatever you do.'

'Well,' I said. 'That all sounds like good advice, and your father's a very sensible man.' Which he was, obviously. Locking up your daughters has never been a wise solution. I searched her face. 'You're not...I mean, it is good advice, isn't it?'

'Of course it is! Isn't he splendid?' She laughed gaily. 'Don't look so worried, Philippe. I'm not in love with you.'

'Oh. Well, that's good, isn't it!' I said, not sure whether to feel relieved or deflated.

3

It took another fortnight for Rick to get over his resentment – or anger or bitterness or whatever precise feeling it was that caused him to keep on avoiding me for all of that time, thereby revealing a streak of obstinacy which I had never felt in full force before. I must confess that during that time I too felt hurt by his attitude, much as I sympathised with him. After all, I told myself, I had told him the truth, or as much of it as I could. It wasn't my fault if we lived in a situation which neither of us, nor Surya herself, could control, and Surya was free to pick her friends as she chose – almost free anyway. It wasn't as if I'd gone and stolen his girl from under his nose. But this wasn't a happy time for Rick, and the strain of isolation and ostracism had no doubt made it worse. Fortunately he had the sense to see this in the end. I don't know if he missed me as much as I did him, but when an opportunity came for a reconciliation we both took it eagerly.

It took the form of a memorable binge, on one of those nights for which Phnom Penh seemed to have a special recipe. The occasion was Shagger Forbes' farewell, at the end of his posting in Cambodia: not a moment too soon, by the look of him. Forbes had reserves of energy far above the average, but even he couldn't keep up his riotous way of life forever, and his efforts to live up to his own reputation were beginning to take their toll, deepening the pouches under his eyes and lining his face to the point where you could see, without too much imagination, what he'd look like in ten or fifteen years' time, if he didn't retire soon from the stud.

Ironically, his last day and night in Phnom Penh were spent in remarkable chastity. Perhaps the looming rigours of Canberra life had begun to dampen his spirit, though in fact it was more a lack of opportunity, as he was hardly left alone for a moment. Departures were a serious business, it would have run against his moral code to leave the boys at a time like this in order to go womanising. Already by mid-afternoon he had distinguished himself by getting remarkably drunk in the house of another Australian, until Rick, passably under the weather himself, took him off to his place to sleep it off, before starting again in the early evening.

I didn't know any of this, having spent the day virtuously at work, and it wasn't until I met them that evening at the house of Colonel Purdue the Australian military attaché, that I learnt of their exploits. By then I had started to catch up on Colonel Purdue's seemingly endless supply of duty-free Scotch, which caused me once again to speak rashly in public.

The guest of honour at the military attaché's that evening was not Shagger, but an American reporter who had been given a three-week visa into Cambodia to make a film about Viet Cong sanctuaries along the border: on the understanding it seemed, that anything he produced would exonerate Cambodia from all those nasty accusations from Saigon that it gave free run of the country to the Viet Cong – or so it looked to me in my growing alcoholic haze. The film, which had clearly been taken in areas previously vetted and if necessary cleared of their illicit occupants by the Cambodian army, showed nothing but a pleasant land full of happy villagers peacefully going about their business, whose only complaint was of unprovoked aggression by the American imperialist troops and their South Vietnamese lackeys from across the border. If I'm laying it on a little thick this is not to condone the kind of border incident with which I was becoming only too familiar. But the increasing weight of rumours and indirect evidence from the border regions, near Snuol and Mimot and Kompong Cham, left little doubt that the Viet Cong were making extensive use of Cambodian territory, and probably with Cambodian connivance. In short the film seemed to me little more than a white-wash, a cynical little piece of public relations – and what's more after the screening I went up to the American reporter to tell him. He was a pleasant enough young man with handlebar moustaches and a harassed expression, and ordinarily we would have got on fine, but I'd had my fill of propaganda that day, and I was past caring. I accused him of taking out insurance for the future, and making sure that he could obtain another entry visa any time he wanted one, and no doubt would have gone on to say even worse things about his lack of professional integrity, if Rick, who by then had reappeared his usual urbane self, hadn't stepped in. He grabbed me by the arm and led me to an isolated corner of the garden, where he rounded on me.

'Of course it's public relations! So what? Do you think he doesn't know that, or feels any better about it? I know what he thinks and what he really saw near the border, and believe me, what he has to say about that in private more than makes up for anything he's said in public.'

'Then why doesn't he say so? Why all this hypocrisy? Can't somebody for once say the truth about these things, instead of covering them up all the time? You saw the film. Don't you agree?'

'Listen! Are you trying to get yourself kicked out of the country? You're lucky there's no one here to report you where it hurts. And as for professional integrity, you're in no position to talk after some of the garbage you've been writing lately.'

Which was true, and very chastening, but neither here nor there because the next thing I knew we were off, Rick and I, to accompany Shagger on a last sentimental round of the bars: not a very cheerful exercise as it turned out, because the sight of all his former girl-friends only served to make him maudlin, until he looked as if he might start crying in his beer.

It was raining heavily that night – the dry season was unusually late – and some of the streets near the Phnom and the Hotel Royal were awash in two feet of water. Rick's car stalled and we left it where it stood, on a strip of lawn in front of the hotel, and waded knee-deep in the swirling water and the pelting rain back to Rick's house, where we spent the rest of the night carousing. Shagger showed signs of wear, but at first light we roused him and went back for Rick's car and drove quietly around for one last look at the town, along empty, new-washed streets, up near the Phnom and down past the Royal Palace where elderly Chinese in singlets and underpants performed their Tai Chi exercises among the riverside shrubbery, lost in concentration, a silent, slow-motion ballet incongruous in the grey light. We watched the sun rise over the Mekong and urinated in the river from the Yacht Club pontoon, and then, after two hours' sleep, accompanied Shagger to the airport with his luggage. Driving back with Rick afterwards I felt depressed suddenly by Shagger's departure. He'd been a good mate, as we say in Oz, selfless and true in his friendship, and if he hadn't repaid all he owed me who cared? It had been worth the pleasure of his company. But I had Rick's friendship again, and that was something: a bulwark against departures, betrayals, insincerities and other minor tragedies of living.

Chapter Six

1

Did I detect a certain reluctance on Nicole's part when the Marchands duly returned from their holiday – a week later than expected? I rang her at once, for I was impatient to see her. Surya notwithstanding I had in fact missed her a lot, and I felt a little anxious too about the possible effect on her marriage of a second honeymoon through Hong Kong, Manila and other exotic places. It was Nicole I thought who seemed less eager to see me. She hesitated, gave moderate reply to my cries of welcome, asked me to ring back in two days' time. I had to wait another week before she was free to meet me on the houseboat. I wondered what to tell her about Surya.

My fears were exaggerated. The holiday had done them both good, but it takes more than four weeks to mend years of gradual estrangement; and although at first with my usual pessimism I sensed a degree of resignation on Nicole's part, we got over that and soon we were back to the familiar setting of the houseboat as if she had never been away. But the moment to tell her had passed, and I didn't know how to bring it up after such a long delay. I hesitated, I postponed it further and in the end, not very bravely, decided to keep quiet and wait until it came up of its own accord – which it did, simply enough, when Nicole drove past one afternoon as I was escorting Surya to the gate. She looked, and waved, and next time we met reacted with surprisingly mild curiosity.

'Wasn't that Rick's girlfriend?' she asked. 'I didn't know she was a friend of yours too.'

'More of a neighbour, really,' I said, trying not to sound defensive. 'She lives just down the street.'

'I know, we've been there.'

'She comes in from time to time,' I continued. 'She borrows books. She's trying to practise her English.'

Nicole smiled roguishly. 'You've never told me this before.'

'Probably because I didn't think of it,' I lied casually. 'She doesn't come very often.'

'And how's her English?'

'Not as good as yours, my love,' I said, which was true enough. And there, for the moment, the matter rested. Nicole made occasional, light-hearted reference to my 'Cambodian girlfriend', and I was careful to mention Surya's name from time to time, so she wouldn't think I was hiding anything, but her curiosity seemed satisfied and there was no longer any danger in it – or so I thought. It was a relief. I had not enjoyed the strain of keeping up a permanent lie and wondered how Henri found the strength for it. I lay back on my bed of half-truths instead and looked forward to a simpler life.

2

False security. I should have known I couldn't get away with it.

'You're still seeing that girl Surya, aren't you?' Nicole asked casually one evening.

'Yes, occasionally. Why?'

'Oh, nothing much. I'd just like to know if you've been telling me the truth, that's all.'

'Of course I have. Why, do you think we're having an affair or something?' I stared at her, but she avoided my eyes.

'It's just that I heard an unpleasant rumour this afternoon.'

'About Surya and me?'

'I suppose it was about her, although her name wasn't mentioned.'

'Tell me more!'

'Nothing very detailed. Just that you seem to be having a sweet romance with a Cambodian student, who visits you at home. You don't know many students, do you darling?' This last she said in the faintly rasping tone she reserved for her more ironic comments. I answered in kind.

'Surya's the only one I can think of, off-hand. You don't really believe that, do you?'

'I don't want to,' she said frankly. 'It's not true, is it?'

'Of course it's not true,' I replied, and this time I let a note of annoyance come through. 'May I ask who's going round saying those things?'

'Well, you know how these things spread, by the time you hear a rumour you never know where it started…I must say this one cut a little too close to the bone.'

'Look,' I said. 'Apart from the fact that rumours are the last thing you should believe in this place, you know me well enough by now to know that if I were having an affair with anyone else you'd be the first to be told.'

'Would I?'

'Yes. Didn't we say that whatever happened we would always tell each other the truth, and never pretend?'

'I said that,' she replied.

'And I agreed.'

'There's no need to raise your voice, darling. I simply asked you a question. From the way you protest, one might think…'

'Might think what? Of course I'm annoyed. I don't care what people say about me, if they feel like throwing mud. But it does hurt when your friends get maligned in the process. Particularly someone like Surya.'

'What's so special about her?'

'Nothing!' I cried, exasperated. 'Except that she's young and vulnerable, and she's far more likely to be hurt by that sort of scandal-mongering than…than someone like you, or me.'

'So you think I'm not vulnerable!'

'No, but you know how to defend yourself. You know what to expect from people. She doesn't.'

'Don't you bet!' she retorted angrily.

'Look, she's just a kid –'

'She's all of nineteen, Philippe. And people are precocious about these things here. Or haven't you noticed?'

'Oh, stop being sarcastic. Don't you remember what you were like at nineteen? What would you have felt if someone had started a rumour like that about you?'

'Of course I would have been angry, And hurt. And I'd probably have done something about it.'

'Like what?'

'Like stopped calling on the young man in question. Any girl who calls alone on a young bachelor like you, in this place…'

'So now I'm a sex maniac, am I?' She said nothing, just glanced at me with that mocking, infuriating smile. 'And I suppose I should just tell her to stop coming, is that it? Well, I don't intend to. I'll tell her to be careful but I'm damned if I'll let my life be ruled by stupid rumours. Anyway,' I went on more calmly, 'I'm sure it's nothing as serious as you make out – just someone who drove past one day and saw her talking to me, as you did, and thought he'd have a joke at my expense.'

We closed the argument, that night, in the classic manner: on the bed, where I used all my skill, all the tenderness and passion I felt for her, to make her forget the heated words we'd thrown at each other. It worked, that evening. But as we left, I thought about some of the things she'd said. They sounded familiar. It wasn't the first time I'd been warned of the possible dangers.

'That rumour you heard,' I asked before we separated. 'Was it Rick, who told you?'

She hesitated, before replying.

'Yes. It was Rick. Don't tell him though. He obviously couldn't see the effect he was having.'

3

So it was Rick who'd betrayed me to Nicole. Unwitting betrayal of course. He couldn't know the damage he was causing. But I couldn't help wondering what he would have thought, whether he would have got any satisfaction from it, if he had known how easily he had just evened the score.

Unfortunately that little outburst, between Nicole and me, only cleared the air temporarily. There was a period of calm. But the subject hung between us, and I knew it would come up again. What I didn't foresee was the violence of it.

4

One day Surya invited me to dinner at her father's house. I accepted with pleasure. I had been expecting some move from him, some attempt to get a closer look at the young foreigner who kept seeing so much of his daughter, and I looked forward to

170

meeting him on his own account. From the little I knew I pictured him as a kindly old gentleman, reserved with foreigners but intelligent and open-minded – which indeed he was.

Perhaps Monsieur Boun Savann – that was his name – wanted to make me feel at home, and enquired first about my friends; or, more likely, he decided to kill several birds at one sitting. Whatever the reason, there were several other guests there, including Henri and Nicole, and the first I knew was when I stepped in the front door and saw them.

Of course nothing happened that evening. We were all too well-mannered for that. I minded my step and behaved as the model guest, covertly watching Nicole and trying at the same time to be friendly to Surya without appearing besotted with her. Not so easy in the circumstances. Nicole was more subtle, and after enveloping us in a gentle smile in which I could detect a hint of mockery – or reproach – she turned her attention to the other guests and ignored me for the rest of the evening. Surya was too excited to watch anybody much, and Henri, peacefully oblivious of all this romantic comedy potential, talked old-time politics with Surya's father. I was relieved when the evening broke up.

But two days later, when next we met on the houseboat, something had clearly happened. For one thing Nicole only agreed to come with reluctance. For another she was over an hour late; and although delays weren't uncommon – some evenings she didn't turn up at all, when Henri changed his mind at the last minute and stayed home instead of going to the office or his mistress or whatever – on this occasion it seemed ominous. More ominous still her reaction when she arrived and I tried to put my arms around her. I had decided that the best way to avoid another argument was to make passionate love to her from the moment she arrived. Reassure her about the strength of my feelings, and the place she held in my life. Not the cleverest tactics perhaps, especially as I felt too tense myself to play the ardent lover with much conviction, and in any case a waste of effort. She brushed my fumbling advances aside before we'd even reached the bedroom door.

'I'm not in the best mood for that,' she said tartly. 'What we need is a good talk, you and I.'

171

'What you mean is a good fight, by the sound of it,' I said, annoyed at my stupidity.

'That depends on you, Philippe. But we'd better sit down. There's nothing like standing to generate heat in a discussion.'

So we sat facing each other across the cane table, like chess players about to start a game. She looked at me, bit her lip, frowned and launched straight in.

'Philippe, I'm serious. You need to stop seeing that girl.'

'So you really think we're carrying on, Surya and I, despite what I said.'

'No, I don't.'

'That's very trusting of you.'

'But I do think you will be before long. That girl's in love with you.'

'Look, we've been over that already. And don't call her 'that girl'. She's not a pick-up.'

'Surya then. But stop pretending that you don't see it! If only you could have seen her as I did at that dreadful dinner. The way she was watching you, you'd think the sun was shining out of your face.'

'Come on Nicole, that's not very original. Your style's usually better than that. And so's your sense of observation.'

'And you're half in love with her already, and it doesn't take the eyes of a jealous woman to see that either.'

'I wish you'd stop!' I cried. 'For the last time, can't you see you've got it all wrong? So you are jealous. Alright, you've admitted it. I'm beginning to know enough about that particular feeling to sympathise. It's not pleasant, is it! But for goodness' sake be realistic. *I* have cause to be jealous, but you don't. Not one bit. So stop it Nicole. You're making life impossible for both of us.'

'Have you finished?'

'No. There's one other thing you've got to see. Even if she and I were having…something, I don't know, not an affair but some sort of feeling for each other. Don't you see what you're asking is monstrously selfish? For months now I've been living on the strength of one evening a week with you – when you're available that is. Have I complained? Have I pried into your life with Henri, told you who you could or couldn't see, thrown fits of jealousy? Alright, that was part of the deal. Agreed from the start. But it was you who trotted out all those fine theories of equilibrium, of being able to love two people at once. Well, why can't I have my share of the theories too? Or do they only work for you?'

'No, they don't. And I deserve having that thrown back at me. But you know? At the risk of sounding very selfish again, in your case I don't think it can work. I don't think you're capable of loving two people at once.'

'How do you know? You don't know what I'm capable of...any more than I do. I've never tried it. Maybe I'll be very good at it.'

She smiled, as if amused at some flaw in my reasoning.

'Not you, Philippe. I know you, you're too much of a piece for that kind of subtlety. Your affection's not meant to be divided. You may think you could carry it off now, but it wouldn't last three months before you were forced to choose.'

Nicole stopped, and stared at the canvas blind which I hadn't bothered to roll up. I thought for a moment that she might start weeping. But she didn't, instead she set her jaw a little harder and turned back towards me.

'You see, Philippe, I don't think I can wait another three months. Now I've got the strength. I don't want to lose you, but now I can do it. But not in three months or six or later. I'm getting too old for that. Don't you see? I'm almost old enough to be her mother. I haven't the strength to live with doubt like that. That's why –' she paused, and took a breath. 'That's why I'm asking you now, for the last time, to give her up and stop this childishness. Before we all get hurt, Philippe,' she said with sudden urgency. 'You're too young to marry, and that's what'll happen to you, with her. And if you don't...'

'Yes?'

'Then that's it, isn't it. We won't be needing any of this...this silly melodramatic décor again.'

She stood, gathered up her handbag and her cigarettes, and looked at me, but I simply sat there looking back. After a moment she walked to the doorway and stopped again, hoping I'd say something. I looked away, and then back at her and suddenly I wanted to rush to her and hold her and tell her that none of the things we'd said mattered, that I loved her, more than anything, more than ever. But she stopped me.

'Not now, Philippe. It's too late. Whatever you said now you'd regret it later.' And before she left she said another thing. 'Jealousy's excusable when you're young. But when you're old...it's ugly, isn't it Philippe?'

5

I did it the next day, before I weakened. And I made a mess of it.

It would have been kinder if I'd had the courage simply to tell her I didn't want to see her again. But I'm the sort of person who couldn't kill a kitten neatly, and to ease my conscience as much as anything I borrowed Nicole's pretext, and told her about a rumour. I said that people had started to talk about her behind her back, it was just a matter of time before they pointed to her in the street if she didn't stop coming to see me. She refused to believe me.

'It's you...you don't want to see me any more, because I'm too young, too stupid. You've lost interest in me, I'm not brilliant enough, I know I –'

'How can you say that?' I cried.

'It's true, isn't it?' she said with such misery that I wondered if, after all, Nicole wasn't partly right – if Surya, without knowing it, hadn't got herself infatuated with me. Flattering? It made me feel like the sort of man who poisons other people's pets.

'It's not my reputation,' she said. 'Do you think I haven't thought about it? Why do you think I'm so careful to come here when no one's about? I know this town better than you do, and you're not telling me the truth. Otherwise you'd just tell me to be more careful. You're just tired of me, that's all.'

'You're wrong, Surya. I'm not.'

'Aren't you? Or else you're in love with someone else, and you're afraid if she finds out about me she'll be jealous,' she said, hitting just a fraction off the bull's eye with her simple child's logic.

'No, that's not true either,' I said.

'Well, I half wish it were – it wouldn't hurt so!'

174

Faced with her reproachful stare, I changed my tactics. I went to the other extreme instead, to pretend that I was too interested in her. I spoke crudely, impatiently.

'Alright then! You're right, and I'm wrong. It's not a rumour. But it's for your own good, all the same! Look: you're young, and nice, and you like making nice innocent simple friendships. Without complications. Because in a few months' time you'll be off to France, and that'll be all, you can walk away from here with nice, simple memories. But what about me? I'm not like that, Surya. I don't want nice simple memories in a few months' time. I'm just like the others, all those young men your father's warned you about. I want to sleep with you! Make love to you! Do you understand? So far I've managed to keep my hands off you, but I don't know how much longer I can hold out. Before long, if you keep coming here, I'll be making a pass at you, and you'll either slap my face or end up in my bed. And your father would not like that!'

It worked. She stared at me for a moment, as if not sure she'd heard me correctly. She put down a couple of books she'd been clutching nervously while I talked, picked up her little black purse, and walked to the door. I made to accompany her downstairs, but she shook her head. 'There's no need Philippe.' She gave me a last curious look. Then she turned and went out. I watched from the window, but she didn't look back at the gate.

6

Nicole, to do her justice, took her triumph very humbly when we met again three days later – at my insistence. She didn't want to see me again so soon and I had to plead with her over the phone. Still drawn and tired from our quarrel, and a little ashamed I think of her outburst, she listened quietly to my brief explanation, and didn't ask for any details. Perhaps she sensed the fragility of her victory. But I mistook her silence for indifference, and though she tried to be gentle with me it didn't work very well. I was too angry with myself, too full of resentment and self-reproach. Even the sex lacked conviction that night.

The next three weeks went by very slowly. By coincidence it was a slack time all round, with scarcely any political activity, not even an anonymous article to liven things up a little. Social life was at a standstill, even Henri had nothing better to do with his evenings than spend them at home, and I only saw Nicole once during that time, a quick furtive meeting where we both tried too hard to make amends. Left to myself I alternated between fits of boredom and gloomy self-analysis, wondering how and where it was all going to end: for end it must, of that I was increasingly certain, we couldn't go on like this. Would it be Nicole who brought it to a stop, when she finally found the strain of fitting me into her life too difficult? Would it be through discovery, accident, some emotional law of diminishing pleasure in each other's company, culminating in one final bitter quarrel? I was no better equipped to deal with the terminal stages of an affair than I had been three months earlier to start one, all I knew was that it was going to be painful. Would she take another lover in due course, someone she didn't have to coach for the part, who could look after the mechanics of the relationship better than me? The thought of a successor – on the houseboat or elsewhere, in Phnom Penh or back in France – was even more painful than the prospect of losing her. I too knew the sharp gut-bite of jealousy. But that didn't excuse my behaviour towards Surya, the memory of which rankled and filled me with shame. Why had I given in so weakly, like some hen-pecked husband? Nicole had no right to make such demands, had I stood firm she would have relented, come round in due course to accept the situation. Was she so unsure of herself, so afraid of Surya's competition? The more I thought about it the more unnecessary and cruel it all seemed. But it was too late to undo the damage. Surya had her pride too – and as if she could read my thoughts, she stayed well out of sight. I couldn't even catch a glimpse of her as I drove past her house on the way home.

One evening I felt particularly depressed. It was a Wednesday, ten days since I'd last seen Nicole, and we had arranged by phone to meet at eight on the houseboat: one of Henri's Rotary dinners. I also had a party to go to, but I had to take my opportunities as they came.

By nine o'clock it was clear she wasn't coming. I told myself it wasn't her fault. She always made an effort to come on time and had never stood me up deliberately. Something must have gone wrong with Henri's plans, or one of the children was sick. But it seemed symptomatic of the whole relationship that I should be the one who had to wait around on the off-chance that she might be available. I felt distinctly rebellious as I put away the cane chairs I had dragged out of storage an hour earlier, rolled down the canvas blind. As if I had nothing better to do, I thought sourly.

The trouble was that I didn't have anything better to do, as I well knew. I hadn't even wanted to go to the party in the first place – a birthday for someone I hardly knew, on the other side of town. Nevertheless it was better than sitting at home with my gloomy thoughts. It might even give me the illusion that I wasn't entirely dependent on Nicole for my happiness.

I would have done better to go straight home. The party was a dimly-lit affair on a rooftop, complete with a band, and the first person I saw when I got there was Surya. She was dancing with a young Frenchman, a weasel-faced *instituteur* with long side-whiskers and a fatuous way of holding her hand high above his head, his elbow at chin level. It must have been highly uncomfortable for her. I saw with satisfaction that she left him as soon as the dance was over. But my pleasure was short-lived. She was walking towards me when she saw me, and froze, and for a moment we stared at each other. I started moving towards her. But someone bumped into me with a drink, spilling half of it down my shirt and holding me up with unnecessary apologies. By the time I had shaken myself free she had disappeared. I spent minutes searching for her on the roof when I should have been chasing down the stairs after her. When I was finally sure she was gone it was too late to catch up with her. Tasting defeat for the second time that evening I decided bitterly to follow her example and go home.

The next two days were even more dismal. Too busy during the day to try and see Nicole, too resentful anyway to make the first move, I waited in vain all day Thursday and all day Friday for her to call me. It wasn't until Saturday morning that, unable to bear it any longer, I tried to ring her; when the phone didn't answer, in desperation I called round to the house, knowing that Henri would probably be there too. I found it empty and shuttered, deserted except for one of the maids who lived round the back. She told me the whole family had gone to Kep for the week-end and wouldn't be back until Monday.

I was furious, but there was nothing I could do. It was partly my fault, I'd forgotten it was a long week-end. Faced with having to wait another three days before I could see Nicole, I did the first thing that came into my head: I went home, picked up my tennis gear and drove at reckless speed to the *Cercle Sportif*, the Phnom Penh sports club of which I was a member, where I spent the next hour in the hottest part of the day bashing a ball against the concrete wall where beginners practised. There wasn't another player in sight, but what I wanted was violence, not sport, and I kept at it, with more strength than skill, grimly smashing at the ball as if it was a human head, until the sweat poured off me and I reeled with exhaustion. So what do I do now? I asked myself. Dash madly to the coast, hunt the Marchands down in Kep, have it out once and for all with Nicole in front of Henri and the children? Easy enough to find them there, unless they were staying at a friend's villa. Or wait in dignified silence until she returned, and then treat her with the curtness she deserved? Whichever way it went, I knew I'd had enough! As if to emphasize my impotence the racket slipped from my hand, looped gracelessly over my head and fell with a clatter behind me. I turned to pick it up and found myself face to face with Surya, who stood staring at me from the other side of the netting enclosure.

'My goodness!' she exclaimed. 'What's wrong with you?'

'Why did you run away the other evening?' I cried out; and suddenly all violence was drained out of me and I was just a sheepish red-faced man struggling to get his breath back.

'Because I didn't want to see you.'

The obvious answer of course. The simple truth.

'Well don't run away this time. Please!'

'But I have to get home. It's nearly one.'

'I'll drive you.' Masterful. No nonsense, won't take no for an answer. Not a word of apology yet: that would come later, when I could speak whole sentences out without gagging. But she let herself be led compliantly enough back to the restaurant near the swimming pool, where to judge by her wet hair and the bag in her hand she had been spending that glorious morning while I tore at my breast and covered my head with ashes. And the sheer pleasure of having her there opposite me, with her customary gentle smile – *le sourire khmer* – breaking out at the corners of her mouth.

'You know I said a lot of stupid things the other day. Very stupid and thoughtless, and to be frank not entirely true. I am not oblivious to your charms, far from it. But I am not a beast, and I do control myself, except verbally on occasion. I had been working hard, and there were personal problems as well. As you guessed. But they're over now. Do you believe me?'

'Yes.'

'I think also one of the problems was a touch of claustrophobia. The way we met I mean, only seeing each other like that, in my flat. We should get out, meet in the open, like this. It's unhealthy to be cooped up inside at our age.'

'Do you think so?'

'I do. If your father agrees I think we should go out together, go for drives in the country, somewhere where your aunts won't see us of course.'

'I'm not sure he'll agree.'

'If you ask him nicely.'

'It sounds a good idea. I don't really get out of Phnom Penh very much. I've never been to Sihanoukville, did you know that? But it's too far.'

'Not if we leave early.'

'Kep is nearer.'

'But Sihanoukville is prettier. Why don't we go there tomorrow?'

She hesitated.

'Ask him,' I prompted.

'I will.'

Chapter Seven

1

Our departure the next morning was like an escape. We left early, before the heat and the rush of week-end traffic, the back of the car packed like a survival kit for some long and hazardous journey: food and drink for the road, straw hats and plastic mats for the beach, even a bottle of water for the radiator and two litres of oil. Surya, afraid of her aunts no doubt, who seemed capable of posting spies along the road, had wrapped a scarf around her head and wore huge sunglasses which she wouldn't take off until we were past the airport and had left all risk of recognition behind.

We made good time along the highway, in the relative cool of the morning, as we climbed up into the foothills of the Cardamom Mountains. The road to Sihanoukville ran through some rugged country, much used by the Khmer Rouge in later years, but it was a good road and perfectly safe then. Within an hour we'd reached Pech Nil, up in the hills. I stopped the car over the pass to check the oil and took out drinks and we stood for a moment to look at the view. The road curved down in a wide sweep, wooded hills and valleys sloping away into the distance, green merging into dusty blue. Already the sun was hot on our shoulders. There was no one in sight but the ring of a forester's axe echoed faintly up the valley.

'I love this country,' I said. 'I wish I could stay and live here for a while, before it gets too civilised.'

Surya smiled.

'I mean before they cut all the trees and plant holiday houses instead along the road,' I went on. 'Did you know you can still find wild elephants in these hills? I saw some tracks once near Kirirom. And tigers. There's even a story about a man who ran into a tiger with his car one night, on this road. It killed the tiger but he very nearly died of a heart attack.'

'You should go on a tiger hunt one day,' she said. 'On elephant back. If you like I can ask my father to organise one. He often comes to the logging camps here.'

'Have you ever been on one?'

'No.' She laughed. 'I've only been on an elephant once, and it made me sea-sick. Besides, I'd be too frightened.'

'I think I would too. And I'd rather leave those tigers alone. They're too beautiful to be killed, even on elephant back.'

Scrupulously I put Surya's empty bottle, and my beer can, back into the ice-box. The can was an Australian brand, one of a dwindling supply left me by Shagger Forbes in part payment of his debts, and it gave me added pleasure to be thus reminded of the man. Like the tigers, he too was an endangered species.

We arrived soon after ten. The first thing I did was to take Surya for a tour of the sights, such as they were: first the harbour, still in its early stages then, with two ships tied up at the end of a long pier. One was French and the other, it seemed in the distance, had a Chinese flag. Beyond that a headland, then a neat park with a miniature lake and an old bungalow on the edge of the beach, surrounded by trees. I drove up to it and stopped for a moment.

'This is called *La Plage*,' I said. 'It's a restaurant. Not very original, but the food's good and we can have lunch here later. The owner keeps a leopard tied up at the bar.'

'Will there be many people?'

'Not if it stays like this.' The car-park was empty, there was no one about – too early for the Sunday crowd. Only the breeze in the palm trees gave the scene any movement.

'Anyway, it doesn't matter, does it? It's mostly foreigners who come here. Your aunts would never be seen dead in this place.'

'I suppose not. But I'm not used to going out with foreigners in public – you don't think people will take me for a bar-girl or anything?'

'No one would ever do that. Now let me show you the city centre, and then I'll take you to the beach.'

'Can't we swim here?'

'There's a much better one further along – and even fewer people.'

Sihanoukville – or Kompong Som, to give it its original name – has changed a lot since those days, but at the time it was a good place to avoid other people. Started ten years earlier as one of the Prince's more ambitious projects but hampered since by lack of funds, it looked more like a giant vacant lot than a growing city.

The harbour, the motel, the unfinished luxury residential quarter, were so many islands flung down in the wilderness and connected by stretches of empty roads which were the most modern feature of the place. The city-centre itself, so-called, was a shanty town more than a kilometre inland, a market place and bus terminal surrounded by dingy shops and jerry-built Chinese hotels. On the far side the shops gave way to a series of bars and dance halls, grotesque structures painted pink and green and yellow (one all black), like a setting for some surrealist western, too hideous against the background of jungle green and raw red earth embankments even to be funny: La Cave, Hawai, the Zig-Zag, the Zanzi-bar!

'Why are they so ugly?' Surya asked innocently.

'God knows. I suppose because drunken sailors aren't very particular. They look even more sinister at night.'

A young girl, barely Surya's age, leaned out of an open window and waved at us as we passed. Surya waved half-heartedly back.

Away from that dismal place however our spirits quickly rose. We sped up and down hills, through dappled woodland, past a new suburb, rows of half-finished concrete bungalows with no one in sight. A long view of beach stretched away to distant headlands. I stopped the car under a clump of casuarina pines, unpacked and led the way among the sand dunes towards the water.

There were no changing huts and here, alone on this vast beach, I expected some coyness from Surya. But Cambodians have a practical method for changing clothes in the open and we used this, wrapping a sarong around ourselves and holding the top between our teeth. The sarong came down to knee level and left ample room inside to move around and still preserve modesty. We only had one sarong between us and I was first in the water. I swam out a few yards, feeling the sun beginning to bite on my pale skin, and watched as Surya came down to the water. She was still wearing the sarong, this time tied in a knot over her breasts to leave her shoulders bare, and the hem swirled around her knees as she waded out.

'Don't tell me you forgot your bathing suit!' I called out.

'I've got it on underneath.'

182

'So what's this for?' I pointed at the sarong.

'Don't you like it? It's very Cambodian. That's how village women go bathing.'

'And very fetching it is too. But village girls don't own bikinis, and they don't come to Sihanoukville. You couldn't swim twenty metres in that outfit. Go and take it off.'

'But people will stare –'

'What people? There's no one around.'

'Yes there is. Look!' She pointed towards the far end of the beach, where a cluster of tiny figures stood at the edge of the water, too far off to be counted.

'They couldn't see you even with binoculars,' I said. 'But they will stare if you come swimming like this. If you must stick to tradition think of Angkor and what the women wore there. Nothing above the waist. This way you really look like a bar-girl on her first day at the beach.'

'Do I? Alright then…as long as you don't stare.'

'God forbid!' I said with patent insincerity, as she struggled out of the garment. And indeed it was difficult not to stare, for she was truly beautiful, standing half-naked in the water, finely shaped with small firm breasts and long slim legs tapering away to the sand, her bikini a pale turquoise against the rich honey of her skin. I was a little surprised by her sudden shyness, for a girl who didn't mind exhibiting herself at the swimming pool, but I put it down to the fact that she was not used to swimming on deserted beaches with young men – least of all someone who had made such a fuss over her reputation three weeks earlier. She soon got over it. She was a good swimmer and we went out as far as we dared, then came slowly back inshore, and floated on our backs squinting up at the sky, and had a water fight, throwing up a cloud of spray and making a joyous din of it, until exhausted we crept back on the beach and spread out our towels. Then Surya did another curious thing: instead of flopping down on her stomach like me she took up the sarong once more, and lying down on her back draped it carefully over herself from her shoulders to her shins. Next she took a wide-brimmed straw hat and put it over her face so that it covered her neck and shoulders. Then she tucked her arms beneath the cloth and lay still, with only her feet at the other end pointing at the sky.

'Now what!' I said. 'Scared of the sun, or something?'

'It's too hot,' she answered, her voice muffled by the hat. 'I don't want to get too dark.'

'Don't tell me you've got a colour complex, at your age.' She didn't reply, and I edged across to her. 'It's silly to worry about the colour of your skin, didn't you know?'

'Is it?'

'Yes. Very silly and very old-fashioned. Especially when you're such an attractive colour.'

'You're just saying that. I'm too black.'

'No you're not!'

'Yes I am. I'm so black you can't see my nose in the middle of my face. You couldn't even see my face at all at night, except by my teeth and the whites of my eyes.' I laughed. 'Look,' she said, putting her hand out. 'And I only go swimming twice a week.'

She pulled her hand back, but I caught it and held it fast.

'Certainly not like mine,' I admitted. 'You could see me very clearly at night – like old cheese, faintly luminescent. See? Camembert, against Cambodian honey.' Propped up on my elbow, I looked down at her shrouded form. The hat moved slightly as she turned her head, and a single eye peered out from under the brim – as if to prove her point, the only sharp detail in all that soft shadow.

'You are very white, aren't you,' she said frankly. 'And you'll get badly sunburnt if you stay like this.'

'I told you. I'm the one who ought to be covered up, not you.'

'But I still wish I weren't so black.'

I sighed. 'Well if you don't like my skin and you don't like yours, what colour would you like to be then?'

'Like those Frenchwomen you see in magazines...all cream and gold, with blue eyes and a very light tan that would go away in winter.'

'What nonsense. It's all make-up, didn't you know? Make-up and make-believe. You don't see many of those in real life.'

'Yes you do. Look at Madame Marchand. Don't you think she's got a lovely skin?'

'I suppose so. But no better than yours. Just different, that's all.' I released her hand and stared at it as it lay on the sand, wishing she hadn't brought up the name. Then I took it up again. 'Anyway, what makes you think she's happy with her skin? Perhaps she wishes she had yours. Look at the time she spends at the swimming pool.'

'But that's just what I mean!' she suddenly cried, flinging away the hat and propping herself up to stare at me. 'I mean she can spend hours at the pool if she wants to, can't she, and all she does is get a better and better tan – but when I do that I go coal-black in one morning. You think I'm joking, don't you. Making a fuss about nothing. But you'd feel differently if you were my colour. Having to be careful with the make-up I use, never staying in the sun too long...when you're white it doesn't matter, you can lie there all day, you can darken your face artificially if you want to, because you know it'll disappear when you want it to. But I can't change, I can't get any paler, only darker and darker until I can't even see my face in the mirror.'

'Now I understand why Cambodians always pick a rainy day to go for a picnic,' I said with heavy banter. Surya gave me a hurt look, lay back against her towel and covered her face again, shutting me out of her sight. She remained silent and still while I cursed my clumsiness. How could I know she felt so sensitive about her colour? She'd mentioned it before but in a light-hearted manner, I'd never guessed it ran so deep. Now what could I say to reassure her? That it was in fact the European women who felt jealous, envious of the local girls who stole their men with their soft velvety skins which didn't dry up and wrinkle from too much sun and too much make-up? She wouldn't believe me, I thought, looking down at the hat, she wouldn't believe that it's the truth...even with the *Madame Marchand* she admires so much.

I looked around. The beach was still empty, except for those distant dots – closer now but still too far away to worry about. I hesitated, then leaned forward and took away the hat, replacing its shadow with mine. Her eyes opened, dark brown, almost black, brilliant eyes that should never want to be blue, questioning me silently as I bent to kiss her. For a moment her lips were stiff against mine, her hand on my shoulder ready to push me away –

then her mouth softened, her arm came trustingly around. 'Philippe,' she whispered.

2

I must have dozed off. Suddenly the sun was hot on my shoulders, I could hear voices and Surya was sitting up, clutching the sarong against her.

'What is it?' I asked.

'People coming.'

'Lie down and pretend to be asleep. They won't recognise you with your hat on.'

'They've already seen us. It's the Marchands.'

Oh Lord! Like a kick in the ribs! Wide awake now I peered round Surya's back at the group of people coming towards us along the shore. No doubt about it, it was the Marchands, in full force, not thirty metres away: Henri, Nicole, the two children, and a Vietnamese maid carrying towels. What were they doing here? My first impulse was to throw Surya back against the sand and pretend we hadn't seen them. But it was too late, the children had already seen us, the elder, Jean-Claude, trumpeting loudly:

'*Regarde, Maman! On dirait Philippe, là, avec une fille.*'

'*Tais-toi Jean-Claude! On ne montre pas les gens comme ça.*'

Nicole's instant rebuke. But she looked up at once, and stopped still.

'Don't keep holding that thing in front of you,' I whispered urgently. 'Or they really will think you're naked underneath.' Reluctantly I stood up and waved, and Henri called out and came across the sand towards us.

Nicole had a lot of self-control. By the time everyone had gathered round she'd recovered from her surprise, though her face was pale. Mine, I felt, was blushing furiously. We stared at each other for a moment, before social roles took over. Then she nodded at Surya, I shook hands with Henri, and the children came forward with handfuls of shells, mercifully chattering.

'Look what we picked up on the beach,' said Jean-Claude.

'That one's from Kep,' said his brother. 'We've just come from there.'

186

'They're very pretty,' I said mechanically. I looked at their father. 'We saw you in the distance, but didn't know it was you. Didn't see your car anywhere.'

'The driver dropped us off, he's picking us up at the other end of the beach,' he explained. 'It's such a fine morning for a walk.' His legs were even whiter than mine against his khaki shorts. 'You're just down for the day, I take it?'

'That's right, we're going back this afternoon,' I said hastily, Surya looking at me as if afraid I might say the wrong thing. Nicole had stepped back a few paces, ostensibly to talk with the maid, and appeared to lose interest in our conversation. 'What about you? Are you staying here?'

'Yes, until tomorrow. We're booked in at the motel. We went to Kep yesterday but it was very crowded and we decided to come here instead. The children like it better here anyway.'

'You were lucky to get rooms at such short notice.'

'What? Oh yes, I suppose so,' he said vaguely, as the younger Henri broke away from his mother's grasp and ran back towards me.

'We're going to have lunch at the beach restaurant,' he cried excitedly. 'There's a tiger there.'

'A panther, not a tiger,' his brother scoffed. 'Tigers have stripes.' The younger boy ignored him. 'Are you coming too, Philippe? And...and you?' he added shyly to Surya.

'*Mademoiselle*,' his father supplied. 'Mademoiselle Boun Savann. Yes, Philippe, why don't you join us for lunch?'

'That's very kind –' I began, and saw Nicole raise her head sharply in our direction. 'I wouldn't press if I were you, Henri,' she called out. 'I'm sure those youngsters have other plans.' As I suspected she hadn't missed a word. Surya looked at me again, with apprehension this time.

'Oh come on, Philippe,' Jean-Claude broke in. 'Come and see the panther.'

'It's up to you, Philippe,' Henri said patiently. 'I don't want to cut across any other arrangements of course, but you'll be very welcome. And there'll be plenty of time later for another swim, before you go back.'

'Alright then,' I nodded. 'We'd love to come. Thanks.'

'Good. That's settled then. About one? We have to call in at the motel first, it'll take us all that time to get there.'

He gave us both a large approving grin and then set off after Nicole, who was already striding up the beach ahead of the others as if anxious to get away from us. We watched them go in silence for a while.

'She didn't seem very friendly,' Surya remarked when they were out of earshot.

'I wouldn't worry. It's probably the heat. I'm sure she didn't mean it.'

'I'm glad you accepted though. For a moment I was afraid you were going to say no.'

I laughed, and sat down abruptly in the sand. Reaction was setting in, my legs were giving way.

'What's so funny about that?' she asked.

'Nothing,' I said. 'I'm sure you're right. It was the only thing to do in the circumstances.' But I couldn't help laughing, at the irony of it. She looked at me curiously, as if the sun had gone to my head.

3

I'm not very proud of myself over that episode. The best I can say about it is that none of it was premeditated, that I hadn't planned any of it. On the contrary, even in the heat of the moment the day before I had been careful to avoid the opportunity so innocently offered by Surya to inflict some sort of revenge on Nicole, by forcing on her the kind of scene which had just taken place. Sihanoukville was separated from Kep by more than a hundred kilometres of winding coastal road, I had no wish to humiliate Nicole, and even less to hurt Surya or use her to prove a point. Only sheer bad luck could have brought the Marchands there at such a time. But that isn't much of a defence, and it doesn't excuse the way I behaved for the rest of that day, towards Nicole or Surya; and the older I get, the less I like the self-absorbed, callow young man that I was on the beach that day – distant ancestor of my present self – even if at other times I recall him with friendship and even affection.

An hour later I led Surya into the restaurant. I didn't feel so cheerful then. I'd had time to reflect on the absurd impulse which had made me accept Henri's invitation on the beach, rising to it as if to some hidden challenge in Nicole's expression, and it seemed to me that I had been very foolish. What did I hope to achieve? My furious indignation of the day before had quite evaporated during the morning, and it would have been more intelligent, I told myself, safer, and certainly more loyal to Surya, whatever she might think, to pass it up and wait some other time for my inevitable confrontation with Nicole. But something in Nicole's manner had made me sense that there might not be another time, if I didn't act very quickly – and now I had to find the strength to face the next two hours and one of the most uncomfortable situations in my life. Much more painful than that evening, months earlier, when I had first met Henri again after Siemreap. At least then, I thought sourly, the game was still fairly simple, and Nicole was my ally – whereas now she had become an opponent who knew the rules better than I did, and all I had to help me was Surya's innocence. She, poor girl, simply wondered why I had become so taciturn all of a sudden.

Under the circumstances lunch was bound to be something of a strain – though it passed without incident, if not without heartache on Nicole's part and mine. We were both too skilled at our roles, and too much was at stake, for us to take any risks. The children were excited but a little scared of the panther at close range – only a cub, safely tethered to the bar, but a surly animal – and so we ate on the terrace outside, facing the sea, under the shade of a casuarina tree. Behind us the restaurant, noisy with talk and laughter, in front of us the small sheltered bay, with a wooded island rising straight from the water on our left, the end of the pier and the two ships away to the right, beyond the headland. Down along the beach a group of hairy Eastern Europeans from Phnom Penh, minor diplomats or technicians from one of the aid projects, played with a beach ball on the sand, their plump women bouncing around like schoolgirls, threatening at any moment to burst out of their bikinis. It was a lively, happy scene, very different from the vacant postcard stillness of the morning. There was even a breeze to temper the heat, and the red-check tablecloth had to be tied down at the corners with pieces of tape, as if on a holiday cruise.

Nevertheless there was too much tension at the table to do justice to this scene, and the food that went with it, even if Nicole and I were the only ones to be fully aware of it. Away from Phnom Penh Henri seemed to be making an effort to relax and enjoy himself, though even here he couldn't altogether escape from his cares, and there were moments when he simply sat in silence staring out to sea, lost in thought. As for Surya, she was clearly more at ease in the Marchands' company than if she'd been alone with me to face the stares of the restaurant crowd. But she wasn't one to sparkle without prompting, and she remained generally subdued. It was Nicole who surprised me. I'd come prepared for coldness and hostility – I half expected her to miss lunch altogether – but she was calm, composed, if not exactly thrilled at my presence at least prepared to be civil about it, as if she'd come to terms with the situation since our encounter on the beach, or at least decided there was nothing to be gained by further displays of temper. She even took pains to be friendly to Surya, offering her food, asking her about herself, as if to make up for her earlier curtness. I knew this was largely a pose, I could see effort behind it, and she looked weary and drawn. But I was grateful to her for it, whatever her motives.

Meanwhile lunch dragged on, slowly taking the proportions of an orgy as one course after another appeared on the table. The restaurant was known for its seafood, and Henri had ordered the full menu: *palourdes fraîches au citron* (fresh clams, which a waiter, his trousers rolled to the knees, fetched for us from a large basket out in the water), followed by *crabes aux poivres verts*, spicy and hot and their red shells already cracked and dripping with sauce, and then grilled soles caught that morning by some offshore fisherman, the whole culminating in cries of joy from the children as the cook himself carried an *omelette flambée* to the table and the scent of burning rum competed for an instant with the breeze. By that stage I was replete, lighting a cigarette, pushing my chair back, no longer sure if I was dreaming – except that at the end of it all, I knew, I would have to sing for my lunch. I hoped the coffee would wake me up in advance.

Finally the moment came – with the coffee, which Surya didn't drink and the children weren't allowed to. Freed at last they bounded off their chairs to go and romp in the sand. After a moment's hesitation Surya went with them – they had become fast friends by then. Then Henri went off to talk to someone inside the restaurant, and I was left alone with Nicole.

We didn't speak at first. Nicole was staring after the children with an odd, wistful expression, while I wondered uneasily how to begin. All the elaborate defences and justifications I had been rehearsing in my mind over the last hour sounded very hollow suddenly. But I couldn't think of anything else, and the silence stretched out between us, until it became almost unendurable. Then Nicole turned to me.

'I suppose you feel pleased with yourself,' she said tartly. I sighed.

'No I don't. The opposite in fact.'

'Aren't you? I would have thought this was just what you wanted.'

'Well it's not. I never meant things to happen like this. Anyway, thank you for being nice to Surya. It's not her fault.'

'I can see that. The trouble is she's such a sweet girl I can't even hate her. How did you manage to talk her into coming down? She strikes me as the kind of girl who'd worry a lot about her reputation.'

'She does a bit. I was surprised when she accepted. But it was all very much a thing of the moment.'

'Really?'

'Yes. I bumped into her yesterday at the *Cercle Sportif.*'

'Just like that.'

'There was a bit more to it. I was of course very angry. I'd just found out that you'd left for the week-end, without so much as a message, after trying all week to see you.'

'It was all arranged at the last minute. There was no way I could tell you. And I've been so busy all week I've hardly had a moment to myself. I tried to ring you at home a couple of times but no one answered and I didn't want to keep phoning you at work.'

'I thought you were in Kep. I'd never have come here otherwise. I certainly didn't intend to flaunt myself.'

'Very considerate. But you did agree to come to lunch.'

'What else could I do?'

'You could have refused.'

'And passed up the chance for this conversation?' I glared at her. 'No, Nicole. I didn't mean it to happen like this. But you can't expect me just to sit quietly waiting for you when you're not around. I'm yours, for all you want of me, when you're available. But frankly that hasn't been very often of late.'

I simmered down. 'I'm sorry. I know that's not your fault. But please, don't take it out on me either. I've got my own life to lead too, as you once told me.'

'Oh, stop apologising. You're right. It was bound to happen. I should never have asked you to stop seeing her.'

She relapsed into a moody silence. Over her shoulder I could see Henri inside the restaurant, standing up, about to leave his friend.

'Look, let's not quarrel,' I said. 'Tell me when I can see you again.'

'Are you sure you want to?'

'Of course I am!'

'Alright…stay the night then.'

'Be serious!'

'I am. Not together of course. But you could stay with us. She can sleep with me and the children and you can share a room with Henri. There were still a few cabins left when we booked in earlier.'

'Come on. She'd never agree. There's her father, her family – besides, it's hardly fair to her.'

'Don't talk to me about fairness! It's up to you. Otherwise I don't know when I'll be free again.'

Then Henri was with us again, precluding further comment.

'Hello you two,' he said cheerfully. 'You look very serious. Anything wrong?'

'No – not at all,' said Nicole quickly, recovering and looking up at him with what could pass for a smile – though she looked pale and, it seemed to me, had not been far from tears. I felt sudden remorse at the way I had spoken. 'We were just discussing a little *difficulté sentimentale…*'

For one wild second I thought she meant to blurt everything out. One glance at her face and he was bound to guess at the truth! But he was looking at me instead, with amused concern.

'Philippe? My dear chap, don't tell me you're having problems with Surya?'

I opened my mouth to speak but Nicole cut in. 'In fact,' she went on smoothly, 'I was just telling Philippe they should stay the night. Instead of driving all the way back this afternoon. Don't you think, Henri? It's such a long way, twice in a day, don't you agree?'

She outlined her idea to him. He listened sceptically at first, then with growing interest.

'What about her family?' I said. 'And we've brought no clothes –'

'We can fix that,' said Nicole. 'We've brought more than enough, and Surya's practically my size anyway. And Henri can ring her father in town and explain the whole thing to him. Don't you think darling? I'm sure he'll agree if you speak to him.'

'Why not,' he said, as I was about to protest once more. 'He's a sensible man, there's no harm in trying. What's the matter, Philippe? Wouldn't you rather stay? Tomorrow's a holiday, there's no need to rush back.'

'I don't think I brought enough money,' I said weakly. 'And Surya's sure to say no –'

'Don't worry about the room. I'll look after that.'

'And I'll talk to Surya,' Nicole added, getting up and walking over to where Surya now laughingly restrained the young Henri from leaping fully clothed into the water. The child squealed with delight at this new game. Surya looked up with – it seemed to me – a shade of apprehension, but Nicole was at her most engaging, and soon they were talking earnestly. I watched in awe, and a growing sense of unease. Henri mistook this for doubt and reassured me.

'Nicole's amazing, you know. She always has her way in the end. And you have very good taste. Surya is a delightful girl.' Then his expression changed, became curious and ironic. I followed his gaze, to the group of Europeans on the beach. They had stopped playing ball and one of them was busy setting up a camera on a tripod, with a long telephoto lens which he aimed in the direction of the harbour and the two ships at the pier. He took his time, with total unconcern for any spectators, and then slowly and methodically began to photograph the ships.

'Who is that man?' I asked wonderingly.

'I don't know,' Henri said. 'A Yugoslav or a Czech, I think, but I haven't seen him before. He's not a Russian, I'm pretty sure.'

'He's going to get run in, if he carries on like this. Hasn't anyone told him they don't like spies in this country?'

Henri smiled wryly. 'Apparently not.'

We watched as the man finished his roll of film, and then carefully unscrewed his camera and folded his equipment away, without so much as pretending to be interested in any other subject. Then Nicole and Surya were back with us, chattering like old friends.

'It's all agreed,' said Nicole.

5

That afternoon I waited in vain for a chance to talk to Nicole again. After lunch we went to the motel, where Henri managed against all odds to get another room – the last one available, half a bungalow tucked out of sight from the main building and separated from Nicole's room by a hundred metres of concrete footpath, but he didn't seem to mind – and followed this up, when he rang Surya's father, by getting both an immediate line to Phnom Penh and the old man's approval. Then we had a siesta, Surya with Nicole and the children, Henri and I in our room, and afterwards we went to the beach, until dusk and the first sand-flies drove us back. Throughout the afternoon Nicole maintained the same unfaltering front of friendship towards Surya, treating her almost like a younger sister, until I wondered if she wasn't deliberately forming an alliance against me – their common male

194

and in many ways their sole common denominator. I would have liked to probe that smooth forehead of hers and read her thoughts: for it was a front, I knew, I could tell anxiety or unremitting thought behind her eyes. But she skilfully avoided being left alone with me even for a moment, and I was left to guess as best I could her secret intentions.

Instead I talked with Surya. We sat on the beach while Nicole and Henri swam with the children. She'd been quiet since lunch.

'You're not unhappy, are you?' I asked. 'That we're staying here the night? It's all very proper. Even your aunts couldn't object.'

'It's alright. My father didn't mind. And they're both very kind.'

'They like you a lot.'

She was silent, looking out towards them.

'Are you in love with her?' she asked suddenly.

'Me?' The question took me by surprise. I pretended to be amused. 'What makes you say that?'

'Oh, I don't know...The way you look at her sometimes. You seem very close.'

'You're imagining things. She is a close friend, and I like her a lot. But not the way you think. More like a sister than anything else.'

Whether that satisfied her I couldn't tell. She didn't pursue. Instead she said:

'You don't love me, though, do you.'

'Oh you! You're in a different league altogether.'

'What does that mean?'

'It means that you're just about the most attractive young woman I've ever met. And the nicest.'

'But that's not the same, is it,' she persisted. I sighed.

'Look, Surya. I'll be honest with you. It would be very easy for me to fall in love with you. But I don't dare. That would be the worst thing I could possibly do. For you, and for me.'

'Why do you say that?'

'Because there'd be no future in it. You're going off to France in a few months. You'll probably be there for years. You don't want to be tied to someone like me. You need to be free. Free to fall in love with someone else if you want. Some handsome young Frenchman maybe. Or another Cambodian, who's also studying there.'

She mused on this for a moment.

'Why did you kiss me this morning?'

I thought about my answer.

'Because I am very close to falling in love with you. I know I shouldn't have. But please don't be angry with me. I think it was the nicest kiss I ever had.'

So help me, I meant it all, almost every word. That didn't stop me from feeling like a traitor.

That evening we ate in the motel dining room, for a repetition of lunch: the same menu, the same faces from the restaurant, their numbers increased by a wave of latecomers from Phnom Penh. I recognised the Eastern European spies and saw, at a table of Russians, Kalyakin's gleaming forehead, Rassimov who stared at me for a moment before he waved. With a return of her earlier timidity Surya looked around anxiously and Nicole made a joke at my expense.

'Sit next to me, and everyone will think you're with me. And stop worrying about your reputation. I'm sure Philippe will do the honourable thing if it gets in danger.'

'He may have to yet. I can see several friends of my father's,' replied Surya, and then she blushed at her audacity, and Henri laughed and even I managed a smile. To all appearances we were just another happy family group, tired and sunburnt. But dinner dragged on, the children began to fret, Henri looked at his watch and became irritable.

'I wish they'd hurry,' he said. 'I wanted an early night. It'll be ten by the time we've put the children to bed.' He turned to me. 'But don't let us spoil your evening, you two. If you want to go out or anything.'

That wasn't my intention. I wasn't going to give Nicole the masochistic satisfaction, if that was what she expected, of watching me whisk Surya off into the night. Besides I couldn't afford to, after my talk with Surya. But with Henri there it was delicate work and better if the refusal came from her. I hedged until we left the dining room and I accompanied Surya to her room, walking behind Henri and Nicole and the children (the maid, who kept reappearing between meals, having retired for the night somewhere in town with the driver). Henri was off soon after, and then fortunately Surya herself decided she wanted an early night too. She probably thought it was safer as well. And once again it was impossible to see Nicole alone.

The light was on in our room when I went in. Henri was standing by a small writing desk under the window, unpacking an overnight bag. He looked up with – I thought – a touch of irritation.

'I thought you'd be on the beach with Surya,' he said.

'She wanted to go to bed early. And I don't blame her. I think I will too.' I yawned. 'It's been a long day. Got up at five this morning, would you believe.' Henri smiled perfunctorily, and I wondered if my welcome wasn't starting to wear thin. 'If you're not using the bathroom…'

'No, go ahead.'

I undressed, wrapped a thin motel towel around my waist and went to the bathroom. The water was warm, which was more than I expected, but the soap was local, pungent and spicy but with no lather, as I discovered when I stepped under the shower. I was about to get out and ask Henri if he had anything better when he called out:

'Philippe? I'm going out for a walk. I need some fresh air. Don't wait up. I'll take one of the keys.'

'OK. Enjoy your walk.'

The sound of the door closing. The water was now quite cold.

Afterwards I lay naked on my bed with the light on, trying to sort some meaning out of the day. My tiredness had gone, but my teeth, cleaned with a finger, felt gritty and my mind refused to concentrate. What should I do now? I wondered. Was there any point in trying to see Nicole, now that Henri had gone out?

As if in answer to my question, there was a knock at the door and I heard her voice:

'Are you two presentable? May I come in?'

'Wait a minute.' I seized my beach shorts and hurriedly put them on, and then opened the door. She came in and stared about.

'Where's Henri?'

'He's gone for a walk. He said he wanted some fresh air.'

'I thought he wanted to sleep early!' She placed the bundle she was carrying on the writing desk. 'Will you tell him I brought these? They're his towel and his sleeping pills. He forgot to take them.'

She turned to go, but I moved quickly to the door, standing in her path.

'Don't go – please. We need to talk.'

She stood for a moment with head bowed.

'Please,' I urged. 'Isn't that why you wanted us to stay? So we could talk?'

She nodded wearily.

'Alright. Wait for me near the car. I'll see the children are asleep first.'

6

It was well after ten, and the motel was quieter now. People were going to bed in the little bungalows, curtains were drawn, here and there a cigarette glowed on a darkened veranda. We made our way to the beach, skirting the paths and the pools of light from the street lamps.

'Did Henri say where he was going?' she asked.

'No, he just said he was going out.' Useless answer. Where else would he go but the beach? But I was afraid that she might change her mind, and anyway it was safe enough in the darkness, with the sound of the sea to cover our voices and only the stars and the edge of the water to guide us, faintly phosphorescent where the waves broke. Nicole took off her sandals to walk in the sand.

'Be careful of the sand-flies,' I said, for she wore only a light dress and her arms and legs were bare.

'The breeze will keep them away.'

'Yes. It's a bit chilly though.' I made to put my arm around her shoulders but she pulled away, which wasn't a good omen. And we walked like this in silence for a moment, each it seemed waiting for the other to begin.

'Alright,' I said at last. 'Come on, Nicole. Say it.'

'What do you want me to say?'

'Anything! I don't know. Anything rather than this...this wall of silence you've been building all day. Tell me why you wanted us to stay the night, for one thing. What were you trying to do? You didn't expect us to tumble into bed, did you, just to prove you were right after all?'

'Certainly not!'

'Then what? Revenge, to pay me back for this morning? If so you certainly succeeded. I don't think I've ever spent a more uncomfortable afternoon.'

'Poor Philippe,' she said drily. 'Yes, I don't expect it was very pleasant...no, to tell you the truth I really did it so that I could get to know Surya better.'

'Get to know her better? Why? You already know her.'

'Yes, but only through your eyes. I wanted to see her for myself, in more detail, close up – if you like, I wanted to see why you find her so attractive.'

'I see,' I said, though I didn't. She still spoke in the same dry, ironic tone, though I could feel my irritation mounting with every comment. 'And did you?' I asked.

'Yes...yes I think I did. She's very likeable, you know.'

'I know that!'

'And she's sweet, and innocent without being stupid, not very sure of herself, and far less coy than I expected. You do have good taste. Of course she's also very pretty, but I'm sure that's not what matters most to you.'

'Nicole, stop it!'

'Yes. There's no point in being bitchy, is there! But I still mean what I said: she's very close to falling in love with you, she's halfway there already, and you're going to have to be very careful with her, to see that she doesn't get hurt. Because, poor girl, she doesn't yet know very much about that sort of situation...but it

199

won't do you any harm, to have a little responsibility for a change. It may be just what you need to make a man of you.'

I stopped, and turned to her. We had almost reached the end of the beach, dark rocks just visible against the sand ahead of us, where the headland began, still with no sign of Henri. I tried to make out her expression, but all I could see was the pale blur of her face in front of me, within reach and yet very remote, separated by all the things which hadn't been said, the implications in her words, that maddening ironic tone.

'What are you trying to say?' I asked.

'Just this, Philippe,' she said quietly, and paused. She crossed her arms tightly around her chest and bent her head for a brief moment. Then she lifted her chin to stare back at me. 'I want it to end, between us.'

It was like a punch, knocking the air out of me. So that was how it came, I thought, the scene that I'd foreseen, God knows how many times I'd asked myself what form it would take. A few words on a beach, with everything over the past few weeks leading inexorably up to them. What I hadn't foreseen was the pain, the cold water shock that made me want to double up, gasping for breath. I turned away from her, until I could trust myself to speak normally. 'Just like that,' I said at last. 'Isn't it...isn't it a bit sudden?'

She shook her head. 'No, it's not sudden. I've thought about it.'

'When? This afternoon?'

'Yes – no. This afternoon, and before.' Her voice rose, no longer so remote now, more human and vulnerable as a note of urgency crept into it. 'I'm sorry Philippe – it's hard to say it, and I don't want to hurt you. But it's got to stop. We can't keep going.'

'Why? Just because of Surya? Because you saw the two of us on a beach, when you thought I was safely in Phnom Penh waiting for you? Is that it?'

'That's got something to do with it, yes!' she retorted. 'But it's only one of the reasons. I can't go on, Philippe. I want to end it, to start being faithful to Henri again -'

'It's the holidays, isn't it – when you were away. Something happened then –'

200

'No, Philippe. It's not that. I wish it were, it would make it easier. But it's not that.'

'What is it then?' I cried in exasperation.

'It's us! Don't you see? Look at us, Philippe. Look at what's happening to us. My jealousy, your resentment – we've reached the stage where we spend half our time saying cruel things to each other. We don't even trust each other any more. Do you see what I've done to you, to myself, with my stupid jealousy? Forced you to hide from me, to keep things from me and see her behind my back? You may be right about her. I don't know any more, all those things I said – but even if you're not, what right do I have to stop you from seeing her? From falling in love with her even, or anyone else if it comes to that? After all, as you said, what am I giving you in return? Half, less than that, of an ageing, dissatisfied woman who can't decide what she wants and even if she could wouldn't have to courage to set about taking it –'

'Nicole, you're twisting everything I said. I didn't mind that –'

'Ah, but you see, I did. Are you surprised? After all my fine theories, all this talk of loving, of coping with two people at once, of making allowances and not demanding too much. You wouldn't believe me at first. Do you remember? You thought it wasn't possible. Well, you were right. I can't handle both you and Henri at the same time. I can't stand by calmly and watch you get attracted to other women – whether it's Surya or anyone else. Yes, Philippe. You thought I was stronger than that. And so did I. But I'm not, and I can't keep it up. Not any more.'

She stopped, and took a long breath. The moon had risen during this exchange, giving us our first clear view of each other – Nicole still hugging herself tightly, as if to gather strength for what she had to say, while I stood staring at her, trying to read her face. There was no mistaking the anguish in her voice, the effort of making this admission came from very deep within her. But I was equally determined to stand my ground. I knew from experience how skilled she was at presenting her arguments, at rationalising her emotions. And this time I wasn't going to accept it. My own anguish was as deep as hers.

'I'm sorry,' she went on, less vehemently now. Perhaps she took my silence for agreement. 'I know I'm hurting you, and I don't want to. It's not your fault. But it's no use pretending it'll go away. It won't – not this time. It'll just go on and on and get worse and worse until we can't stand the sight of each other – and I don't want it to end like that, Philippe. I've got just enough strength to give up now, while there's still time. Let me do that.'

'No!' I said, exploding into anger at last, channelling my pain and my frustration into this more manageable emotion. 'This will not do! It's too easy! You know what you're doing, don't you! You're behaving with total and absolute selfishness. You think you can just have an affair with someone, with me, a younger man you can dominate, and then pull out when the going gets rough, when things no longer go according to plan. Well that's just not good enough. I won't accept it, whatever your argument. I'm not a plaything for you to pick up and then discard when you've finished with me. I told you this morning that I'm not your property. That doesn't mean that you can just walk away from me now. I'm not ready to give you up, Nicole.'

'Philippe! Please don't talk like that. Be reasonable –'

Sois raisonnable! The ultimate cry of all Frenchwomen, mothers, wives and mistresses, shouted down the ages in the face of Huns, Goths and Visigoths, and all those invaders since the days of Rome. Be reasonable! Cease this uncouth behaviour! Nothing could have been better calculated to make me lose my reason! No doubt it had had the same effect on the other barbarians.

'Reasonable?' I shouted. 'No, I will not be reasonable! Not with you. Reasonable for you simply means listening to your point of view, agreeing with everything you say. Well, there's another point of view on this matter, there's mine as well, and it's time you listened to it for a change. Because I'm not going to let you go, Nicole. Do you hear? Even if...even if I have to make a scandal about it!'

'Philippe, this is stupid! I will not listen to this. Let's go back. We can discuss it some other time.'

'No we won't. We'll have it out here and now.'

'It's no use! All we're doing is shouting at each other. And Henri will be back soon.'

'Damn Henri!'

She flared up. 'You have no right to say that –'

'Right? What right have I had from the beginning?'

'Philippe, that's enough! I'm going back.' She started to turn away, but I caught her wrist.

'No. You're not going to run away like that. I won't let you.'

'Let me go! You're hurting my wrist!' She broke loose, but I reached after her, catching her sleeve as she turned – there was a tearing sound as the material gave way – and then we were grappling and swaying together like drunks in the moonlight, finally collapsing in a tangle of legs on the sand. 'Philippe, what are you doing? Control yourself!' 'I will not let you go, do you hear? I will not! I will not!' She fought to get free, but I held her down, my anger fired by her resistance.

'Quiet!' she suddenly urged. 'I can hear someone.'

We stopped, and lay perfectly still, ears straining against the thumping of our hearts and of the sea against the shore for whatever sound had alerted her – but it wasn't repeated, and we were well sheltered as we lay by the rocks around us; and then we resumed our silent struggle, but in a different key now, anger sliding into lust, resistance into something else – reluctance, complicity, a last shred of caution as I rucked her skirt up about her waist and fumbled at her hips.

'Philippe, you can't – not here –'

'Yes. Here and now. If it's the last thing I do.'

I made love to her, there and then on the sand. It wasn't a rape – I'm not a rapist by nature, in my wildest moments I couldn't force myself on a woman against her will. But there was a violence about it which had never before existed in our lovemaking. It was I think the indignity which she resented most. She had never before been thrown down and taken like this. She struggled for a moment longer, but my blood was up, the pale gleam of her thighs excited me, old-fashioned desire and the pent-up tensions and frustrations of the past month mingled and made light of the paltry obstacles of our clothes. Soon we were half-naked, rolling fiercely about, heedless of anyone who might by then have chanced upon us. When she finally climaxed and her grip tightened on my neck and around my waist I felt like howling my triumph out like some primeval beast.

Afterwards I couldn't help laughing out loud – with joy, and relief, and at the sheer incongruity of it all. We lay side by side, her head pillowed against my shoulder, in the manner of all lovers after the storm has passed. It was as if all the harshness and bitterness of the past weeks had been swept away in that vast gust of lunar madness, leaving us lying naked on the shore like pebbles or seashells tossed up by the tide, under a moon so bright that it hurt the eyes to look at it. I felt closer to her than ever before: and slowly I put into words a thought which had been lying in wait for that very moment.

'We don't have to go on like this, you know,' I said. 'There is another way.'

'Is there?'

'We could live together.'

She was silent for a while; then:

'Don't think I haven't thought about it.'

'I mean it! Leave Henri and come and live with me. Get a divorce. Put an end to all this…this terrible nonsense. This hiding, and the quarrels and the lies, and having to wait and wait just to see each other.'

'Philippe, Philippe, do you know what you're saying?'

I took a deep breath. 'Yes, perfectly. I'm asking you to marry me.'

It took a long time that night to make her see that I meant it – that this wasn't some madcap idea of the moment, some impulsive moonstruck notion born out of the turmoil of the past weeks. It's true, I said. I love you, can't you see? I can't bear the thought of losing you. I want to live with you, openly, by day as well as by night, not have to lie and hide like this. What does Henri offer you anyway? Position? Money? I'll have those in due course. Your children? I'll look after them.

'But I can't just leave Henri. He needs me too.'

'Does he really? And what about you? What do you need?'

'Oh, I don't know – I don't know, Philippe. All I know is I don't want to lose you either. Don't ask me to think beyond that. Not now. I can't.'

But I could, and I meant it, and now that I'd said it I knew it was the best thing to do, the obvious and only solution. The simplicity of it was overwhelming – I couldn't understand why we hadn't thought of it before. I used the most persuasive arguments I could muster, emotional and physical; and when she finally agreed I felt as if I had won a long and arduous battle against tremendous odds.

Chapter Eight

1

Henri was still out when I got back to the bungalow, but I hardly noticed. I was too tired to think and I dropped into bed, to wake up the next morning more refreshed and at peace with myself than I had felt for weeks. At first I couldn't understand why. Then as memory came back I almost burst out laughing again. I told myself that my behaviour towards Nicole had been quite inexcusable and thoroughly uncivilised, and that I had acted very rashly too, rushing in to propose marriage where a cooler head might have paused first and weighed the consequences. But nothing could shake that sense of deep satisfaction, the sort of physical and moral well-being which comes from having at last found the solution to a difficult problem; and any doubts I might have had were swept away when I faced Nicole's tired, bitter-sweet smile over breakfast, next to Henri's dour morning countenance. Those two had not slept well. Henri's muddled complexion spoke of bad digestion (though there was nothing alarming about his manner, nothing to suggest that he had any inkling of what had happened) and Nicole looked bruised about the eyes and oddly shy and vulnerable. For the first time since I had known her it struck me that she didn't know how to handle the situation. I told myself as I looked at them that it wasn't too late to pull back. I was the interloper, the stranger in their marriage, and I knew that Henri would be cruelly hurt by what we were about to do to him; but I felt no compassion, only relief that it was over; and all I wanted to do was put my arms around Nicole and reassure her that everything would be alright. I had to stop myself from blurting it all out there and then.

Perhaps in retrospect that's what I should have done. It might have saved a lot of unpleasantness later on. But we had agreed during the night that it was Nicole's job, she would do the talking, at a time of her choosing; and all I could manage was a few quick words with her afterwards, before I left with Surya. She smiled wanly back, half-convinced.

206

My only regret was Surya, and the way I had unwittingly used her as ammunition in my running battle with Nicole. I felt towards her too a kind of sweet protectiveness, but I saw it now as something else, a kind of brotherly affection, a tenderness very different from anything I felt towards Nicole. I did not want her to be hurt again. But she had sensed the change. Though I was gentle with her there was a distance in her manner, a coolness between us as I drove her back to Phnom Penh and the safety of her father's house. It made me sad. But I pushed it aside, and concentrated instead on the problem ahead. For all my new-found confidence I knew it wasn't going to be easy.

The rest of the week went by very quickly.

2

On Tuesday Rick came to see me. Normally I would have been happy to see him, but he only brought unwelcome news, in the shape of yet another article from *East of Suez*, hidden inside a copy of the *Revue*. I have the text of it still – an argumentative little piece, overwritten like the others but well-informed as always and nicely calculated to get under the Prince's skin if he read it – which, as Rick assured me, was a certainty. But I had other things on my mind and I couldn't take it seriously. Rick was irritated.

'I wouldn't laugh if I were you,' he said. 'They still haven't found the author, you know, and you're not in the clear yet.'

'I know, I know,' I said impatiently. 'What do you want me to do, issue a public statement?' Rick gave me an odd look, decided that my company wasn't worth the effort, and started to leave. At the door he paused.

'I hear you were in good company in Sihanoukville,' he said. 'Did you have a good time?'

'Who told you that's where I went?'

'Your maid. I came round on Sunday and she told me you'd gone there for the day.' He smiled briefly. 'Actually it was your friend Rassimov who filled in the details. I bumped into him this morning. He was uncommonly chatty, I had to tear myself away.'

I stared at him. 'I'd be surprised if he was doing it out of friendship,' I said.

'My sentiments exactly.' He hesitated. 'But don't worry. If he was trying to sow discord between us it didn't work.'

His tone of voice left me in some doubt about that. I shook my head ruefully. 'You wouldn't believe me if I told you,' I said, and started explaining the circumstances of my visit there – leaving out three quarters of the story. His eyes assessed me as I spoke, and I foresaw that he too would need a lot of convincing, when the truth came out, that I hadn't deliberately used Surya's friendship for my own selfish ends. In a way, I thought, he would find that harder to forgive than a straight-out seduction.

3

On Thursday I had a more disturbing experience. I was sitting at my desk, writing an article about the Cambodian pepper industry – a nice safe subject, calculated to raise no one's blood pressure – when the phone rang. I picked it up, hoping it might be Nicole. But it was someone I'd never heard of, an *Inspecteur* Than Souk from the *Police Spéciale*, inviting me politely to come round and visit him at Police Headquarters.

Inspecteur Than Souk was a very polite man. The way he apologised, after keeping me waiting in his anteroom for half an hour, the soft drink and the cigarette he offered me in his office, showed polish, good manners, and ease in dealing with foreigners. I had a good idea what he wanted to see me about and I observed him curiously. He was a small, dapper, finely-featured man with Chinese blood, dressed in white trousers and a short-sleeved shirt, with a gold tie-pin and a Valentino moustache. He could have been a bank clerk or a floor-walker in a smart department store. But there was a sharp intelligence in his eyes and authority in the way his subordinates treated him.

The *Inspecteur* placed a plain manila folder on his desk and came round to sit facing me, and I remembered the discussion I'd had in Rick's office months earlier. He smiled at me and I waited patiently as he ran through the ritual preliminaries and asked me polite questions about my job, my life and whether I was happy in the country. Then he came to the point.

'My dear *Monsieur Roche*,' he began in his precise French. 'You must be wondering why I asked you to come. The fact is that I've been asked to enquire into a delicate matter – which is why I insist on the informal nature of this discussion – and as it's something about which I'm not well informed, I thought perhaps you might be able to help me form a clearer picture. I take it you're familiar with this publication.'

With a deft movement he took the folder from his desk, pulled out the contents and handed them to me. They were, as I'd already guessed, the copy of *East of Suez* which Rick had shown me two days before. I made a pretence of studying its cover, opened it – almost accusingly it fell open at the article in question – examined that briefly, and handed it back to him.

'Yes, I know it,' I said. 'Isn't this the one which has been publishing a series of articles about Cambodia?'

'That's right. You've read them?'

'Some of them. I've also heard the Head of State's comments over the radio, from time to time.'

The *Inspecteur* closed the folder, put it back on his desk, crossed his short legs and sat back. His smile still held the same friendly intention, but his eyes seemed to become more alert.

'What do you think of them in general?'

'I...well, if you want to know whether I agree with them, the answer's simple. No. They're well-written and they appear to be well-informed, but I find them biased and often inaccurate and at times plain objectionable.'

'Thank you,' he said, with no visible irony, 'Of course I didn't suspect you of agreeing with them. You know the magazine is banned in Cambodia?'

'Why, yes. I suppose you're wondering how I came to read them.'

'Not at all. It's your job, after all, you have a perfect right to keep yourself informed about that sort of thing, being a journalist. And anyway, that sort of restriction isn't meant to apply quite so literally to foreigners.'

'I guess not…in any case, it's no secret. A friend showed them to me.'

'A foreigner?'

'Yes.' I hesitated, debating whether to be more specific, and decided against it. But I also decided that I had better come forward with as much information as I safely could, given the shape this interview was talking. 'He asked me more or less what you've just asked me. In fact he went further and asked me if I'd written them.'

'You? I thought he was your friend?' And the *Inspecteur* allowed himself a small smile of incredulous amusement.

'He didn't know me very well then. I'd only been here a few weeks. Besides, I think he was only asking for the record. You know, he didn't really suspect me but just wanted to clear the air. He soon found out that I agreed with him – and with you too, obviously – that they're rather nasty little pieces which aren't worth the paper they're written on.' I paused, wondering if I wasn't laying it on a little too thick. 'Then he asked me if I knew who had.'

'And did you?'

'No, and I still don't.'

'Now why did he ask that, I wonder,' the *Inspecteur* mused. 'The magazine's published in Hong Kong. Do you have friends there?'

'No, not in press circles. But you see, he thought it possible that they might have been written by someone here – or at least with some local help.'

'That's very interesting. May I ask why?'

I began to wonder if I hadn't gone too far. The discussion was subtly changing into an interrogation, even though the *Inspecteur*'s manner remained affable. But I had decided to stick to the truth, as closely as I could without involving Rick, and in any case if the *Inspecteur* had done his homework – and he looked the kind who would – there was little I could teach him. It would do no harm, and might stand me in good stead if their suspicions turned towards me: something which seemed very possible just then. So I summarised for the *Inspecteur* some of the discussions

I'd had with Rick on the subject. When I finished the *Inspecteur* nodded, smiled and said:

'Your friend was very perceptive, I must say. Is he a journalist?'

'Just a friend.' The answer was too bald. 'I'm sorry, *Monsieur l'Inspecteur*, I'd rather leave him out of it. I'm sure you understand.'

'I see. Yes, yes of course. Though if I may be indiscreet, why should he have shown such interest? Was he perhaps worried about it?'

'No, simply curious.' I considered that reply, and decided to give out a little more line. Or swallow a little more bait. 'No, that's not quite true. He wanted to warn me. He thought that there might be enquiries, and that I might be suspected of having had a hand in the articles myself.'

'Why you?' The *Inspecteur* seemed genuinely surprised.

'Because I was new here, and I speak English, and I'm a foreigner.'

'I see.' The *Inspecteur* pondered this in silence, taking his gaze off my face for a moment. I relaxed my cramped knees. Then his eyes swivelled back to me, and his next questions were sharp and to the point:

'Well then, just for the record...did you write them, Monsieur Roche?'

'No! I told you –'

'Do you know who did?'

'No!'

'Do you suspect anyone?'

'No.'

Another pause. 'But you seem to think it's a foreigner. Why?'

'I don't know precisely...perhaps because some of the journalists here are foreigners, and the Cambodians I know don't seem somehow to be the kind who would.'

'But the foreigners are, is that what you mean?'

'I didn't mean that,' I said hastily. 'Let's say I was just working out various probabilities. In any case, it needn't be a journalist at all – assuming there is local collusion. It could be anyone, provided he's well informed and has means of communicating with Hong Kong,'

'A diplomat then?'

'Surely not!'

'Why not?'

'Because...well, why should a diplomat do that? That's not the sort of activity they go in for, surely. And they're not short of pocket money.'

'You'd be surprised...though I expect you're right. If a diplomat were involved, it's more likely that he'd get someone else to do the actual writing.'

'Put like that, perhaps...' I nodded, non-committally, and remembered the clumsy attempt Kalyakin had made, months earlier, to hire my services. I wondered how much the *Inspecteur* knew of my friendship with Rick, and waited uneasily for the next question.

'You haven't told me why you don't think a Cambodian may be responsible.'

'I didn't say that. I simply meant that I'd be surprised.'

'Why?'

'Because...well, it would seem out of character. Cambodians strike me as too loyal for this sort of thing. Especially those I know in the job.' Or too frightened, I thought. But there was no harm in a little flattery – not that it had any visible effect on the *Inspecteur*.

'I wish I could be as sure of my compatriots as you are, Monsieur Roche,' he said drily, and looked speculatively at me for a moment longer. One point which he had not touched on, if it was a local man, was how he managed to send his notes out of the country. The problem was clear enough – mail censorship worked both ways, out as well as into the country – but I suppose that was scarcely the sort of thing a policeman would admit to a foreigner, and a journalist at that. In any case it wasn't my job to put ideas into his head. I had probably done enough of that already.

As if on cue the *Inspecteur* looked at his watch and stood up, signifying the interview was over. I followed him to the door. He thanked me for my assistance and apologised for taking up so much of my time. But in the corridor he turned to me.

212

'I trust,' he said, 'that if at any time you should have further ideas on the subject you'll keep my interests in mind?'

'I'll certainly do that,' I said. Then a foolish notion seized me – a mild revenge for his inquisition. I smiled wryly. 'But you're not asking me to be your informer, I trust?'

'That's too strong a word, don't you think?'

'Because I couldn't really play that role, you know. Not with my own colleagues.' He nodded thoughtfully, keeping his eyes on me. 'I'm sure you understand,' I went on lamely. 'Of course I would like to help –'

'Yes, quite, quite.' He shook my hand formally. 'But you will of course treat this conversation as confidential.'

'Of course.'

The *Inspecteur* offered me a police car to drive me back to the office, but I declined. It was only a five minute walk, and I needed it after an hour in that gaunt building. My shirt was wet under the armpits. There was no reason, I told myself, why I should feel guilty, and the admission that I had read some of the articles wasn't in itself incriminating. But there'd been something about that interview which made me feel uneasy. And why should he have picked on me to discuss all this – unless he already had suspicions about me? I wondered if he was putting any of my colleagues through the same wringer. Perhaps I could ask Marcellin. Then I remembered the *Inspecteur*'s parting request: better keep quiet about it. Though of course I would have to tell Rick. I owed him that at least – my promise of discretion had been conditional.

Marcellin was out when I returned. I asked Mademoiselle Sovannareth if there had been any calls, but she said no, and gave me a wary look. She knew where I'd been of course. As I went up the stairs I thought from now on I'd better avoid phoning Rick – or Nicole – too often from the office. It was quite possible the *Police Spéciale* had asked her too to be an informer – and whatever she might feel about it, unlike me she was in no position to refuse.

My mind was still full of the interview, and it took me a while to understand, and another to make sure: but at last I was reasonably certain. Papers not quite in their usual position, my

Larousse dictionary not where I had left it. My room had been searched in my absence. Now I understood why the *Inspecteur* had kept me waiting so long, and glanced at his watch before letting me go. For a minute I thought of rushing downstairs and questioning Mademoiselle Sovannareth. But I remembered her expression: she knew, and she wouldn't speak. I leaned against the window-sill and smoked a cigarette to still my nerves. For the first time I felt afraid.

<h1 style="text-align:center">4</h1>

By Saturday I was starting to get rather worried. I still hadn't heard from Nicole, the *Inspecteur*'s interview was weighing more and more on my mind, and I hadn't had chance to speak to Rick.

That wasn't quite true. I had seen Rick, the night before, at a small cocktail party given by one of Rassimov's colleagues from the Soviet Press Bureau, but only briefly and in circumstances which didn't allow for much private conversation. The cocktail was a modest affair, a few press attachés and local journalists with a sprinkling of communist diplomats, thirty guests at most crowded into the chap's living room, and it would hardly rate a mention if the Russians hadn't used it to introduce the recently-arrived East German press attaché – something which they hadn't mentioned in their invitation. That didn't bother me particularly, but it was a calculated embarrassment for Rick and a couple of other western diplomats there, whose governments in those days didn't recognise East Germany. And as if to drive the point home Rassimov had then made a violent speech against – I quote – *the neo-fascist and neo-militarist clique of the Bonn regime*, an amazing little tirade studded with all the clichés of the Cold War. Rick had listened to it in silence, prevented from making a scene by the presence there of several Cambodian officials; but as soon as Rassimov finished he put his glass down and came up to me. 'I'd be grateful if you'd keep my name out of it, when you write this up for your magazine,' he said stiffly, and marched straight out, followed by the French and British press attachés. Rassimov looked after them with an ironic expression, as if he had deliberately engineered the whole scene – which, to give him his due, he probably had.

By contrast the next reception I went to, on Saturday, was a much more ambitious affair. It was a national day for one of the third world countries, one of those diplomatic spectaculars where everybody got invited: the government, the press, local dignitaries, and every other embassy in town. And this included such adversaries of the day – apart from East and West Germans – as North and South Koreans, Russians and Chinese (this was at the height of the Sino-Soviet split), North Vietnamese and Australians, Israelis and Arabs, and no doubt more besides. Luckily diplomats on the whole tend to avoid confrontations, or the place would have been a warzone. Instead it looked more like a slow-motion ballet, as these people gravely circumnavigated each other on the lawn and amidst the shrubbery, only occasionally coming face to face in the crowd: then there would be a brief pause, eyes and hands would stop in mid-movement, before moving on as if nothing had happened. All very foolish no doubt, but preferable to beating each other up in public (though that too has been known to happen).

Six months earlier I would have found this *manège* highly diverting. But I'd seen it all before, and I was too concerned with my own problems to pay much attention to it. I knew Rick would be there, and I ran him to earth in the crowd. He looked anything but festive.

'What's the matter?' I asked him. 'You look as if someone's poured champagne down your pants. Still angry about last night?'

'Don't laugh,' he said sombrely. 'Do you know what I've just heard? On top of everything else that prick Rassimov's going round telling everyone those articles are an American plot to destabilise Sihanouk, with the help of one of the western embassies here and some of its friends.'

'Hey! That's getting close to the bone!'

'The bastard! He's all but named us! Just when Sihanouk's started to put more pressure on too, over that bloody declaration of his. You know the latest on that? He's threatening to pull his ambassadors out of the countries that don't come good.'

'What are you going to do about it?'

'Nothing! What can we do, except stick it out? Of course we'll go round saying it's just a lot of rumour-mongering, but a fat lot of good that'll do!'

'Well,' I said, 'if you think you've got problems, listen to this.' And I told him about the *Inspecteur*'s interview, and the search of my office. He listened gloomily.

'That'll teach you to take me seriously,' he said. 'But at least that search should put you in the clear.' He ruminated darkly. 'You know, there's something I don't like about all this.'

'How do you think I feel!'

'No. It's something else. It's odd – all this happening at the same time. It seems too much of a coincidence.' He gave me a serious look. 'Maybe we should stop seeing each other for a while. I have a feeling we might be being watched a little closely.'

Once again I felt that chill up the spine.

'What if I need to get in touch with you?' I asked.

'Oh, you can always give me a ring at the office, provided you've got a good reason. And we'll see each other on the cocktail circuit. But I think we'd better keep it at that for now. At least until things cool down a bit.' He gave me a cheerless smile. 'Not much fun, I know. Think your nerves can stand it?'

I shrugged, half-angry with myself, unwilling to show how vulnerable and isolated his words made me feel. At least he'd made his feelings plain, I thought unfairly, he's more concerned about his job and his precious position than anything that might happen to me.

'Don't worry about me, I can take care of myself,' I said, and left him to go in search of Nicole. I had seen her arriving a moment earlier with Henri. I found them amidst a group of officials and diplomats, Nicole looking cool and elegant as always in those gatherings, Henri grizzled and distinguished as any ambassador. I stayed out of range, not particularly keen to face Henri just then, until I caught her eye. She came over and we moved away to talk more discreetly. Close up she looked just as tense and tired as I felt.

'I suppose you still haven't talked to him,' I started, trying not to sound reproachful. She shook her head.

'I can't, Philippe. Not now, not yet. It's…Henri's too tired, there's something worrying him at work. It's the wrong moment.'

'It's always the wrong moment, Nicole, and he's been tired for a long time. Do you really think waiting will help? How long will you have to wait anyway? Until you go back to France next June?'

'Please, Philippe. If you were serious –'

'Did you think for one moment I wasn't?'

'I know. But we can wait a little while longer, can't we? Please, Philippe, trust me. And besides,' she added gently, 'Christmas isn't the best time for that sort of revelation.'

I nodded resignedly, and forced a smile. 'Yes. You're right. I'm sorry. It's just that I won't feel really secure until it's happened, you know.' And even then, I thought, as I debated whether to tell her about the interview, and Rick's news. I decided not to. She had enough to worry about.

'Can I see you tonight?' I asked softly.

'No, we've got to go to a dinner. Monday night perhaps. I'll ring you.'

'Okay. I'll try and live until then.' She smiled back, and we stared at each other for a moment. I wanted desperately to hold her in my arms.

Over her shoulder I saw someone bearing down upon us.

'Watch out, we've got company,' I muttered, and we reverted instantly to small talk. It was Kalyakin, dressed like a scarecrow as usual, with his shambling walk and death's head smile. Nicole nodded briefly and left. She didn't like Kalyakin, though to my mind he was less noxious than Rassimov, and that evening I even felt a sneaking sympathy for him. There was something so pathetic about him – that gaunt bony face, his forced bonhomie, and the unhappy myopic eyes behind his goggles, which spoke of failure and invited commiseration. I could never detest him like Rassimov, with his cold clever eyes and the smile that flicked on and off. Kalyakin was human, he suffered, it showed in the sweat on his forehead and the folds of his long face, and there was something wistful in the way he looked after Nicole and murmured: 'What a beautiful woman.' For once I agreed with him.

It was nearly eight, the guests were leaving. I saw Nicole and Henri making their way towards the host. I was about to follow them when Kalyakin caught my arm.

'If you're not doing anything tonight, why don't we go out and have dinner somewhere. Away from this official circus.'

I looked at him, amused in spite of myself. It wasn't often that I heard any of his lot making a simple human statement like that. I thought of my empty flat, where Chi Hai would have set the table by now, and left a cold salad in the fridge before going off to some Chinese cinema; and of Rick's advice too. It might be safer if I showed myself a little more with the opposition, from now on. I might even learn something.

I returned his smile, as cheerfully as I could.

'Good idea,' I said.

Kalyakin chose Chez Martin, which suited me fine. Martin's food was good, and his place rarely crowded. In fact we were his first customers. The only sign of life outside apart from the doorman was a girl sitting in a cyclo in the shadows, waiting for clients. She looked hopefully at us as we walked to the front door, and the cyclo-driver edged his machine forward so that the light from the neon sign fell slanting on her face, giving her an ephemeral beauty. But Kalyakin had no eyes for it.

'Prostitutes!' he exclaimed irritably. 'What a plague they are in this town, always soliciting. Go away, we don't want you!'

'Don't be unkind,' I said. 'She's probably got a family to feed.' Kalyakin snorted.

'It's the French who started all this – with their loose morals. One of the evils of colonialism.'

'It's over ten years since the French left,' I said. 'Surely by now the Cambodians are old enough to know what they want. And don't tell me you don't have any in Russia.'

The girl dropped back in the shadows, relapsing into indifference. She was no doubt accustomed to abuse. I recognised her – she had once worked in one of the bars. Perhaps she found it more profitable to work the streets, or else she didn't have the patience to play the customers along until closing time. On the pavement it was straight from the hip, no hovering, no mock courtship, and with luck she might pick up two or three clients in an evening. Not tonight though. Eight thirty, and not a cat stirring.

Ten thirty. We'd worked our way through several *apéritifs* and a bottle of Algerian wine, black as ink, past the cheese and our first Armagnacs. Kalyakin insisted on paying and I remembered an earlier occasion. I wondered if he was going to renew his offer! But so far there was no sign of it, all he'd talked about in the small dining room at the back of the bar was the Soviet education system, *Trud* and the *Komsomol*. I listened with fading interest, bored by the old-style jargon. Didn't they ever stop? Then Martin came and sat with us, and Kalyakin asked if he had any vodka.

'Where could I get it?' asked Martin wistfully. 'There's no money left in this country, and you lot don't come round very often – not like the Americans, in the old days.' Before Martin could start another round of reminiscences someone came in and he went back to the bar.

'If you could get me some, now,' he called over his shoulder, not very hopefully. Kalyakin swallowed the last of his Armagnac.

'Come on,' he said to me. 'I've got some vodka at home – the real stuff, just received it from my wife. Want to try it?'

'Why not? As long as I can leave my car there. I don't think I'll be able to drive home if I have much more to drink.' I felt flushed from all that drink, and my head was beginning to spin, but I was past caring. Kalyakin himself had only become paler, but he was sweating heavily, despite the air conditioning, his lank hair sticking in strands across his bony skull. Was he ill? Another one who's been here too long, I thought. He'll crack up if he doesn't go home soon.

Kalyakin's flat was small, even by Russian standards: a ground floor *compartiment* in a side street off the Boulevard Monivong, where few Europeans lived. There was a tiny front garden, more concrete than grass, with an empty cage in a corner. Inside the furniture was cheap local white wood, the chairs hard and overstuffed and covered in yellow vinyl. The floor was tiled in large squares of blue and white.

'You could play chess on this,' I said. Kalyakin looked at me hopefully.

'Are you a player? Would you like a game?'

'Certainly not. Aren't you all Grand Masters over there?'

I hopped across the floor like a knight, slid like a bishop, incidentally identifying a smell of sour armpits which took me back to crowded *métros* in Paris. But when Kalyakin went out for glasses and a bottle the smell went out with him, reassuring me that I wasn't the cause of it. Then he came back, with a monkey on his shoulder – a young gibbon which clung to his neck like a hairy spider, with long slender black claws and soft grey fur. It looked apprehensively at me.

'Is that what the cage is for?' I asked, and reached out to caress it, but it shrank away from me and buried its head against his shirt. Kalyakin put the bottle down and stroked it gently.

'I don't keep him there any more. Last week some Chinese boys went past and threw stones at him – see? They hurt one of his paws, poor little beast. *Atrocités chinoises!*' He gave a wry laugh. It wasn't long since Soviet diplomats had been jostled and spat on in Peking, and jeered at on the way to the airport to be evacuated. 'His name's Hanuman,' Kalyakin continued, 'like the Cambodian sacred monkey. It's made him very afraid now, he won't go out of the house at all, even when I hold him, except at night. But he'll start walking about in a minute, when he's used to you. He's very affectionate.' Carefully he picked the animal away from his shirt front and put it on the floor, talking to it like a child. It walked about uncertainly, swaying like a tight-rope walker with its endless arms stretched out for balance, staying prudently out of my reach.

'Now I'm going to teach you how to drink vodka.'

He poured the colourless liquid into balloon glasses, then on top of it and with great care so that the two didn't mix, added an inch of tomato juice. He stuck a thin plastic straw into each glass, right to the bottom.

'I've never seen it prepared like this,' I said.

'The idea is you suck the vodka up gently, working your way up towards the tomato juice. Isn't that what you call a Bloody Mary in English? We ought to have some food with it – dumplings, to act as blotter. But I didn't think to make any, and my cook doesn't know how. The problems of living like a bachelor. My wife could soon prepare some if she were here. Cheers!'

'Cheers! How do you say that in Russian?'

'Na Zdorovya!'

'Na Zdorovya!'

It was cold in the mouth – like ether, I thought, and about as potent. I'd have to beware of having too many with this man. No wonder they went berserk and dashed their glasses against the wall afterwards. How many hours of Cossack dancing could a man do on a pint of the stuff? I looked across at Kalyakin, stretched back in his chair with a faraway look in his eye. There was a silence, then Kalyakin smiled.

'We don't see much of you these days,' he said. 'You ought to come out more often.'

'I've been leading a quiet life lately. I don't have the stamina any more for all those parties and the bars.'

'It's the climate, isn't it,' he said sympathetically. 'It's so trying. But you should come round to one of our evenings at the Cultural Centre. We're showing a film there next week. Plissetskaia. Do you know her? She's one of our best ballerinas.'

'I've already seen it.'

'Have you? That's right, I remember. What did you think of her?'

'Perfect. I could have watched her for hours. Certainly a change from Khmer ballet.'

'Yes. It's alright, and very decorative, but too static for my taste. You should see her on stage. There you've got something. Ah, Philippe, you should come to Russia some time.'

'Maybe I will – if you get me a job with Tass!'

I was beginning to feel drowsy, but I let Kalyakin refill my glass. 'You can't appreciate this until you've had a couple,' he said. I smiled affectionately. The chap must feel lonely for the

Soviet Union, I thought, with his wife away, the children that he'd discussed earlier – Kalyakin wasn't one of those cheerful opportunists, like some of his younger colleagues, who could make the most of capitalist decadence and still retain their ideological purity. For him this place must be very outlandish, with its corruption and its Frenchified manners, though he'd understand better than most the subtle atmosphere of fear and wariness which came from living under the shadow of the Prince. I was aware of his eyes on me, speculative, almost sad.

'You know, I like you Philippe,' Kalyakin said suddenly.

'I like you too, *mon vieux*,' I risked, my voice a little thick. We beamed at each other, all peaceful coexistence across the tiled floor.

'Do you?' he said musingly. 'Then why wouldn't you help me, when I asked you?'

'What? Oh, you're referring to those articles you wanted me to write for you. Good God, don't tell me you're still thinking of that!'

Had it weighed on him all these months, like a rebuff, or was he simply making use of every opportunity, never entirely giving up, at work even when drunk?

'It wouldn't have hurt you to do that for us. You must know how few friends we have here – they're all either pro-American or pro-Chinese.'

'Well, I'm neither of those, but you know I couldn't do that,' I said a little tartly. 'I work for the locals, I can't work for anybody else – you, the French, Australia, or anyone. It wouldn't be right.'

'But you are working for a newspaper in France too.'

'That's not the same thing.' So you know about that, I thought. 'Besides, the Cambodians are aware of it.'

Kalyakin shook his head slowly, unwilling to concede the point. 'I still don't see why you had to take that attitude. We weren't asking for anything very difficult – just your help with a few articles.'

'Look –' I began, but he persisted.

'You're sure you wouldn't like to change your mind? The offer still stands, you know.'

'I'm quite sure, thanks Yuri. Look, it's one o'clock and I've got a heavy day tomorrow –'

'Don't go yet – have another one first. Go on, one for the road. You're a young man, you can take it better than I can.'

'Oh alright, one last one then,' I said gruffly, annoyed and embarrassed. Like a foolish virgin caught in a doorway, who doesn't know where to put her hands. Didn't they ever let up?

Kalyakin poured two more glasses, with a steady hand that said much for his capacity. 'Cheers', he said again, and waited until I was stuck into my drink before he spoke again.

'You know, Philippe, what I'm going to say is rather difficult.'

'Why? What do you want to say?' I stared at him owlishly.

'I like you, that's the trouble.'

'Sure. You've said that already.'

'I really would like you to change your mind and help us.'

'Look!' I exclaimed in exasperation. 'I told you I couldn't. Why do you have to insist? If you like me, then leave it at that, for heaven's sake. I like you too, but I don't want to be made to feel that you've offered me all that vodka simply to ask me for my help. That's not very friendly.'

'Unfortunately it's not a very friendly world,' he said gloomily, his forehead creased as if with painful thoughts. He stared at the floor, while I hastily finished my drink. Then he looked up, and his eyes were sad and unsmiling.

'What would you say if I told you that we have the means to make you work for us?'

'What? What are you saying?'

'I told you it wouldn't be nice. I'm sorry you wouldn't listen earlier, and I have to say this now. But I'm afraid, my dear Philippe, that you haven't been quite as discreet as you thought you were.' He sighed, and I put my glass down. I watched him carefully.

'You see,' he went on, and wagged a thick finger at me. 'We've been watching you. We've known about your little affair with Nicole Marchand for some time now. What would you say if I threatened to tell her husband? He's a gentle chap, I know, a decent man, but I wonder how he'd react. You don't believe me? My dear fellow! We've got all the evidence we need, not only tapes, we've even got photos, films to go with them. Yes, on the houseboat! Now that wasn't very friendly to Henri Marchand, was it! You seem surprised. You can't believe it's happened, after all those weeks of security, of thinking you had it made – you want to go and think it over? By all means do, and talk it over with her too if you want. It won't change a thing. You'll agree in the end. We've got all the proof we need. You'll come to us.'

The odious voice had stopped, like an old scratchy record, but its words echoed through my head. So that's how it comes, I thought, not with a flourish, just an unkempt smelly man making a business proposition over drinks. Take it or leave it. But if you leave it, at your own risk. We've been spying on you for weeks, we've got you on film fucking your friend's wife, complete with sound track. No way you can escape now.

The rest happened very fast. No word of denial, of protest. Kalyakin tried to make me sit down again, but I was beyond that now, to real anger, a welling up of hysteria and disgust from deep inside, a nausea of hatred. The vodka, the dregs of tomato juice ran in rivulets down his face before I realised I'd thrown my glass at him. 'Is that how you get your recruits?' I screamed at him. Coat in hand, at the door a look back, a last view of Kalyakin sitting there, and the liquid on his face could even pass for tears in the dim light, or spittle. 'You filthy Russian cunt! You know what you can do with that fucking monkey of yours!'

Nausea caught me at the gate, and I vomited my disgust over Kalyakin's concrete garden.

5

I saw Nicole the next morning. I rang first, then called at the house, while Henri was out at tennis. We talked in the little sitting room near the foot of the stairs where the servants couldn't hear us. Bluntly I told her what had happened. She became very pale.

'It's horrible,' she said.

'Yes. It's frightening, I know. Those cunning bastards! But it's not as bad as it looks. All they're doing is forcing us to tell Henri now rather than later, that's all. There's nothing they can do then.'

'But how did they find out?'

'God knows. Maybe they saw us in your car one evening, and followed us, or a servant talked...there must be a dozen ways they could have done.'

'But we were so careful, all those months!' she cried.

'Not careful enough, apparently!' I said bitterly. 'Oh God, Nicole, it's not you I blame, please. For all I know it may not be our fault at all. Perhaps they came on it some other way.'

'How? Through Henri?'

'No, through me. I've never told you this, but it's not the first time they've approached me. Six months ago they tried to get me to work for them – well, that's what it looked like then, but they didn't have anything like this to use against me, and I just laughed it off and refused. I thought that would be the end of it. But they must have kept on watching until they got another opportunity. Though why they should have bothered...How do you mean, through Henri?'

'I just said that. He knows several of them...'

'Yes, but he doesn't know, and even if he did he'd scarcely go and tell them. No, it must have been sheer bad luck, they stumbled on to it and decided to make use of it. I was stupid last night. I should have laughed at him, and stayed on to hear what he had to say. That way I might have learnt something. Now we don't even know what proof they have.'

'Does it matter?' said Nicole wearily. 'They know, surely that's enough.' She shuddered. Then she got up and pressed a little bell-push on the wall. 'We both need a drink. A whisky?'

'Yes, a strong one.'

A Vietnamese maid came to the door. She smiled at me. It was the girl who had accompanied the Marchands to Sihanoukville. I wondered how much she knew, or guessed. But it was pointless to raise it. Even if she was the source of the Russians' information, we could never prove it. And there were so many other possibilities. We waited until she brought our drinks. Nicole drank hers with a lot of soda, but I took mine neat. It tasted vile.

'When are you going to talk to Henri?' I asked.

'How long do we have?'

'He said a week, to think it over. Just like an employer discussing a job! But anything can happen now. My reaction was pretty clear.'

'I'm glad of that,' she said quickly. 'I'd hate myself if you had got into their clutches because of me. But that doesn't solve the problem.' There was more colour in her face now, and her voice was stronger. 'Do you really think they'll tell Henri, if you don't cooperate?'

'I don't know. Don't you want to tell him first?'

'Please. Answer my question.'

I stared at her. 'I'm not sure, Nicole. It's a big risk to run.'

'If only we knew what they know! Perhaps they only suspect, do you think? Perhaps it was only a shot in the dark?'

'They wouldn't have gone so far without something pretty firm to work on,' I said. 'Of course they're running a risk too. If I went to the Cambodians and told them…there's a chap I know in the Police.' I thought of *Inspecteur* Than Souk, and our interview. 'But they know I won't do that.'

'But they must realise that if they tell Henri, then there's nothing to stop you from going to the Cambodians.'

'That's true. It doesn't make sense, does it!' I finished my whisky. 'If only there were someone I could talk to. But there's no one is there.'

'Oh God!' she said suddenly, and hid her face in her hands. I walked over to her and put my arms around her. 'What are we going to do?' she said, her voice muffled against my shoulder. I stroked her head. 'You'll have to tell Henri,' I said. 'Before they do.' She stayed very still for a moment, while I held her and kissed her hair. Then she shivered, and gently pushed me away.

'No,' she said, looking at me with an effort. 'No, I'm not going to tell him.'

'What do you mean? Have you changed your mind?'

'Yes.'

I sat down, and stared at her.

'Philippe, this is going to hurt you. I'm sorry, believe me I am. But I've decided to stay with Henri.'

'When did this happen?' I asked. But that was a silly question. 'What made you decide? Was it the children?' She shook her head. 'Yes,' I went on. 'You've known all along, haven't you. You knew all along it wouldn't work.'

'Please, Philippe. Don't be bitter. He's my life, my husband. It's with him I belong. He needs me, much more than you. I have to stay with him.'

'Do you think you'll be happier with him?' I asked heavily. I knew I was saying all the wrong things, but I couldn't think straight, my mind felt stiff and wooden. 'Happier than we would have been?'

'How long do you think we would have lasted? Me, fourteen years older than you. The children. How long before you started to regret it?'

'I wouldn't have done that.' Already I was talking of it as a lost cause, accepting the inevitable.

'You don't know. You can't say.'

'Is that what's frightening you? The uncertainty?'

'The certainty, Philippe, that I'd make your life miserable. And mine. You're young and idealistic –'

'Not so much these days.'

'You think you can change things, people, yourself, just by an act of will, a decision.'

'Do you think you'll change Henri?'

'I know that unhappiness. I know I can live with it. But another sort? I'm not strong enough, Philippe.'

'You knew all along, didn't you.'

'It couldn't have worked.'

'You knew all along that it was just a daydream, an illusion.'

'Don't be bitter, Philippe. Please, please don't be angry.'

'I'm not angry. Maybe I even expected it too, deep down. But it hurts all the same.'

'I know. I'm sorry.'

I don't remember much of the rest of that conversation. I was too numb to think. We held each other one last time, she kissed me, then I left. Henri would be home soon. I went straight home, and drank until I fell asleep.

PART IV

Chapter One

1

There were several new years in Phnom Penh, reflecting its multiracial, multi-coloured character in those last years of the *ancien régime,* before racial hatred drove the Vietnamese out in 1970 and later on the Khmer Rouge reduced the country to the horrors of the killing fields.

First came European New Year, hard on the heels of Christmas in a round of parties, culminating in a ball given by the French Military Mission, to which I wasn't invited.

In late January came Chinese New Year. Based on the lunar calendar, it could fall any time between mid-January and late February. In Cambodia they called it *Tet,* like the Vietnamese: *le Tet vietnamien,* and once upon a time it was held as sacred there as in Vietnam, where friend and foe made a ceasefire of it, like Buddha's birthday. The streets, decked in red and gold streamers, throbbed for days on ends with drums and fire crackers while the dragon dancers snaked their way along the Chinese quarter chasing the moon on a stick, never quite fast enough to gobble it up. When two dragons met there was a long, elaborate combat dance; and in Vietnamese households apricot branches came into bloom, decorative as a new year greeting, fragile as any resolution. In recent years, since the worsening of relations between Phnom Penh and Saigon, Sihanouk had dropped *le Tet vietnamien* from the official calendar and the dragons were smaller, the blossoms stayed indoors. But the Vietnamese and the Chinese still clung to their traditions, powerful enough between them to cripple the country's economy if repressed too hard; and the Vietnamese girls once again found the courage to parade in the streets in their *ao dai,* their long coloured tunics fluttering in the breeze like the wings of dragon flies – at other times they risked arrest for it – while businesses and restaurants closed, embassies depleted of local staff worked at a snail's pace, and in European households servantless matrons sweated and cursed over their stoves, or more wisely took their families to the coast for the duration. The Year of the Horse became the Year of the Goat.

Unlike their neighbours the Khmers followed a solar calendar and their own new year, *Chuol Chnam,* came later still, in mid-April. National holidays this time, three days off for everyone, with full-page advertisements in all the papers wishing the Prince, the Queen Mother and all the Royal Family a year of good fortune, glory and happiness. The Chinese, the foreign firms were the first to send in their copy. But the festivities this time were uniquely Khmer: very religious of course, for the Khmers were devout Buddhists, and there were pagoda feasts and gatherings all over the country; but also very secular. Cambodians like most Asians had a passion for gambling amounting to a disease, which the Prince restrained for most of the year by banning gaming altogether – except for the state lottery, from which the government derived a healthy income, and the casino at Bokor near the coast, which was only open to foreigners (not to mention the illegal gambling dens and private casinos which flourished in the back streets of Phnom Penh, some of them it was said run by members of the Royal Family). The Prince wisely turned a blind eye to these; and once a year he showed his love for his people by lifting the ban altogether for the duration of *Chuol Chnam.*

The result had to be seen to be believed. For three days the town went without sleep. Treasured packs of cards, mats and dice carefully hidden during the long months of prohibition came out in every house; cockfights were held in country villages, and in Phnom Penh every street had its improvised gambling den, a shack or a house taken over at exorbitant rentals by the professionals, with barkers outside to draw in the crowd. All sorts of games were played, many of them strange to a European: packs of 120 cards, or dice with animals instead of numbers, the thirty-six beasts, counting the beans, *fantan* perhaps and in Chinese houses the rattle and click of mah-jong. For those three days even prostitution and smuggling took second place as the country's leading forms of recreation: the brothels stood empty while the whores played away their earnings, while in lonely frontier outposts smugglers sat together with customs officers, too busy exchanging their respective parts of the loot to worry much about anything else. Sin for once was made legal, though not long enough to grow tedious and respectable. It was as if a drought had broken.

Only one incident marred this delirious interlude: when the Prince, seeking perhaps to refurbish his popularity, decided to extend the period of grace by a fourth day. This was greeted as a gesture of extraordinary benevolence, but the instructions unfortunately did not percolate through to one of the police stations in Phnom Penh – presumably the officers responsible were out at the time, to be found instead around the nearest card table. When at the end of the third day the police resumed their official role and bravely tried to close down the gambling houses in their precinct an angry mob, better informed, sacked the police station and burnt it to a shell.

Closer to home my landlord, an otherwise sober man, managed in the course of those four days to gamble away his recently imported BMW: a loss of which he boasted mournfully for the rest of the time I knew him.

Later in the year there were other celebrations still, but by then I had lost interest in them.

2

Somewhere between *Tet* and *Chuol Chnam* I emerged from a period of deep depression, about which the least said the better. It was a dark, bitter time, full of anger and self-pity, during which I drank too much, whored, and tried hard to pretend that nothing much mattered any more, while waiting anxiously for the axe to fall. I wasn't very successful at it, and when it didn't I became even more apprehensive, and spent sleepless nights trying to understand why; but I couldn't make any sense of it, except to tell myself that somehow Nicole had come out of it better than I had. How I managed to do any work during that time I have no recollection. I shunned my friends, turned my back on every Russian I met, and saw almost nothing of the Marchands, except at a distance, from time to time, unavoidably; and then I looked the other way and tried to think of something else.

By what process I came out of it I'm not entirely sure. Surya had something to do with it, for it was about that time that she surfaced again, after a period of silence and invisibility following our return from Sihanoukville. What she thought or guessed about it she never told me. She simply appeared at my door one day, with her brother, on some pretext – I think it was to return a book she had forgotten – I managed not to be too surly, she came again a few days later, without Sarin, and soon her visits became regular once more, as if they'd never stopped. For a while they didn't have much effect. But somehow I stuck through it – pride maybe, or pig-headedness – and gradually I began to recover. Under her influence my bogeys began to fade and look less sinister – even *Inspecteur* Than Souk took on a more benign air when I learnt that he was a cousin on her mother's side – and as we slipped back into our earlier friendship I stopped looking on her as an intruder into my private misery; until one Sunday morning I became aware that the sun was shining, birds sang outside, and if all was not for the best in the world, it was not perhaps as grim as I had been persuading myself. Horowitz played Scarlatti on the record player, and Surya sat reading a book while I tried to sketch her. I wasn't very good at it, but that didn't matter. I could manage to smile, and start thinking again about the future.

3

But there were still battles to be fought, demons to be exorcised. Whether it was that Sunday or another like it I can't remember for certain. Suddenly there were footsteps on the stairs, a knock at the door, and then Nicole stepped into the room, asking unnecessarily 'May I come in?' She stopped as she saw Surya, and instantly apologised.

'I'm sorry – I didn't mean to intrude –'

'It's alright,' I said automatically, getting to my feet. 'Come in. We were just listening to music.' But Surya too had got up, and looked as if preparing to leave, instinctively making room for her rival. Nicole stopped her.

'No – don't go Surya. I'm not staying. I only dropped by to say hello –'

She looked uncharacteristically confused, and genuinely dismayed too that she had disturbed us, and that Surya should so meekly step aside for her.

'Please – I'll call again some other day.'

'I'll come down with you,' I said, making no attempt to keep her. I felt half-angry with myself, and with her, as I escorted her down the stairs. Why had she come back? Hadn't we been through enough? But already I didn't want her to leave, and I guessed there must be a reason for her visit. I looked at her back as we walked down the stairs, but she didn't turn round until we were well outside and she had regained her composure.

'I'm sorry Philippe,' she said again more formally. 'I should have rung first. But I was afraid you mightn't want to see me.'

I didn't take her up on that. She was probably right, but I didn't have the heart to admit it, and I didn't want to lie to her.

'What is it?' I said.

'I wanted to talk to you. I think I need your help.'

'What about, Nicole?'

'I can't explain. It would take too long. Could we meet later?'

'Aren't you afraid of being seen with me?'

She bit her lip, and looked away, then she squared her shoulders and looked back at me. 'I can understand if you don't want to see me, but this is serious. I really need to talk to someone, and you're the only one I can turn to. If you won't help nobody else will.'

I relented. 'Alright then. This evening if you like. But you'd better not come here. Is there somewhere I can pick you up instead?'

'Yes, meet me…meet me near the Cercle Sportif. About eight. I'll be parked in the side street.'

'I'll be there.' She gave me a pale smile, to which I responded briefly. Then she was gone, and I walked heavily back up the stairs to Surya and Scarlatti.

'It's Henri,' she began that night, as I drove her out of town, on the road towards Oudong. I had picked her up at eight as arranged, her car was parked in the shadows near the sports club, no one saw us as she darted across the road into mine. I hesitated at first where to go. The houseboat was out of the question, but there weren't many roads out of Phnom Penh, and fewer still that didn't pass through the city centre, with all its lights. Finally I decided to head in the opposite direction. 'There's something wrong. I don't know what it is, but he's going to pieces.'

'Do you think the Russians have told him?'

'No, it's not that.'

'How do you know?'

'Because I could tell if it was. There'd be something – some change in his manner at least, even if he didn't say anything. But there's been none of that, nothing of the...the suspicion you'd expect, the analytical looks, the feeling that he'd be watching, trying to understand. As far as that's concerned he's remained perfectly normal – no, whatever it is it's something else.'

She fell silent while I picked my way through the outer suburbs, past the Catholic village of Russey Keo, scene of pogroms and massacres a few years later when the Khmers, freed from Sihanouk's restraining hand, turned on the Vietnamese community. Out in the countryside the road became a narrow strip of bitumen following the Tonle Sap north towards the ferry crossing at Prek Kdam, beyond that Oudong and Kompong Chhnang. On the right towards the river the road was lined with hamlets and houses but on the left there was only a void, with a three metre drop to the rice fields below.

'Do you remember one night I told you Henri had a mistress?' Her words came at me suddenly in the dark.

'Yes. I wouldn't believe you at first.'

'Do you remember why?'

I cast my mind back to that episode. It seemed so distant, and yet wasn't so long ago. 'Because it seemed so...out of character somehow,' I said. 'I couldn't imagine him as a woman chaser. Not like me,' I added wryly. 'And also it seemed odd that you could accept it so calmly. But no doubt I was being very naïve.'

'No, you weren't being naïve at all. You were right.'

'What do you mean? Have you found out something?'

'No, I knew all along. You see…oh dear, this isn't as easy as I thought. I'm not sure I should be telling you at all…' She drew in her breath. 'Henri…is more interested in men.'

I almost stopped the car in my astonishment. So that was it! No wonder Nicole had hesitated to tell me, stumbling over her words. Now it was my turn to fall silent, while I digested this revelation. Why was it that I'd never guessed? I went back over my memories of him, looking for signs, any indications, but even with hindsight I couldn't find any. And yet why was it that deep down I wasn't totally surprised?

'It doesn't show, you know,' I said gently. 'Or else I really am very naïve.'

'No. You're right. He doesn't let it show very much.'

'How long have you known this?'

'A long time.' She brooded for a moment. 'Like you, I'd never have guessed,' she went on. 'I only found out by accident, after we'd been married nearly two years – the classic way, when I found a letter from one of his friends. At first I couldn't believe it. It seemed so enormous. I'd heard about homosexuals of course, or bisexuals, but I'd never thought I'd be married to one. But when I finally asked him about it he admitted it readily enough.'

'What did he say?'

'Oh, he explained that that was the way he was, he'd always been like that, he didn't like it very much but he couldn't help it…He said it had taken him a long time to come to terms with it, he'd fought against it at first, when he was younger – he'd had girlfriends before we met – but as he got older he realised that wasn't enough, it wasn't something he could repress, or ignore…I think he was relieved to be able to tell me about it. He told me he hated to lie and keep secrets from me, that was the worst thing about it, what he regretted most, he was very apologetic about that. He said he'd never wanted to hurt me. But he wasn't ashamed of it. He kept insisting it didn't threaten our marriage, it was a separate thing altogether, it wasn't like having mistresses, there was no competition...In the end I believed him.'

It couldn't have been easy, I thought, trying to concentrate on what she was saying, while keeping an eye out for the occasional oxcart or unlit village motorbike. What a shock it must have been. I tried to think of something to say, something helpful that wouldn't sound trite or patronising: though there was little point, she'd already had ample time to come to terms with it.

'You know,' I said, 'I'm not very knowledgeable about this, but from all I've heard I suspect it's not unusual. Do many people know about it?'

'No. Very few. Fouchet, I think, perhaps one or two others. He's very discreet, you know, not like some others – thank God! He's not the type to accost young men in public lavatories – I don't think I could cope with that! In fact I don't think he's had many lovers at all over the years, and some of them seem to have lasted a long time...I wouldn't be surprised if it was more platonic than physical, at times. I suspect with Henri it's more an emotional need than just a physical one. But I'm not sure...'

'Don't you discuss these things with him?'

'No. Not very often. He...he keeps a lot to himself, and I – I respect his privacy. He's told me more than once that these...these attachments don't compete with our marriage, with his feelings for me. And somehow I believe him. I don't feel jealous or threatened by them. Not any more. And I know he's very careful – he doesn't want to embarrass me, or hurt me in any way. He's very considerate, in lots of ways. More than you, Philippe. I know he has a friend, but I don't know who it is, and I don't want to know – not until he decides to tell me.'

'So you didn't follow him.'

'No.'

'Why did you tell me he had a mistress then?'

'Because you were asking too many questions, and I – I wasn't ready to tell you then.'

'But now you are,' I said gently.

'Yes.' She sighed. 'Oh, I know I shouldn't be talking to you like this about him, it's not fair to you, or to him, but I need help, and you're the only person I can talk to. Somehow it doesn't feel quite as if I'm betraying him.' She sniffed, and gave a little laugh. 'Isn't it silly? Because we've been lovers…I know it's over, Philippe, and I don't want to hurt you by dragging it all up again, but I trust you, you're the only person I can trust, and I need your help.'

Nicole had been speaking calmly enough, keeping her explanations undramatic and matter of fact, but there was a note of strain in her voice, an underlying tension not far below the surface, which had become more noticeable as she talked. I thought of all the questions I wanted to ask, the details of their life between them: what was it like when they made love? Did the knowledge of his lovers come between them? What was he like in bed for that matter? But I didn't want to invade his privacy further, I had penetrated far enough into it already…

'Alright then, you'd better tell me what the problem is, Nicole.'

'That's the trouble, Philippe. I don't know.'

'You said something was bothering him.'

'Yes, but that's all I know.'

'Do you think he's being blackmailed?'

'It's possible, though I don't see how. I mean, I know about it, and it's not a crime – I don't see how anyone could blackmail him.'

'Are you sure he's not just going through a rough patch with…his friend?' I said. 'That they might be breaking up?'

'Maybe. But I don't think so either. I don't think it's just that – if that's what it is. Oh, how can I explain? Look, I know him, Philippe. I know his moods, the way he thinks, the way he acts when he's worried about his work, or when he's going through a rough patch, as you call it. I've lived through them with him before. We don't have to say things out loud. I know when he's angry, or disturbed, or annoyed, or when he's got problems…even if he doesn't tell me about them, he lets me know, in his way, and I help him through them. But this time it's different, it's worse…oh, I've seen it building up over a long period, since last year at least, before we went away, before you came even…but I've never seen him so moody before, so bleak! It's as if I can't reach him any more. I've tried to get him to talk, I've done everything I could to make him see, make him feel that I'm there to help him, if only he'll let me, but I can't get through to him, it's as if he's built a wall around him, that I can't get through. He says it's his work, he needs a rest, but I know it's not that – he – oh God!' She stopped, as if to gather breath. 'Do you know,' she went on haltingly, 'the other day he said something I've never heard him say before. He said, 'if anything ever happened to me'…and then he stopped. I think he was embarrassed as much as anything – it sounded so melodramatic. I asked him if he was sick, if he'd been to Fouchet or anything. I thought he might have cancer, and just found out – but he swore it was nothing like that, he was just saying that, because it had entered his mind – and he tried to laugh it off. But I could see there was something very painful about it, there was almost a desperate look about him. Oh God!' she said again, and all of a sudden she put her head in her hands and burst into tears.

I found a place to pull up by the roadside, turned the engine off, and put my arms around her, until she recovered.

'There's something else,' she said. 'I'm pregnant.'

'By me?' I asked in surprise.

'Yes.'

'Are you sure?'

'Of course I'm sure! What do you think? Since that night in Sihanoukville. When you almost raped me on the beach.'

'I did no such thing! And you didn't stop me.'

'No. You're right. I wanted you too.'

'Anyway, how do you know it's me? It's not Henri?'

'Because we – we hardly have sex any more. The last time was in Japan, during our trip – and even then it wasn't very successful.' She gave a wry snort. 'I'm sorry. I shouldn't be telling you that either.'

'Does he know about it?'

'No. I haven't told him.'

I was silent, as I absorbed this news. For some reason it shook me less than her revelations about Henri – mainly I think because it wasn't the first time we'd discussed the possibility that Nicole might get pregnant. But until now I'd never taken the risk seriously. She'd always assured me she had things under control, she knew her rhythms, and we'd always been careful…until that night! And now here I was, faced with the consequences of my impetuousness. I wasn't sure whether to feel terrified or elated. I thought with bitter irony of what Henri would say, once he found out. If he found out.

'So what are you going to do? Are you going to tell him?'

'I'll have to. I can keep quiet about it for another month or so, but after that it'll start to show...'

'You're not thinking of having an abortion then.'

'Is that what you want me to do?'

'No. I'm just asking.'

She shook her head.

'No. I don't want to. I thought about it. I know this is silly. I could easily have one, without Henri knowing. It's no big deal. But...this child, this small thing that's growing inside me – even if it was an accident...we made it together. Out of love. Later on, when we've moved on and you're living your own life somewhere else, this will be all that's left of you. Of us, of our time together. Maybe that sounds very selfish. I know it will hurt Henri terribly. But I want to keep it.'

I felt deeply moved when she said that.

'Thank you,' I said. 'I'm glad you said that.'

'But please don't tell Surya.'

'Listen. I don't know what you're imagining, but there's nothing between Surya and me. She's a lovely girl, and I like her a lot. She's been very good to me. But I'm not in love with her, and we're not having an affair.'

'It's alright. I'm not jealous any longer.'

'But we're not. I'm not lying to you. And even if we were I'd never tell her.'

We sat in silence for a while, digesting all this. Then I turned to her, caressed her face, kissed her forehead.

'Now you'd better tell me what you want me to do about Henri.'

'Follow him. Find out what it is – and then help him.'

———————————

I thought about it hard over the next couple of days. To be honest, I wasn't exactly thrilled by it. Whatever my feelings about Henri – and they were pretty confused just then – the thought of following him about, of spying, for whatever reason, on a man I'd cuckolded, seemed unpleasant, an even deeper intrusion into his life than I had already committed by sleeping with his wife. But I'd promised Nicole I would do what I could, and whatever my scruples I felt I owed it to her. So when she rang me a few days later I was ready. As ready as I'd ever be.

Chapter Two

1

Following someone about, even at night and in a town you know like your own living room, is no job for an amateur. That much I learnt over the next few weeks. It takes patience, luck, and a great deal of determination. It also takes a lot more experience than I had at the time, or indeed at any time since. I prepared for it as best I could, borrowing from my extensive reading of spy thrillers: dark clothes and soft-soled shoes, and nothing in my pockets which might rattle, such as coins or keys. Despite my distaste for the job I couldn't help feeling a thrill of excitement – or apprehension. I even topped up the car with petrol in case he decided to go for a spin in the countryside.

I reasoned that Henri, whatever his plans for the evening, would probably want to call at his office first, if only to give some plausibility to his story; and so I decided to go straight there, rather than start following him from his house. I arrived ten minutes early, chose a dark spot some distance away, and settled down to wait. Not long afterwards headlights appeared, and turned in at the gate. I recognised the Citroen, and a minute or two later, saw one of the upstairs windows light up.

It was a long and uncomfortable vigil, screwed up in the front seat with my head down below window level. I didn't dare smoke, for fear that the glow would give me away. Then I had a thought: there was probably a back entrance to the building. What was to stop Henri, if he wanted to cover his tracks, from leaving his car there and his light on and simply slipping out the back? But short of circling round the block there wasn't much I could do about it. I decided to stay put instead, and trust to that upstairs light; and there I sat stolidly through the next two hours, yearning for a cigarette and staring at that window until my eyes smarted and all feeling of suspense had well and truly disappeared. If I hadn't made a promise to Nicole I would have packed it in there and then. The longer I stayed the more convinced I was that it was all perfectly straightforward, and that when Henri had finished working he would go straight home and sleep the sleep of the just.

Which is precisely what he did, that night and the next time round a few days later. At about ten thirty the light went out, a moment later his car emerged from the grounds and he drove sedately home, not even stopping on the way for a drink at one of the bars. I followed him as far as his front gate, careful to keep my distance without letting him get too far away from me – though I found that easier than I had expected; and then I drove home myself, oddly disappointed.

I reported all this dutifully to Nicole, who listened non-committally. By that stage I was ready to call it off: but she insisted that I should try one more time. She wanted to be absolutely sure. I couldn't see how that would make any difference, but I agreed. Three days later she called me again.

'I think it must be tonight,' she said in a strained voice. 'He's been pacing up and down all afternoon like a caged bear, and he's taking my Fiat. He says the Citroen's giving trouble.'

'Alright,' I sighed. 'I'll be there.'

This time I varied the routine by parking in a different spot, further away and across the street, where I could have a better view without getting a crick in the neck. Just as well. I'd been there half an hour when I saw what looked like the car, moving across an intersection a hundred metres down the street. I stared after it, puzzled, then checked the window. The light was still on. I sat still for a second or two. Then I started the engine and went after it.

I caught up with it 500 metres down the road, held up at the lights on the Boulevard Monivong. This time there was no mistaking it, I recognised the shape of Henri's head against the light. So there had been a back exit after all! And no doubt on this occasion too that he wasn't taking the quickest route home. I let him move off and followed at a safe distance as he headed south towards the Bassac and the Monivong bridge. At one of the large avenues Henri turned left, towards the Independence Monument, and left again at the next corner; and then began a series of turns and zig-zags among the smaller streets which lay between the Boulevard Monivong and the Boulevard Norodom, in a complex, apparently aimless pattern which brought him gradually back towards the centre of town but made it hard for me to follow without getting too close. There weren't many lights in that part of town but not many cars either, and it took all my concentration to stay far enough back without losing him. As a further precaution I dimmed my lights, but that too was risky, for I could easily ram a cruising *cyclo*. Nearer the market there was more traffic, odd lights bobbing up and down, and I moved in closer. But I became uneasy. He varied his speed a lot, and kept turning into side-streets and going back on his tracks. What would I do if he stopped suddenly?

Henri turned another corner, into a dark street where, I remembered, there was hardly ever any traffic. I had a feeling something might happen now. I pulled up short of the corner, got out, and peered as casually as I could up the next street. It looked empty, and for a moment I thought I'd lost him. Then further up a car door opened, I saw his shape against the ceiling light. He got out, shut the door and started to walk back towards me. I scarcely had time to admire the cunning of it, if it was forethought and not simple coincidence. I dived back into my car, crouched down behind the front seat, and waited for him to pass. Fortunately there wasn't a street-light for thirty metres, and he was in a hurry, or he couldn't have missed me. I waited until he'd gone past, counted to five, then came out again, just in time to see his tall shape plunge down towards the Rue Pasteur. I left the car unlocked and went after him, more than ever grateful for my choice of clothes and Phnom Penh's deficient electricity supply. Short of an accident there was no way he could guess I was behind him. I went by hearing as much as by sight, relying on the sound of his footsteps to warn me if he stopped or turned back.

Then I truly lost him. One moment I had him in my sights – he had almost reached the end of the street, I could dimly make out the blob of his shirt up ahead – the next a car was turning into the street and coming for us, headlights blazing. I barely had time to look for cover as its lights swept around the corner. I saw a tree, a parked car, and bent down quickly in its shadow, then edged around as the car went past. I doubt that anyone saw me. But when I stood up again Henri was gone. I ran to the end of the street: no sign of him. Fifty metres away, the tail lights of another car moving off, too far off to be identified.

Gingerly I set out to explore my surroundings. It was a street I knew well, only a few doors up stood one of Phnom Penh's best known brothels, *La Mère Nam*, very discreet and shuttered. I circled round for ten minutes or so, barking my shins in the dark against various obstacles, then went back to my car. Wherever Henri had disappeared to, I couldn't imagine him going into that establishment. I debated whether to wait until he returned for the Fiat, but there seemed little point now. Instead I drove home, feeling dispirited. What could I tell Nicole? I asked myself. That I had failed? That Henri had gone for a walk?

I slept badly that night, my mind full of nasty thoughts, trying hard to make sense of it all. I wasn't very successful. But by morning I had reached a decision. I wasn't going to tell Nicole anything.

Quite why wasn't very clear. Uncertainty no doubt, a desire not to alarm her unduly. After all, what was there to report? And a lingering sense of loyalty to Henri too. Whatever he was up to, it was his business, his life, I had no right to go following him about in the depths of the night. But most of all I needed more information, more clues, before I could work out what to do. Some of my thoughts of the night were just too far-fetched to contemplate.

I decided to do my own investigation.

2

Easier said than done. Up to then I'd had Nicole to help me, to warn me in advance when he was going to the office. Now I would have to do it on my own, I could hardly ask her to keep me informed of his movements, after telling her for the third time in a row there was nothing to report. Already she sounded suspicious – some of my answers had been vague. I didn't even know what time he'd got home.

I decided that the best way to do it was simply to drive past his office, of an evening, when my own social life allowed it. That wasn't every night, obviously. Though I wasn't as gregarious as I'd once been I still went out from time to time. I had stopped playing the hermit. Nevertheless there were enough free nights in the course of a week to make it worthwhile, over a period of time. And I really couldn't think of any other way.

In this manner I spent the better part of a month, alternating between my work, Surya, the ordinary, visible part of my life, and my new, solitary night-time pursuit: between daylight and darkness, it seemed at times, normality and secrecy. At about eight or eight thirty I would drive past his office, check if his light was on, and as I went past cast a look inside the grounds to see if his car was there – or Nicole's. I'd noticed there was one spot along the road behind the building where I could get a good view through the gate. If he wasn't there I sometimes came back half an hour or an hour later, on the off-chance that he might have been delayed. But as I gained experience I learnt that there wasn't much point in trying any later than eight-thirty. He was a punctual man.

Then if I saw his light, I went and parked further up the street, as discreetly as I could. With further reconnaissance I had found one or two other places from which I could observe the building and the intersection with less risk of being seen. Then, depending on what happened, I either tried to follow him, or sat quietly in the dark for one or two hours, waiting for him to go home. If nothing else I learnt the art of waiting.

By the end of that month I wasn't much further ahead. I had only managed to follow Henri twice more, with the same result each time. Only the route changed. Once he led me into the Chinese part of town, between the Boulevard Monivong and the Sports Stadium, before he got out and started walking. The second time we went all the way south to Takhmau and back to the centre of town. But on both occasions, though I was getting better at surveillance, I lost him in the crowd or the darkness. I cursed my luck, or my incompetence, and wondered how I would ever get to the bottom of it: because it was now increasingly clear that he wasn't going to the same place each time, and also that he was taking great precautions to cover his tracks.

On a third occasion I thought for a moment that I was being followed myself. I was behind Henri, careful to keep my distance, when I noticed another car in my rear vision mirror. We hadn't been going long, and I wouldn't have paid much attention if the car had had its headlights on, and had been going at normal speed.

But I caught sight of it two or three times, and each time it seemed to me that, when we turned a corner, the car behind raced up, and then slowed down just before it too reached the corner, as if to peer round first before turning. This was so much like what I was doing that I became suspicious. When it happened yet again I became frightened. I restrained my first impulse, which was to put my foot down and head for home, and told myself not to be stupid. If I was being followed, the best thing to do was to behave as naturally as possible. Find a plausible reason for what I was doing.

As it happened we weren't far from the railway station, another area I knew well. I thought hard, and at the next corner, instead of following Henri, who kept going straight, I turned right, and right again, and drove slowly on until my headlights picked up what I wanted: a cruising *cyclo* with a female passenger. I overtook it and stopped just beyond. The *cyclo* pulled up in a squeal of brakes, I opened the passenger door and the girl flitted over and sat down beside me, her feet hardly touching the roadway in her hurry. I couldn't see the other car but managed to get snarled up with the *cyclo*, and make a slow departure: anyone watching, I thought, couldn't fail to see what I was doing. Then I drove straight home.

For good measure I kept the girl until late that night, and made sure she earned her money. You couldn't be too careful. But my heart wasn't really in it. A lot had changed since the early days.

3

I suppose at this point the wisest thing would have been to go and talk with someone else. Someone I could trust, like Rick or Fouchet. It might not have made much difference to the final outcome, but some of the intermediate stages at least might have been avoided. But apart from the fact that I didn't have many friends of Rick's sort, whose discretion I could rely on, it wasn't exactly clear what I was getting myself into. Whatever my suspicions might be – and they ranged far and wide, from the trivial to the absurd – I had nothing to base them on except two things: first, Nicole's concern, based on her own understanding of her husband's character; and second, the fact that he was prone to wander about the town at night – taking some care admittedly to cover his tracks – when he'd told her he was at work. For all I knew, all he wanted was to take the cool night air, by himself, to get away from things for a while. God knows, that could happen to anyone in Phnom Penh! Perhaps he did have assignations from time to time, or just liked to pick up young boys – perhaps he really was in trouble of some sort, though I couldn't imagine what – but perhaps, equally simply, he just wanted to be alone. And tempted as I might be to read deeper mysteries into his behaviour, I didn't have anything to back them up.

The second reason of course why I didn't want to consult Rick, let alone anyone else, was that it would have meant revealing everything to him, including my affair with Nicole. And that I wasn't prepared to do, at any price.

That left me with little alternative, except to keep on trying – or quit. I must admit I was tempted to do just that. But my curiosity was too strong. And whatever I had said to Nicole, I felt I owed it to her as well to find out what he was up to. If only I could follow him once to his destination – even if that meant walking the whole night through, while he collected his thoughts along the river or wherever his fancy took him, before seeing him invisibly home like some apprentice guardian angel – then at least I would have something to tell her. Something to reassure her with or truly frighten her. In the meantime I had gone too far to back out. I had to go on.

4

In the midst of it all there remained Surya: innocent, unknowing, virtually the sole ray of sunlight in what had become a dark and solitary pursuit. She came often to see me, in the late afternoon. And now that a precedent had been set we made frequent use too of my week-ends, going for long drives in the countryside: to Kirirom, or Neak Luong, or to little out-of-the-way places like the Monkey Pagoda near Kompong Kanthuot, named after the troupe of monkeys that lived in its grounds in peaceful cohabitation with the monks. Old stone lions guarding a crumbling staircase, a pond covered with waterlilies like stepping stones. It was while strolling through the grounds that we came upon two monkeys vigorously copulating by the side of the path. I tried delicately to draw her attention away but she, true child of the east, didn't blink an eye as we walked past.

Quite why we ourselves didn't follow their shameless example I'm not entirely sure. It wasn't shame, or lack of wanting to. I hadn't lied to Nicole when I'd said I wasn't in love with Surya, and I was careful to keep our friendship at that level. But we were young, and warm-blooded, and often only the thinness of a shirt stood between us and temptation. But somehow it didn't seem right. It was only a question of weeks before she left for France, there couldn't be any permanence in the relationship, and I didn't see myself in the role of a casual seducer. But I often thought of how much I would miss her when she'd gone. Life would seem very empty without her, Phnom Penh would lose a lot of its colour.

Then, finally, I had a break – if you can call it that.

Chapter Three

1

It was a Monday, and I had a feeling, based on the pattern of the past few weeks, that Henri might be out and about again. I had managed to keep the evening free and about a quarter to eight I took up a position at one of my observation posts near Henri's office. Despite my last experience I was determined to have another crack at him. Shortly afterwards Henri himself arrived, as I had predicted, and half an hour later he set off again. He was driving the Citroen this time, and he turned the light off before leaving.

I expected another round of hares and hounds through the back streets of Phnom Penh but this time Henri wasted no time in preliminaries. He headed almost at once for the waterfront and then turned left and made off at a sharp pace along the Quai Sisowath, following the line of the river up through Russey Keo and the Catholic village. Before long we were out of the suburbs and heading north towards Prek Kdam, along the road which I had taken nearly six weeks earlier with Nicole.

Once out in the countryside Henri put on another burst of speed and I dropped back a little. By daylight the road was safe enough, but at night and at high speed it was downright dangerous. As the only road north out of Phnom Penh it carried all the traffic to Kompong Cham and Siemreap, and its surface was badly rutted by the overloaded buses and rice-trucks which used it constantly. Henri seemed determined to drive as fast as he could but he had the advantage of a heavier car and I was hard put to keep up with his tail lights, a hundred yards ahead. With my own foot flat to the floor the small car groaned and wheezed under the strain, occasionally hitting a pothole with a sickening crunch or swaying too close to the edge of the road, and several times I felt the hairs prickle on the back of my neck. One mistake and I would be in no shape to follow anyone for a long time. But I was equally determined not to lose him this time. Now and then I took my eyes off the road to check the rear vision mirror. But there were no lights behind me, and anyone trying to keep up in the dark would soon go over the edge. We passed huts, dirt tracks, old buildings, rice mills and brick kilns briefly lit up by our headlights, and went roaring over a hump-backed bridge with an old watch tower. For the hundredth time I wondered where Henri could be headed at such speed, so far out of his way. I had the feeling that this night I was on the verge of learning something at last – perhaps even the truth about him.

We were nearing Prek Kdam, I could see the lights of the small settlement at the ferry crossing over the Tonle Sap. Briefly I wondered what to do if Henri decided to cross the river: try to sneak on the same ferry as him, and hope he didn't see me? If I waited for the next one I would lose half an hour, and might as well turn back for all the chance I'd have of catching up again. I moved up closer.

My indecision didn't last long. Henri stayed on the main road, the ferry turn-off dropped back to our right, and we were heading for Kompong Chhnang. Somewhere to our left lay Oudong, site of an earlier capital, the last before Phnom Penh, now no more than tumbledown ruins in the dark. We passed the turn off, Henri still holding his lead. Then I braked hard: fifty metres ahead, Henri's car had slowed down, was turning left along a dirt road. I recognised where we were: this was the old road, built in the eighteen eighties, linking Oudong with the coast. Twenty kilometres of rough track before it joined the highway to Sihanoukville.

This time I switched off the headlights. From here on, we would have to drive at a more reasonable speed, and Henri would quickly notice if anyone was following him. I waited a minute or two, then followed him. There were no further turn-offs here, he would have to stay on the track until we hit the highway. I could trust to the pale light of the stars to avoid running off the track or into the back of his car.

There was a small village near the turn-off. I drove through it slowly with my parking lights on, then, once I was clear of habitations, turned these off too. There was just enough light to make out the pale ribbon of earth ahead of me. Two little red spots ahead, jigging up and down: Henri.

For the next ten minutes I drove at the same pace, concentrating on the road. While a slip here would not prove fatal, I had come too far to be put off by a meeting with a palm-tree. Up ahead, the two red spots glowed brighter for a moment, then disappeared. Now what! Had Henri stopped, or gone round a bend? I tried to remember the configuration of the road, but it was months since I'd last taken it, all I could remember was that it ran generally in a southerly direction. I drove on for a hundred metres. Then, alarmed at the possibility of running into him, I stopped by the side of the road. I switched off the engine, got out, took care not to slam the door, and proceeded cautiously on foot.

Just as well. I'd gone on for perhaps another hundred metres when I heard voices up ahead. I tried to make out how far they were, but all I could hear was a vague mumble. Slowly I walked on, bending low, although this was hardly necessary. I could have stepped within a metre of someone without being seen, the trick was not to be heard. The voices gradually grew louder, and then I paused. There had been a gleam, instantly lost – I shifted a little until I caught it again: yes, unmistakably, the gleam of a car fender. I crept slowly ahead, placing my feet soundlessly on the soft ground, my legs aching with the strain. Another ten metres, and I stopped. There was the vague shadow of bushes on the right. I inched over to them, went around them and lay down on my belly. Then I focussed all my attention on listening.

There were, as far as I could tell, three men, one of whom was Henri. They were still too far away to make out any words, but I could hear his voice: its low, growling tones carried clearly to me. There was not a breath of air. The other two voices puzzled me: there was something familiar about them, but I couldn't place then. They weren't French, however, to judge by the intonation, nor Cambodian. I tried to work out how the two men had got there: no other car had passed us since leaving the tarred road. Had they come there ahead, and waited for Henri to arrive? That meant another car, and that was a worrying thought: what if it faced the way we had come? Once they got moving it would only take them a minute to come to mine along the track. I was debating whether to turn back and start reversing all the way to the tarred road – an impossible task in the dark, and bound to alert them – when the voices were raised in what sounded like an argument. And this time I clearly heard the words.

'*C'est absolument impossible!*' Henri's voice, angry and defiant.

'*Mais il le faut!* (And I stiffened: there was no doubt now about the ownership of that voice.)

'But I can't,' Henri went on. 'Do you realise what you're asking?'

'You must,' the voice went on, firm and even. 'I know it's unpleasant, but we have no choice. And probably not much time either. Let's hope we haven't left it too late.' There was a mumble, which I didn't catch. I held my breath. My heart was beating hard, I felt as if it must be reverberating through the night. Once again the voices were raised. 'It's your neck! And we can't risk that. Besides, everything's set. It's just a question of opportunity.'

Silence, until I thought that the men had gone away on foot. Then, briefly, Henri again.

'Alright. I'll do what you want.'

'Good. Now come along, I'll take you as far as the highway. George can follow in your car. We still have many things to discuss.'

The creak of a car door opening. I quickly got up, went as fast as I dared back along the track to where I had left my car. I paused, decided it would be safer to wait in the shadows nearby until the others had gone. It would not do to be caught inside with no means of escape. I waited a moment, heard engines start up ahead, saw the glow of headlights, facing away: one car, moving off down the track. I waited again: it hadn't sounded like Henri's car. One minute, two minutes: then the second car, Henri's this time, also heading away. I breathed more easily. Presumably they didn't want the two cars to be too close together. I waited a little longer, until all lights had faded on the horizon. Then, slowly, I got into my car, and started off again. No need to hurry now, or follow anyone. I knew all I needed to know. My shirt was sticking to my back, but I felt cold.

This time there was no doubt about it. I had to do something, and probably fast. My first impulse as I drove back to Phnom Penh was to go at once to see Rick. Only he, with his job and his background, would know what to do. But I soon rejected the idea. I had once promised Nicole I would never do anything to harm Henri, or her, and this could only have the opposite effect, with disastrous consequences for them both. The more I thought about it, the more I knew I had to tell Nicole first, before anything else. She would be devastated by it, she might even hate me for it. But I saw no alternative, if I was to keep my promise, if I was to help her as well as him.

It was too late to ring her when I got back to Phnom Penh. In any case Henri would have got home ahead of me. And as luck would have it I couldn't contact her for the whole of the next day. We were very busy at work, I had to wait until lunch time before I could ring her from home, only to be told that she was out and wouldn't be back until late. When I tried again later I got the same answer. I decided to wait until evening.

That night I had a reception to go to, another diplomatic spectacular – my last in Phnom Penh, though I wasn't to know it then. I felt as much enthusiasm for it as for a funeral, but I thought Nicole might be there, and forced myself to go. Henri was there, together with Rick, Marcellin, almost all the diplomatic corps and half the government, performing their usual ballet on the lawn and amidst the shrubbery, but there was no sign of her. I searched for her in the crowd, trying to read some meaning into her absence. Was it because of her pregnancy? In my obsessive hunt for Henri I had almost forgotten about it, but she must be approaching the time when it would start to show. That made me feel guilty. Maybe she was right to have chosen to stay with Henri. How could I hope to look after her, when I was so self-absorbed? Henri himself I had no wish to speak to. What would that achieve? It was weeks since I'd seen him face to face, and I was shocked at his appearance. His face looked ravaged, he seemed to have difficulty even in speaking. At one stage our eyes met, and I thought for a second he meant to come and talk to me. But someone else intervened, he moved away. A moment later I saw him leave.

I left myself soon after, thoroughly depressed, unwilling to go back to my empty flat. Chi Hai had gone out for the evening, the place would be like a tomb. But the range of Phnom Penh's bachelor distractions was even less appealing. I drove round aimlessly for an hour or so, before going home.

Chi Hai was still out, but there was a note under the door, addressed to me. It was a laconic message, written apparently in haste and in eyebrow pencil on a sheet torn from a small notepad: '*I need to see you urgently. Can you come to the old place tonight? I'll wait as long as I can.*' It was unsigned, but I didn't need to be told who it came from. What was it that couldn't wait until the next day? Had she come upon something too? Wearily I set out again.

I had second thoughts, on my way to the houseboat. What if the message was a hoax, to draw me into a trap? There was nothing to prove it was genuine, anyone could fake a scribble, and the houseboat had been known to 'the enemy', as I called them, for months. But I was halfway there when I thought of it, and I felt too tired to change course now. I looked in the rear-vision mirror, saw nothing suspicious, told myself to stop being paranoid.

All the same I took the precaution when I got there of driving past first, to see if her car was there. I couldn't see it at first, and went on for some distance before turning back. I spotted it then, a pale blur near the gate, hidden behind a low tree. I parked further along and walked back to check the number, then went up to the gate and set off down the track.

Nothing had changed since visits of this sort were part of my everyday life. The warehouse wall, the vegetable garden, even the barking dog were still there. I walked slowly, for the path was dark, and paused at the top of the bank. The houseboat seemed much lower in the water than I remembered it. Then I remembered too that this was the dry season, the river was at its lowest level. And new steps had been cut into the earth, which made the descent easier.

At the edge of the water I paused again, and listened. All I heard were the normal sounds of the river against the poles and the drums, harmless eddies and gurgles, muted now with the slower current. I stepped across the gangplank.

Inside everything was as it should be. The creaking door, the soft glow of the hurricane lamp at the end of the corridor, the old reassuring smells of rotting wood and stale petrol fumes. I heard a movement from the bedroom, and called softly. 'Nicole? It's me, Philippe.' I turned the corner. The cane table and chairs were already out on the veranda, but I couldn't see anyone. I called again. 'Nicole? Are you there?' Still no answer. Suddenly unnerved, I started to back away.

Too late. The bedroom door opened, and Henri walked out in the veranda.

'Don't go, Philippe,' he said. 'I want to talk to you.' Then, as I looked anxiously around, expecting others, he raised his hand.

'Don't worry. I'm quite alone.'

'Where's Nicole?'

'She's at home.'

'She didn't write the note then.'

'No. I did.'

'I see,' I said. Clearly there was no point in further dissembling. For a moment we stood staring at each other. His face was grim, and there was a dark brooding look in his eyes, but he no longer looked so haggard. There was even an air of self-assurance about him, or of firmness. Perhaps it was simply the bleak satisfaction of seeing a gamble pay off.

Henri came away from the door, and I noticed the glasses and whisky bottle in his other hand. He sat down, poured himself a drink, and looked at me.

'Care to join me?'

I shook my head, and wondered how many he'd had. The bottle was half full. After a while I moved across and took the other chair. I took out my cigarettes, lit one, then sat watching the smoke, and waited for him to speak.

We must have sat like this for several minutes without speaking, like children in a game, to see who could last longest before breaking the silence. Occasionally I glanced at him, but his face was impenetrable, and his eyes fixed on me made me uncomfortable. It was one thing to sit safely at home preparing for the day when we finally came face to face over the truth, and another to be there. Strangely enough, my new knowledge of Henri was no help to me. All I could feel was that dismal sense of being caught out. My own guilt stood out far greater in my mind than his.

The silence had grown intolerable. I cleared my throat, and squared myself to face him.

'Are you waiting for someone?' I asked.

'No. I told you I'm alone. And unarmed too, if that's what you're thinking.' I couldn't help smiling. It was so unlike the old Henri I knew to be carrying a gun or a knife in his pocket. But he misunderstood my smile and flushed angrily.

'Don't laugh,' he snapped. 'I do have a pistol at home. The only reason I didn't bring it was the thought that I'd probably use it. So let's start, shall we? I wrote that note. I know how I phrased it. In case you're still in doubt, I know you've been Nicole's lover, and perhaps still are. I haven't known very long, but that's usually the way, isn't it? The cuckold's always the last to see the horns on his head. And until tonight, until you came in a moment ago, I kept hoping it wasn't true. Which is why I went to this childish rigmarole, instead of asking you straight out. Now I'm not going to rant and rave like the traditional wronged husband – even though I'm doubly hurt that it was you –'

'Would you have preferred someone else? Another of Nicole's admirers, all muscles and tan?'

'In a way, yes,' he retorted. 'Not someone I considered a friend.'

That made me angry. He was right, of course. It didn't lessen my share of...of betrayal in any way. But to talk of betrayal, Henri! But I kept quiet. He was entitled to his bitterness, and I owed him pity, not anger. Instead I asked:

'Have you talked about this with Nicole?'

For the first time he dropped his gaze – only a second, enough to show that he wasn't as cool and tough about it inside as he pretended. It also told me she hadn't told him yet of her pregnancy. That made it a little easier -- just.

'No. I wanted to see you first.'

I nodded. I wanted to ask when he'd learnt, who had told him, but that could wait. In any case it was pretty obvious, and also why.

'I take it you don't deny it,' he went on.

'No,' I said. 'Except that I'm no longer Nicole's lover. We did have an affair, but that was last year. It's been over for months. She broke –'

He gave me a curious look. 'Go on,' he snapped.

'She broke it off, more than three months ago. Before Christmas. I won't go into the circumstances just now, she can tell you herself when you decide to discuss it with her. What matters is that she was the one who broke it off, and the reason she did was that she found that she loved you, more than me. I think for her it was more a kind of...compensation than anything else, though perhaps she didn't see it quite that way. I wasn't really in love with her myself when it started. But by the end I was, and I'm the one who got hurt most over it. That's all. We met here, as you know, on nights when you stayed late at work or went out by yourself. We didn't dare use my flat. She was afraid we'd be discovered, and she didn't want to hurt you. She was going through a pretty bleak time when it started, for which I think you're at least partly responsible. Now if you want any more details you'd better ask her. I've told you my end of it.'

I hadn't told him the whole truth. There was obviously more to it. But I didn't feel like raking over all those memories now, and I didn't see why, in the version I gave him, Nicole shouldn't appear as loyal as the circumstances made possible. She was the one who would have to live with Henri from now on, not me.

He was looking at me with an odd expression, part disbelief, part something else which I couldn't understand. I challenged him.

'You don't believe me?'

'Oh, you make it all sound very plausible,' he said. 'Though it doesn't explain everything. When did it start, by the way?'

I hesitated. 'At Siemreap. Or rather coming back from it.'

'I see. That explains why you didn't come round so often afterwards. Your conscience get the better of you?'

'Something of the sort,' I nodded, and he smiled thinly.

'What about Sihanoukville? When you were down there with Surya.'

'That was just before the end. We'd been going through a bad patch. Surya got caught in the middle.'

I didn't intend to tell him about that. That was my business, and had nothing to do with him.

'And?'

'That's it. A week later it was all over.'

'Are you sure?'

'Of course I'm sure! Why should I lie to you? I'm not trying to protect Nicole, or myself. It's over. It was a mistake, maybe, but it's the sort of mistake people make all the time. Your wife had an affair with a younger man, and found that she preferred her husband after all. End of story. Too bad for the young man.'

'Too bad for the husband too, at least about that particular young man.'

'What do you mean?'

'Oh come on, Philippe! You make it sound so simple,' he said drily. 'So simple that all I have to do now is go home and live happily ever after, knowing that my wife preferred me after all.' Henri pushed his chair back and stood up. He paced up to the end of the veranda, stood for a moment staring at the canvas awning, then turned and came back. He leaned against the wall with his hands behind his back, facing me.

'Now why don't you stop pretending and tell me what really happened.'

'But I am telling you what happened!'

'You haven't told me why you've been following me.'

'That's another thing. Nicole asked me to. She was worried about you.'

'What? Don't take me for a fool!'

'But it's the truth!'

'Like hell it is! About Nicole, yes, I'm prepared to believe you. At least in part. And maybe I did drive her to it. But you, Philippe? Aren't you carrying your act a bit far?'

'What are you talking about?' I cried. 'I've told you what happened. If you don't believe me ask her! If you must know we broke up because someone tried to blackmail me, and when I asked her to leave you and live with me she decided to stay with you. Go on, ask her. It's been over for months! And if you're worried about tonight, for God's sake, I had no idea what she wanted to see me about, except that I thought it was about you. So stop torturing yourself, and believe the truth. It's not pretty, but there it is. And you've asked for it, if you don't mind my saying so.'

'God damn you Philippe, shut up!' he shouted. 'I know the truth, and it's not nearly so nice!'

'But I tell you, Nicole –'

'Leave Nicole out of it! It's you I'm talking about.' This was no longer the cool, calm Henri, discussing his wife's infidelity with her ex-lover with such seeming acceptance. His face was flushed, and his hand shook as he pointed it accusingly at me. And I couldn't help thinking how melodramatic we become when we want to express a strong emotion.

'You! You conniving little bastard! I know what you were up to. All that talk of being attracted to an older woman, of falling in love with her! I'm not surprised she broke it off, when she saw how you'd used her.'

'Used her? What on earth are you talking about?'

'You know exactly what I'm talking about! From the beginning you've plotted your way, carefully working out how to get close to me, find out what you needed to know. And you've done it in the sneakiest way possible, by sleeping with my wife, by using this sordid little place, bringing her here and gradually worming out of her what you wanted to find out...I bet she was the one who told you about me! As if you didn't know before. Why, you little hypocrite, you don't have to worry about me, I know I'm finished anyway. But just tell me Philippe, before I'm through, who are you working for.'

'What? But I'm not –'

'Is it the French? Or the Americans? Who is it who's put you on to me? Is it Rick perhaps? Now there's a thought. Rick, you two are thick as thieves. Is he the one? Who couldn't find out the sordid details himself, and got you to do it for him?'

'Did they tell you this?'

'Yes, *they* did! And look how right they were! Yes, they were the ones who told me about you, who gave me the clues. How you used to come here. How you made good use of the nights when I couldn't look after my wife. They'd warned me. And they were right, weren't they.'

I didn't answer. Henri had lost control of himself, he was shaking, sweat stood out on his forehead. What could I say now that would convince him? I waited for him to work out of himself what he had to say – he was speaking to himself more than to me, I had become a spectator, a live audience at last for the things he had never been able to say before to anyone but himself – and then hope that, when he calmed down, I'd find the words to convince him what had really happened.

'I know,' he was saying. 'I know them. They didn't tell me this for my benefit, there's always a reason for what they do – but they did tell me the truth, whatever their reasons.' He sat down suddenly, placed his head between his hands, and looked at me from under his forehead. 'Philippe, Philippe, I liked you,' he muttered. 'Why did it have to be you?'

There was no answer to that. I tried to meet his eyes, but it was too painful, and I looked away again. He'd probably take that as a sign of guilt, an admission that what he's said was correct. That I was the treacherous shit who didn't have the basic humanity to seduce his wife for good earthy reasons, but instead had worked through her to reach at him and destroy him.

'When did they tell you all this?' I asked quietly.

'Does it matter?'

'Maybe. Was it yesterday?'

'Yes. But they'd warned me before.'

'About me?'

'About you, about others. They didn't have to though. I knew it would happen one day. I knew it couldn't last.' He shrugged, looked ashamed. 'It was stupid of me to rant like that. But I was hoping you wouldn't turn up, tonight. I kept hoping they were wrong. Not you, Philippe. I didn't want you to be like them.'

Then I understood. The only explanation, which made it possible for someone like Henri, basically so kind, so thoughtful, and who only wanted to live peaceably with himself and his books, to become the sort of man he now was, bitter, twisted, hating himself.

'Blackmail?'

'Yes.'

'How long?'

'A long time. Years. I've lost count. Before I came here. Not like you. I suppose you do it for – what, Philippe. Patriotism? Idealism? It couldn't just be money, could it, you're too young for that. A taste of adventure?'

I didn't answer, and he looked up after a while. And curiously, there was almost a gleam of sympathy in his eyes, of apology even, for the way he'd broken out. As if he saw that – according to his lights – there was nothing else I could have done in the circumstances. That I was as much an instrument as he was.

'Tell me, Philippe,' he insisted. 'I've so often wondered, what it's like to be on the side of the angels. Does it feel good, do you feel proud of yourself, or do you dislike some of the things you do?'

He poured himself another drink, helped himself to one of my cigarettes – rare for him, he hardly ever smoked – and waited for my answer.

'I don't know, Henri,' I said at last. 'You see, I've told you the truth.'

'Is it? How can I believe you?'

'It doesn't really matter, I suppose. Except for your peace of mind. But you ought to try. Because I'm not working for anyone, you know. Not the French or the Americans or my own government, nor the British or the Chinese or the North Vietnamese or any of the dozen intelligence services that must be operating in this place. Does that surprise you? It does me now, rather. I must be one of about ten people in this country who really prefer to mind their own business! Not that I've done that very well. I wish I had, now. I wish I'd never listened to Nicole, and started to follow you.'

I looked at him, to see what effect my words had on him. But he just stared back, his dark eyes gleaming oddly in the light, and I couldn't even tell whether he was listening.

'I'm not sorry I've been Nicole's lover. You should know that. I'm only sorry it's over. She's such an amazing woman. And she taught me so much: how to think, how to see myself more clearly...She's very brave, you know. And I did love her. I still do. I wouldn't have done it otherwise. Spy on you like that. I didn't like it.'

'Why not?'

'You should understand. We argued about it at first. I didn't want to do it. And she accused me of complicity with you. Of male complicity. Of considering her as a possession I'd taken away from you. She kept telling me that I shouldn't feel guilty towards you. That if I'd become her lover it was because she'd wanted it too, it was her decision, from the start. She wasn't the kind of woman to let herself be seduced against her better judgment.'

He smiled. As if that struck a familiar note.

'When did you have this discussion?'

'About following you? Nearly two months ago. She came to see me. I hadn't seen her for weeks – not since we'd broken off. She asked for my help. She was afraid you might be in trouble, she thought you might need help -'

'Help?' His mouth twisted wryly. 'What sort of trouble, did she say?'

I shook my head. There were some indignities I wanted to spare him.

'She didn't say. She wasn't even really sure. But she was very worried. You were under great strain, and she didn't know why, because you wouldn't talk about it. And you weren't always at work when you said you'd be.'

'How did she know that?' he asked quickly.

'I think she followed you once or twice. She didn't really want to discuss it. She simply said she was very anxious about you, she knew there was something wrong, I was the only person she could turn to. Finally I agreed to help, and do what she wanted.'

'Which was?'

'To follow you, and find out if you needed help.'

Henri looked at me speculatively for a moment, as if still debating whether I was telling him the truth.

'And now? What does she know?' he asked evenly.

'Nothing.'

'Nothing at all?'

'No. You see, I didn't find out until last night.'

'Last night? You were there?'

'Yes. I followed you.'

He sighed, and his shoulders slumped. 'Yes,' he said, as much to himself as to me. 'They thought they heard something, but when they looked they couldn't find anything. You must have been lucky.'

Or unlucky, I thought, depending on how you looked at it.

'How much did you hear?'

'Not everything, but enough. I guess I can fill in the rest.'

'Yes. It's not a pretty story, is it.'

'How did it all start? Do you want to tell me?'

Once more he paused, as if to gather strength this time. He got up, walked to the end of the veranda, then came back and sat down again, finished his glass, and poured himself another. It was his fourth or fifth, I'd lost count, not counting any he might have had before. He had regained his self-control but his speech was getting thick, and I couldn't foresee his next change of mood.

'I had an affair with a young man once,' he began. 'A charming little idyll, with a naïve and fresh youngster, I thought. Oh don't be surprised, Philippe. These things happen, you know. Even in the best marriages. Just because I don't walk with a mincing step and wear eye-shadow...And I was much younger myself of course. But it turned out the young man wasn't so naïve and charming after all. Only long enough to get the evidence they needed. It happened in Prague, which may explain things. I was with a trade delegation. Nicole had stayed in France. We'd only been married a year.'

'And they...'

'They confronted me. They had all the evidence – photos, the young man's alleged confession. They said homosexuality was illegal, and threatened to have me arrested and put on trial. But they gave me an option. Tell them everything I could about the French position on the negotiations. In exchange they would let me go. I accepted.'

He'd seized the cigarette packet, and absent-mindedly twirled bits of the wrapping around his finger, his eyes focused on some spot in the centre of the table. I felt like a confessor – odd, that a man twice my age should be telling me his innermost secrets – but he'd been in need of confession a long time now, and he didn't have many candidates to choose from.

'What happened after that?' I prompted.

'Oh, pretty well what you'd expect. They waited until I got back to Paris, then they re-contacted me. Very discreetly. A friend of Gregor. Gregor had been the young man. They weren't especially nasty about it. But they made it clear that I would have to keep on 'helping them', as they called it. Or else. They even offered me money. I refused. I didn't want anything from them. They said they would keep it for me, for my retirement. No doubt they hoped I'd become venal as well. But I wasn't going to do that.'

He paused again, lost in thought.

'So what are you doing in Cambodia?' I asked. 'Did they send you here?'

'You won't believe this. But I deliberately asked for this posting, and others – Brazzaville first, before we came here – simply because they were less important. I wanted to limit the damage. Even traitors can feel scruples from time to time.'

'Do they know this?'

'Oh yes. I told them. When I realised that although they had me in their power, I could damage them too. And when I learnt that truth, it gave me a certain courage. How to deal with them. They didn't like it, but there wasn't much they could do. I'm still useful to them. They keep asking me questions. I meet them every couple of weeks. In cars usually, the way you found out. Now and then we change the pattern, and meet out in the countryside, or down at the coast. Like that week-end at Sihanoukville. That was all pre-arranged. Oudong was just bad luck. It was only the second time we'd used it. After Sihanoukville they became very worried. I think they thought you were on to me then. And they decided to change the pattern, and meet less often. I must say, that's something I've always loathed, all that skulking about in the dark, and taking precautions, to make sure I wasn't followed.

Sometimes I got so sick of it I deliberately made mistakes. Blundered, missed some of the procedure. Almost as if I hoped I'd get caught. But I didn't really have the courage to go through with it, to go and tell someone. Sometimes I wish I had. It would have simplified things long ago. Maybe I would have too, if it hadn't been for Nicole. But I didn't have the courage. I was terrified of losing her, and the children. She's what's kept me together, all this time. Isn't it ironical? I guess you could call me a pretty reluctant traitor. But a traitor all the same. A bloody traitor. And a failure at that too, like all the rest.'

He was rambling, a note of self-pity had come into his monologue, and I listened with half my mind. That explained a lot of things, I thought. Why he'd gone for a walk so suddenly at Sihanoukville. And why he'd been so keen for us to stay, after Nicole proposed it. I was his alibi, it made it easier for him to get away. I felt my blood rise when I remembered that evening, my walk with Nicole on the beach. Nicole had been right when she heard a noise. The bastards had followed us even there, to make sure we didn't interfere with their meeting with Henri. What else had they witnessed? Our wild coupling on the beach? Was that when they'd first known?

I turned my mind back to him. We hadn't reached the end yet.

'It can't have been easy, living with this secret,' I prompted. 'It must have taken a lot of strength.'

He laughed, so suddenly that his glass shook. 'The worst irony is that she knows about me. A year later she found out – not about this, but about my...my tendencies, I suppose you'd call them. The fact that I prefer men. And I admitted them. And what's more she accepted them!'

'But why didn't you tell her then?'

'It was too late! Don't you see, Philippe? Don't you think I would have told her if I could? But it was too late. It was one thing to have boyfriends on the side, that was hard enough for her to accept, though she did in the end – but to learn that her husband was a traitor? No, that was one thing I could never tell her. Not that –'

'But she could have helped –'

266

'How? Come to gaol with me? Waited ten years until I came out? Or just sweated it out with me for the rest of our lives? No, Philippe. Maybe I was too much of a coward to face the music, to face the look in her eyes when she found out the full truth about me. But I loved her. I loved her too much to put her through that. It wasn't all self-preservation on my part.'

He stared moodily at his glass.

'It's a strange thing, patriotism, you know Philippe. It's a bit like sex, it hits you below the belt, when you least expect it. When it first started I didn't really mind so much. I rationalised it all fairly easily. I told myself that it didn't matter very much, I was only a small cog, what I told them wasn't important, they could find out anyway – it was a small price to pay to save my marriage. And they agreed of course. Anything to keep me happy, to stop me from fretting too much. They've always been good at that.'

He snorted, whether in derision at them or at himself I couldn't tell.

'But later on,' he continued, 'the strange thing is that later on, it didn't seem so insignificant, so easy to rationalise away. As I got older, ironically I found I didn't need male company so much any more. It was as if I'd got over it – I needed it less and less, to the point where I could do without it for long periods. As if somehow being married to Nicole had slowly converted me. It was the other thing that weighed more and more on my mind. And I couldn't talk to Nicole about it, of course! I could feel it eating deeper into me, like some...some cancer, and eating deeper and deeper into our marriage, knowing that Nicole thought it was my homosexuality that kept us apart, that she didn't have any idea of the truth. I wasn't so blind that I couldn't see the effect on her too. Her need for youth, and affection, when I couldn't give her those things in sufficient quantities. Oh, I could see the attractions, the young men circling around, the way they looked at her, and at me, calculating their chances! I could see the flirtations, the playing around, the temptations...But I knew Nicole, I knew how strong she was, and I trusted her. She wasn't the type to console herself with cheap thrills and little affairs – there was too much still between us.' He paused, and looked at me.

'What I didn't reckon, Philippe, was that she'd fall in love. Because that's what she did, isn't it. I see it now. In the end it wasn't thrills, or fun, or a way to fill the gaps in our marriage – she really fell for you. It wasn't just a cheap little fling. She's not the type, and neither it seems are you. Which makes it all doubly tragic. And the irony of it is that we can't even talk to each other about it. She can't tell me about this – her affair with you. She doesn't want me to find out. And I want to leave her with that illusion. I owe her that! And I certainly don't want to talk to her about this! All these bloody secrets...'

His speech was getting blurred, but there were surges of toughness in him still. He turned, with a touch of bravado, a defiance in his stare.

'Ten years I've lasted. Would you believe it, Philippe? Ten bloody years. But it won't be long now, will it! Just a little longer, a few more months maybe, even less. I'll soon be caught.' He stared gloomily at his hands. 'I should have sent Nicole back to France long ago. It wouldn't be so bad, if she weren't here, to have affairs with the likes of you. But I didn't have the courage for that either!' He shrugged. He took his drink, but rammed the glass too hard on the table, and some of it slopped over. He turned to me.

'And now what, Philippe?'

'Now?'

'Aren't you going to turn me in? That's what you have to do with traitors, you know. Like TB carriers. They don't shoot them any more, which is a pity. Only thing to do with a traitor. Shoot him before he infects the rest with his maudlin confessions.'

'You should go home, Henri.'

'You haven't told me what you're going to do. Don't you think I ought to know, so I can prepare myself?'

I sighed, and shook my head. 'Come on, Henri. I'm not going to report you. You know that. I can't tell anyone about this. Maybe I should, maybe I owe it to Nicole to tell her...but I can't. Not now. It's not much help, I know, but it's the best I can do. It's your problem.'

I paused, trying to pull my thoughts together, while he stared at me, as if trying to understand me. I felt drained, emptied, incapable of anything except pity. After what he'd gone through, I owed him that, as well as silence.

'I'm sorry,' I went on. 'I wish there was some way I could help, but I don't see how, other than keep quiet about it…You'll have to take my word for it of course. But you're safe with me.' I shrugged. 'Maybe I'm not so great on morality. I don't like treason any more than you do. But I'm hardly in a position to make a song and dance about it. I'll make up some story for Nicole. I'll tell her I didn't find anything, you just went for drives in the moonlight…' I was seized by a ludicrous thought. 'Maybe you should have brought your gun after all,' I said. 'You could have shot me and no one would be the wiser. Call it a *crime passionnel,* you'd probably get away with just a few years.'

'Don't say that, Philippe. You're too young to die. Think of all the women yet to be seduced in your life.'

He stood up, and walked to the bedroom.

'Now go, Philippe. I appreciate what you're doing, but I really want to be alone right now.'

I picked up my cigarettes, and my tie off the back of my chair, where I had left it earlier in the conversation, and started towards the door. I was exhausted, and had one thought in mind: go home, and sleep forever.

Then I stopped, for a man stood in the entrance. His face was in shadow, but I knew who it was even before I heard his voice.

'Don't go just yet, Philippe,' he said softly, and pushed me gently back. 'We need to talk too.'

He moved forward, his eyes glinting against the light as he surveyed the scene. Two other men loomed over his shoulder. Behind me the canvas awning stretched from the floor to the roof, cutting off any chance of escape. He saw my glance and smiled.

'Sit down, Philippe, and relax.'

Henri had come out, and stood staring in the doorway.

'I thought you were alone!' I said, as cuttingly as I could, but he ignored me and looked at Rassimov.

'What are you doing here?' he cried.

'Just checking that everything's under control.' Rassimov's smile was as urbane as if we were at the reception. 'Making sure you get home safely. But I see everything's gone well.' Satisfied with his effect, he lit a cigarette, while Henri and I kept staring at him – both of us equally astonished.

'Go home, Henri,' he said, and there seemed to be genuine concern in his voice. 'We'll talk about this later. George will escort you to your car.'

'What are you going to do with Philippe?'

'I just want to talk to him. Don't worry. We'll look after him.'

He said something to one of his acolytes, who stepped forward into the light – I recognised him then, I'd seen him at various *bloc* functions, he had the face and the build of a bouncer, but for all his size he moved quickly. He took Henri by the arm, his mate picked up Henri's coat, and together they marched him off the houseboat – leaving me with Rassimov. I wasn't having any of this, and started to get up, but Rassimov pushed me back.

'Not you,' he said, and brought his hand up. And I saw that he had a gun pointed at me, a strange looking weapon with an abnormally thick barrel. I guessed it was a silencer, never having seen one before.

'Just like the movies,' I said sarcastically, to hide my fear.

'Shut up!' he said crisply. 'I can kill you very easily, and no one will hear a thing. So keep quiet and sit still.'

One of the two men had returned. Rassimov said something to him in Russian, and he moved up behind my chair. There was a crashing pain against my head. I had a vague notion of falling, and then nothing.

3

I woke up by slow and painful stages, to find myself tied to my chair, with my hands behind my back and a handkerchief under the ropes to prevent chafe marks. I had a racking headache which centred behind my right ear, there were lights in my eyes, and at first I thought I was in bed with a monstrous hangover and Chi Hai was shaking me awake – but it was Rassimov, shaking me by the shoulder and shining a torch in my face.

'Are you alright?' he asked solicitously. 'I told him he shouldn't have hit you so hard.'

'Oh Christ,' I muttered, and tried to touch my head. That was when I discovered that I couldn't. Rassimov gave an order and George moved into view, the cosh hanging from his fist like a thick comma. Instinctively I flinched. But he put the cosh on the table, where it lay curled like an obscene black slug, and untied my right hand. Gingerly I raised it to my head and explored the area behind my right ear. There was a large lump the size of a pigeon's egg and the skin was so tender I could barely touch it. But when I brought my fingers to my face I couldn't see any blood. Rassimov smiled.

'George is quite good at his job, you know,' he said with self-conscious pride. 'It won't show at all in a couple of days.' He laughed as if he'd made a joke, but I couldn't see it. Waves of pain and nausea came and went like surf on a beach. I tried to look around, but that only made it worse.

'Where's your other friend?' I asked thickly.

'Outside keeping watch.' Rassimov lit a cigarette and passed it to me. I coughed over the first lungful but I began to feel better. He looked at his watch.

'Just after twelve,' he said. 'We'd better not waste any more time.'

'How long was I out for?'

'Just a few minutes.'

I groaned. The pain had receded to the dimensions of a normal headache, and with it too that odd intimacy when he had passed me the cigarette. I squinted up at him. I still couldn't focus properly. He sat opposite with the gun in his lap, as if waiting for me to give him cause to use it. At that moment nothing was further from my thoughts, or what was left of them.

'Can you tell me what this is all about?' I asked. 'What you intend doing with me?'

'Nothing much,' he replied nonchalantly. 'I just want to ask you a few questions.'

'And then?'

'If you answer them nicely, we'll take you home.'

And if I don't? I digested this in silence. I'd believe it when it happened, and wondered if he was going to torture me. Up to that point I'd been too busy fighting my head to think of fear, but the prospect filled me with panic. He'd have to gag me then, because I certainly wouldn't keep quiet. But what was the point of it all?

'What is there to talk about?' I asked.

'I just want to check over some of the things you told Henri earlier. I take it you were speaking the truth?'

'Why do you ask? Did you hear what we were saying?'

'Most of it. As you know we've had some practice.'

As if on cue George reached up to one of the veranda rafters, from which he detached a small black object and a length of wire, which he put in his pocket. It was too far to see clearly, but even in my fuddled state there was no doubt what it was.

'Not a very sophisticated device,' Rassimov explained. 'Only good for a short range, but that was all we needed.'

I closed my eyes, and wondered how I could have been so naïve. I summoned up my courage. 'Don't expect me to answer any of your questions,' I said at last.

'No,' he smiled. 'I didn't really. Pity, because there's a couple of things that interest me in all this.' He paused, and I waited. 'For instance, why you didn't go straight for help when you found out about Henri, or earlier, when you started suspecting him.'

'What makes you think I didn't?'

'Come on, I know what you told Henri.'

'You don't think I'd be so stupid as to come here without taking some precautions, do you?' I said, wondering wretchedly why in fact I had been. 'Such as making sure that if anything happens to me a full account of what I know will reach at least two people.'

Rassimov drew on his cigarette, blew the smoke out slowly, then smiled again at me. 'You can do better than that.'

I shrugged, and tried to look confident. 'Don't you believe me?'

'*You're safe with me, Henri,*' he mimicked. '*You could have shot me and no one would be the wiser.*' He laughed suddenly. 'I liked that bit about the *crime passionnel*,' he said. 'That was very witty.'

Rassimov stopped smiling. He brought his face closer.

'My dear Philippe, you really must stop taking us for idiots now, or amateurs. Even if we do slip up sometimes. That was

272

clever of you last night, to sneak up on us like that. But you can't expect to get away with that kind of luck twice in a row.'

'Are you going to kill me then? My disappearance might be hard to explain, you know – or even more my reappearance somewhere with a bullet in the head. I wouldn't bank on Henri accepting that, for one thing.'

Rassimov looked at me speculatively for a moment. 'Rest assured,' he said at length. 'We have other plans for you. We'll let you walk out of here alive.' He looked at his watch again. 'And now we'd better get going,' he said. 'We haven't got all night.'

'I've got a question, before you go.'

'Yes?'

'I'd like to know whether Henri knew you were out there tonight.'

He shot me an amused glance. 'That bothers you, does it?'

'We used to be friends.'

'Ah yes, I'd forgotten. So friendly with his wife too.' He puffed at his cigarette. 'Fine thing, friendship. And loyalty too. There should be more of it.'

'I'm surprised you know the meaning of the words,' I said, and he laughed.

'My dear Philippe, you mustn't try to insult me, if that's what you're doing.'

'Have you ever had any friends?'

'Oh yes. Back home, I have many. But you're being childish. A relationship such as mine with Henri has nothing to do with friendship. It's simply part of my work, and that's another thing altogether.'

'Henri's a fine man, or used to be, before he fell in with your lot,' I went on. 'Has it entered your head that you've destroyed him?'

'Of course it has,' he retorted sharply. 'Do you think I'm a fool, or totally inhuman?'

'No, you're not a fool. As for being human, that's another matter.'

'Now you're being stupid,' he said again, but calmly, as if trying to dispel some erroneous theory from my mind. 'Can't you see, for me this has nothing to do with being human, any more

273

than…say, building a bridge has for an engineer. It's my job. I'm good at it, which explains why I've lasted so long at it. But I don't let myself get overcome with pity for a man like Henri. Though I agree it's a waste of a fine man in a way. Henri had to be used, or someone like him, and that's all there is to it. If you must know, most of the time I find him rather irritating, with those sudden little rebellions that he hasn't got the courage to push through.'

'I suppose you sneer at people like Henri, don't you, after using them and squeezing them dry. After all, what is he to you, an instrument, a weak man who didn't have the strength to resist you. You shouldn't take it as a personal triumph, you know, Rassimov. It's not you alone who's made Henri what he is. It's your system, and the fact that he's alone. I wonder how you'd cope if you had to face what he's gone through all these years.'

'I'd probably crack up,' he said cheerfully. 'And that's what you don't understand, Philippe. Henri's a man, like any of us, and I can see it as well as you. The difference is that he's trapped, and I'm not. The roles could easily have been reversed, and Henri been using me for the last ten years. It's just a coincidence really, from the human angle. I don't see why you should waste any pity on him, when there are people suffering for much nobler reasons. Over the border for example. Just take a look. Or better still remember what we saw, that dead woman, those children. Didn't they have a right to live?'

'Now who's getting sentimental!' I said. 'Why don't you say what you really mean? You don't care about those people, any more than about Henri. It's the power you enjoy, that's what you like about your job, the power to control other people and make them do what you want. Oh I can believe that it's a cold impersonal game, and that you don't feel any hate for your victims, but spare me your noble sentiments!'

'You've made another mistake, you know,' he said, no longer smiling. 'I do hate some of my victims. You, for example.'

'Me?' I was surprised. 'What on earth for? I've done nothing to you.'

'For what you are. You're everything I despise – a man who thinks of nothing but his pleasure, his conscience – if you had any guts you would have reported Henri long ago, as soon as you

274

suspected him, instead of wallowing in your scruples. That's decadence if I ever saw it. All you're fit for is to bumble through from one little adventure to another, never achieving anything important – you're nothing, and you go on about the virtues of the individual as if that was all that mattered.' He shrugged. 'So you see, I do have feelings. And if at times my job gets a bit tedious, it has compensations. And to have you sitting here in front of me is one of them. You're nothing but a fool, Philippe, and you deserve everything that's happening to you…Ah dear, I'd have thought you had more sense.'

I studied him in silence for a while. It's not pleasant to hear such truths about oneself, even if they're only partly right, and the person saying them is himself far more odious. The fact that I was under duress didn't make them any more palatable. Some of what he said was accurate enough, even if on other points his views and mine were irreconcilable. Not in a million years could I accept that I should have turned Henri in. Finally I said:

'One day, friend, someone will get you. I don't know how, or what shape it will take, but one day you'll make a mistake, and you'll be through. And that day you'll see that your work isn't the only thing that counts. But then it'll be too late. And you'll suffer.'

Rassimov looked at me, and his eyes were just blanks in his face. Then he stood up, nodded to his friend, and came over towards me. I braced myself for the expected blow. But instead of the cosh, the man took my right hand and twisted it behind my back while Rassimov untied my left wrist. Then they both tied them together again behind my back, still careful to leave the handkerchief under the ropes.

Then suddenly Rassimov punched me in the stomach. The shock made me gasp, and before I could recover a hand had shoved a wad of cloth into my mouth and tied it with another piece of cloth around my head.

'We're going now. We'll have to untie your feet, but if you give us any trouble George will hit you again with his cosh and make you feel really sick. The only reason he's not doing it now is to avoid having to carry you.'

They untied my legs and hauled me up. Rassimov held me face to the wall while George put the furniture away and cleared up all trace of use. He took out a torch with a tiny beam, blew out the lamp, put it back in the bedroom and locked all the doors. Then they marched me off the houseboat.

4

The rest was straight from a B-grade movie. Dragged up the bank and along the path to the road, where they held me in the shadows for a moment while they checked the scene, then thrown into the back of a car which wasn't mine, my head striking the doorframe as I went in. I grunted against the gag and almost passed out again with the pain. Rassimov followed me in while George slid behind the wheel. I felt the muzzle of the gun behind my left ear. 'Lie still,' he said softly, 'or this thing could go off.' He pressed my face down against the seat while George started the car. For destinations unknown.

Despite my discomfort I tried to keep track of our movements. The car had been facing south when we started, but George did a U-turn soon after, which meant we were heading back towards town. From the corner of my eye I could just see the back of his head framed against the windscreen, silhouetted from time to time by the lights of oncoming vehicles. The lights became more frequent, I heard the muted sounds of late-night traffic and guessed we were approaching the city centre, probably on the Boulevard Monivong. Later we turned left, the sounds and the lights decreased and became rarer. After a while George accelerated and the car settled into a cruising speed. From the smoothness of the ride I guessed we were on the airport road.

I lost track of time. My headache returned, I had difficulty breathing. I struggled against Rassimov's grip. The muzzle pressed against my skull, but he understood my message. 'I'll take the gag off, if you behave yourself,' he said. I nodded, the gun was removed, the knot at the back of my head unfastened. As the cloth came away from my face I gasped for air. Another few minutes and I would have choked.

More lights, a burst of music and laughter as we passed the *Dancing d'Etat* at Pochentong. Then darkness and silence again.

The car maintained its speed, as if set for a long drive. Rassimov let me sit up and I leaned back against the cushions.

'Where are you taking me?' I asked, my throat tight with fear.

'I just want to show you something. It's alright, not very far.'

'What have you done with my car?'

'Aleksei's driving it. He's just up ahead.'

I fell silent once more. I had no illusion now where they were taking me, or why – nor about my chances of escape. The question was whether I went kicking and screaming or meekly and quietly, proverbial lamb to the slaughter. I can't do that, I thought wearily, I must at least give them a run for their money, if only I get a chance. I closed my eyes, and opened them again.

The inside of the car had grown lighter, I could see the back of George's head, the colour of his hair. Too early for dawn, I thought stupidly. George kept looking in the rear-vision mirror, his eyes shining every time he looked up.

He said something over his shoulder, and Rassimov twisted to stare through the back window.

'What's the matter?' I asked. 'Afraid of being followed?'

He didn't answer, and I turned to look for myself. I caught a glimpse of distant headlights, which disappeared round a bend. Rassimov said something to the driver, and the car slowed down. To let him overtake, I guessed, see who it might be.

The car behind didn't seem to catch up at first, and Rassimov kept looking back with a worried expression.

'Who do you think it might be?' I asked. 'The cavalry? I thought you would have taken care of that.'

'He's coming nearer,' he muttered to himself in French. He turned to me, and with a quick movement grabbed me by the shoulder and jerked me off balance, so that I fell once more across the seat. He lay down over me and jabbed the gun into my ribs.

'Don't make a move, you, or you'll get badly hurt.'

Not that I had much choice, with his weight across my shoulders and my head buried against his leg. I could hardly hear a thing, but my face was turned to one side and out of the corner of one eye I could see a little of the ceiling from under Rassimov's coat-sleeve. I breathed quietly, and tried to relax – though my heart was beating hard inside my chest and my mouth felt dry.

This is my last chance, I thought, my only chance, and felt none of that desperate courage which saves heroes *in extremis* – very much the opposite. But I kept my eyes glued to that patch of ceiling and prayed, prayed desperately that it would work, because there would not be another chance, of that I was certain.

The patch of light on the driver's head grew brighter, larger, slid down his neck and shoulders as the car behind drew nearer. I tried to think who it might be – someone going to the coast after a late-night party? A truck driver? It had to be a car, travelling at that speed – the light dimmed, as the driver dipped his headlights, and my heart beat faster. Should I try it now or later? Was he going to wait forever? Rassimov I guessed must be having the same thoughts, because I felt his leg move slightly to ease some cramp or other, and he whispered into my ear:

'Not a move, little one, not a move.'

Suddenly the headlights shot back up on high beam, and I knew this was the moment. I breathed out, pushed with my shoulders against his stomach and my feet against the door, and thus braced shoved with all my strength, just enough to shift his weight a fraction. For a second I thought he'd hold me; but by some miracle I'd caught him off balance, I'd slipped off the seat and was up again before he could pull me back, and I was hammering with my shoulder against the side window as the other car came abreast. I shouted and screamed, anything, formless sounds and hysterical yells to attract the driver's attention – though that was almost certainly in vain, with the engine roaring and the window closed – and struck viciously back with one heel time and again, squirming like an eel and going berserk with fear and hysteria.

That's probably what saved me from an immediate blow on the back of the head – that and the risk that Rassimov's hand would be seen through the window unequivocally raised. But that was the best I could expect – the headlights were now abreast of me, the car seemed to pause there for a second as if gathering strength to overtake, while our own driver I could feel instinctively braced against the wheel and Rassimov, losing all restraint, pouring out a mixture of French and Russian behind me and trying to drag me down while I struggled like a madman in a straightjacket. The car beside us suddenly shot ahead and I stopped shouting and struggling, for I knew now that it was no use, all I could expect was that smash on the head, which would be the last thing I would ever feel. Rassimov would not be merciful.

It all happened very fast. I'd hardly sunk back against the seat, twisting my head to avoid the worst of the blow, when there was a heaving crash and a tearing sound, shouts and screams – mine probably, I didn't know what I was doing any more – the car lurched tightly to the right, and we were plunging headlong, higgledy piggledy humpty dumpty all over the back seat with my teeth fastened on Rassimov's hand and his scream of pain ringing through my mind, and the driver in front shouting indiscriminately as we lurched sickeningly off the road and down the embankment with a scream of mad tyres and a rending of metal as the two cars parted – a flash of white in front, with a cry of joy I recognised the Fiat, leaping all over the road like a rabbit with a broken leg in the headlights, hurling itself from side to side as we went over and the car rolled over and over and I sank my fangs deeper and deeper – thank God for those solid fillings – through skin and sinew into the bones of Rassimov's left hand, hanging on like a terrier with a rat in its jaws kicking and jerking, and the sweet exhilarating taste of his blood in my mouth, until – bang! There we were immobilised against a palm tree, on our side, with my head against Rassimov's shoulder and my jaws knocked loose at last by the jar – and nothing, not a sound, as we lay there, and I thought, thank Christ I'm still alive, and what do I do next?

Time enough to kiss a woman, or think out the plot of a novel, or utter a curse, or look at one's watch, or play the Emperor Concerto three times through in your mind – does it matter? A lull, a total peace on earth -

Then off again, with me squirming to get upright and reach that door above me before the whole thing lights up like a bonfire, kicking Rassimov with ever-increasing pleasure in balls and stomach and perhaps even on his potato nose at the same time, while he clutches at my legs and even – the bastard – tries to bite me back, but my legs are faster than his teeth and I bet I loosened a few gold caps with that last kick, and the door finally jerks open and a hand drags me up through the hole and over the side and throws me on the ground and a familiar voice says run you bastard like you've never run before, and I don't ask for a repeat, I'm on my feet scampering like a horse through the stubble rice and over the lumpy ground, one shoe on and one shoe off and my right trouser leg ripped to the waist hanging loose behind me like a roll of toilet paper. I can hear thudding footsteps close behind, shouts and a shot – and I'm on my stomach, flattened by a shock of pain in the back. Darkness falls with a sound of church bells.

A long night. Heaved arse uppermost through the undergrowth on a man's shoulder, grunts and whistles in his pipes, and muttered oaths and words of encouragement. Pauses to slide to the ground, and fight against the nausea, and try not to weep through clenched teeth. Once or twice, alarms, shots, close by and distant. Darkness again, and that thirsty feeling that wakes you up from the deepest sleep, and more marching, on my feet this time, with my hands free and a handkerchief shoved against my shoulder and the distant stars above and the lights of cars stopping and pausing along the highway over to the right, stumbling over dykes and kicking against stumps and trying desperately not to scream every time my bare foot strikes another of those blasted roots.

Chapter Four

Convalescence was a confused, uneasy time during which I groped fitfully back towards reality, too late to be of use to anybody.

Henri was the first to come and see me on my sick bed. It was late the following afternoon. I was in an upstairs bedroom in Fouchet's clinic, protected from the world by a screen of efficient nurses. I had only a hazy idea of how I had got there.

'How are you feeling?' he asked anxiously.

'Alive, thanks to you. What's happening?'

'Has Fouchet spoken to you?'

'Just a few words. He keeps wondering what the hell it's all about. What did you tell him?'

'Not very much. What we agreed, more or less. But it's alright. He'll keep quiet, and that's the main thing.'

'Pretty decent of him. To look after me like this. He's not going to get into trouble?' I closed my eyes, too weak to speak for long.

'No. Don't worry. He knows his way around. Apart from him no-one has any idea what happened. Officially you're suffering from nothing worse than contusions and lacerations and a cracked rib from a hit-and-run driver.'

'He said.' I knew there were more questions to ask, details to work out, but my mind refused to focus. It felt as if it as well as my body had taken a battering.

Henri gave me a reassuring smile. He looked as if he hadn't slept for a week, but even in my befuddled state I could see a new air of calm and confidence about him.

'It won't happen again, I promise. I've taken the first precautions. But we'll talk about that later. You lost quite a bit of blood. I can't stay for long. I'll come back as soon as I can.'

It was Fouchet who explained how Henri had brought me to him in the middle of the night, slowly bleeding in the back of his car, and how they had smuggled me into his clinic, where he had operated on me, alone with his head nurse. Henri was almost incoherent with anxiety and Fouchet had wanted to give him a shot as well, but he refused and disappeared as soon as he knew I was going to make it, to return three hours later, looking like death himself but oddly satisfied, before he finally went home.

'What did he tell you?' I asked, while Fouchet dressed my wound.

'Enough to make me shut up, but not nearly enough to satisfy my curiosity. Was he the one who shot you?'

'Did he say that?'

'Not in so many words. He said it was an accident, but it was his fault, and if it came out he'd probably have to go to gaol for a long time.' His eyes became intent while he examined the wound, disinfected and dressed it again. Other than his head nurse he didn't want any of his staff dealing with me.

'Did you have a fight?'

I kept a still face, unwilling to speak.

'Anything to do with Nicole?'

I gave a reluctant nod. That was part of the story I'd agreed with Henri. 'But she mustn't know! Please, Aristide, make sure she doesn't! It's more than their marriage is worth. And I owe him that. He saved my life.'

He looked at me sceptically for a long moment in silence, his eyes serious and sad.

'You've been up to no good, haven't you.'

'I'm sorry Aristide. I can't discuss it. Please – if it comes out it'll wreck their life. I don't want that to happen.'

Too bad if he thought I was the cause of it all, if he put it down to a *crime passionnel*, as I'd flippantly suggested to Henri. Better that than the truth.

He sighed, and rolled his eyes a little.

'Well, maybe it's better I shouldn't know. It's alright, I'll protect you, and him. But you're lucky, in more ways than one. It was a close call, you know. The bullet didn't hit anything vital but it came pretty close and made quite a mess on the way out. You'll have to keep that scar out of sight, for your sake and mine. Thank your lucky stars Henri's the same blood group as you. You're carrying a lot of his blood, you know.'

So I owed him that as well. It made me feel very close to him, and strangely content, as if somehow that gift from him had restored the balance between us, reduced my share of guilt and responsibility. We were blood brothers now!

'What about your nurse?'

'She won't talk. She's been with me for years. But I don't trust some of the others. As soon as you're strong enough I'll send you home.'

Rick was harder to fend off. He came round as soon as he heard. Although he didn't know about the shot, and accepted the story of the cracked rib without question, his suspicious mind focussed on other aspects. He nodded unconvinced when I told him how lucky I was that Henri had passed by so soon after the accident, and had taken me straight to Fouchet.

'Very lucky indeed. Where did you say this happened?'

'Not far from here. I was just getting out of my car.' That was one detail I hadn't yet sorted out with Henri.

'Bad time for accidents, all round.'

'What do you mean?'

'Haven't you heard? There was a major prang on the highway the other night. Rassimov, and one of his friends. Ran off the road. About the same time as your own accident, by some coincidence.'

I closed my eyes, remembering that grinding crash, the combination of panic and joy as the car went plunging over the embankment. After that I had only confused memories – of lying in a ditch patiently waiting for Henri to come back for me, while I stared up at the pale stars above and the strength oozed out of me in a sticky fluid between my fingers; of another ride, back to safety this time, during which I moved in and out of consciousness like an exhausted swimmer and confused Henri's shape at times with that of George, and I shouted feebly and kicked against

Rassimov's restraining hands; of other, gentler hands helping me up the stairs and into a room, and the pin-prick in my arm which finally sent me into oblivion. It was during my brief moments of lucidity that I had urged on Henri the need to work out a cover story, and not expose himself any further because of me – he was all set to blow the whole thing wide open, regardless of the consequences for himself.

'How's Rassimov?' I asked.

'Broken ankle, and badly cut about the face, I believe. Luckier than his friend, who was driving and got the steering wheel through his chest. Died on the way to hospital.'

'A real holocaust,' I murmured, and slid gratefully back into sleep. Fouchet was handy with a needle, and kept me under sedation much of the time – a convenient way to keep most visits short, under the pretext that I was still suffering from concussion – which, overall, wasn't far from the truth. I wore a bandage around my head like Apollinaire and I looked as if I'd been dragged through a hedge.

Nicole was the hardest to convince. She was frankly disbelieving, and her visits were the most painful of all.

'Did you fight with Henri? What on earth happened?'

'Of course not! Why do you ask that?'

'Because there's a great bloody dent in the front of my car, that's why, and some cock and bull story about running into a *cyclo*. And all that story about a hit-and-run sounds very fishy to me. And to Rick too, I might add. He's been sniffing around with questions no one's got any answer to.'

'For Christ's sake keep him out of it!'

'What in heaven have you been up to?'

'Nothing! I told you. It was an accident. A mad driver ran into me just as I was getting out of my car and knocked me down. It could have happened to anybody. It was pure luck that Henri came along soon after and picked me up.'

'I bet! And what has he been up to? Why didn't you keep me informed about him, as I asked you?'

'Because there was nothing to tell. I told you. You were dressing it up. He just went for drives from time to time. For goodness' sake stop being so suspicious about everything and everyone. And I don't owe you an explanation for everything I do!'

She stared at me, and I apologised.

'I'm sorry. I didn't mean that. But it's been a rough time, and I didn't enjoy following him around. But you don't have to worry about Henri. He's a good man. He loves you. I'm sure of that.'

'That's not what I asked you. I asked you to see if he needed help.'

I shook my head, unable to answer. Too many lies, too much evasiveness. What could I tell her, that wouldn't make things worse? In any case there was nothing either she or I could do about it. I closed my eyes, half-feigning exhaustion, and after a while she got up and went away.

Surya by comparison was straight therapy. She accepted my story without blinking, asked no questions I couldn't answer, and came often to see me, after Fouchet allowed me to go home, bringing me records and books and flowers and fruit in the best convalescent tradition and holding my spoon for me at meal times, which placed her conveniently close to my right arm – fortunately unaffected by all this and valid enough to encircle her waist. Inactivity was beginning to prey on me, I was regaining strength quickly – Fouchet said I had the constitution of an ox – because I had to exert a lot of self-control not to whip her into bed beside me.

On a later visit Henri was more informative, and filled in some of the blanks.

'It was touch and go for a minute,' he said, and explained how he'd managed to get me back unobserved – stopping a little way up the road and then hurrying back to the car just in time to get me out – then the running, with several shots being fired, including the one that had got me. He didn't know until later that Rassimov couldn't run after us. He'd done a long loop through the rice fields, carrying me much of the time, until we came to a small side road, and had left me there to get back to his car. By then other motorists had stopped near the accident, but fortunately no one connected him with it – his car was just one among several, he was able to drive off soon after without drawing attention to himself, came back to where he'd left me, and just drove me back to town. As simple as that, but a lot of luck had been involved, good as well as bad. The good had won, and I was back on my feet, more or less.

'I owe you a lot, one way or another,' I said. 'It's obvious that they meant to kill me, though not with a bullet. My guess is they were going to stage an accident, somewhere up in the hills. Car running off the road, or something. If you hadn't come along that's where I'd be now. What made you follow us? Did you suspect what they were going to do?'

'Pretty well. It didn't take long to figure it out, after I left you. They took me back to my car and told me to go home, everything would be alright. I was very worked up as you know, and I suppose in a state of shock, and at first I just did what they said. Force of habit I suppose. But then I started thinking. I pulled up off the road and tried to calm down. I told myself at first that they couldn't possibly be thinking of killing you. It seemed so cold-blooded, so brutal. But the more I thought about it, the more obvious it was. From their point of view it was the simplest solution. You'd admitted that no one else knew about me. It was just chance, and the fact that you'd been so close to – to Nicole and me, that had made it possible for you to find out. Whatever you said they couldn't take the risk that you mightn't tell someone else later on. By killing you they not only got rid of that risk but they made me an accomplice as well, and got me even more under their power.' He smiled, and some jauntiness even crept into his voice. 'Much as I hated you at that moment, I didn't wish that on you, any more than on myself. And so I turned back.'

'I'm certainly glad you did,' I said fervently. It was in my mind to ask how long he'd waited before turning back, whether he'd hesitated, but it wasn't the sort of question to which I really wanted an answer. 'It's lucky they didn't spot you then too.'

'I was careful this time. I took a chance, that they'd probably head back to town, and so I drove the other way for a bit, around the next bend. Then I came back on foot and waited. I didn't have to wait long. As soon as they brought you out I knew I was right. Especially when I saw one of them get in your car. They moved off pretty fast and I almost lost them at first. I had to run back to my car. But I caught up with them before they reached town, and after that it was just a question of opportunity. Luckily I knew their car, I was able to follow them at a distance. Until you took the airport road. Once you were past Pochentong I knew I had to act fast. So I just came up and – bang! Not very imaginative, but I couldn't think of anything else. And it worked, luckily.'

'What about my car? Who brought it back?'

'The chap who was driving it, I suppose. I saw a car come back the other way soon after, while we were getting away. It looked like your car, and I guess it was him who got rid of Rassimov's gun, and got them to hospital. After that I forgot about it. But it was back the next morning, outside your front gate. I told everyone I drove it back myself, after your accident.'

I looked at him with affection. In a very short time there had grown a new kind of friendship between us, a camaraderie such as I would not earlier have thought possible. The fact that he knew I had kept his secret clearly had a lot to do with it. And that he had saved my life. Whether these two acts balanced each other out was immaterial. What mattered was that they had brought us together, made us feel very close to each other, without the need for any words of acknowledgment, which would only have been embarrassing. It was as if we had pulled off an enormous prank, the two of us against the world. For a moment it almost made me forget the seriousness of his situation.

'You know, I've been thinking,' I said suddenly. 'About that blackmail episode. You remember, when Kalyakin tried to get me to work for them, by threatening to tell you about – about Nicole and me. That wasn't the first time they'd tried something like that.' And I told him about that distant episode. He listened with interest.

'I couldn't work out why they didn't carry out their threat. But I know why now. It wasn't to make me work for them. That wasn't their purpose – not the second time around. All they wanted was to frighten me away from Nicole – and you. I think they were getting pretty worried by then that I was getting too close to you, and somehow would find out what you were doing...'

Or that I'd succeed in taking Nicole away from you, I added to myself. I didn't know how close I'd come to that, and I didn't propose to discuss it with him. But they must have been worrying about that possibility too. They would have known that would just about finish him. They must have been desperate at the end to tell him themselves. Whatever they'd told Henri, during that meeting near Oudong, it was obvious they'd known for some time that I'd been following him, and that time was running out.

It was strange, I thought, how my relationship with Henri had changed, since our confrontation on the houseboat, and the attempt on my life. The news of his homosexuality had surprised me at first when Nicole told me, but I hadn't thought much further about it. In my youth homosexuality was only timidly beginning to come out of the closet in Australia – the word *gay* was still used in its original sense, to mean simply 'merry' – and homophobia was still fairly widespread – that's another word which wasn't in use in those days. In rougher parts of Australian society poofter-bashing was considered almost a national sport. I'd never been homophobic myself – a couple of my friends at university had been almost openly gay, including one of my teachers, a man I greatly admired, and I was appalled at the thought that they could be victimised in that way. But I'd never felt anything remotely sexual in my affection towards them. If anything like most heterosexual men I found the idea of male couplings rather repugnant.

Now, given what I now knew about Henri, I found myself thinking again about that question, and wondered if my feelings towards him were more complex than I'd previously thought. Was I in any way physically attracted to him? I felt a deep affection for him, deeper than at any time before, and not only because he'd saved my life; as if his admission, his revelations, had created a new bond between us, almost a kind of love. But try as I might I could find nothing sexual in it. Indeed, the thought of physical intimacy with him struck me as more ludicrous than repugnant. Nicole was the only person I wanted to have sex with (apart from Surya, and that was clearly not going to happen). And with Nicole too that prospect now seemed diminishingly small. Since our break-up, since her decision to stay with Henri, a gulf had opened between us, which no amount of yearning could ever bridge; to which Henri's admissions, and my promise to him, had now added a wall of mistrust. I watched with great sadness as the woman I loved, more than anyone else, moved ever further away from me.

Whether by coincidence or design, it was Inspecteur Than Souk who called by, to investigate the accident. I was home by then, in Chi Hai's motherly care. He asked me details of where, when and how it had happened, and whether I could identify the car or its driver in any way. He was sympathetic and said how regrettable it was that this sort of thing should happen in Phnom Penh. 'Maybe it was a foreigner,' I said, to ease his national sensitivities. 'I'm sure a Cambodian would have stopped.'

He gave me another of those odd looks I was getting used to, which seemed to say they knew I wasn't telling the whole truth. Perhaps it was just my guilty conscience – or perhaps with his policeman's mind he really thought someone had tried to do me in. There was no mention of Rassimov's accident, and no suggestion that he doubted Henri's role in all this, or Fouchet's explanation. As it happened Surya came by for a visit as he was leaving. They smiled at each other and exchanged a few words. She seemed to trust him.

I had no end of visitors. Even Marcellin had come to see me, unusually expansive. 'You should take some time off,' he said genially. 'You look peaky. Get out of the place. Go to Singapore. I'll get Sovannareth to make the bookings. You deserve a break. You were working pretty hard, before your accident.'

Not a bad idea, I thought. Forget all this, have a change of scene, come back and start afresh. Turn my back on all these problems, in the hope that they'll have sorted themselves out by the time I get back.

But I couldn't put them out of my mind, or the feeling that there was more to come. For it was not over, at best a lull, there were too many things left hanging. Henri knew it, despite the smile of encouragement which he put on when he came to see me. His worried look had returned. I might be out of the firing line, as he said they wouldn't try anything else against me, but what did they hold in store for him?

'There's nothing they can do,' he reassured me. 'If they try to do me in, and they succeed, it'll all come out. I've taken steps – the classic solution, letters to be opened only after my death, etc. But for a classic situation there's nothing better. They're worried alright.'

'Have they replaced Rassimov?'

'Yes. Kalyakin. He was blown anyway, I guess, the way they used him for you, so they're not losing anything with me this way. But it's pure form. They haven't asked me for anything new.'

'I still think you should tell Nicole.' I had tried several times to persuade him that he should do that – that Nicole was stronger than he gave her credit for, that she would stand by him, whatever happened. But he was adamant.

'Out of the question. And I want your promise that you won't tell her either.'

'But what if they try to get you to work for them again? Are you going to let them blackmail you to the end of your days?'

290

'That's my problem, and I'll deal with it in my own way. I will not have her brought into this.'

'You're not being fair to her,' I tried to argue, but he grew impatient. 'I want your word, Philippe,' he insisted. 'You owe me that much.'

I sighed. 'You know you have it.'

He smiled at me, and again that strange look of calm, almost of contentment came over his face.

'You know I'd rather die than have her find out,' he said simply.

Two days later, my week-long beard had started to become a nuisance. It itched like mad, and Surya complained it scratched her when I gave her a brotherly kiss – though she agreed it made me look romantic. I still couldn't move my left arm very easily, so she'd helped me shave by holding the mirror for me, and pulling the skin on my instructions while I held the razor with my good hand. Result: blood all over my pyjamas, and I looked even scruffier than before.

Nicole also came again that day. 'Henri's been recalled to Paris, for consultations,' she announced.

'When's he going?'

'The day after tomorrow. He's going to ask for another posting, he says.'

'You don't look very happy about it.'

'No – there's still too much I don't understand. And I know you're hiding something from me. Your accident – I don't think it was an accident at all.'

'Of course it was! Why, do you think I staged it on purpose?'

She shrugged, and we stared at each other for a while without talking.

With Henri's future hanging on my silence, there seemed almost nothing left to say between us, but I felt a growing hollow under my ribs at the thought that she might soon be gone altogether out of my life.

'Have you told him yet that you're pregnant?'

She shook her head. 'I keep putting it off. But I'll have to soon. It's just starting to show. I can't keep it hidden much longer.'

She came close to my chair, and let me put my hand on her belly. I put my arms around her waist and held her close for a moment, before she pulled away.

Saturday. Ten days since the 'accident'. Henri was due to go on the Sunday night plane, to Paris. He came again that afternoon, and the gaunt look was there again at the back of his eyes. It was as if he knew that the past few days had only been a brief respite, that soon he would be back as before, if not worse. He'd come to say good-bye, to wish me luck.

'I don't know how long I'll be gone,' he said. 'But I'll write to you. I have a few things to arrange. May I have your word that you'll do anything – anything within reason – that I ask you to, and not tell anyone?'

'Of course.'

He came over to the bed, shook my hand, looked at me for a while, as if he knew we wouldn't meet again for a very long time.

'You know, I think you're very wrong not to have talked to Nicole,' I said, trying one last time. He shook his head, and his eyes burned into mine.

'Remember your promise.'

I sighed. 'I'll try to be at the airport,' I said. 'Fouchet says I can start to get about tomorrow.'

He nodded, seemed about to say something else, then turned and left.

During the night Henri drove down to the coast, to Kampot and up to the casino at Bokor. To try his luck one last time at the roulette with the two zeroes? That was one of Sihanouk's inspirations, to

292

double the odds for the bank. The casino was built on a peak, overlooking the coast for fifty kilometres in every direction, when it wasn't shrouded in mist – Wuthering Heights, the French called it, *Les Hauts de Hurlevent,* a gaunt, echoing shell of a building on the edge of the cliff, off-limits to Cambodians but open to everyone else, with forlorn little altars in every room to placate the spirits of desperate gamblers who threw themselves over the edge from time to time.

What went on in Henri's mind in those last few hours no one will ever know. Did he genuinely go up there to gamble, to stake everything on the spin of the wheel and the roll of the dice, and stand by their decision? They certainly went against him, the management said, because he lost heavily during the night, and drank heavily too, which could have explained what happened next: coming down the mountain side at three in the morning, with its hairpin bends and its sheer drops, the car skidded in the mist and on the wet roadway, left the road, somersaulted half a dozen times off rocks and tree-stumps and finally came to rest, half its former size and five hundred metres further down. A short cut to oblivion. Henri was still in it, but barely recognisable by the time the rescue teams worked their way to him, for they had to cut through thick jungle for a whole day to get to him, and the flies and the heat and a few jungle animals had just about finished off what the accident had started.

Accident? That was the official verdict, while my own thoughts ran at once to murder. They'd done him in, as they'd tried to do me in, regardless of the consequences. But just as my mind was grappling with the awful implications (not to mention the improbability, of this hypothesis – how could they have organised it?) Chi Hai brought the mail up; and with it a plain envelope with an even plainer message, incomprehensible to anyone else: 'Remember your promise: you owe me that. PS: there weren't any letters. But they don't know that.' It wasn't signed, but there was no need. This was one message which couldn't be faked – or traced, or used in evidence.

The funeral service held for Henri in the ugly concrete cathedral in Phnom Penh, which the Khmer Rouge subsequently razed in a rare act of inspired destruction, was one of the largest

I've ever attended. A testimony to the number of friends Henri had made in the country, Cambodian and foreign, most of them genuine to judge by their expressions. Only the Russians were noticeable by their absence: Rassimov had returned to Moscow, ostensibly invalided out, more likely I thought recalled to face the music. A very small consolation, in the circumstances, almost infinitesimal. And Kalyakin no doubt had better things to do. I've sometimes wondered what happened to those two since those days, but I've never heard any more of either of them. Perhaps they were simply transferred to their training department.

I saw Nicole twice more. Once in public: at the funeral, where she was heavily surrounded, by Fouchet, and the Boisjolys, and the embassy staff. We hardly said a word to each other. I didn't have it in me to utter any of the usual banalities for such occasions.

And once, at her house, when she finally let me in, after remaining incommunicado for nearly a week. In shock, said Fouchet, himself not far from it. It was the day after the funeral. She herself rang me at home and asked me to come by. She had left the children with friends, sent most of the staff away, the house was almost deserted. We spoke one last time in the small sitting room near the foot of the stairs.

'Do you have any idea, any idea at all, what might have made him do it?'

'Did he leave a message?' I asked.

'No. But I know it wasn't an accident. Henri was a good driver, he would never have done something stupid like that.'

I shook my head. 'I'm sorry Nicole. I tried. Please believe me, I tried. And I wish it had been me instead of him in that car.'

'Isn't there anything you can tell me? When he came to see you, after your accident, didn't you talk with him? Didn't he say anything?'

'Nothing that could have made me think about suicide, Nicole, if that's what you think. The last time he came to see me was the day before he was due to leave, and he seemed sad at going, but that's all.' I hesitated one last time. I'd thought hard about what I might say to her, and had prepared a speech – an alternative version of the truth. 'He did say one thing which I think you should know. Not then, some other time. He said he knew about our affair. He had known for a long time, he said, almost since the beginning. He said it had hurt him at first, but he had understood it, he felt in a way he deserved it, he had come to accept it, and in the end he said he was happier that it was me than someone else.' I uttered a small silent prayer to Henri's soul, wherever it might be. Forgive me this lie, I said, but she deserves better than silence, and I can't tell her the truth, you've stopped me forever from telling her that. 'He said that he didn't want you to know, because it would only make you feel guilty, or remorseful, and he didn't want that. And when I told him how it had stopped, and that you had decided you loved him more than me, and that you didn't want to leave him, he didn't say much, but I think it made him very happy. Deep inside. I don't know what makes you think his death wasn't an accident. But I can tell you that if he did commit suicide, it wasn't because of that.' And that, I thought, had to be the truth.

She looked at me in silence, as if trying to decide herself how far to believe me, how much of what I said was genuine, how much deception, Henri's or mine.

'I'm leaving tomorrow,' she said. 'With the children. We're going back to France.'

'What will you do?'

'I'm not sure yet. Go back to Normandy, probably. I have a house there, we can live there for a while, until I work out what to do...'

She looked at me, long and hard, with great sadness as well.

'One thing I've decided. Whatever you do, I don't want you to follow me there. If you were thinking of it. I don't... I want to start afresh. I don't want the children to know about us. I want them to remember Henri as he was, as we were when we were all happy together. I don't want them to know about our affair. And I don't want this new child –' she touched her belly, which even now was barely starting to show – 'this boy or girl, I don't want it to know or suspect that Henri wasn't its father. I think that's the most important. I know this must hurt you, and it hurts me, you have no idea how much it hurts me. But I know this is the right thing to do.'

She came and put her arms around me, and we held each other for a long while. This woman, for whom I still felt so much love, so much tenderness, the one person I knew I could always talk to and be understood, and yet to whom I was forever barred from telling the truth. I wanted to argue, to protest, to tell her to wait, not to take any decision yet, let things settle down, before she made any final choices. But I didn't. Deep down I knew she was right, for my own reasons, which I couldn't share with her. I knew I would never be able to live with her without telling her the truth, and that I'd promised not to do. And I knew that I had to keep that promise: not only for Henri, but for her sake as well, and that of her children, including the one who was ours. None of them was to know the full truth of what their father had done, and what had driven him to suicide. So I just kept quiet, and wept inside. Then, as she had that earlier afternoon when she had told me she was staying with Henri, she held me tight one last time, then sent me away.

Chapter Five

After that, what followed was almost an anticlimax – but a painful one all the same.

Three days after Nicole's departure I left Phnom Penh myself, on the regional tour that Marcellin had promised me: Saigon, Bangkok, Singapore, in that order, following the vagaries of airline schedules. Not a holiday, nor an attempt to forget, but a necessary diversion, an emotional convalescence, after the pain and the turmoil of the last weeks.

Of the three Saigon in wartime was the most fascinating. It reminded me of an anthill when I was a child, and used to delight in kicking them to make the ants go berserk: Saigon was a sprawling ant-heap gone berserk, for twenty hours out of every twenty-four – a deafening disorderly anthill, with half its population at any one time dashing about at breakneck speed on their hopped up Honda and Toyota motorbikes, four, six or ten abreast down every street and lane, spilling over on the footpaths, on their way to work, from work, to earn their daily rice by any means legal or illegal, for it was a merciless struggle in that cut-throat city just to scratch a living. Thousands of people at all hours, bursting out of every tea-house, trampling over each other at the thieves' market, trampling over the big sewer rats that didn't get out of the way fast enough, stealing, scrounging or being stolen from, and trying desperately to pretend that the hundreds of tall sullen men in olive uniforms with the round eyes and the long noses who took the sidewalks to themselves weren't really there. I stayed with a friend of Rick's in a flat on Yen Do street, the old *rue de Champagne*, listening to the roar and thud of this endless scurrying, and when it stopped, late at night, during the brief curfew from twelve to four, tried vainly to sleep against the glare of the night flares that fell like the Northern Lights around the city, and the thunder of artillery beating out squares of the countryside, the bumble-bee drone of aircraft taking off and landing at Tan Son Nhut airport, less than a kilometre away, every few seconds. A thunderstorm would have passed unnoticed in all that racket. After three days I was haggard from lack of sleep but strangely happy. There was something in that frenzied rat-race, the smell of the sewers and the heaps of garbage rotting by the road-side, the festoons of cables draped over trees and lamp-posts linking up one military strongpoint to another, the shrill whistles of sentries behind their sandbags frantically waving everyone aside, the stuttering jeeps and the roar of military convoys, the flag-draped pagodas and the riot of slogans and banners, all the sights and smells of a city not so much under siege as run amok, that caught me by the throat, held me captive and exhilarated.

After Saigon Bangkok was a disappointment. The behind-the-lines city, fattening on the war from a safe distance. Perhaps in reaction to a surfeit of Khmer culture I stayed away from the temples and palaces and explored instead its night-life, thereby no doubt acquiring a very distorted view of the place: every girl a whore, every taxi-driver or hotel bell-boy a pimp in uniform, everywhere the same refrain, echoed from mouth to mouth like a chant or a slogan: girl-boy-massage-blowjob-blue-movie-very-good-very-cheap. The masseuse at the Snow White Massage Parlour was pretty in a rubbery sort of way but didn't have the first clue about anatomy – not for a massage anyway. She gave my dorsals a perfunctory tap, slithered her hands up my biceps, triceps and calves. Then she offered her specialty, which I declined, and immediately offered herself as a permanent maid, *une bonne a tout faire*: anything to get out of that miserable occupation. I overtipped her, fled into the warm night air and went to see a bad version of a Lartéguy novel on the screen, where the Vietminh all chewed gum and snarled continuously, and spoke English with a Filipino accent. For the first time in my life I saw a pornographic movie: alone in a room in an empty villa, the sole spectator among rows of empty chairs with the projectionist behind me, a cheerless man who didn't seem at all surprised when after two ancient one-reelers in black and white I cried enough and walked out, rather relieved, through the deep depression into which the sight of these sexual gymnastics had thrown me, to discover that I had nothing of the voyeur. A striptease, or the sight of two bodies intertwined in ridiculous or sordid combinations, left me cold. I preferred to practise sex rather than look at it. And as for genital organs, they were best kept out of sight until required. I failed to find anything attractive in their display.

That was Bangkok, that was: as the ineffable Forbes had once said, a city that truly lived up to its name.

Singapore by comparison was an efficient supermarket, where I caught up with my shopping and drank milk by the quart – an orgy, after months of abstinence. But I got bored with it, and after three days cut my trip short and caught the first plane back, an elderly *Royal Air Cambodge* Caravelle that took hours to creep up the Gulf of Thailand, with no cigarettes on board but unlimited champagne. This helped me sleep. Later I wrote a letter to my parents on a blue *sac vomitoire*, which, split open and stripped of its plastic lining, could pass for a new model air letter. Another item in short supply. Then I was looking down at the island of Phu Quoc, humped like a prehistoric beast under the port wing, the thin strip of coastline, the rugged slopes of the Cardamom Mountains, and finally the flat delta plain as we slid down to Phnom Penh. In the late afternoon sun thousands of sugar-palm trees cast long pencil shadows over dry brown rice-fields pockmarked with empty ponds. I recognised the stretch of road where Henri had saved my life, saw villages and pagodas loom up under our nose, and wondered how I would face the next few months. I felt as if I'd never left the place.

Rick was in the terminal when I walked in. He was chatting with someone, a departing visitor he'd escorted through customs and immigration with his diplomatic pass. I went up to say hello and get from him the cigarette I'd been craving for the past hour. His manner was cool and strangely formal but he supplied the cigarette graciously enough, and introduced me briefly to his friend. After a few words I left them to go through immigration. I'd only gone a step or two when he caught up with me. 'You've forgotten your matches,' he said, handing me a box. I knew at once it was a feint, as mine were still in my pocket, but I took it from him unblinking. He dropped his voice. 'Come and see me tonight, after dark, as quietly as possible,' he said quickly, and went back to his friend.

His explanation that night was quick and to the point.

'You're in deep shit!' he said as soon as it was safe to talk – leading me at once to his study, where he drew the curtains and turned on the radio to cover our voices.

'What have I done now!' I cried, more in desperation than alarm. Had they found out something after all about my accident, and Henri's death? Forewarned, I had taken care to make sure I wasn't followed to his house. I had also refrained from going at once to see Surya, to give her the small present I had brought back from Singapore – a pair of jade ear-rings which I could ill afford, but whose effect on her I was impatient to see. With Chi Hai there was no need for such caution and her pleasure at the somewhat cheaper wrist-watch I had brought her had seemed genuine enough; but so too had been the wariness in her manner, which even without Rick's warning would have struck me as odd. There was usually nothing furtive about her.

'It's not what you've done, it's what they say you've done. Didn't you read the papers while you were away?' And he went on to relate how, a few days after my departure, another of the articles had come out. 'You haven't seen anything like it – it really went over the edge.' Everyone hopping mad, he said, rebuttals in all the papers, long editorials read out over the radio before the news, even a princely speech, a real scorcher this time, with everyone swearing they'd uncover the traitor in their midst if they had to search every office desk in Phnom Penh to do it. 'Three days later – I hear this from a friend, it hasn't come out in public yet – they start searching through newspaper offices and premises; and lo! what do they discover in your desk drawer, my friend, but enough notes and rough drafts to prove beyond a doubt that their owner is also the author of those articles – all neatly typed and annotated, in a handwriting which looks remarkably like yours. Even the typing matches your type-writer. So: no announcement, everyone lies low, waiting for your return, except that fairly soon it's all over town that they've caught the culprit, it's just a matter of time.'

'What about you? Are you involved?'

'No. My name hasn't been mentioned, it seems it's only you they're after. And if you hadn't come back early they'd have had you under the spotlights the moment you stepped off that plane.'

'You're taking a risk telling me all this.'

'My ambassador would have a fit if he knew I was talking to you like this. I tried to contact you in Singapore, through a colleague there, but I couldn't get to you in time. It was pure luck meeting you at the airport.' He paused. 'Look, I know you didn't do it, Philippe. It's a set-up, for whatever reason. Very possibly something to do with that phony accident of yours, that you didn't want to tell me about. I know, it's none of my business. But somebody's gone to a lot of trouble to lay a trap for you, my boy: and there's nothing you can do about it. They've got you. My only advice is to brazen it out and deny everything. They won't believe you, but it may make them think twice. And good luck. There's nothing else I can do for you, not here. But at least this way you won't walk into it cold.'

———————————

Rick was right. I tried to argue the point, not with him so much as with the Cambodians, the Ministry of Information, Marcellin, the Minister himself. The evidence, they said, was incontrovertible, I had broken their deepest trust, there was no alternative, I had to leave the country. They gave me forty-eight hours to pack, and, for reasons best known to them, decided not to make it public – perhaps my protestations of innocence, as Rick had guessed, had given them food for thought; or perhaps they felt some residual sympathy for the young man who stood and argued his case so passionately before them. Marcellin told me the Prince had felt personally hurt by my actions, as he had taken a liking to me; and Marcellin himself, to his everlasting credit, spoke well on my behalf, saying that whatever the reason for my actions, I had always served him and the magazine well, and I had been a valued colleague. To this day I don't know for certain if it was he who slipped those papers into my desk. But if he did, he went some way towards redeeming himself on that occasion.

Perhaps too it was something like that which explained Than Souk's attitude towards me, as he escorted me to the airport to make sure I left on time. He was too much the professional to show his feelings, and there was no hostility in his manner. But he went beyond the call of duty when, in desperation, I turned to him: for I had been unable – and unwilling – to contact Surya since my return. The last thing I wanted was to implicate her in any way; and I could no longer rely on Chi Hai to carry even a simple message. She, poor soul, had been so shaken by the circumstances of my departure that she had retreated to her room and only came out to take from me the money I owed her, puffy-eyed and trembling with apprehension. The police, I guessed, had given her a hard time in their investigation.

But I couldn't leave without saying something to Surya, a few words at least to ease the pain and the bewilderment which she would necessarily feel at my departure, whatever explanations for it she was given or eventually deduced. (Rick I knew I could rely on to defend my reputation with her, but that was scarcely enough.) I had written her a short letter, in which I simply said that I had to leave the country urgently, for reasons beyond my control, without going into them; that, whatever she heard about me, she shouldn't think badly of me, at least until I had a chance to explain myself; and that I hoped I would be able to do so one day. Until then I wished her well, and a great deal of luck. It wasn't written quite in those terms, but that was the thrust of it; and on an impulse I turned to Than Souk as we sat together in a small room at the airport, isolated from the other passengers.

'I don't expect you to believe me when I tell you that I'm innocent,' I said to him. 'But I do have one favour to ask, a personal one, for a friend who is totally unconnected with this. It's your cousin, Surya Boun Savann. I haven't gone to say goodbye to her, as I didn't want to get her into trouble. But I have a present for her, which I wanted to give her, and I've written her a short letter. Can I ask you to give them to her? I know she trusts you, and I can assure you that whatever you think of me she had nothing to do with any of this. And please make sure that nothing happens to her because of me?'

Than Souk didn't say anything for a while, and I thought for a moment that I had misjudged him. But then he nodded, took the envelope and the small packet from me, and said simply: 'Yes, I will.' Then he put them out of sight in the pocket of his jacket and we didn't refer to them again. A few moments later he walked out with me to the plane, conscientious to the end. He didn't shake hands with me at the foot of the steps, conscious no doubt of people watching, and I didn't offer to. But the look in his eyes was not unkind as he said, 'Good-bye, Monsieur Roche – and good luck.'

Rassimov's revenge, I thought bitterly, and laughed ironically when, a few months later, as I was struggling with my new life in Melbourne, I received a letter from Rick – and with it a more recent number of the magazine *East of Suez*, published well after my departure; in it was another article on Cambodia, written very much in the same vein as its predecessors, and clearly by the same author. There was no way I could be accused of having written this one; and I took some pleasure in cutting it out and sending it to the Ministry of Information in Phnom Penh, with a short note in which I pointed this out and suggested they might wish to reconsider their verdict.

Somewhat to my surprise, the Minister himself replied, in person, three weeks later; in a rather pleasant letter, couched in his impeccable French, in which he said that while the latest evidence did suggest that I was innocent, and the victim of a regrettable miscarriage of justice, unfortunately there was no prospect of reinstating me in my previous employ, as budget cuts had forced his ministry to reduce the number of foreign staff to the bare minimum. Nevertheless he had the honour – and the decency – to enclose a glowing reference and testimonial to my services in Cambodia, which he hoped would assist me in finding further employment. I was tempted for a moment to tear it up, and I've never used it; but I kept it, and I have it still among my papers, a

303

yellowing memento of my time there, during what feels sometimes like the last days of my youth.

Epilogue

'I'm so glad you've told me about my father,' says Lise. We're sitting in her fragrant kitchen, drinking herbal tea and sipping a fiery local spirit called *poiré*. I have to go easy on the stuff, as I have a long drive back, but it's helped loosen our tongues. I feel like a fraud.

I am a fraud. I've only told her a small part of this story: a severely truncated version of it, almost an alternative version in a way – what might have happened if I'd never made a pass at Nicole by quoting Apollinaire, if we'd never driven back together from Siemreap on that warm and humid night and had only remained friends. True to my promise – my promises, to Henri as well as to Nicole – I've told Lise nothing of our affair, nor of her father's treason, given her not a hint that his death might have been other than a tragic accident. She's asked me questions about life in Phnom Penh, all those years ago, and about her parents, especially her father, the man she thinks of as her father, and I've answered as truthfully as I could. I've told her of the colour and excitement of the life we led, as privileged expatriates, of the receptions and the dinner parties, the Sundays on the river at the houseboat, the pomp and glamour of de Gaulle's visit, and the excitement of my own life, my first exposure to Asia, my work for Marcellin. I've also tried to explain the underlying tensions, the looming menace of the Vietnam war next door, the growing threat from within too, that we were then unaware of. Would the Khmer Rouge ever have come to power in Cambodia, if the country hadn't been sucked into that war? But of the essential part of our lives, in those months of 1966 and early 1967, I've said nothing. Instead I've talked rather more of Surya than perhaps I should have, but that was almost a reflex action, an instinctive protective measure to deflect any suspicion she might have about my feelings for her mother.

Lise has asked me what happened to the various people I knew in Phnom Penh, and I've told her that too, as best I could: most of them are dead now of course, or retired. Some, like, Marcellin, went back to France after Sihanouk's overthrow in 1970, others like Fouchet stayed to the end, finding refuge in the French embassy when the Khmer Rouge marched into Phnom Penh in April 1975 and overnight emptied the city of its inhabitants. There they stayed for a month, until the KR finally let them out through Thailand, in sealed buses with the windows blacked out so they couldn't see the scale of the massacres and devastation, after first taking out for execution any Cambodians among them. She's listened soberly, fascinated, at times horrified.

'*Et votre petite amie*, Surya? What happened to her?'

'Luckily she was in France when Phnom Penh fell. She went there as planned, soon after I left, to pursue her studies, eventually she met a young Frenchman there and married him.'

'That must have been sad for you.'

'Oh, not really. She was never really my *petite amie*, you know. Just a very good friend. And I was much too young to get married in those days. It would never have worked.'

Another lie. I'd been ready enough to leap into marriage with Nicole, if she's agreed to leave Henri when I asked her. But of course I can't tell her that.

'Luckily her brother was with her too by then. Sarin, the young boy I told you about. Her father sent him to France before the end, to be with his sister. But her father, most of her family died under the Khmer Rouge.'

'And Rick? That other Australian you mentioned, who worked in the embassy?'

'Oh, he'd left long before, at the end of his posting. He's retired too now. He became an ambassador in due course. We still keep in touch, though I haven't seen him for a couple of years.'

As the questions have become more personal I've slipped in a few of my own, curious to know how Nicole had fared on her return to France with the children, the two boys and her unborn child. I've made up a story to explain my visit – Lise wanted to know what had prompted me to call on the family so long after. I've said that some years earlier, Nicole had written to me. She'd apparently come upon a long in-depth piece I'd written about Cambodia, and she was curious to know what had become of me. She'd asked me to come and visit her if I was ever in those parts.

That was pure fabrication. Nicole had written to me, once, but much later, and in very different terms.

Lise at first has been very general in her response. As she points out, she wasn't even born then, and she was too young to

307

register anything much in the first years. It was the boys who filled her in later.

'It must have hit her hard. The boys told me that she cried a lot at the start. But she was a strong woman. She adapted. My grandmother was still alive then and we all came to live here – this was the family house. She'd been a secretary when she married my father, and she requalified and got a job with a firm of solicitors in Alencon. She worked there until she retired.'

'She never thought of remarrying?'

Lise shakes her head.

'No,' she says briefly. Then: 'I asked her once. She had a close friend – the *notaire* she was working for. I think – I probably shouldn't be telling you this –'

'It's alright. You don't have to. But she did mention she'd met someone.'

'That must have been him. I asked her once why she didn't marry him. They were – I think they were lovers. She could have, he was divorced… but she said she never wanted to marry again. She said her relationship with my father had been too deep, and while this was her new life, she couldn't envisage living like that with anyone else. She still missed my father too much.'

I nod, sincerely moved, not doubting the truth of what Lise has said, or what Nicole said to her, though I also know there's more to it than that, which Lise can't know, and must never know. I also can't help feeling a twinge of jealousy at the thought of Nicole in another man's arms. After all these years.

But there's another reason behind my questions, apart from prurient curiosity.

Some years ago, Rick came to see me. He was passing through Melbourne, where I live, on his way to his last ambassadorial posting – making the usual round of high-level calls ambassadors-designate make before setting out, on state governors and captains of industry. He called me and invited me to lunch at the Melbourne Club, whose august precincts I've only ever graced a few times in my life, when I've been invited there by my elders and betters. Over roast pork with apple sauce we reminisced as we often did when we met, about the old days in Phnom Penh.

'Did I ever tell you what happened about those articles?' he said suddenly.

'No, I don't believe you did. I heard some stories, though, that eventually they did find out who it was. Somebody from another embassy, it seems.'

'That's right. But you'll never guess who.'

'No, who was it?'

'Parodi, the press attaché from the French embassy. Do you remember him?'

'Of course! But what on earth for? What was in it for him?'

'Just a bit of pocket money, I suppose. Also I suspect he fancied himself as a journalist, and that was the nearest he got to it.'

'The bastard!' I said, still capable of indignation after all those years. 'He must have laughed himself sick when I got thrown out.'

'If he did it wasn't for long. It was only about six months later that they caught him.'

'How did that happen?'

'Just bad luck I think. Somebody at the magazine in Hong Kong was stupid enough to write to him through the open mail, and it got caught by the censors.'

'What did they do to him? Did they throw him out too? It must have been done very discreetly.'

'That's right, they kept it very quiet, but they did make a protest, and he was asked to leave soon after. I guess everybody felt a little embarrassed about the whole thing, after what they did to you...Did you ever find out who it was who put those papers in your desk? It couldn't have been him, surely.'

'No, I guess not,' I said briefly, clear enough in my mind who had been behind it all, even if I didn't know how they'd managed it.

'You had quite a raw deal, over that episode,' he said sympathetically. 'First that accident, and then to be set up and expelled like that...though of course that was nothing compared to what happened to Nicole, and to Henri. That was really sad.'

'Yes.'

'Though in some ways I'm not sure if it wasn't for the best in the end. His accident. If it was an accident.'

'What do you mean?'

'You were always pretty close to him, Philip. Didn't you ever feel there was something a little odd about him?'

'No, I...I thought he was rather sad in some ways, and introverted, but he was a very private man, and he never spoke much about himself...Why, why do you ask?'

'And Nicole? Didn't she ever say anything to you?'

'No, not at all. Why? What did she tell you?' I asked, my throat tightening a little in spite of myself.

'Oh, not very much, but she made the odd comment...' Once again he looked at me, and I had the feeling that he was judging me, trying to see what effect his words had on me.

'I probably shouldn't be telling you this,' he went on. 'Even after all these years. So you'd better keep it to yourself. But did you know that Henri was a homosexual...and a spy?' Before my startled expression he went on. 'He was working for the Sovs. They were blackmailing him. A classic case. His own government had found out and he was about to be brought back to France to face charges when he died.'

'How do you know this?' I asked, aghast.

'I read a report about it when I got back home. It came out quite by accident. A defector. It seems the chap who'd compromised him in the first place later defected to the Americans. And in due course they told the French. Do you remember he was due to go back to Paris, the day he died?'

'Yes, I remember, he came to see me the day before, when I was still recovering.'

'It just seems too much of a coincidence, don't you think? His death, just before he was due back...'

I was silent for a moment, remembering those sad, confused last days, so long ago.

'Perhaps someone back home tipped him off,' I said, as calmly as I could. 'Did Nicole ever find out any of this?'

'I don't know. I hope not, for her sake. She was quite in a state of shock after his death, and then she left soon after, I didn't see much of her...'

Once again I had the feeling that Rick was weighing his words.

'Have you seen her at all since those days?' he asked.

'No. Have you?'

'No. But I heard that she retired back to Normandy, where she came from. I don't think she ever remarried. Fouchet kept in touch with her, and he would have mentioned it...' He paused, then suddenly: 'You know, Philip, I'm surprised you know nothing of that. You were closer to him than any of us, at one time. To them both, in fact.'

Rick, as he got older, had acquired a lot of presence. His hair, always sparse, was now thin and grey, and with his glasses made him look rather professorial.

I was tempted, for a moment, to tell him everything – the whole story, my affair with Nicole, how I had followed Henri, how guilty I still felt that I had not been able to help him, that I had not helped him save himself. Perhaps it was true, as Rick said, that it was all for the best. I remembered how passionately Henri had rejected all thought of telling Nicole. I hoped for the sake of his memory as well as for Nicole's sake that she had never found out, that the authorities, those who were in charge of such things, had had the decency to keep quiet about it, and bury his secret with him. Rick, I could see, was more than a little suspicious about me still, and my role in that sorry episode; I'm sure he thought in retrospect that I had been much more involved with both of them than he had suspected at the time. It would have been a relief to tell him the truth, to set the record straight, after all those years. But I had no desire to talk about Nicole, much less reveal anything of our affair, which lay so much at the centre of things, and still in some ways at the centre of myself. And I still remembered the promise I had made to Henri. It had been unconditional, and it was totally binding, in death as in life, irrespective of what anyone else knew or suspected.

'No,' I said, making my voice and my face as gentle and kindly as I could in return. 'No, I never knew any of this. But if what you say is true, it's one of the saddest things I ever heard.'

That, I thought afterwards, explained something which had always puzzled me about Henri's death: why had he waited until that moment to commit suicide, if indeed that was what he had in mind. What had driven him to it? I knew full well, as I'd told Nicole, that it wasn't because of our affair. Was it to do with his recall to France? And why recall him for consultations like that, if he was going to be sent off on another posting?

The answer now seemed pretty clear, even if I couldn't be entirely certain. Whether someone had tipped him off, or he simply sensed it, he knew his time was up. This way, he must have thought, he'd not only avoid having to face the music, but by staging an accident, he might not only save his reputation, but also Nicole's memory of him, and his children's. And that, I knew, was what mattered most to him.

But that in turn raised another question: what if anything had Nicole been told? She clearly didn't know when I last saw her, the day before her departure for France. But what about later, after her return? Had the French authorities, their security service, left her alone, in merciful ignorance, or had she also been drawn into their investigation, questioned even?

That concern lay behind my questions to Lise. By now I knew the answer, because Nicole herself had told me. What I didn't know, but could only imagine, was how she had coped.

My dearest Philippe, she'd written in that letter, the only letter I ever received from her. She'd entrusted it to the firm of solicitors she'd worked for, with strict instructions to make sure it reached me and no one else, which was why it had taken so long.

It's taken me a long time to write this letter, and I'm not sure even now that I should be sending it. It's so long since we last spoke, and so many things have happened since. You're married, with a family of your own, you may not thank me for raking over the ashes of the past. I'm not even sure it will reach you. But I must write it, I must try to speak to you, one last time, while I still can. I hope you'll forgive me, and somehow read it to the end.

I'll start at the beginning.

When I first came back to France all those years ago I was very confused. I missed Henri dreadfully, and I was very angry with you. I felt you'd let me down. When we last spoke, that dreadful afternoon in the little study, I knew there were things you weren't telling me. I was sure you knew more about Henri's death, or at least what had caused it, than you were saying. I was dreadfully unhappy. I knew, or sensed, that there were things I should have known, and I blamed you for that.

It was after my return to France that I began to understand at least part of the truth. But it took a long time for me to grasp the full extent of it.

As I told you, I had decided to come back to Normandy, and that's what I did. I settled down with the children in my mother's house, in the little village near Alençon that I told you about. I started to plan for my new life, without Henri, and without you.

Then, about a month after our return, I had a visit from two security officials. They were polite, courteous even, but very professional. They asked me a number of questions about Henri and our life in Phnom Penh, about his work and his activities, to which all I could say was that it had been perfectly normal. They then told me that they had information that Henri had been spying for the Soviet Union for years. They asked me again what light I could shed on this.

I was shocked when I heard this. At first I refused to believe it. I said there must be some mistake, they'd got the wrong man, Henri would never have done anything like that. But they said they had incontrovertible evidence. They said it appeared that Henri had been blackmailed into it. They asked me again if I knew anything about it. Of course I denied it. In fact I was horrified when they told me. They seemed to accept this, but they made me surrender my passport. They said I must tell no one about it, and that I would probably have to go to Paris for further interviews.

I was called there a month later. Different people were involved this time and it was more like a series of interrogations. I was asked again what I knew or suspected of Henri's work and activities, and again I was unable to tell them anything. Finally they accepted that I was probably telling the truth. I asked a few questions myself and finally they revealed that Henri had been blackmailed into it following a homosexual incident in Prague not long after we were married. They also said that they believed Henri's death had not been an accident. They thought it most probably was suicide. They asked me again if I could cast any light on it. I said I couldn't. I said I had loved my husband, I still loved him, whatever he had done, I wished I had known about it when he was still alive, because then I might have been able to help him.

Finally they returned my passport. They said I was in the clear. They apologised for the distress that they had caused me, but said it had been an unavoidable part of their investigation. I said from my point of view what mattered most was that my children should be spared. I did not want them to suffer the distress of learning these facts about their father. They agreed, and said they would not be making any details of the case public. They asked me in return not to talk to anyone else about it.

I didn't tell them that I had already known that Henri was part homosexual, nor that I had asked you to follow him. I didn't tell them anything about you, and our affair. Whatever they might have made of it, it had nothing to do with their case, and I felt too deeply that it was none of their business, or anybody else's.

I did what they asked: I told no one, not even my mother. I made some pretext that I'd had to go to Paris to help sort out some of Henri's affairs at the Ministry, and I left it at that. She could see I was upset, but I put it down to my grief over his death, and she accepted that. But what it did do was make me even more angry with you. I was certain now that you knew something, something more than you'd told me, perhaps you knew the whole story already. I even thought for a time that you might have been involved in uncovering Henri, that somehow you had threatened to report him and that was why he had committed suicide. Eventually I concluded that you could never have done this, or that you would at least have told me about it. But I stayed angry with you for a long time. I also began to have doubts about your story of your accident.

It wasn't until some years later that I learnt more about that – from Aristide, when he came back to France. He'd been Henri's friend more than mine, but we'd always got on well and he came to see me on his return. He wouldn't say much about your accident at first, but I pressed him and eventually he gave in and told me what he could.

He said there had never been an accident – not the way you'd said. You hadn't been run down by a car, you had been shot. He didn't know how it had happened – all he knew was that Henri had brought you to him in the middle of the night, in a state of shock, afraid that you might die. He'd asked you both what had happened, but you'd both refused to give any details, other than to say it had been an accident, and you'd pleaded with him to keep quiet about it, for fear that otherwise Henri might have to go to gaol. From that he deduced that it was Henri who had shot you, but there were some aspects which puzzled him: it looked as if you'd been bashed, and dragged through some bushes, and it didn't look as if you'd been shot at close range. But when he pressed you and Henri for details you both continued to say it was an accident, and you pleaded with him to keep quiet about it. Reluctantly he'd agreed, for Henri's sake. His final conclusion was that you and Henri had had a fight, perhaps over me, and whether by accident or not Henri had shot you – then in remorse had rushed you to the clinic, afraid you might die.

I didn't tell Aristide about Henri's work for the Russians, and I didn't confirm his suspicion about the possible cause of a quarrel. I didn't tell him anything about our affair. Once again I considered it was nobody's business but ours. But I began to think further about that whole episode. At first I thought Aristide might be right, that you and Henri really had had a fight, about me, and I remembered what you'd told me, that Henri knew about our affair, and had forgiven us. But again it didn't make sense. If it hadn't been for his work for the Russians I might have accepted that. But it didn't fit in with what else I knew about Henri, and the fact that you'd been following him. Why would you have run away from Henri? And why would he have had a gun with him in the first place? If he had tried to kill you because you'd found out about him, why did he then rush you to Aristide's clinic and seem so desperate to save your life? And how did that tie in with his suicide? It seemed too much of a coincidence that Henri would have shot you, either by accident or in a jealous rage, somehow come to his senses, rushed you to safety – Aristide said Henri was almost beside himself with anguish over you – and then, as a

315

totally unrelated event, have committed suicide rather than come back to France to face the music over his treason.

Eventually I concluded that the two things were almost certainly related. I didn't know how, I still don't know, but I began to think that maybe it wasn't Henri who'd shot you – but if so who, or why? Rick McPherson I remembered had said something about another accident, by some coincidence, at the same time as your supposed one, on the airport road, involving some Russians. He thought it was odd, that it should happen at the same time as yours, but he put it down to coincidence, and at the time I hadn't paid much attention to it. But I began to think that maybe it was all part of the picture. And I remembered too that you'd had your own brush with the Russians, when they'd tried to blackmail you as well.

So then I started asking myself: is that what happened, Philippe? Were you shot at by some Russians, and did Henri then try to save you? And is that why you wouldn't tell me anything? Because you were trying to protect Henri? Or me, from the knowledge of his actions? Was it because he asked you not to say anything? Did you even know he was planning to commit suicide?

I thought then of writing to you, to tell you what I knew, and ask you for the truth. But Aristide had told me you'd got married – to an Australian girl, not Surya – and I thought you probably would not welcome an intrusion from me into your present life, so long after the event. After all, I was the one who had told you not to follow me to France, not to try to contact me again. What right did I have to interfere with your life now? And even if you could confirm what I suspected, what would it achieve, other than to revive painful memories? What comfort would it give? Whatever satisfaction it might give me to know the truth for certain, it wouldn't resurrect Henri.

Well, I've now decided I should tell you, after all, and for one reason. I have cancer. I was in remission for a time, but it's now come back with a vengeance, and I have months to live, if that. So, selfishly, I've decided that I must try one last time, to contact you, before it's too late. It will be too late for you to reply, as I've given instructions that this letter should only be sent after my death, and in the strictest confidence, to be delivered only to you in person –

if not, it should be destroyed. I've asked a former colleague at the notaire's office where I worked, someone I trust, and I know she'll do as I ask. I'm sorry if it causes you pain. But I could not rest easy without making this last effort.

I have another reason for writing: to tell you that you have a daughter. Her name is Lise. She's now a grown woman of course, a fine woman, with a family of her own. She knows nothing of this. Like her brothers – her half-brothers I should say – she thinks Henri was her father. I would like you to meet her one day, if you could. I know I have no right to ask this, and I can understand if you feel reluctance. But at least you should know of her existence, and have a chance to meet her. You'll have to make some excuse – I don't want you to tell her anything of this, or in any way suggest that Henri was not her father. It would have a devastating effect, on her and her brothers. I rely on you to keep that promise you made, I extracted from you, all those years ago. But it would make me happy to know that you have seen her, and she you, even if it's only the one time. Somehow it would give meaning, continuity, to what we had. She lives in the small village where we settled back in Normandy. It's called Champfleur, near Alençon.

If you do meet her, she may tell you something of my life. She may tell you for instance that I met another man. He's since died, leaving me widowed in a sense for the third time. I didn't marry him, though he asked me to, because I didn't want to lose my independence. This way, I could remain in a way more faithful to Henri, and to you. But he was a loveable man. I remember telling you once that it was possible to love more than one person at a time. Well, it's certainly possible to love more than one person in succession. I never told him any of those things about Henri, and I never mentioned you to him. But he was sweet, and kind, and he helped me a lot through what otherwise would have been very barren years.

And yet, during all that time, I never stopped missing Henri, and I never stopped loving you.

Nicole

I wanted to weep when I read that letter, and I'm grieving now as I re-read it in my mind on the drive back to Paris. As Nicole discovered, I did marry, I have a large family, all of whom I love deeply. I've been reasonably successful in my chosen career of journalism, I've had a happy life. But I can't help wondering what would have happened, if I'd behaved differently, all those years ago. If I'd disregarded my promise to Henri, and told Nicole the truth: if not that last afternoon in Phnom Penh, then at some later time, if I'd disobeyed her too and followed her to Normandy after I was expelled from Phnom Penh, before she fell in with that *notaire* and became his mistress – even now stirring up an ancient jealousy. If I'd told her the truth about Henri, about his reluctant betrayal, and the penalty he'd paid. Would she have forgiven me, for my role in it? For telling her, even? Would she have accepted me back, would we have lived happily together, pretending that the children were all Henri's even though one of them was clearly mine – would it have worked at all? Or would she have been angry, so terribly upset that she repudiated me and all that I stood for, and forbade me ever to try and see her again? I'll never know. Even after receiving her letter I can't tell for certain. What I do know is that for a long time afterwards I kept thinking of her, dreaming of her, even now I still have an occasional dream where I lose her all over again, where she walks away from me and I know I'll never see her again, and I wake up with a feeling of irreparable loss.

And then I grit my teeth and get on with the business of living.

The End

Acknowledgments

This book could not have been written without the help and support of several people.

I wish to thank:

Sir Leslie Fielding, KCMG, British Chargé d'Affaires in Phnom Penh 1964-66, whose book 'Is Diplomacy Dead?' (among others) published at the end of an illustrious career, contains searching insights into Cambodia of the mid-sixties, including a masterly portrait of Prince Sihanouk; for his encouragement and most useful advice, and a friendship spanning half a century.

Dr Jack Dempsey, American writer, historian, editor, and author of two remarkable novels about Minoan Crete, *Ariadne's Brother* and *People of the Sea*, for his continuing and unstinting support.

Margaret Renaud, retired judge and fine judge of words and ideas as well as of humans, for her long-standing interest and words of wisdom, and her and Max's detailed contribution.

Patrice Malavieille, retired industrialist, sculptor and lover of the arts, for his enthusiasm and his heroism in translating the book into French.

Dominique Lacoste, another lover of the arts, for her much appreciated support and interest over the years.

Laksana Chamroeun, whose memories of Phnom Penh are from a much darker time, for her trust and her tireless efforts on my behalf.

My cousin Didier, for having the patience to listen to my long recital as we tramped through central France on hot summer's days.

And most of all my wife Kieu, herself an old Cambodia hand, for her unwavering support over the decades and for giving me the strength to finish the book.

Its strengths are largely due to them. Its weaknesses are my own.

As noted, the plot and characters of this novel are imaginary and not based on real events or persons. Nevertheless I have striven to depict Cambodia in the mid-sixties as accurately as possible, including the very real role and influence of its ruler at the time, Prince Norodom Sihanouk, whose presence is felt throughout the story. Much has been written about him since, but for anyone wishing to know more about this remarkable man I would recommend as well as Sir Leslie's book, *Sihanouk – Prince of Light, Prince of Darkness*, by Dr Milton Osborne, who also knew Cambodia during the last of the golden years.